LOVE ME LOVE ME KNOT

DEB LEE

SOUL MATE PUBLISHING

New York

LOVE ME LOVE ME KNOT

Copyright©2019

DEB LEE

Cover Design by Anna Lena-Spies

This book is a work of fiction. The names, characters, places, and incidents are the products of the author's imagination or are used fictitiously. Any resemblance to actual events, business establishments, locales, or persons, living or dead, is entirely coincidental.

Published in the United States of America by
Soul Mate Publishing
P.O. Box 24
Macedon, New York, 14502

ISBN: 978-1-68291-853-1

ebook ISBN: 978-1-68291-830-2

www.SoulMatePublishing.com

The publisher does not have any control over and does not assume any responsibility for author or third-party websites or their content.

For my dad,

who taught me to love recklessly.

To love people, to love God, and to love art.

All art.

And to my sweet daughter, Sydney.

You may be in heaven,

but your coos sing forever in my heart.

Thank you for sharing your short life with me.

Acknowledgments

Writing is hard. Like planting a fertile seed in the Sahara Desert without photosynthesis hard. But I hope to have the honor of planting that seed many more times, until my eyes go crossed or my fingers give out—because some days I feel like one or the other will.

I want to first acknowledge my twinsie, my partner-in-crime, my very wonderful friend, Rachelle DeNecochea. Without her, and her almost otherworldly editing magic, my book would have been burned like the first-draft evil nemeses it was. But I make her laugh, force her to talk to strangers (stranger-danger does not exist in my world), and I buy her all the wine . . . so we're even. A million thanks for your friendship, your love, and your tolerance of me—I can be #extra!

I don't have to words to adequately describe my full measure of gratitude to my wonderful friend (can I call you my friend? Um, my book, my words . . . definitely going to call you my friend) Kristan Higgins. Your generous and incredibly helpful critique was invaluable. RWA New York will always be the most memorable conference ever! You make me feel like I'm more than I am at this little pen & paper gig. I'll probably fan girl you on some level for life, but there could be worse things in the world. Seriously, a million thanks will never be enough. So, I'll start by paying it forward and sharing your kindness with others.

For my sbux girls who write with me, and laugh with me and make me pee a little (six births helped with that too). I want to throw a shout out to you, Kristin Miller and T.J. Kline. Oh My Gawd . . . what would I have done without out you? You make me better!

To my critique group—Hillari, Marla, Dirk . . . you have traveled many chapters with me and sharpened these pages with the most beautiful shades of blood-ink ever. Thank you for making me a better writer and sharing your time with me.

Ms. Debby Gilbert—thank you. Thank you for laughing at my stupid jokes, for reading this book too many times, for sharing your wealth of knowledge, and for your faith in helping my story have a place in this written world. I'm grateful to you and Soul Mate Publishing for this opportunity.

Don, you are my breath. You are my hero. You are my first and last line of defense, and I can't express my love to you enough. To do any part of life without you would be pointless. Thank you for the support and the love you freely give, even when I can't remember how to spell 'the'.

And to my kids (including my wombmate). You give me great writing material, but we can tone it down a bit now. I'm good for a while. I love you all with a fervor I will never be able to quench. Real love is us. And for your baby sister, who sits on Jesus's lap until we all group-hug/smother her with kisses together, know that she is the muse that keeps us real.

Name Cred: Thank you, Amy, for your name so I could develop a character. Your happily ever after is what every woman deserves. A real life love story.

Thank you, readers, for spending time with this book. We all have stories, and I'm honored you spent a few hours with some characters who, though are not real, you invested in. Thank you.

Best,
Deb Lee

Prologue

Only two other young journalists have ever accomplished such a feat. Call it viral fever, call it a fluke. But we call it a hole-in-one! And to all the Sophies out there . . . we see you!

It's not so much what the dreamy Ryan Pike wrote, but its raw content. In less than 500 words, his real-life personal account captured America's heart. In a world that only looks at the brawn and beauty, Ryan found the Achilles' heel of our industry. And he beat us to a pulp with it.

Taking a neglected subject, and adding some editorial magic, he shot *Sports Now,* the leader in Over the Top, Inc.'s periodical conglomerate, into a new category. Of course we brought a snippet to share. It's only fitting that we release Ryan Pike's new *Sports Now* app with a sample of the article that sent him right to the top. Congrats, Ryan. All of us here at *Sports Now* know you are the industry leader.

~ ~ ~

September 28, 2008
Larger Assets, Lesser Access: How Women in Sports View Themselves
America's pastime has taken a lot of hits. And I don't mean a piece of wood striking a fistful of yarn.

We're talking about an epic play. Bottom of the ninth, bases loaded, two strikes—everything on the line. The home team is down by one. Yankee stadium is so quiet you can hear the pitcher's knees quivering. You've replayed this moment in your mind so many times that you know failure is not an option. Unless you want to let the entire world down. You laser focus on five ounces of a nine-inch sphere. The pitcher winds up and throws a curve ball.

Whoosh!

Your momentum spins you a complete one-eighty. Yet, you only hit air.

The crowd gasps, having expected—no, anticipated—a homerun. But when the catcher's glove echoes the hollow sound from a mile's worth of yarn slamming into it, that's when you know you missed the mark.

And once again, Sports Industry, you have done just that. **Missed. The. Mark**. Pressure within the industry for a woman to look a certain way is leaps and bounds different than what it looks like for men.

A right fielder with a .350 batting average will have several major sponsors lined up to sign him.

But a female with the same level of sports proficiency must first check the hourglass figure box before possibly landing a temporary sponsor for female sports deodorant.

Which begs the question, are we being fair in our approach to sign female heavy-hitters who may lean a little heavier on the universal scale of success?

A girl can handle a fastball. But we want to know if she can she handle fast food?

She will surf after a shark attack, but will her picture on the cover of a national magazine also attract web surfers?

These are questions we have to ask ourselves. It's second nature for a male athlete to eat a greasy hamburger and wash it down with a beer. He'll sweat it off on the court or field. But for a woman athlete to do the same, the stigma is that she's fat. She may even believe it herself. It's a lie. But don't tell her that. Or she'll say *you* think she's fat. Have we created the same shaming in sports as we have in Hollywood?

Take my ex-girlfriend, Sophie. Beautiful. Filled with potential. Wicked smart. But she thought her pretty face was hampered by her size. Put some fries and a Coke in front of her, and she binges. Then she turns into a reclusive hermit crab, scampering to find a larger shell in which to hide. She becomes more insecure and more insincere in a never-ending cycle of self-hatred. Bigger can mean beautiful. But it can also mean bitter. We need to teach our young female athletes we are better than this. Or they will continue to find bigger shells.—*Ryan Pike*

Chapter 1

About ten years later—give or take a few months.

A man who drinks peach schnapps has secrets.

Of this, Sophie Iris Dougherty was certain. Sometimes it meant he bat for the other team, sometimes it meant he couldn't handle hard liquor, and sometimes it meant he was a low-down, no-good, scum-of-the-earth boyfriend. In this instance, it was the latter. An all-too-familiar case of a new office romance gone awry.

Sophie picked up a dart and nailed the bull's-eye just as the crowd cheered. Sure, game three of the National League championship series was showing on all six of the pub's TVs, and the Giants had just hit another two-run grounder deep in left field, but she'd hit the bull's-eye. Same thing.

Sophie rewarded herself with a bite of Sergio's finest Italian cuisine by the Bay—or so it said on the box, all melted in mozzarella and enough calories to last a week. She checked the time on her phone. 8:57 p.m. Exactly forty-eight hours since she and Asher had split.

Sophie scanned the room in hopes her BFF had come in. When she checked the bar, she caught more than she bargained for. The pizzeria's lighting cast Ash-face and his new play toy, Trixie-Way-Too-Frisky Bell, in a sickening yellow glow. They sat at the bar just a half dozen tables over. Trixie's skirt was almost long enough to cover her thigh. Except it wasn't, which was probably why Asher's hand was covering it as he nibbled on, or more likely drooled in, Trixie's ear.

Sophie gagged, her pizza threatening to make an encore appearance. She grabbed her sangria and chugged three-quarters, enjoying the *I don't give a damn* essence it provided.

When a bleated yelp escaped Trixie's mouth, Sophie cringed and wondered if somewhere far off in the San Leandro hills an innocent doe died from a burst eardrum. She grabbed another dart and flung it at the board.

The arrow struck right under the bull's-eye. Close enough considering the wine and all.

Sophie leaned back in her seat, grateful for the faithful fans crowding the pub and providing the perfect camouflage. Then she dropped her eyes to the daunting stack of grant applications she'd printed before coming. She was determined to get them finished. Sophie sipped her wine, and then, as if by some magnetic pull, she chanced one more glance at her ex and sighed.

Amy Reedy zigzagged her way through the tables and plopped down in the vacant wood chair next to Sophie. She followed Sophie's gaze to Asher and harrumphed. "Stop staring at him. Unless you're marking him for a hit. If that's the case, I'm in."

"That's not such a bad idea." Sophie agreed. "They'd never find the body."

Amy nodded toward the neon exit sign, a hopeful glint in her eye. "I have a shovel and lye out back. Do I hear an impending road trip?" Amy may top out at five-foot two, but add in the two-inch heels she lived in and her bulldog bark, and you get a beautiful partner-in-crime with incredible calves. Amy's goldilocks hair was frizzier than usual tonight, but so was Sophie's mood, so they were basically matchy-smatchy.

"And I wasn't staring." Sophie waved off the ridiculous—okay, somewhat truthful—notion. "I was thinking . . . and working, thank you very much."

Sophie stuck her pen against her tongue and then pressed it back to the grant application. She wrote Chicks 'n' Slicks, the name of her community outreach café, where indicated. Beneath her eyelashes, she peeked at Asher again. His hand had moved up Trixie's thigh. Another gag threatened its way up her throat.

Sophie swallowed the lump and looked at Amy, whose eyes had followed suit. She raised her brow in question.

"I'm not pathetic, if that's what you're thinking."

Amy raised her hands in defense. "I didn't say anything."

Subject change. Pronto. "What took you so long anyway?"

Amy yanked the scarf from her neck and shoved it in her purse, then patted her moussed hair in place. "B.A.R.T. is what. And of course you're not pathetic. Does he know you're here?"

"No. I don't think so. I'm a needle in a haystack thanks to the playoffs." She checked her phone. "I can't stop watching the YouTube video of him kissing Trixie right in front of everyone."

Amy crossed her arms. "Okay, *that's* pathetic."

"Sorry if my public humiliation caught on camera and turned viral is a kink in your BFF's social status."

Amy gave Sophie a motherly glare. "How many times have you watched it?"

"I'm a moth. It's my flame. But I promise I won't watch it again."

"You said that yesterday."

"I said a lot of things yesterday. But this time I mean it."

Amy sighed. "Give me your phone."

Sophie narrowed her eyes. "Why?"

"Just hand it over."

Sophie slowly slid the phone across the table.

Amy snatched it up. "I'm deleting your YouTube app."

"Hey!" Sophie grabbed her phone and slipped it in her purse. "Fine. I'll stop. I just can't stop replaying the part when I accidentally took Trixie down. The look on her face brings me such joy." She grinned evilly.

"As evident by the number of views."

"Is it bad I'm not horrified by tripping over my own feet and taking all one hundred and nothing pounds of her to the floor with me?" A moment of silence thanking Mr. Murphy's Law was still in order.

"As in going she-bat crazy?" Amy offered a scandalous grin. "Serves her right."

"Right," Sophie said. "Because it looked like I did it on purpose." She picked up another dart, aiming carefully. She struck the upper right quadrant. "Eighteen points. Not bad."

Amy glared at the dartboard and then Sophie. "It was totally on purpose and you know it."

"It was an accident. Otherwise my Catholic guilt would have me Hail Marying 'til I'm blue in the face."

A thunderous cheer earthquaked through the pub. Sophie glanced at the screen. The Giants had scored another two-run hit.

"Drink your wine and stop obsessing," Amy yelled over the sound of hoots and hollers.

Sophie sipped. "I really did trip, but it was Trixie's fault is all I'm saying." Or rather the fault of Trixie's obnoxiously ample—and oh, so fake—rhinestone ring.

Sophie *may* have been trying to confront Asher and *happened* to accidentally push Trixie away when the gawd-awful ring snagged Sophie's shirt, tripping them both. Trixie went down, plastic boobs first. *Ah, fond memories.*

Amy plucked an artichoke from Sophie's pizza and dangled it over her mouth before dropping it. "Totally Trixie's fault. And her synthetic boobage."

It always warmed Sophie's heart when Amy said

something so inappropriately blunt. "I'm totally friend crushing you right now."

"Ditto. So"—Amy nodded at the pile of applications—"where're we at?"

"The same place as yesterday. And the day before. Five grand short for the café's rent by the month end."

"Well, all we can do is fill out these puppies and pray your sob story is sobbier than the next." Amy took her chance with a dart. She flung it, striking a man's calf two tables over. She winced and hollered over the crowd's cheers. "Sorry!"

The man, obviously three sheets to the wind, laughed at the pinhole-sized mark in his leg. He tossed the dart back. "Double bogey."

"Darts, not golf, but whatever," Amy said with a wink.

He grinned, then began yelling profanities at the TV.

"Sobbier?" Sophie lined up the dart with the board and flicked her wrist, striking the middle. "Bull's-eye," she cheered, and then bit her lip not wanting to draw unwanted attention from a certain scuzz bucket and his harlot.

"More sobby? I don't know." A server brought Amy an iced mug with something from on-tap and set it in front of her. "Thank you." She tipped the server. "Sadly kids with eating disorders are a thing now. Not really a call to action."

Sophie flinched. True as that may be, the teens at the café lit Sophie's world. She knew their struggle and the very real consequences if not addressed. "May I remind you, you have never been the one to pick out a toothbrush based on its capacity to reach the back of your throat to gag."

Amy laid her hand over Sophie's. "Sorry. I didn't mean it like that. I just mean a café training teens how to eat properly may be an uphill battle as far as funding is concerned."

Sophie closed her eyes. Clearly she was taking out her Asher angst on Amy. "No, don't apologize, I'm not being nice. I didn't expect Asher to be here. And bring *her*. Luckily the place is packed tonight."

"It's the magazine's local well . . . and a home game. Probably should have expected it. We could have met at the café and filled these out there."

Sophie lifted her shoulder somberly. "I'm not ready for the gang to know we are hanging on by a financial thread. It may make one of them purge . . . or worse. Plus"—Sophie pointed at her nearly empty wineglass—"this is the only place in walking distance from the café that has fifty-calorie sangria and free darts." She risked nausea by lifting her eyes to Asher one more time. "And it's a wine sort of night."

"Priorities and all," Amy agreed, picking up her mug and clinking it against Sophie's glass before taking a sip.

"Exactly. Besides, I was here first. If I leave, he may see me and he'll think it's because of him."

Amy narrowed her eyes at Asher. "He's an ass."

"That's the problem. Apparently everyone wants a piece of it."

"Listen." Amy slammed her mug on the table and stabbed her finger in the middle of Sophie's stack of paper. "No more office romance and no more distractions. We will find a way to come up with the money. Asher will be old news. The teens at the community café will continue to get the help they need. And God willing, this humidity streak will lay off my hair. They did not create enough mousse, spray, or gel to tame this wild beast."

Grateful as always for the pigpen mess of Amy's hair to lighten the mood, Sophie shoved a handful of the grants in front of Amy. "Grab a pen and get to work."

Amy winked. "That's my girl."

Sophie stared at Asher once more as if participating in the fine art of self-torture would ease the twisted knife to her gut. She had to admit it was only six dates. Hardly worth batting an eyelash over, but somehow, in the pit of her stomach, the familiar pang of rejection eroded through her.

Sophie sighed, subconsciously patting her Ellie Award on its back. Whereas her column had won the "Oscar" for magazines on health and humor, Trixie was a measly freelance photographer at *Up Front.* She wasn't even an employee. Talk about trading in filet mignon for ground beef—the off-brand kind, no less.

The problem with working full time as a columnist for *Up Front,* an all-encompassing magazine focusing on life and leisure, and then moonlighting at her community café for teens with eating disorders was it didn't give her a lot of time to find "Mr. Right." Not that she was searching, but could it kill her to meet a good guy? Sure, she'd fallen in love once with "Mr. Nice," but that was eons ago, and he'd completely humiliated her, so he wasn't so nice after all.

"Is this what we're doing now?" Donovan Charbert asked, joining their table. "Stalking the plaintiff over darts and carbs?"

"And wine," Sophie said, breaking her brooding glare from Thing One and Thing Two, to smile at her favorite Y chromosome. Too bad he was the only man she'd ever met who could make a girl swoon and laugh before she caught on he was gay. All the good ones usually were. "No one's on trial here. He is free to go out with whomever he wants."

"Well," Donovan mused, setting down his glass of red, "in my opinion he's a little too pompous for his own good." He stroked Sophie's cheek with his thumb. "Now, I only have an hour before I'm taking Mother to the show. *The Lion King* just opened last week and Mother is getting her hair fixed now."

Sophie took in Donovan's three-piece, pinstriped suit. "A man who takes his mother to off Broadway . . . swooning even more now." She batted her lashes, and Donovan blew her a kiss.

Amy raised her mug. "It's the best show Off Broadway. I should know, I wrote a review last week."

"And a beautifully executed review you wrote." He rose his glass in return. "So how many grants have we applied for already?"

"Sixty-seven." Sophie tapped her fingers on top of the current list of potential donors—or future rejections if this pile was anything like the last batch she sent out.

"Sixty-seven?" Donovan's eyes widened. "That many?"

Sixty-seven was a drop in the hat. There were thousands of available grants. She'd been filling them out for weeks now, and she'd earned a blister on her finger from the pen as a battle wound. So far she hadn't heard back from any.

She hadn't seen her ailing grandma in two weeks either, and her current column was due tomorrow, yet it wasn't even close to ready. Sophie took a deep breath. "Well, you know what they say: Throw spaghetti against the wall and see what sticks. I'm applying for everything."

Donovan held up an application. "This one is for teenage mothers who want to go back to school."

"Intense competition," Sophie said. "Which is why I have to keep applying to everything with the word 'teen', 'eating disorder', 'education', or 'starving artist looking for a break.'"

Amy tapped one of the completed applications. "That's why you have a degree in journalism. These submission letters make those animal cruelty commercials seem unworthy in comparison."

"There's enough to go around," Sophie said, taking the application from Amy. "I just don't know why the magazine cut our funding. It's *their* outreach and our biggest sponsor."

"Have you talked to Red?" Amy asked.

Red Goldman. Though she absolutely adored *Up Front's* editor in chief, he was a dinosaur in the industry who barely owned a smart phone. Recently he'd been incredibly distracted, so she didn't rely on him getting the word out to corporate that they needed their funds completely reinstated. "I tried. He said he was looking into it, but you know Red."

"Hi, Sophie." Asher's voice grated on her ears. She forced her body not to squirm.

Her throat went bone dry. "Asher." Sophie returned the same flat tone.

"I didn't realize you'd be here. But I didn't want to be rude and not say hi. We're just leaving."

Sophie closed her eyes. Asher's hand in ungentlemanly places on Trixie's body replayed in her mind like a broken reel that wouldn't jump to the next scene. "Okay. Bye."

Asher saluted the table. "I guess I'll see you all tomorrow."

"See you tomorrow," Donovan said.

When he was finally gone, oxygen slowly seeped back into Sophie's brain.

Donovan rubbed her back. His warm hand comforting her. "You okay, toots? He's not worth the effort of one salty tear."

"Peachy," Sophie murmured. Totally not worth the effort. She had more important things to deal with. Like . . . "Back to carpal tunnel syndrome," Sophie ordered. "Let's get these applications filled out, and hopefully we'll hear something positive soon."

"Way to stay focused, toots."

"Of course, finding life on Mars may have better odds than actually getting a grant."

Chapter 2

Sophie pressed send, and all the applications she'd scanned into her laptop fluttered off into cyberspace. Now it was a matter of hurry up and wait.

Her hand shook. She'd like to blame it on the aftermath from punching Asher in his kisser, but alas, the tremor was the result of well-earned writer's cramp. She could have typed the grants, but something about writing the requests, in actual penmanship, held a certain dignity she hoped would weigh in her favor.

She anticipated hearing something soon—or else. At least it couldn't get worse.

Until, that is, she spilled out of the elevator door and into the office.

The low buzz went silent the minute she walked into the office.

Julie from graphics winced at her as she made her way to her desk. "How are you, Sophie?"

"Fine," Sophie assured.

Jocko, their Swedish intern who acted as a contributing editor, hung over her cubical partition. "You need anything?"

Oh, his accent. "Nope, I'm good."

"Are you sure? You're up to four hundred thousand views."

Sophie shook her desk mouse, and her computer hummed to life. "I'm aware." Her voice cracked behind gritted teeth.

"Shoo." Donovan sent Jocko away. He set a love offering—a ginormous cup of coffee—on her desk. "One large, sugar-free, vanilla soy latte with extra foam for my YouTube sensation."

Sophie scrunched her nose at Donovan the Great and his ability to make all things right in the world. "You sure I can't marry you?"

"Sorry, if my mother doesn't scare away all my prospects, I have my eye on someone with a tad more stubble."

Sophie sipped her delicious cup of goodness. "Don't check out my legs then, because they'd have you fawning."

Asher's laugh echoed from across the room. Sophie side-eyed in that direction, her lip curling in utter repulsion. "He'd better stay on his side of the ficus tree. Or else."

"Want me to hire a hit man?" Donovan offered.

"You do love me, but you'll have to fight Amy on who gets to hire the hit. Remember, the offer to marry you stands."

"As does hiring a hit man, toots."

"Tempting as the offer is, you wouldn't look good in orange."

Donovan shrugged. "This is true. Okay, then, off to finish my piece on that new vineyard in Napa. Word is they still press grapes with their feet."

"Ew, gross."

"Don't knock it till you try it." He leaned over her shoulder. "What are you working on?"

Sophie groaned. "That stupid hernia piece."

Donovan read aloud. "How to make hernias less harmful." He let out a guttural sound.

"I know. Tell me about it."

"What'd you do to piss off Red?"

"It's a favor for his bridge group or something. But turns out it's probably the nail in my coffin."

Donovan the Great winked his unfairly long lashes. "You'll make it shine."

Sophie fluttered her own lashes. "Yes, I will."

He flung his thick dark locks back over his shoulder. "Love ya, toots. See you at the café later?"

"Where else would I be?"

When 1:00 p.m. rolled around, Red e-mailed her a request for hard copies of her hernia column. He said it was this month's *exciting* piece. Having an old-school editor who liked printed copies of his articles was not only uneconomical but on a day like today when the copy room was across enemy lines, or rather on Asher's side of the ficus tree, it produced a bit of a geographical challenge.

Maybe she could get one of the interns to make her copies. Then again, did she really want them looking at her hernia headline when she was already the topic of gossip?

No, thank you.

Just stride across the room, make the copies, and drop them off with Red. No big deal.

Sophie clicked the keys to send the article to the printer, then pulled herself to her feet. Feigning great interest in her pumps—they really were cute with the wedge and slingback straps—she avoided eye contact with anyone who wanted to give her one more sympathetic look.

She slipped into the copy room and rushed to the massive machine and pushed in her password.

It beeped at her.

She tried again.

It beeped again.

She pounded the keys harder. "I'll beep you—"

"Hi, Sophie," Asher's pretentious voice came from behind.

Ficus. She forced herself to swallow the lump suddenly choking her. "Asher," she hissed, refusing to give him the gift of eye contact. She held her breath and punched in the password again. The printer sprang to life, spitting out her article. *Oh, God, please don't let him see my hernia piece.*

From the corner of her eye, she saw him rest his arm against the wall a foot or so from where she stood.

Sophie could practically feel bile seep up.

"I have a box of your things. I can drop it off at your apartment later today."

Sophie's throat tightened. No chance she'd let him anywhere near her apartment. "I'll be at the café after work. You can drop it by there." She snatched the printed copies from the tray and folded them in half, then turned to leave, but Asher stood in her way. She sat back on her heels, refusing to back up. "Instead of infuriating me, why don't you go play with your new toy?"

Asher smirked. "Her name is Trixie, she's off on assignment, and it wasn't personal, Sophie."

"Good to know, and I don't really care."

Asher didn't budge. She considered a well-placed knee that would make him move, but she was above violence. For now.

"You're in my personal bubble, Asher."

"You have a bubble?"

"Amy!" she hollered over his shoulder. "Asher's in my bubble."

Almost instantly, Amy stuck her head into the copy room. She assessed the situation and raised a critical eyebrow at Asher.

"You should leave," Amy advised. "I only see that look right before she makes her kill."

He kept his amused gaze on Sophie. "According to your boundary lines, you're on my side of the tree."

Sophie's eyes grew wide. *Ficus.*

Amy stepped into the room and held the door open. "You must not have hear me. I said get out." A few silent beats passed. "Please," she said, barely containing a growl.

"Whatever," Asher grumbled. "I'll leave your stuff at the café."

The simultaneous bing of all three cell phones broke the tension.

Sophie reached for her phone, careful to keep her article hidden. It was from Red calling a mandatory meeting. *What could it be this time?*

Sophie followed her fellow journalists to the conference room and took a seat as far away from Asher as possible. Amy plopped down in the chair next to her, and Donovan winked from across the table.

Red stood at the head of the long table. In his right hand he held a fistful of pamphlets advertising the team-building trip orchestrated by their parent company, Over the Top, Inc. "Those of you who have already signed up for the company cruise, thank you. For those who haven't registered yet, here's some added motivation." He drew his glasses from his plump face and rubbed his eyes.

An unsettling fear knotted inside Sophie's gut. *Why was he stalling?*

"Ryan Pike from *Sports Now* will be flying in on Wednesday. He has agreed to head the training on board the cruise as Jack Batson from Human Resources has become unavailable."

At the mention of Ryan's name, Sophie's chest tightened as if an ice pick had stabbed her in her sternum. *Why Ryan?* She hadn't seen him in ten years, and for good reason. Was there not one other person in the company they could send?

"I want all hands on deck—pun intended." Red laughed at his own joke. "If you're ill, I need a doctor's note. Unless you're the primary caretaker for your children or a relative, you're going."

Sophie's breathing accelerated into short puffs. Mandatory meant she couldn't weasel out of it. She'd have to spend four days trapped on the same ship as Ryan.

Red scanned the room. His eyes landed on Sophie. Red treated her like a daughter. Always asking about her grandma, taking extra time to mentor her with her articles, going out Friday nights after the café closed. His eyes appeared remorseful, and he sighed. "And due to some personal circumstances, I won't be attending."

Sophie and Amy's eyes locked. *What?* She turned back to Red as if to look for him to say, "just kidding" only he didn't. Sophie slumped. First Ryan, then mandatory, and now Red wouldn't be there to provide her the buffer she needed.

Not happening.

Sophie's hand shot up. "I can't go. Not with the café struggling."

Red's rueful look said, *I'm sorry, darling, but I can't help you this time.* "We need all the training we can get, and Ryan's the best. With the way our subscription rates have plummeted the past three quarters, I don't want any further negative attention."

"Not a problem for me, Red." Asher's dimple popped when he played kiss up. Sophie was pretty sure she saw a sparkle ricochet from the Twit's perfectly whitened ivories.

"Way to be a team player, kid." Red slapped Asher on his shoulder. "But no need to suck up. I'm not happy about this, either."

Sophie sulked as Red passed out the pamphlets. When he tried to hand her one, she just glared at it.

Red dropped his chin. "How do you kids say it these days? Who pooped in your Cheerios?"

Sophie couldn't help the grin. Hipster lingo was not his forte.

"That's better," he said.

Sophie leaned in and whispered, "You know what Ryan wrote about me."

"I do." He pressed the pamphlet into her hand. "And you're not that girl anymore. You're an amazing journalist and an even more amazing woman. He'll see that."

Sophie frowned. "My column covers hernias this month. I highly doubt that screams amazing."

"We write about health, life, and leisure. Your health and humor column is very important. Remember, you earned the Ellie, he didn't."

Sophie played with the pamphlet's corner edge. Something in Red's tone was off. He was normally so lively. "Is there something we should know? Why the sudden change in training?"

Red sucked in a deep breath and squeezed her shoulder. "Nothing you need to worry about. Just remember to never put your career over your heart."

Sophie cupped her hand over his. She couldn't count how many times he'd told her that. "Never."

"I have some calls to make." He tapped her chin with his fist and walked out of the room, leaving Sophie somewhere between "This can't be happening" and "I feel like I'm going to toss my cookies." The copies of her editorial fell from her grip.

Asher scooped them up and handed them to her. "Nice hernia there, Soph," he said, then waltzed away like a cat that just sprayed.

Ficus.

Sophie shuffled back to her cubicle and slumped into her chair. She studied the colorful brochure, which glamorized the Baja Californian escape like it was paradise at sea. Considering the rock and the hard place she found herself between, paradise may as well have been purgatory.

Her thoughts subconsciously drifted to Ryan. A forever reminder that no girl forgets her first heartbreak, or in this case, her first backstabbing.

Chapter 3

"So you never actually met Derek Jeter, right?" one of the junior journalists said. This question happened to come from a twelve-year-old whose screeching voice made Ryan Pike's ears bleed. He hated these office tours.

He felt suffocated despite his four-thousand-square-foot office on the thirty-fifth floor of Stark Tower with a killer view of San Antonio's famous River Walk. He could play golf in here, but whenever a band of aspiring journalists arrived, they made him sweat . . . something that not even a coveted interview with the president of the NBA could do. Kids were out of his league.

"I had a telephone interview with him right before his final game."

"*So you are a poser,*" he screeched. A couple of the other kids snickered. "I knew it!"

The squealing lad was pressing his luck. His hair looked like a beaver had cut it, and the gap in his teeth almost made him look cute.

Almost.

"I am not a poser, I was paid a lot of money for that interview." He nodded at an autographed picture of the great Jeter that hung on his wall, accompanied by photos of a few dozen other sports legends. His reflection from the glass frame caught his eye. He looked tired, and a five o'clock shadow darkened his chin. Time to wrap up this *sports journalism tour turned accusation hour*.

"But you didn't actually meet him. Hang out with him. Get his autograph on a real baseball."

Sizing the boy up, Ryan imagined the amount of force it would require to launch the boy through the massive double-paned window. If aimed just right the kid would land in the River Walk's mucky water. Four feet deep was plenty of cushion, right? "There's a lot more to journalism than getting baseballs signed."

The boy crossed his arms. "Well, my dad has a ball signed by Babe Ruth and Jackie Robinson from the 1947 World Series."

"Impossible." Was the argument worth the effort? He knew firsthand the pressure dads put on their kids. And if he could alert this brat to that hard truth, his civic duty would be done for the day. "There's no such thing as a signed Ruth-Robinson ball. And if it did exist, it would be worth more money than I make in a year. And that's a lot."

The kid glared at him. "Well, my dad also has George Washington's sword from the Battle of Trenton."

"Equally doubtful," Ryan mumbled.

"And the first coin ever minted."

"Okay, we're done here." Ryan pressed the intercom to his secretary. "Lola, do we have parting gifts for these young men?"

"Wow, fifteen minutes," she answered with bright enthusiasm, all of it sarcastic. "A new record."

He stifled a grin. "You're fired."

"Ha ha. You couldn't find your left foot without me."

So true, but he'd never own up to it. "Will you see these boys out?"

Dead air and the tapping of a keyboard came from the other end of the intercom. "Lola? Parting gifts."

"You owe them another fifteen minutes. Fifteen minutes I've set aside to order you a throw rug for your bleak, man cave office. Oh, and thank you for the daffodils you're also ordering me. Your generosity knows no bounds."

"Lola." Ryan squeezed the bridge of his nose.

"Fine." Ryan could hear her smiling on the other end of the intercom. "I'll have the gifts ready."

He released the button. "Boys, it's been a pleasure." He glared at the beaver-haircut boy and added, "Of sorts. On your way out, my assistant will give each of you an autographed photo of the Dallas Cowboys."

Beaver Boy frowned. "My dad has a real—"

"I'm sure he does." Ryan tousled the kid's hair. He escorted the boys through his office door.

Lola handed them their photos and whispered, "Phil wants to see you."

He scrubbed a hand over his stubble. This was going to be his day. It was the pennant, after all and he was just waiting for the green light from Phil to cover what could be the final game in highly sought after championship.

"And Ryan." Lola lowered her voice, creasing her forehead.

Ryan knew that look. "Hmm?"

"Your dad called. Again."

~ ~ ~

After waiting for the boys to disappear down the hall, Ryan veered for the corner office where a silver plaque on the door read "Phil Grites—Editor-in-Chief." Equal parts respect and admiration for this man crossed Ryan's mind. Phil had given Ryan his first job as a young journalist right out of college and personally mentored him into the A-list writer he was today.

Ryan opened the solid oak door and let it close on its own behind him. "Hey, Phil."

Phil waved him into an oversized leather chair facing a mahogany desk. "You survive the boys?"

He shrugged. "And they survived me." Why the delay tactic? Phil was always direct and to the point. Was he trying to build up to good news? Or hesitating to deliver bad news?

Phil sat. "I appreciate you stepping up today. You know how we value the youth in our community."

"Sure," Ryan said, locking his hands together behind his head. "But I'm sure that's not what you wanted."

"Listen, Ryan," Phil said amicably, shuffling some papers from a stack on his desk. "Red Goldman from *Up Front* has accepted an offer for early retirement effective Friday."

Retired or fired? Ryan wondered. He'd never seen an editor retire with four days' notice. What was he missing?

"The board has asked I assign my best employee to cover in the interim until he's replaced. You're my number one and you have experience, so naturally I've assigned you." Phil's smile widened as he passed a folder across the desk.

Ryan paused, absorbing the news. Red Goldman was Sophie's boss. He hadn't seen her in years but showing up as her interim boss after how she left things may cross more than a few hairs. And how he reacted to how she left things may cross her left hook to his chin.

And then the nagging question of why Goldman would retire on such short notice bothered him. There was more going on here.

Clearing his throat, he took the file and composed himself. He needed an excuse to decline. "Next week's the pennant," he said, knowing Phil was well aware Ryan was scheduled to cover it.

"Johnson can cover it."

A heated stab of adrenaline shot up Ryan's spine. *The hell he can.* The pennant was one of the most coveted sporting events. Over fifty thousand people followed his personal sports blog, and he couldn't just *not* write about the pennant. Up until now he'd made accurate predictions and called games based on relief pitchers. That sort of thing couldn't be taught. It was instinct. Something Johnson lacked. This meeting was turning to crap fast. "Johnson?"

Phil tipped his head, as if he'd thought this through. *Except details, Phil. You can't play the rookie when the game is on the line.*

"You still get the World Series, don't worry."

At that Ryan clenched his jaw. Johnson's articles were crap, but his father was chairman of the board, which meant he often scored top assignments. "With all due respect, sir, ever see a turtle on top of a post?"

Phil combed a hand over the few strands of hair on top of his head. "I know, but think of this as a great opportunity."

Yeah, and I actually earned my position here. Ryan checked his tone before responding. "Why me?" What Ryan really wanted to ask was why not send Johnson as the interim? The guy had his lips permanently glued to whoever ass was in command, so this position was perfect for him.

"Why not?" Phil ambled to the wet bar. He poured two fingers of whiskey and handed one to Ryan before raising his glass. "To a new promotion."

Ryan almost dropped the tumbler. "A promotion?"

Phil clinked Ryan's glass, and then swallowed its contents. "The position's open. Why not throw your name in the hat? Consider this your on-the-job interview." Phil poured a second round. "I'll put in a good word for you."

Ryan nodded in thanks and stared out the massive window overlooking the Alamo. The whiskey's spicy and vanilla notes burned his nose. He tossed the drink back and pressed the back of his hand to his mouth. The familiar burn grounded him.

The last thing he wanted was to work out of the San Francisco office. After all, he'd done a fine job not visiting that office more than absolutely necessary, and Sophie had been conveniently absent each time he'd flown in. But he wasn't in a position to tell Phil no. Besides, he loved his job. There was nothing better than being in the middle of the action, feeling the players sweat and hearing the grunts as they became America's heroes. All he wanted was to tell their stories and follow their careers. He interviewed every athlete he wanted. The job was daunting and living out of hotels was exhausting, but the chase kept him going.

Ryan sighed. "I don't know, Phil. I'm not sure running *Up Front* is for me." He turned and faced Phil. "Don't get me wrong. I'm honored. But I interview athletes. I have a pre-pennant interview with Buster Posey in two days. *That's* what I know. *That's* my job."

Phil poured another shot of whiskey. Ryan already felt the liquor numbing all the right places and he held up a hand, signifying a half shot was sufficient.

"Don't sell yourself short, son." Phil's smoker's voice graveled. "Your *Sports Now* app put us in contract with the largest smart phone company, making it the fastest downloaded sports app ever. That's the sort of mind we need running one of our magazines."

Ryan smiled at the compliment. He worked two years on that app and was thoroughly enjoying the residual income each download offered.

Phil slid another file across the desk. "You'll also join the *Up Front* staff on their team-builder excursion in a few days and assist with some of the training. I've already let Red know you're flying in."

Ryan nearly choked on his drink. Did Phil not get it? Not only was Ryan just informed that he'd no longer cover the pennant, but now he'd miss *watching* the final games. Sure, he could watch the highlights on his app, but apps didn't show live action details—the fierce look in the pitcher's eyes after the catcher determined whether to call a curve ball or splitter, how the third baseman rarely planted his heels on the ground after the pitch, and most importantly, the excruciating pained look in a thousand fans' eyes when a batter made contact. Would it be a homerun, a base hit, an out?

Writing about pounding heartbeats in athletes who blew out their knees and suffered concussions was a privilege. Being an editor for a magazine that covered fashion, entertainment, and health didn't exactly call to him.

Phil crossed his office again and poured himself a seltzer. "Johnson's going to be madder than an old wet hen that we passed him over. He looks good on paper and all, but we need a man with your digital experience and someone who knows this industry inside and out. It's a new ball game out there, and we have to stay ahead of our competition." Phil's eyes narrowed. "We feel you're the best for the interim."

Ryan scrubbed a hand through his hair. There was something more Phil wasn't saying. Why was Red quitting? Why reassign *him* when there were dozens of more qualified candidates looking to jump in at *Up Front*. What was he missing? "Level with me, Phil. Is he quitting or is it something more?"

Phil sipped his water and stared at Ryan. He set his glass down and tapped the rim. "I've heard talk of a merge with *Jazz*. But it's doubtful. Blending *Up Front* with *Jazz* doesn't feel like a good mix. Not only is *Jazz* only in digital form, it'd require a whole new facelift. Marketing is looking into that now. But we need you there." He tipped his chin and raised his brow. "Is that clear?"

Ryan nodded. "Crystal." He set his drink down and picked up the file, fanning through the specs. The first few pages explained the itinerary. Ensenada, Avalon, a day at sea. *That* he could manage, especially the stop in Avalon where he owed a friend a long, overdue visit. Flipping through a few more pages, he stopped at Sophie's employee fact sheet. Memories flooded his mind, twisting in his gut the way only painful ones can. It had been ten years. She'd made it abhorrently clear she was over him. *This* would be a little harder to manage. But he was a professional. This was his job. A routine business trip where they'd work separately. Period.

Phil slapped Ryan on the shoulder and he stiffened. "Relax, son. This is a good thing. Aligning your career in a direct path that's both good for business and lining your pocket—that's what separates the go-getters from the has-beens around here. And I'm not going to be around here much longer. So, pull this off successfully and when you return from the West Coast, the two words you'll here from me will be"—Phil held up his glass—"Congrats, Chief."

Chapter 4

Sophie tapped a brad nail into Chicks 'n' Slicks wood paneling and hung the vintage sign she'd picked up at a garage sale last weekend. This one quoted Laurel Thatcher Ulrich: 'Well-behaved woman seldom make history.' She angled it in an effort to conceal a crack on the café's gray-tinted wall. Yet another thing her sleazy landlord hadn't fixed.

Being six blocks from the publishing office, the café's location was an easy after-work walk. She had fallen in love with its 1950s malt-shop inspiration. With money earned from a fundraiser, they'd put in a black-and-white-square tile floor, red jukebox, and a frozen-custard machine, AKA Suzie—fondly named after one of their girls here. They even paid extra to have it restored to its original 1955 condition.

Despite a few holes in the walls, some dents in the cold box, outdated fixtures, and the unsightly smoke damage on the ceiling above the grill, the café was perfect. Its flaws mirrored the imperfect teens that volunteered here. Sophie wished she had money to fix everything, but then again, securing five grand this month for rent to keep the program running was money she didn't have. And it could be weeks before she heard back from the recent batch of grant applications.

She popped another hip-o-licious chocolate morsel into her mouth, trying to ignore the looming, gray cloud reminding her that if this place closed, the teens had nowhere to go. The chocolate sat on her tongue, engaging her taste buds the way only sugar crystals could. Was that her fifth? No, probably more like her eighth . . . or eighteenth.

Familiar squabbling from the kitchen grew louder as Charlie Williams, her favorite teenager in the world, and Donovan pushed through the kitchen door. Donovan carried a fresh batch of sweet potato fries.

"I'll hear something when I hear something," Charlie said on a laugh. "It's not even that big of a deal."

"You bet your bum it's a big deal," Donovan insisted. He set the tray of fries on the bar top and transferred them to a basket before sliding them toward Sophie. "Try these. New recipe."

"What is or isn't that big of a deal?" Sophie tossed a rag on a recently vacated dining table so she wouldn't forget to wipe it down.

Donovan dusted his hands, shed his hair net, and hung up his apron. "Nothing. Charlie likes to argue, especially when it involves senseless reasons why she hasn't heard back from any of her choice colleges."

"I could've told you that." Sophie, popped a fry into her mouth. "These are good. Need salt though."

Donovan's eyes cut to hers. "Not everything needs salt."

"That's debatable," she said and then wiped down the table. "Anyway, I agree with Charlie. She'll hear something when she does, and hopefully it will include a full-ride."

Donovan's eyes lit. "Wouldn't that be great?"

Charlie seemed to reserve her smile as if any sort of positive emotion would jinx the acceptance letter, forcing a hard no. Though a small grin slipped past her lips as she pushed a vinyl chair up to the table, collecting the $4.32 tip left under the receipt. "Want half?"

"All yours, my dear." Sophie waved off the crumpled bills. Charlie always offered to share the tips. But Sophie had never taken money from any of the teens.

Donovan wrapped his scarf around his neck and slipped on his coat. "Okay, the last batch of sweet potato fries are in the warmer, unsalted for now—deal with it—and I've prepped a few more turkey burgers with my secret awesome sauce. Also in the warmer. The cran-walnut salads are prepared and in the cooler, and Jenny and I are off for our pedi-date. Her toes have been banned from sandals until further notice."

"Pedicure, huh? 'Bout time." Charlie tossed a fry in the air and caught it in her mouth. "Pretty good. But I agree. Needs salt."

Donovan twirled his finger between Charlie's eyes. "Watch it, girlie. And tomorrow we're going to separate that unibrow."

"Gross, no. Sophie, Donovan's trying to turn me into him."

Donovan let out a wicked laugh. "You wish!"

Sophie grinned. Tormenting her teens through pampering was a rite of passage she never experienced in her own adolescence. "No sympathy here. I agree with Don Juan. Time for your brows to become two separate entities."

Donovan grabbed Jenny and waved. "See you all tomorrow."

Sophie watched them leave, eternally grateful that he spoke their same hormonal teenage language. She glanced at the only occupied table in the back. Two older ladies, regulars who almost always ordered the chicken-pesto salad, stared back at her.

Sophie smiled and walked over. "Can I get you anything else?"

"Nope, we're just enjoying dinner *and* a show," one of the ladies answered.

Sophie cleared their empty plates. "We aim to please."

"You do it so well," the other lady said, patting her

modern bouffant hairstyle in place. "I just adore this little café. We'll take two of your famous custards to go."

That warmed Sophie's heart more than anything. The custard here represented far more than just an old-fashioned dessert. "Coming right up."

Sophie walked the ladies to the door and handed them their custards. When they left, Sophie shoveled another chocolate into her mouth.

Charlie raised a brow. "Those little Satan's will go right to your hips."

Sophie stuck out her chocolate-covered tongue. "And?"

"You still not over the Twit?"

"Six dates hardly constitute a need to get over someone," she lied. "I'm more heartbroken that I lapsed enough judgment to justify dates two through six."

"Name one woman who hasn't," Charlie said over her shoulder as she carried the empty plates to the kitchen.

"When did you grow up and get all logical on me?" *Le sigh.* Sophie didn't know what she'd do without Charlie. She represented the maturity Sophie required at the café, but dished out just enough back talk to keep Sophie grounded in adulting.

As far as Ash-face, nothing about their ten-minute relationship had been serious. It wasn't like Sophie had picked out a wedding dress or anything. But a spring wedding with her bridesmaids wearing peach and steely blue refused to give up real estate in her mind. It only solidified the awful, not-so-benign tumor that established residency in the pit of her stomach.

The only true time Sophie had heard wedding bells was a decade ago. And that breakup was probably for the best— college romances had the highest divorce rate. Or so she'd read.

Sophie absently popped another chocolate.

Charlie tsked, walking out of the kitchen. "A few more of those and we'll have to change the café's motto from 'a healthier lifestyle' to 'eating your emotions.'"

"Don't judge." Sophie held out the bag. "Want one?"

"Thought you'd never ask."

"Good, now please ask Deidra prep the fruit for tomorrow."

Charlie rolled her eyes, did an about-face, and then marched off. For a seventeen-year-old, Charlie was one part sassy teen and three parts Yoda. Her perceptive Jedi mind tricks didn't come without heartache, however. Maybe it had to do with her pipe dream of going to law school. Thank you, Reese Witherspoon and *Legally Blonde,* for providing that idea, but not the funds!

Charlie's mom, Josephine D'Angelo, had kicked her out of the apartment a month after she turned thirteen because, well, prostitution and parenting didn't mesh. Charlie, fluent in sarcasm, strolled down to the liquor store and called the police on a payphone. She had watched enough TV to know her basic rights. But rather than take Charlie back to her apartment, the police officer took her to an emergency overnight group home that, against Charlie's wishes, turned permanent. Within weeks, Charlie added three misdemeanor charges for vandalism and petty theft to her rap sheet.

During the court hearing, the judge listened as Charlie's court liaison ruefully explained her family situation and recent bulimic tendencies. The judge was a golf buddy with Red and familiar with *Up Front's* new outreach, and how it offered teens, mostly girls, with eating disorders a safe place to hang out.

Then, Charlie's mom kicked her pimp to the streets and completed a 12-step program. Newly reformed, having found religion, she begged Charlie to come home, and the judge approved the mutual request for Charlie to return.

Sophie was immediately drawn to Charlie's hard shell and soft interior, so when Charlie's fragile relationship with her mom remained rocky, and she spent most afternoons at the new café anyway, it worked out that Charlie would often crash on Sophie's couch. Being she was seventeen and pseudo-emancipated anyhow, the unofficial arrangement suited everyone perfectly.

Sophie smiled at the thought, thankful for how things worked out.

The front door opened with a loud thud. Sophie jumped and Amy charged in, bestie style. Mark, her newest fling, walked in behind her, his eyes glued to his phone.

"Miss me?" Amy asked. "Because you're gonna love me now. You'll never guess what I have!"

Sophie looked over Amy's head at Mark. "A bun in the oven?"

Amy scoffed. "God, no. I have something way better." She slammed a check on the bar. "Cold hard cash for the café."

"Ooh, you're right. That is better. Did you sell a kidney? I hear black market value has gone up."

Amy sat at the bar, and Sophie slid around to the front so they were face to face. Mark collapsed in the bar stool next to Amy, eyes still fastened to his phone. Sophie would usually comment on the guy's obsession over a five-inch screen, but she really should be happy for her friend. Finding a boyfriend wasn't exactly Amy's specialty, so who was she to interrupt a budding romance?

"Not exactly."

"Did you mug someone?"

Amy lifted an eyebrow. "Closer."

Okay, that piqued Sophie's curiosity. She leaned in, her attention dialed to full-blown. "I promise to plead the Fifth if subpoenaed. Spill it."

"You know Dirk Green over at Channel eight, right?"

"The guy with the toupee?"

"The one and the same." Amy sashayed her shoulders as one does when the story is about to get good. "Well, he bought my silence for another three years."

Sophie's eyes widened. "Sounds scandalous. What'd he do?" She gasped. "Did he lie about a story? They all do. Their embellishments put ours to shame. Not that I've ever done it. That I'll admit to, that is."

"Better," Amy enticed.

Sophie felt her cheeks burn. She'd had a YouTube video and hernia piece that could be considered for the humiliation-of-the-year award. So this must be real good. "Tell me already!"

Amy's lips pursed. "Ever hear of a Barney?"

Sophie's jaw dropped. "A fake lead that was aired?"

Amy nodded slowly. "Right after college, he bought a story involving a French dossier that was transcribed incorrectly. He thought it was a financial institution that had embezzled millions from its customers. Sort of like a Ponzi Scheme."

"No."

"Yes."

"What happened? And how?" Sophie's voice cracked, almost afraid of the answer.

"Total rookie mistake. But luckily, before the piece aired, I was in the van editing my own work when my then boyfriend, a French nudist model—God I miss his abs—got bored and read the dossier. Turns out, Dirk was being punked by a former classmate and his source was a paid actor out to make Dirk look bad."

Sophie sat back on her heels, only too sure how quickly that story would have ended Dirk's career before it even took off. "How have you never told me that story?"

"That story was never worth fifteen hundred dollars."

"Wow. He didn't mind you blackmailing him?"

"Not for a good cause. He's forever in my debt, and he happens to love your column."

Sophie smiled.

"Meanwhile, we're that much closer to our goal." Amy's optimism revealed a truth. They were still thirty-five hundred dollars short. But progress and all . . .

"Anyway, all that legwork made me hungry." She turned to Mark who was busy building some world on an app. "I'm getting my usual. How about you?"

He remained glued to his phone. "Okay."

Amy shrugged. "Two veggie burgers with sweet-potato fries please."

Sophie wrote up a ticket and took it to Deidra in the kitchen. Only one of the girls was legally old enough to work the grill, so when Donovan wasn't around, most of the food was reheated from the warmer.

With the grant money, maybe she could hire a real cook . . . or at least an adult who could use the grill. Maybe that would bring in more customers.

Sophie brought Amy and Mark cucumber water. She heard the clinking of change being dropped in the jukebox.

Charlie was at the box picking out a song. A few seconds later, Ariana Grande with her four-chord range that made baby cherubs cry broke through the sketchy speakers.

Charlie danced her way to the center of the room and scooted two tables out of the way. It was common knowledge that none of them, save Donovan, had any rhythm, so watching Charlie dance ranked right up there with watching a cat take a bath. But sure enough, the music drew Deidra from the kitchen, spatula in hand, and the two of them jerked around the dining room paying homage to that one kid no one ever picked to play on the team. The girls threw their hands in the air and contorted their midsection in ways Sophie was sure would cause her to break a hip.

Charlie grabbed Sophie's hand.

"Oh, no you don't!"

"Come on," Charlie coaxed. "Don't be a prude."

"I am not a prude."

"Then come dance. Live a little."

"I'm watching the kitchen, sorry."

"I'll watch the kitchen," Amy said with a betraying smile. "Go dance. It's good for the soul."

"So is stabbing best friends in the eyeball."

Amy sipped her water. "Prude."

"Fine," Sophie said, making sure Amy knew the 'F' in *fine* really meant another common four-letter word, saved for moments like these.

Sophie popped her hands in the air and hip-chucked Charlie into a nearby chair. She shimmied her hips so hard, she put the other girls to shame. Laughing and music drowned out all other sounds. Except one.

"Having fun?"

The low voice that sent a sizzle down Sophie's back was one she'd never forget. One she'd longed to hear for years, but now ranked right up there with an onset of herpes . . . or worse.

Chapter 5

Sophie froze like an ice sculpture, and cold pierced straight to her heart. Surely someone was punking her now. Ryan Pike wasn't due for two days.

Sophie dropped her arms and slowly turned. Amy must have seen "the look" because she jumped up and turned the music off.

"Hey!" Charlie protested until she saw there was someone else in the café. "Oh."

"Charlie," Sophie murmured. "Can you and Deidra finish Amy's order please?"

"Sure," Charlie said in almost question form. "You okay?"

"Super."

The girls disappeared behind the kitchen door and Sophie continued to stare at Ryan. He *was* here. Smirking, maybe. Or trying not to laugh.

Either way, he pierced through her with those haunting Caribbean-blue eyes, the exact same shade she remembered from a decade ago. Broad shoulders had replaced that boyish stick figure. His hair was a little shorter and strands of gray peppered his dark roots. He still carried his blessed assurance in his back pocket. Like his ace in the hole. Weren't memories supposed to pale instead of increase in hotness?

Ryan grinned with that same commanding air of self-confidence. The cramped dining room shrank, and all the oxygen drained from the air. "You have quite the knack for dance."

Her skin felt tight, her mind numb.

She was supposed to have until Wednesday to deal with this. Not tonight. Two more days. "What are you doing here?" She wanted her two days back.

He shrugged. "I'm hungry."

Really? Five million cafés in the Bay Area and you waltz into this one? And did I mention it's been ten years? She crossed her arms. "And you come here?"

Amusement flickered in his eyes. "Since *Up Front* has a vested interest in this place, I figured I'd check it out." Ryan looked around, taking in the ambiance. "It's . . . quaint."

Was that a compliment?

Amy slid to Sophie's side. "So, this is him?"

"Yes."

Ryan's lips pressed together in a hard line. "I had a long flight and I'd like to have a sandwich? Or cup of soup maybe?"

"We don't have soup."

"A sandwich is fine."

Leave it to a man to leave for ten years and come back wanting a sandwich. Would it have killed Ryan to warn her he was coming? "Um, take a seat wherever you want."

He sat at the bar, still looking around, allowing Sophie a moment to wipe a gunk of mascara that took this exact moment to blind her. Stupid idea, since that just made her hand black . . . and probably smeared her cheeks. She escaped to the kitchen, grabbing Amy along the way.

Amy followed. "Are you okay?"

About as good as a lightning bolt to the head. "Peachy."

"I know he's a trigger for you."

"I'm good." *Good enough.* "I promise."

Amy studied Sophie's face. "Just say the word and I'll kick him out lickety-split."

"Deal."

"So, you didn't tell me he's gorgeous." Amy's eyes darted between Sophie and the end of the bar, where Ryan was shaking Mark's hand like Rhett Butler himself.

"Mother Nature has clearly been way nicer to him than to me."

Amy socked Sophie's arm. "Stop it. You're gorgeous. Even with raccoon eyes." Amy licked her thumb and index finger and did the mother saliva thing on Sophie's face. "There. We only have a few minutes before those guys start engaging in the fine art of man gossip."

Sophie cocked a brow. "Seriously?"

"Trust me, it's a thing."

Deidra stepped into the kitchen and rubbed her palms together as if she were about to feast on a Thanksgiving spread. "So are you going to tell me who that hottie is or what?"

"Simmer, girl," Amy warned. "He's the opposition. At least for now."

Deidra rolled her eyes. "And you guys consider *me* the child."

Sophie kneaded her temples. Everything was pelting her too fast and Ryan was making himself at home in *her* café. Should she make him go or find out what he wants? Because coincidences were not a thing. He wanted something. "Amy, what do I do?"

"You pull out all the stops and make him regret the day he walked away."

He did walk away. Or ran. At least that's the story Sophie told. Still, he wrote that article about her. But the article didn't specify how fast he typed the hurtful words. Regardless. "I don't play games."

"But men love games."

Gamer extraordinaire she was not. Nor was she twelve. "No. No games."

Amy pursed her lips. "You're no fun."

Sophie's belly twisted. "Not with him."

"Fine." Amy hugged her friend. "You're in the driver's seat. I'll spare you my expertise in back-seat-driving."

The girls walked out of the kitchen, Amy in the lead. She slipped up behind Mark and slapped him on the back of his head.

He rubbed his scalp. "What was that for?"

"Anything you may have said in our absence."

Mark grinned. "Babe, if we're going to make that show, we have to go."

Amy groaned. "Shoot. I forgot. I have a review tonight." She looked dolefully at Sophie, and whispered, "I'll cancel."

"No, go. I've got it here."

Amy wrapped Sophie in a hug. "Call me for anything. I'll be right here."

Sophie smiled. "Thanks, bestie."

"You bet. Just play it cool. Remember, he's on your turf now."

With that, Amy dropped a couple ten-dollar bills on the bar top and took Mark by his arm, leading him out the door.

Sophie counted to ten, hoping the next time she opened her mouth she would sound as confident as Ryan looked. Because he was really here. *Here*, inside her café, even more handsome than when he left. Older. An entire *decade* older than the last time they were together. It seemed like yesterday that he broke her heart, without explanation or a goodbye. She may have shut him out at first, but she knew the real reason. Page seventy-four of *Sports Now*'s September issue, ten years ago.

This time she didn't try to hide the ragged breath escaping her lips. Sophie turned around.

Ryan was staring at her, and she couldn't break his gaze. Her spine tingled, and her heart jackhammered. Could he tell how much effort it took to stop her knees from buckling?

Ryan's raspy sigh broke the deafening silence. "Think I can get that sandwich?"

Her heart slowed to an almost rapid pace. "Right. A sandwich." *Forgive my ogling.* She called to Charlie. "Can you prep a sandwich?"

"Sure, what kind?"

Sophie looked back at Ryan. Had he gotten taller?

"Anything's fine."

"Give him Amy's sandwich. She left without it." Ryan had always been a carnivore. He'd probably choke on a veggie burger. "I take it you want that to go?"

He held her gaze without a hint of levity. "Not particularly. Do you want me to take it to go?"

"Yes. No. I mean you probably should." The longer Ryan stayed in her café, the higher the odds were she'd say or do something she would regret . . . like kill him. His mouth tugged up on one side. Or kiss him. Another minute or two, and she might be willing to forgive him for . . . page seventy-four, was it?

"I need to get ready for my meeting with Red tomorrow morning anyway."

Red's troubled face earlier flashed across her mind. He seemed upset about something. What if this was that something? *If you hurt him, I will track you down and cut you.* "You'll like him. He's a good guy."

"I'm sure I will." He shot her that unfair, heart-stopping smile.

Charlie handed Ryan the sandwich bag, making sure their fingers touched. Sophie tried hard not to roll her eyes.

But Ryan's eyes remained fixed on Sophie's. "It was good to see you, Sapphire."

Her old nickname, the way it rolled off his tongue and lingered in her ears . . . it took her back. Sophie shook her head. She had to get herself together. Now. "Yeah." Her voice caught her in her throat. "See ya."

Ryan pushed open the door . . . and smacked Asher right in the moneymaker.

Blood drained from Sophie's face. *Thank you, Mr. Murphy, for coming through again*!

Ryan held the door open for Asher. "Oh, hey, man, sorry. Are you okay?"

Sophie bit down on a laugh, wishing a real-life "replay" button existed.

Asher rubbed his nose. "Fine."

"Pity," Sophie said, mostly under her breath. Could it have hurt anything if Ryan broke Asher's nose?

Asher carried the promised box containing Sophie's things, the potted plant she'd bought for his kitchen window right on top. Sophie winced, remembering how she watered it just few days ago.

"Hey, you're Ryan Pike," Asher said.

"Yes." Ryan offered his hand.

Asher shifted the box to his hip and shook it, a cheesy grin slapped across his face. "I'm Asher Hughes, in *Up Front's* entertainment department. Good to finally meet you. I follow your blog religiously."

"Thanks. And thanks for reading my blog."

What sort of bromance was this? Was Asher drooling? And no, they couldn't be friends. Asher was still holding her box. Ryan was holding her sandwich. Both held a broken piece of her. This wasn't right. *Get out! Both of you!*

Asher still gripped Ryan's hand. "No, thank *you*. I've won a few bets based on your predictions."

"Oh." Ryan frowned, wiping his palm on his jeans.

"You're pretty much a legend around the office. You really think the Giants are going to take another series?" Asher's eyes grew to silver dollars. "Did you watch Posey's hit last night? I thought—"

"We're closing." Sophie stepped forward wringing a terry towel so tight she thought the fibers might split. "So, if you guys are done—and believe me, you're done—I need to lock up."

Ryan's soft eyes swayed toward her. "Right. I'll see you tomorrow. Good night." He turned back to Asher. "Sorry about the nose."

"No problem."

When the door closed behind Ryan and Asher moved two steps inside, Sophie held up her hand. "That's far enough. You can leave the box and go."

"Where do you want it?" His cheery attitude grew stale. Apparently he didn't have any of that kissass boy charm he used on Ryan reserved for her. Not that she cared.

She pointed to the table closest to the door. "Right there is fine."

He plopped the box on the table. "You sure you don't want to take inventory? I have your vinyl Beatles records and"—he pulled out a colorful box—"your super-absorbent tampons. Still not clear why you put those in my bathroom."

Sophie tasted bile. *Because I needed them one time and had to go to the store since you wanted me to stay and rewrite your column. I forgot to take them home. So, sue me.* "You can leave now."

"Actually, can I order a kale smoothie?"

Sophie narrowed her eyes. Was he purposely trying to antagonize her? "Goodbye, Asher."

Asher held his hands up. "Fine. I'm leaving. But I don't understand why you're so mad. It's not like we were exclusive."

The problem was Asher was right. Sophie was the one reading into the relationship. Asher never said they were a "couple." Dating past the twenty-something age was only beneficial for men. Whereas women are introduced to cellulite and fat pockets, guys become all Richard Gere and George Clooney. Not fair. "I'm not mad," she said flatly, "I just need to lock up and give the girls a ride home."

"So, a rain check on that smoothie then? Maybe Trixie and I will come by next week to try the new cran-salad."

Sophie clenched her jaw, but said in her most even-tempered voice, "You need to leave." *Before I gouge your eyes out with one of those super absorbents.*

"Sorry," he sneered, exiting. The sneer clearly negated his apology. But whatever, he was gone.

Sophie flipped the bolt and sighed. He wasn't worth it. She looked around and felt the warmth this home away from home offered. This was her safe place. The teens' safe place. Asher might not be worth it, but this place was, even if she was bone weary from the day and had to spend the rest of the evening prepping for tomorrow. Like every evening, the rest of her time spent at the café was delegated to sweeping, mopping, washing, chopping, and packaging. It all had to be done.

The best part of afterhours, however, was watching the teens sit at the bar, eating frozen custard, and talking about everything from boys to school drama to personal triggers. Seeing them band together in an effort to heal made the long, hard hours worth it. So, securing funding was not an option. It was a must.

Charlie popped her head out of the kitchen door. "I assume it's safe to come out? Mail's here." She glided across the floor and handed it to Sophie. They usually only received junk mail, since the café's bills went directly to corporate.

One piece of mail stuck out, however, addressed directly to Chicks 'n' Slicks. Sophie's cheeks immediately burned hot. It was from Mr. Tomilson, the landlord. *Now what did he want?*

Sophie's throat tightened. There were only a handful of reasons Mr. *Waste of a Human Being* Tomilson would directly correspond with her café. And not one of them was good.

"Bad news?" Charlie grabbed the bag of chocolate Satans from Sophie's apron and popped one into her mouth.

Sophie ripped open the envelope and unfolded the paper. A hitch in Charlie's breath told Sophie that she was reading the letter over her shoulder. And when Charlie slipped a Satan inside Sophie's palm, she knew Charlie understood exactly what the bad news meant.

A rent hike, effective immediately.

Chapter 6

Ryan stepped onto the sidewalk. The café door swung closed, effectively cutting him off from the chatter inside. And from Sophie.

Though this was the City by the Bay, in this part of town, he'd be hard pressed to smell the ocean over the stench of urine and garbage. Not unlike San Antonio, however, the beauty of the city was not on the surface, but in the diversity of the people.

Although currently, the city seemed to be of one mind, amped up on baseball fever. With the home team up three games, all he saw was the Giant's orange on every surface. He'd be sure to not wear his Dodger's shirt anywhere near this city.

The jagged skyline lit up the city, drowning out the night sky. Yet, Aquarius was clearly visible.

His dad's favorite constellation.

His father would be eager to share facts about the water-bearing constellation, and proud that Ryan still knew it covered 980-square degrees of the sky. Well, that is if Ryan was still nine and cared about that any more.

He took a long breath, trying to settle his nerves. The temperature dropped significantly over the past hour, and Ryan was grateful for the cold bite. No sense in hailing a cab, the Grand Bella Suites, his hotel, was only a brisk walk from the café, and that would give his head, among other extremities, a much-needed cool down. He took off in the direction of his suite. What had possessed him to visit Chicks 'n' Slicks?

He could lie to himself and believe he went to satisfy his curiosity for why Sophie would create such a huge community program when the rest of the affiliate magazines used food drives and office tours to "give back" to inner-city kids. But he knew he wanted to settle other curiosities. And as soon as he read her personal file, he knew exactly why she got so involved with kids suffering from eating disorders. It was deeply personal to her. And if it was personal, it meant a great deal.

Ryan kicked a rock across the road and it thudded against something. When the object moved, Ryan recoiled, only to realize a homeless person leaned against the building, hidden by a sheet. He stared at his sandwich. Chef's choice wasn't much to offer, but it probably tasted just fine.

Ryan walked over and tapped his foot against the piece of cardboard the person was sitting on.

When the sheet lifted, a gray-haired head popped out. Ryan jumped back. Damn if the guy wasn't the spitting image of his dad. He composed himself, hoping he didn't startle the guy. "Sorry about the rock."

"Don't mention it. I've had worse." The man's gravel voice added years to what Ryan assumed was mid-fifties. His age sunspots, faded scars on his arms, and missing patches of hair told Ryan *worse* was likely an understatement.

"You hungry?"

"Starved. You offering?"

Ryan held up the bag. "I think this lacks meat, but it's from that café over there."

The man looked past Ryan. "Good café."

"You know it?"

"Of course I do," he said as if that was a given.

Ryan handed the guy the food. "What's your name, boss?"

The man took the bag. "Thanks. Just call me Wolf. You got custard in here?" He opened the bag to peek.

"Sorry. Just the sandwich. Not even sure what kind to be honest."

Wolf shrugged. "Just as well. Probably healthier, considering where it's from. There's some really fine girls in there."

Ryan flinched. It must have been evident in his expression, because Wolf let out a hearty laugh.

"Not like that, junior. I mean the girls in there are well behaved. Sweet, too. The lady who runs that place must have come from a convent or something, because my own daughter won't give me the time of day. But they . . . well, they're a lot nicer than my Janey."

What Ryan assumed was a painful memory flickered in Wolf's eye. He pulled a twenty from his pocket and handed it to his new friend. "Sorry about the rock. Enjoy the sandwich and have a nice evening." Ryan crossed the street again and gave another long look at the café before it disappeared from sight.

A little more research had told him that Chicks 'n' Slicks funding had been cut by over half. Which didn't make sense. In fact, that was the typical formula for axing the whole program.

Ryan shook the thought. He'd know if they were nixing it. But just in case, he'd ask Phil about it later.

Once at the hotel, Ryan headed to its convenience store. He'd already checked in so he waved at the man at the front counter as he passed by. A pre-made ham and cheddar sandwich, candy bar, and bottle of water would suffice. He paid for the food and then unwrapped the sandwich, taking a huge bite. It wasn't much, but it curbed the low growl in the pit of his stomach. At least the part related to hunger. The other part, well, that was knotted up quite tightly.

Finishing the sandwich in three large bites, Ryan tossed the wrapper into a garbage receptacle next to the elevator, then pressed the button heading to the thirteenth floor. The penthouse was bigger than he needed, but Lola had set up his accommodations, so he wouldn't complain.

He cracked open his water bottle and relaxed on the king-sized bed. His head still spun thinking about Sophie. Watching her dance with the girls in the café awoke something in him he wasn't ready to face. It took him back to the girl he once knew. The girl who, after only dating a few months, he would have married.

He had been young and dumb. It was probably for the best they broke up, even though he still didn't know why she had dumped him. Fast-moving, passionate relationships were doomed to fail. It probably saved them both a ton of heartache. But his heart didn't seem to believe it, even after a decade apart.

Still, seeing her tonight was worth it, regardless of how it threw an incredibly complicated wrench in executing his task at hand. He would ignore *that something* she'd awoke in him and be the professional Phil believed he was. The professional *he* knew he was.

~ ~ ~

After a sleepless night, Ryan prepared for his visit to the West Coast publishing office. He cleared a three-mile run on the treadmill, hopped in a cold shower, and downed a bottle of cranberry juice. Wishing, instead, for the shot of bourbon in his minibar. But drinking for more than a social obligation was a hard limit he imposed on himself. Even if he still couldn't shake Sophie from his head.

At a quarter to six, he grabbed his coat and escaped the hotel. Ten minutes later, the cab pulled street side to a four-floor industrial building. The structure sat level, despite the steep hill it was on. It butted up against similar-shaped buildings and had suffered from sun exposure. But it was a prime location, only a mile or so from Google.

His last visit here was when he interviewed quarterback legend Joe Montana about former football players and prolonged brain injuries. Conveniently, Sophie had been out of the office, but so had Red. He hated that his first opportunity to meet the man was because of what Ryan assumed was a forced retirement.

The elevator spit him out on the third floor. He swept the layout, gathering his bearings. There seemed to be less room in here than a third-string locker room. His cheeks warmed just thinking about his spacious office with a killer view.

On the way to Red's office, he passed no less than twenty cubicles. Each one personally decorated with photos, stationary, notes on features. Which tiny box belonged to Sophie?

He turned the corner of the last row of cubicles and there, leaning heavily against the doorframe of a windowed office, stood Red Goldman. The red streaks in the whites of his eyes told Ryan that he hadn't been the only one who couldn't sleep. "Ryan Pike," Red slurred.

Ryan held out a hand. "Red Goldman, nice to finally meet you."

Red gave a sarcastic laugh, but shook his hand. "Better come in." The putrid smell that socked Ryan in the face made him doubt his sleepless night theory. Brewery and sweat. It reminded him of his father.

Red's office was the biggest room on the floor. He had three times as many framed photos hanging on the walls as Ryan, and probably somewhere around thirty awards strewn throughout the room. A stack of moving boxes sat off to one corner.

Red skirted around his desk, where he all but fell into his chair. He held up an empty glass. "Join me, my good man."

Ryan closed the door and tried to picture Red thirty years younger. It tears a man down from the inside out to have his livelihood threatened. If that's what was really happening. Or he was just a typical work-induced drunk. Under the circumstances, Ryan would give him the benefit of the doubt.

Ryan took the seat on the other side of the desk and held up his hand. "I'll pass, thank you."

Red's rosy cheeks reminded him of Santa Claus. "Suit yourself." He gripped the bottle and read the label. "Twenty-five-year-old scotch. Puts a hair on your chest."

Red's shirt was partially unbuttoned with chest hair sticking out of the V-shape. He had to be pushing sixty years old with a stocky build, offsetting the thin-framed glasses outlining his eyes.

"Are you feeling okay?" Ryan asked.

Red set the bottle down and sipped his drink, ice clinking together as he drained the glass.

"Yes, I'm feeling rather jovial. Ecstatic, if you can believe it." He belched. "Oops. Excuse me." He pressed the back of his hand to his mouth.

Ryan grabbed a fistful of tissue from the box on Red's desk and handed them over. "You want me to call someone for you?"

"No."

"You sure? We can reschedule our meeting. You sleep it off, and when you're feeling better, we'll regroup."

Red went silent, nodding a bit, then his bloodshot eyes shot to Ryan's. "What are you doing, boy?"

Ryan cocked his head. That question came out of the blue, no slur detected. "What do you mean?"

"I mean"—Red picked up a plaque that read, *Red Goldman, Over the Top 2000 Editor in Chief of the year*— "make sure your choices and sacrifices are worth the part of your soul that you can never get back."

Ryan felt his brows furrow. It was barely 6:00 a.m. and Red, or the Scotch, was overly philosophical for the hour. "I'm sure you have a lot more of your soul to offer, Red."

"Pffft." Red spit a little and wiped his chin. "Son, I know why you're here. You don't have to play politics with me. I sent the last editor packing myself. Back when periodicals were respectable and the subjects on the cover earned their place."

Though he was sure Red wasn't privy to the merge—if it was a merge—he assumed based on the garbled speech that the editor assumed the worst. He couldn't blame him, though. Why else would an A-list journalist be summoned to a smaller branch after reports showed declining subscriptions? That was information he'd found by digging, something Phil had forgotten to mention.

"I'm just saying this job can be a soul-crusher," Red continued. "You married, boy?"

"No, sir."

"You got a girl?"

Why did Sophie flash through his mind? He shifted uncomfortably. "Nothing serious."

"Well, one day you'll fall in love. You'll promise her the world, but then you'll get a call to come back to the office right after you get home from a long day at work. Then another call ruins your anniversary dinner and sends you on an urgent trip across the country. And another call that your wife's cheating on you . . . not that you'll care, because, hell, your marriage was over years ago. The calls won't stop. You'll see your kids grow though pictures, or, for your generation, your cell phone screen. They didn't have those when my kids were learning to walk, and talk, and graduating high school."

Ryan dropped his eyes as Red's words seared him like a hot knife through butter. Red might be drunk, but even in a stupor, especially in a stupor, a man feels his past regrets. But Ryan couldn't linger on his regrets or this whole thing would be a disaster. "Red, I'm here to discuss training details since you won't be attending the trip. But you're in no state to have a meeting. Let's reconvene later."

"I know you are, son. I had this same meeting twenty-three years ago with a guy named Chuck Maury. I'm not an idiot." He laughed, picking up the bottle of scotch. "And contrary to how it looks, I'm not a drunk either. But, I know times have changed and people want their news on a six-inch screen the instant it happens. Hell, they want it before it happens. And mark my words, the industry as a whole will be compromised." Red shook his head. "Just promise me one thing."

Ryan lifted his head to meet Red's eyes.

"Don't put your career over your heart. This job will suck you dry faster than a combative third wife during an asset mediation hearing." Red chuckled to himself. "Trust that thumping organ. It'll break but it'll never lead you astray the way that big ego in your head will."

Ryan nodded. What could he say? His heart went out to this man. "Understood."

Seconds later, Red's head bobbed a few times before it rested on his chest. Drool pooled at the corners of his mouth. The deep grunt signified Red was down for the count.

That was intense. "I'm calling you a cab."

Chapter 7

Two hours after Sophie boarded Colossal Cruise's *Epic Dream*, a series of ear-piercing tones signaled the start of the mandatory safety briefing, sending her group of passengers to the top of the Lido Deck with their life preservers in hand.

"Saved you a seat, toots," Donovan said, patting the empty spot on the whitewashed bench next to him. His life jacket seemed to fit flawlessly, whereas Sophie thought she'd might accidentally strangle herself with the loose strap on hers.

Sophie sat and Donovan handed her a cup of ice water. "Thank you. Where's Amy?"

Donovan shrugged. "Beats me. Figured she was with you."

"No, I've been cooped up in my room trying to reach Charlie before I lose reception."

Donovan slowly turned his head and gave Sophie the 'look.' "Why?"

"Because I'm certain the roof will cave in or the place will burn down or the cartel will show up and kidnap everyone."

Donovan raised his hand. "Please stop. You're interrupting my chi."

"Your what?"

"Just relax. We only have a couple of hours before our first meeting. I don't want your stressing out about nothing to ruin my treatment."

Sophie cocked her head. "Again, I ask, your what?"

"Vitamin D treatment while the salty breeze exfoliates my pours. Now hush."

Donovan closed his eyes and leaned back. Sophie would have rolled her eyes, but Donovan had grown immune to her judgment. She scanned the deck for Amy. Yet, between the other sardines—some of whom needed to watch where they placed their wandering hands—all she saw was a sea of orange life preservers.

Before the drill started, a crewmember with a nametag that read Roberto from the Dominican Republic thrust a bright pink flyer in her hand and then passed one to Donovan with a wink. Donovan smiled back and scanned the flier. "Ha, not a chance," he said, resuming his treatment.

Sophie read the flier.

Captain Tristan and Colossal Cruise Lines invite you to participate in its fifth annual charity event:
If By Land or Sea Scavenger Hunt!
You find the goods. We write the check!
$5,000 for first place.

Sophie blinked. Was this for real? Nothing in life is handed over so easily—especially five thousand dollars. But then again, just because she wasn't naïve enough to fall for easy money didn't mean someone else wasn't crazy enough to give it away. Five grand would more than cover rent, and when she added in Amy's blackmail money from Dirk over at channel eight, she'd have enough for some repairs.

She'd just have to find a way around the rules. Per the company bylaws outlined in their itineraries, employees at Over the Top, Inc. were prohibited from cruise-sponsored activities. This was a training cruise, so other than free time during port-of-calls, this trip revolved around meetings and training.

However, Red wasn't here. Neither was the human resource guy. And last time she checked, Ryan didn't sign her paycheck, so she didn't need his permission.

Participating in a forbidden scavenger hunt would definitely require a bit of insanity to pull off. But hey, *she* was the woman who had four hundred thousand YouTube hits from a completely accidental take down.

The answer to her problems stared back at her, serenading her name like a heavenly host of angels. She traced her finger over the ginormous red lettering promising five thousand dollars to the grand prizewinner as if doing so would transport the winnings straight to the café's near-empty business account.

Donovan turned toward her, making a judgy face. "I know what you're thinking. And don't."

"Go back to sunbathing. I'm plotting over here."

He lowered his Elton John replica sunglasses and glared. "For what it's worth, there are ways to come up with money that won't get you terminated. And I like working with my favorite toots. I would wither and die if you were fired for something as stupid as a scavenger hunt."

"Not when Mr. Tomilson's rent increase is effective immediately. That bacterial-petri dish of a man sent the letter directly to the café rather than to corporate because that's pretty much what a sleazy, gutless, cockroach does to get around corporate's red tape."

Donovan put his arm around Sophie. "Tell me how you really feel."

"I'm serious."

"Me too. Think about it. If they fire you, who'd run the café? I'm only good for pedis and cooking. You need to think about the girls."

"That's *exactly* who I'm thinking about."

He lifted a perfectly groomed brow. "Oh really?"

"Yes."

"You sure it's not to prove a certain asshat wrong?"

With the background sound of the captain starting the muster drill instructions, Sophie traced Donovan's gaze to Asher who made a beeline in their direction. He stopped in front of a woman in a skirt Sophie was pretty sure had been sized for a toddler. When he planted his arm on the wall above her head, Sophie bristled. *Asshat, indeed.*

"You are the wind beneath my wings!" Amy chorused off key.

"There you are," Sophie said, scooting over just enough to allow her friend to sit—and land—halfway on her lap. "A little early for the schnapps, wouldn't you say?"

Amy whipped her head around, giving Sophie a mouthful of hair. "Actually, it's never too early for schaps . . . shooaaps . . . schnapps. Have you ever said that word?" Amy crossed her eyes, watching her lips pucker in pronunciation, then dissolved into giggles.

Sophie spit out the crunchy, wayward strands of mousse-lathered locks blowing into her face. "Your hair is in my bubble, Amy."

"Hey, you got one of these too?" Amy plucked the same pink flier from her back pocket and scrunched her face. "Who wants to scavenge for dumb trinkets? Now send me on a hunt for some sexy, six-pack abs or the firefighters from one of those charity calendars and I'm in."

Sophie snatched the flier from Amy's hand and waved off her erroneous comment. Except for the firefighters part. Yes, Sophie would definitely be in on *that* hunt. "As if five thousand dollars is anything to snuff at. We're talking divine intervention to have this be the one week out of fifty-two that they're running this contest."

Amy glared at Sophie . . . sort of. Her eyes darted a few times before they locked onto hers. "There are two of you," Amy slurred.

"I'm sure there are. How many have you had?"

Donovan leaned into the conversation. "One too many, it sounds like."

Amy tipped her head back, the bottle pressed to her lips. "Mmm," she mumbled into the bottle. "So good."

"Anyway." Sophie read the flier again. "It's easy money. I could win this contest without even trying."

"They're all rigged you know," Donovan said.

Sophie frowned. "They are not. Stop being a naysayer unless you want to write me a check right now."

Donovan barked out a loud laugh. "I wish I had that sort of scratch."

Amy pointed her finger in the air as if a light bulb lit above her head. "You could always fake an injury and sue the company for damages. Pick a good company though. One with more money than *Up Front*."

"So, pretty much any company," Donovan quipped.

"You two suck," Sophie said. "I didn't say I was participating."

"Good, because it's a terrible idea," Amy said on a drunk sigh. "Unless it's for hot firefighters, that is."

Which is exactly the reason Sophie would sign up after this drill was over. Anything Amy thought was a bad idea meant it was a good one. They were polar opposites—the exact reason they got along so well. Yin and Yang would be pointless if they were Yin and Yin.

"Speaking of terrible ideas," Donovan growled. "Don't look at your ten o'clock."

Sophie's eyes banked left.

"Why do I bother warning you?" he murmured.

Sophie curled her upper lip and made a guttural sound. Asher had apparently finished bothering the woman in toddlers' clothing and squeezed his way through the crowd. Luckily she had her friends flanking her.

"Look what the kraken dragged in," Sophie sneered. "What's wrong? She too old for you? Or perhaps too smart?"

Asher feigned a laugh. "I'm just being friendly. No need to be rude." He raised his drink to his mouth, which was an exact replica of Amy's. Peach schnapps. *Are you kidding me?*

Amy doubled over in drunken hysterics and thudded to the floor. She groaned. "Everything is spinning down here."

Sophie patted her friend on her tower of hair. "It's fine, honey. Just stay down there until the spinning stops."

"I just wanted to come by and tell you sorry about another blow to your crusade."

"Another blow to my . . . " The puzzle pieced together in her head. She looked down at her schnapped friend. Beasties socializing while drunk with the poster boy for Cheaters-R-Us did not make a good combo for secrets. *Oh, Amy, you told Ash-face?* "It's not a crusade. Stop calling it that."

"Call it what you want," Asher continued. "Crusade. Slow death. Drain on society. I'm not trying to be cruel, I'm just calling it as I see it because you're in too deep to see what's going on." He took another swing.

"And I suppose you see everything."

Asher lifted his shoulders. "When it comes to spending much needed company resources on a glorified hobby. Yeah, I like to think of it as my unofficial job." His smirk made Sophie want to dry heave.

"I'll tell you what your unofficial job is. You're the king off ass—"

Donovan squeezed Sophie's shoulder, essentially cutting her off. Sometimes she wanted to squeeze the levelheadedness out of Donovan. "What do you want, Asher?"

"Nothing. Just making conversation while we apparently *don't* pay attention to the crewmember over there giving us directions in case of an emergency. Though maybe we should. It's for our safety and all."

Sophie looked past Asher. Though she couldn't really understand his accent, the safety instructor demonstrated the proper way to wear a life jacket, and what do in the event of pirates—no, fire. Yes, he definitely said fire.

Sophie gave up trying to untangle the knot her straps had created and turned back to Asher. "I don't know what Amy told you about the café, or what you did to her, but it's none of your concern."

His eyes dropped to Amy, who leaned against Sophie's legs. "She sings like a canary, lightweight that she is." He stepped around the Amy blob. "If our outreach is going under I think it concerns the whole office. That money can be used to market new subscribers. We need increased readership, or haven't you noticed the decline with all the time you spend in your exalted cave?"

Sophie narrowed her eyes. "It will never be *our* outreach. It's not like you've ever helped."

"As expected, you missed the point entirely."

"That's because I can't hear anything past that big-headed ego of yours."

Asher simpered. "Well, don't say you weren't warned by a friend who cares."

Donovan stood up, apparently having had enough of Asher too.

Asher stepped back.

Sophie reached for Donovan. "It's fine."

Amy groaned. "I'm not feeling so well."

"Of course not," Sophie said, patting Amy's head again. "You frolicked with the enemy. That's enough to make anyone want to retch."

"Seriously, I think I'm going to throw up."

Donovan stepped between Sophie and Asher and drew Amy to her feet. "Let's go, lightweight." Donovan draped one of Amy's arms around his neck. "I'll find you later, okay, toots? You going to be all right here?"

Sophie glared. "I've dealt with worse."

Donovan helped Amy through the orange mob. "No more schnapps for you."

Sophie watched them leave and then addressed Asher. "Listen, Ash-face. I get the only thing you care about is Asher. But back off, okay? The café's not closing. And not that it's any of your business, but"—she gripped the flier clenched in her fist—"I have resources at my disposal."

Asher leaned in. Nodes of his familiar Old Spice rendered her nauseous. He flicked her flier and whispered, "If you're referring to the scavenger hunt, be forewarned, I'm in the hunt."

A lightning bolt shot through Sophie, momentarily snuffing out her last bit of hope. "You're . . . in?" With Asher in the game, her odds of winning were slim to none. He was the competitive king. From Parcheesi to last month's half marathon, if competition was involved, the slaughter he left in his wake was worse than *300*.

He flexed his biceps. "Yes, I am."

Sophie's dry lips cracked. She sipped from the cup of water Donovan had given her, hoping to loosen the knot in her throat.

"Don't blame your friend for ratting you out. She was worried about you. About Chicks 'n' Slicks, actually."

"Good afternoon." The smoothness in Ryan's voice sent a shiver down Sophie's spine and she all but choked on her water. Rather, she snorted it, causing it to dribble out her nose and down her chin. *Perfect.*

Ryan shook Asher's hand. "How's it going?"

Asher cracked his neck. "Can't complain."

Sophie narrowed her eyes and murmured, "I can."

Asher smirked.

Ryan's eyes trailed from Asher to Sophie. "Did I miss something?"

"Trust me, you haven't missed anything." Sophie maintained her solemnity.

"Now, Sophie," Asher started, cracking his smug smile, "tell Ryan all about our fabulous little café and how it's in dire straits. He should know since he's heading the training. This could be used as a great opportunity to discuss deferred resources."

Ryan's eyes hung on to Sophie's a little too long for comfort. "I'm afraid I'm not following."

There were over eight hundred people on the cruise. She was supposed to be a needle in the haystack. Yet, here she was, and here Ryan was.

"Sophie's little crusade is in trouble," Asher clarified.

"It's nothing." Sophie wiped her chin again with the sleeve of her track jacket. Bright yellow with reflective red sleeves. No wonder everyone seemed to know where she was. She stood out like a scream in a silent movie. Speaking of screaming . . .

"Crusade?" Ryan lifted his brow.

"Our magazine's little do-gooder project Sophie's been playing with. It got slapped with a rent hike."

The heat in Sophie's cheeks sweltered, but she breathed in as much salty air as she could before answering. "It's nothing we can't handle. Just a little internal misunderstanding."

Asher's beady rat eyes stared. "A little misunderstanding?" He forced a cough. "Yeah, little like the state of Texas, or your hips," he muttered.

Sophie's mouth dropped, instinctively dropping her arms in front of her hips.

Ryan glared at Asher like someone had smacked his mother. "Cool it, man."

"I'm kidding. Sophie knows I'm playing. But seriously, I'm just suggesting better use of company funding." Asher killed his drink as a beautiful woman walked passed. "And that's my cue. I'll see you guys around."

Sophie growled. "Prick."

A beat passed before Ryan's deep blue eyes settled on her. He was not just looking at her, but through her. Those eyes. The pit of her stomach tingled. He stood so close the smell of his aftershave made her knees wobble. She stumbled back and a flare of anger ripped through her. How dare he come back and do *things* to her without her logical half's consent.

"Why didn't you tell me about the café?" A passenger bumped Ryan into her and the contact sent a thrill through her.

She closed her eyes. "Why are you here?"

"Company training, I told you."

No, why are you here, right this moment, eliciting unwanted feelings? She opened her eyes and searched his face, hoping to read what he wasn't saying. She had no reason to doubt he was here for training, but her intuition screamed there was more to it than that and making her feel like a love-sick college student again. And her intuition usually excelled around a ninety-seven percent accuracy rating. "There's a whole team of outsourced associates that do our training on a regular basis. Last time I checked, you weren't on that list."

"You check on me?" He smiled.

She felt her cheeks flush. *I used to.* "No, I checked the list."

"Well, lists change. Things change." Was that guilt that flashed in his eyes?

Ding, ding, ding. She was on to something. "Like what? What changes brought you here?"

The drill had ended and people dispersed around them, however, Sophie remained trapped in a bubble with Ryan. She fidgeted with her vest, trying to untie the knotted string.

"Do you need help with that?" His hands brushed against hers, and she instinctively flinched.

Was he avoiding the question? "What do you mean changes?" she asked again.

Pressing his lips in a hard line, his gaze shifted.

"Right. Lips sealed." She fumbled with another knot.

"No, my lips already told you I'm here on assignment."

He stepped closer and she looked up, eye level with said sealed lips. All this talk about lips made her wonder if his were still as soft as she remembered.

Ryan scrubbed a hand through his gorgeous hair. "Asher said something about the café. Is everything okay?"

At his mention of her café, Sophie tugged the strings harder. "What is wrong with this thing? I get it. Use the vest if we hit an iceberg."

Ryan tried to help again and she jerked away.

He raised his hands. "Sorry."

Sophie took a moment to fill her lungs and exhale slowly. Why was she acting so crazy? He hadn't done anything. Except show up at the worst possible time, with the stress of the café weighing her down, and then Ash-face being . . . well, Ash-face, she sighed, apologizing with her eyes. "No. Ugh, this isn't the normal me. I'm . . . I'm not feeling myself lately."

"I'm sorry to hear that. Let me know if I can help with anything." Ryan smiled warily.

Sophie's heart jolted. It pounded so hard she wondered if she'd need the defibrillator attached to the wall. The clean smell of his aftershave enveloped her. "Okay," she breathed.

"Hey, Soph?" A voice came from behind. At least she thought it did. Between the thick fog in her brain and the scattered mumbling from people leaving the muster drill, she wasn't sure she could trust her senses.

Except, maybe for one: That pesky sixth sense that told her she wasn't completely over a certain someone after all.

Donovan gripped her elbow and Sophie fell out of the fog. "Sophie?"

Ryan stepped back, his lips curing upward. "I'll see you later at the training."

Sophie swallowed a lump. "See ya." She turned to Donovan. His brows shot straight up.

"What? It's nothing. I . . . um . . . I'm sorry, did you need something? How's Amy?"

A wicked smile crossed his lips. "I've seen 'nothing' before. And that ain't it."

Sophie shook her head. "Whatever."

"So you know, gay men invented that word. Don't try it on me." He grinned his big Donovan smile, and Sophie averted her eyes before her flushed cheeks gave her away. "Anyway," Donovan said, graciously dropping the subject. "Amy's back in her room. She said to tell you Charlie called."

Sophie's eyes grew wide and she slapped her back pocket, searching for her cell phone. "Shoot, it must be in my room. "I'll go call her now, thanks."

"And, Soph?"

Sophie whipped around, finally ripping off the life vest.

"Watch out for that hottie."

"I don't know what you're talking about."

"Except you do. And he's totally into you."

Sophie hugged the life vest and headed back to her room, dismissing his preposterous assumption. She and Ryan were way past their college days. Him being here was solely for training, and nothing more. She would not let a ten-year-over romance get in the way of her goal. From now on, she would focus on winning the scavenger hunt and kicking Asher's butt in the process.

Too bad it was Ryan's butt she was focused on.

Chapter 8

"Charlie, it's me." Sophie tossed her life vest and bag on the tiny bed and stared at the windowless wall. Why didn't she answer? A hundred worst-case scenarios burst to life on her mind. "How are things? Sorry I missed you again. The place burn down yet?" She slumped into the Barbie-sized chair next to the Barbie-sized desk. "That was a joke . . . unless of course it did burn down, in which case, I hope you grabbed the jukebox."

She cradled her head in the palm of her hand and stifled a sigh. Using sarcasm to suppress the crazy. *Smooth, Sophie.* "Anyway, just checking in. I won't have service once we're out to sea, but I'll check my messages as often as I can, and you know Tanya is there . . . sort of . . . if you need anything."

Tanya Nelson from the—yawn—art and literature department stayed behind due to hyperactive motion sickness. She volunteered to hang out as the "supervising adult" at the café. But she was more of a figurehead. Sophie didn't actually expect Tanya to spend her evenings there. Plus, Charlie could run that place with two hands tied behind her back. Sure, she could have just closed it while she was on the cruise, but they needed the income.

"Okay, hug the other girls for me. Don't really burn the place down. Love ya. Bye."

Only four days to go. Worrying about the girls would only make time slow. They'd be *fine*. Charlie was probably busy working at the café, which is why she didn't answer. Everything was *fine*. She checked her reflection in the mirror and tucked her hair behind her ears. "The girls are *fine*, I will survive this trip, and I will win this scavenger hunt."

Sophie scrolled to the envelope icon on her phone and opened her email. *Ugh, nothing from any of the grant applications.* Could they at least send an automatic reply that they'd been received and were under review? Microscopic hope was better than no hope at all. This whole process frustrated her.

She quickly thumb-typed an email to her landlord, the despicable Mr. Tomilson, to formally request a deferred rent hike. By doing so she acknowledged the rent hike, but by not, the locks could be changed without her knowledge.

Then she'd reached out to a few old contacts that'd helped her start the café, namely local sponsors who'd assisted with the initial opening. Sergio's, for one. The YMCA another. Though one-time support did nothing more than stick duct tape over a gaping hole on a rusty pipe, treading water could buy them another month until a grant came through. So, yes, frustrated was an understatement.

Nothing less than desperation made her go against company policy and throw all her eggs in this one tiny basket over a game that for all she knew was rigged.

Before they sailed too far out to sea to lose reception, she Googled 'winning scavenger hunts' and took notes. She tapped the Colossal Cruise Liner pen against the matching signature note pad and learned everything she could. The girls needed this win.

~ ~ ~

After his first official training meeting, which was more of an informal introduction, and then a quiet dinner alone, which he mostly picked at, Ryan returned to his suite. He'd had plenty of time to run numbers in his head, and something didn't add up.

He loosened his tie and picked up the landline. Though he'd paid for a service package for his cell phone, he wasn't sure of the reception. Despite the time difference between the West Coast and San Antonio, he needed to clarify once and for all what was going on with the café and *Up Front's* future. His gut told him that when things didn't add up, there was usually a reason. And the "M" word came to mind. A merge could be a logistical nightmare. And as "acting editor in chief" a crap storm for him.

He let the phone ring through until Phil's voicemail picked up.

Damn.

He'd leave a message just the same. "Phil, Ryan here. Listen, give me a call on my cell in the morning. We need to discuss some things. Thanks."

When Ryan disconnected, he kept his hand gripped tightly around the receiver. Not good enough. He needed answers. There was only one person he could think of who knew just about everything under the sun related to office gossips and secrets. He unlocked his cell and scrolled through his contacts until he found his assistant's home number.

He dialed the numbers and after the third ring, a gravelly voice answered. "Someone better be dead, or someone will be very shortly."

He glanced at the clock and did the math. Right, 2 a.m. "Hey, Lola, it's me."

"Ryan?" Shuffling ensued before a brief pause, and then Lola's voice was chipper and sharp. "What do you need? Is everything okay?"

"Yes," Ryan said, dropping into the chair adjacent to the desk. He ran his hand through his hair. "Listen, something's going on with *Up Front*. What do you know?"

The dead air wasn't a good sign. Ryan waited patiently.

"Ryan. Dear."

"That bad?"

"Not if you don't want it to be." Her voice was soft. Tranquil. It made him think of how his mom would tell him that his dad had hit the bottle a little hard and she had to run and pick him up.

"Lola, just rip the Band-Aid, okay? I'm a sitting duck here. Is it a merge? Is *Up Front* closing?"

"I don't know anything officially."

"Bull." It was not like him to be so crass with his assistant. After eight years she never once forgot his birthday, or neglected to send the best gifts to his sister on hers. She always sent flowers to his mother's resting place, and she never lied to him. Not once. When she didn't respond, he softened his tone. "Can you tell me what you do know unofficially? I'm literally out to sea with people I expect to trust me and they don't even know I'm here as interim yet. I can't not have all the info in front of me. Phil's a little less than forthcoming."

Lola sighed into the phone.

"Please."

"I only heard Phil talking to the board via Skype a few days ago. Yes, a possible merge with *Jazz*, which would mean a partial layoff . . . and closing the office altogether. But that's not official."

Ryan pinched the bridge of his nose. *What is official?* "So, in summary, I'm here as a catch-all to the crap storm that may unload at any moment. If the board moves through with the merge and possible closure, that is." Ryan recalled the conversation he had with Phil before he left. Phil had told him he'd heard of talk about a merge with *Jazz* but it was doubtful.

This did *not* sound doubtful. "Why won't Phil be straight with me? Why be so surreptitious?"

"It's a gag order. Comes from the top. And until things

are official, there's nothing to say. Otherwise you risk a leak. And if there's a leak, there's damage control."

He squeezed the receiver in frustration. "And I get to *prove* my value through making it look all pretty and packaged with a proper bow? What is this? A set up for failure? One where I get to hear news on TV and then pour myself a drink and justify that it's just the way it is?"

"You're not your father, Ryan."

Ryan cringed. *No kidding.* He'd never be his father. He had too much self-respect to treat people like dirt and run out on them. He would see through whatever was going on here. He clenched his teeth. He'd never raised his voice to his assistant, and he wouldn't start today, no matter what she insinuated. "That isn't relevant, Lola. I'm talking about people here."

"You're very good at your job and an even better man. You know how to talk to people. You have a knack for the game. Whether it's a ball game or the game of life. Just listen to your team, and set them up for success. No matter where the wind blows."

Lola was right. Nothing had been decided, at least not that he knew of. And until he did know, he would move forward with the information he had and trust the system. He was here as editor in chief, though unofficial until Red announced his retirement. He wasn't making decisions or passing judgment. He'd just do his job and help whoever he could in the meantime.

A pulsing nerve in the back of his mind, however, told him what that meant for Sophie's outreach.

"And Ryan?"

"Yeah?"

"Call your dad."

"Bye, Lola," Ryan said on a much-needed laugh.

Chapter 9

Ryan wanted to talk to Sophie. She needed to see where he was coming from. He couldn't very well apologize on behalf of the magazine for what might happen, especially since he couldn't disclose any information. But if he could spend some time with her, gain her trust and help her understand the nature of internal reorganization, maybe she could come to terms with letting go of the café if it came to that. She's been in the industry for years. She knew these things happened. The Bay Area must have dozens of similar outreach programs to offer those kids.

It was well past midnight. According to the itinerary, they'd be docking in Ensenada early in the morning. He'd talk to her then.

Needing to clear his mind, Ryan slipped out of his room and headed to the all-night dessert buffet cruise ships were famous for.

When he stepped onto the Lido Deck he came to a grinding halt. To say it was enormous would be like comparing a football field with a runway at San Antonio International. He'd bet each of the two pools with water slides could fit their own fighter jets. No wonder this ship made *Cruiser's Digest's* June cover, ranking number one in the Must-Travel category. Ryan subconsciously cataloged the information, though this sort of knowledge savagely killed off useful brain cells. How many times had he murdered conversations during a blind date by uttering the phrase "consumer report rating" or "Monday morning quarterback?"

Honestly, not many. He didn't date much.

A lone shadow dressed in dark clothing slowly crept behind one of the hot tubs. The hair on the back of Ryan's neck stood on edge. He watched the shadow slip a piece of paper into his pocket before he disappeared behind a staircase. Earlier he'd seen posted signs with pictures of cameras strewn about. The cruise-wide scavenger hunt had people stalking around looking for something. Apparently that *something* was happening tonight, as he counted no less than four more nomads roaming the deck like cat burglars.

He shoved his hands in his pockets and made his way to the dessert bar, drooling over an array of everything from six-ways-to-die-by-chocolate to a selection of exotic fruit. With two plate sizes to choose from, he couldn't deny his salivating mouth, and didn't hesitate to grab the larger one. A morning run would be in order.

Someone's shoulder rammed into him as he blew by, knocking Ryan's plate out of his hand.

"Watch it, man," Ryan called out.

"Sorry, dude." The guy was covered head to toe in black. Even his face was concealed with a ski mask. If he was a part of the game, his clothing screamed, "I'm forty years old and live in my mother's basement." This stupid game ran the risk of getting someone thrown overboard. Whose idiotic idea was it to plan a scavenger hunt in the middle of a cruise? He'd probably read about it later when it ended in a lawsuit. Good thing his team was forbidden from participating. They didn't have the insurance to cover such distractions.

Grabbing a fresh plate from the pile, Ryan stacked all the right food groups: chocolate, sugar, cheesecake, and fruit—dipped in chocolate. He placed a piece of parsley on the outer edge of the plate so it had some inference of health.

Ryan sat near one of the ginormous pools and indulged.

As the first bite of cherry cheesecake passed the threshold of his lips he heard a piercing scream. A woman's. Then, *"No. No. No!"*

Ryan jumped up so quickly his chair knocked over, slamming against the deck floor.

The high-pitched scream came to an unsettling halt just as a splash cut through the dead of night.

He hurried around a spiral staircase. About twenty feet away another dark shadow jetted past the other pool, ducking behind one of the many poolside bars.

His skin crawled as he raced toward the scream, and squinted through the dim light. Waves rippled at the far end of the pool even though it was covered by a tarp and netted rope. Whoever had fallen in had created a hole in the tarp. A woman's arms broke through the rope, flapping like a distressed bird. She was caught.

"Damn," he mumbled. This side of the deck was a ghost town. Where was the staff? Not thinking twice, he shrugged out of his jacket and kicked off his shoes, then jumped into the tarp opening. He ripped the rope from the side nearest him and swam as close to the hole as he could.

"Help," she screamed, though it was more of a gurgle.

The dark prevented him from seeing where the rope tangle ended and her limbs began. *Stop struggling.*

She kicked at the water, and even though it wasn't deep, she was disoriented. Her arms continued to flail.

Ryan filled his lungs and dove under, grabbing her legs to pull her under. With strenuous effort, he tried dragging her toward the narrow opening he'd made on the other side of the pool, but he didn't expect her to be so strong. She kicked him on the side of his head, momentarily impairing his vision.

But her body started to relax and seconds later she stopped kicking. Ryan's adrenaline kicked in to high gear. *No, no, don't you stop.* This woman was not going to drown. He crushed her against his chest and pushed off the bottom of the pool. When he broke the surface of the water, he scooped his arms under hers and dragged her limp body to the deck floor. He rolled her to her side, revealing her face. "Sophie?" Beads of water glistened on her lashes against the dim lighting. *Oh my God, Sophie.* Anger and fear knotted in his gut.

She choked and spit up water, sucking in huge gulps of air.

He collapsed to his haunches, trying to catch his own breath.

"You almost . . ." The rest of his sentence caught in his throat. The thought of her drowning threatened to unhinge a wrath he would unleash on whoever did this to her. "You okay?"

She coughed up more water, then flipped over and balanced her weight between her hands and knees, dry heaving.

"Hey!" Two crewmen ran over. "You guys okay?" one of them asked.

Sophie wiped her mouth. "I'm fine," she said, then coughed again.

Ryan ignored the men and pressed one hand to her back. "You are not fine. You were just unconscious."

The soft light added a little color to Sophie's otherwise pale face. He clenched his jaw as he offered his arm to help her up.

She took it and stumbled to her feet. "Seriously, Ryan, I'm fine."

The two penguins circled them. "Do you need first aid? We radioed for help," the taller penguin said.

"No. Don't." Sophie coughed a few more times. "I'm perfectly fine."

"Are you sure?" he asked, holding his radio inches from his mouth.

"Positive," Sophie wheezed.

The taller one stepped back and mumbled into his walkie-talkie, likely canceling the medical staff.

Ryan picked up his coat, shook it out, and then draped it over Sophie's shoulders. "What happened? Did someone push you in?"

She wrapped the coat together in her fist and shook her head. "I think it was an accident."

She involuntarily shook and Ryan draped his arm around her, briskly rubbing.

"We need to document the incident," the other penguin said. He looked disturbingly identical to the redheaded kid on the Cracker Jacks box.

Ryan gave Sophie a once-over. Her breathing steadied, and by the way she shrugged away from him, she clearly didn't want this attention. "It's fine, fellas. No harm, no foul." Any incident reported on behalf of *Up Front's* reckless behavior could lead to instant termination. Not that being thrown in a pool was her fault, probably one of those crazy scavenger hunt enthusiasts, but he didn't want to chance it. And he didn't believe for one second it was an accident. Not the way she screamed.

"I fell, that's all," Sophie said, breathing softly. *Thank God.* She caught his eye and held his gaze. "This guy helped me out." Her attention slowly returned to the employees. "I'm fine. Please don't write anything down."

Ryan bit his lip. If his sister had been thrown into a covered pool, you can bet she'd declare World War III on that person. Sophie seemed to be okay, but it was a matter of seconds before shock kicked in. He needed to intervene to prevent that incident report and further investigation from the company.

"Listen, guys." Ryan stepped forward. "We don't want it getting out that the pool wasn't properly secured. I mean, how would it look on permanent record to see that the pool was an accident waiting to happen? What if a child fell through instead of one of my colleagues?" Ryan waited, allowing the reality to soak in.

When the penguins' still appeared unsure, he reached for his drenched wallet and handed one of the men a business card, enunciating his title as a journalist. "Have your supervisor contact me if you have any questions. Meanwhile, let's just call it a night and I'll see her to her room."

The Cracker Jack penguin shot the other one a knowing look. "All right then. I see your point." He waved the business card and walked away, mumbling, "Have a good night."

Ryan filled his lungs and turned to Sophie. Her wet hair hung over her shoulder, framing her heart-shaped face. Though his coat more than covered her, he couldn't but notice how her drenched shirt clung to her slender body. How much weight *had* she lost? All anger he felt moments before dissipated. He wrapped his coat tighter around her. "You okay?"

She didn't answer but he felt her shiver.

Probably shock.

"You should eat something. I have a table over there." He kept one arm around her shoulder, distinctly aware just how perfectly she molded into him, like a custom-cut puzzle piece. He buried the thought deep. *That was over*.

He guided her to the table and eased her into the seat directly across from him, pushing the dessert plate in front of her. "Eat."

She didn't so much as bat an eye. She just stared, shivering. "I'm not hungry."

"Listen, I'd feel better if you ate something. Not to mention your adrenaline will slow down and you'll stop shaking if you put some sugar in your system."

Her eyes narrowed at him. "But I'm not hungry."

"That's not the point," he said pointedly. "You're in shock and if you don't eat you could pass out."

She pushed the plate away from her. "I'm fine. I'll order a sandwich from room service."

Ryan stood. "I'll get you one now."

"But—"

"Humor me. It's the least you can do after I rescued you."

Sophie's mouth fell open, but whatever she was about to say she thought better of and clamped her mouth shut. Crossing her arms, she said, "Fine."

At the buffet, Ryan made her a sandwich with turkey, unlike his veggie burger—and grabbed a bag of chips for good measure, then headed back to the table, determined to get to the bottom of what actually happened.

He slid the plate in front of her and plopped down in his chair. "Okay. Someone pushed you in. Why?"

Sophie froze with the sandwich at her lips. "I fell, I told you."

Ryan leaned back in his chair. He folded his arms across his chest and said, "I don't believe you. The way you screamed . . . it sounded like a struggle. People don't scream like that when they're falling."

"It was a misunderstanding."

Damn. He was right. Which meant his next suspicion wasn't as farfetched as he hoped. Especially with her desperate to make the café's rent. He ran a hand through his hair, hating to make the accusation, but he was worried. Really worried. "Listen, Soph, promise me you're not participating in this scavenger hunt. It's against company policy."

Sophie flinched. "Not that you ever participate, but in the past, company trainings are a good mix of work and play."

Ryan scrubbed a hand over his jaw, scratching the stubble on his chin. She wasn't denying it, but trying to make a case *for* it. This was bad. As her boss, if she admitted to participating he would be required to take disciplinary action. He leaned forward. "You should have fun, but drowning doesn't count as fun. And for the record, no scavenger hunting, okay? There's plenty of other games to play here. It's a little different this year."

"So you've said," she hissed, though he couldn't figure out her sudden animosity. Was she angry with him? "And like I said, I'm not playing *games*. But I'm going to bed."

Ouch. That would be a *yes* with a side of *screw you*. Ryan set his lips in a hard line. "Okay. Why don't I walk you to your room?"

"I'm fine." Sophie stood, shaking off his coat and handing it over.

He slipped it on. It was damp and smelled of her shampoo. A delightful shiver ran down his back. "Are you sure? I don't want to hear that you fell down or passed out later."

Sophie grabbed the sandwich off the plate and then picked up a fork, spearing a piece of cheesecake. She slowly bit down, scraping the fork between her teeth. The hairs on the back of Ryan's neck rose.

"Better?" she said around the cheesecake.

"Much," he said. "Have a good night. We have a lot to accomplish over the next few days."

A determined look crossed her face. "I know. And thanks for, you know, pulling me out. I'll see you at tomorrow's training."

She rubbed her arms as she walked briskly to the elevator. He watched until the elevator doors swallowed her up. Sitting back down, he looked at his dessert plate. She had him reeling and if she wasn't careful, she'd get herself in too deep and there would be no way for him to save her from drowning professionally. He stuffed a huge chunk of chocolate cake into his mouth. The question was, why did he care?

Chapter 10

Sophie watched a bird peck at the railing next to her bistro table on the Lido Deck as she sipped on her coffee and picked at the scrambled eggs. She'd barely slept a wink. Last night's events reeled through her mind nonstop, cycling a good dose of mortification with every rotation.

The scavenger hunt's unofficial kick-off did not go as she had planned. The first event had participants roaming the ship looking for a bonus item. One she did not find.

She cringed at the memory of being pushed in the pool. When she couldn't reach the surface, panic had set in. Everything happened so fast that her fear turned everything fuzzy.

But the real fear didn't set in until she saw Ryan leaning over her, asking her questions. She realized he could have gotten caught in the ropes too. Sophie squeezed her eyes. Death *is* scary. She'd learned that much when her parents died. But the thought of being responsible for someone else's death was downright petrifying.

She pushed the fear from her mind; she had to concentrate. The ship had just arrived in Ensenada, and Sophie figured the day would be filled with tourists, making her job of finding her first items on the scavenger hunt list effortless once she jumped on a tour excursion. The one with ATVs looked the most promising, so she would sign up as soon as this morning's training was over.

"Good morning, toots," Donovan said, slumping down in the seat across from her. With coffee in hand, he looked about a twelve on the fashion scale of one-to-ten.

"Why do you look like you're ready to walk the runway?"

He winked, licking his finger to fix his eyebrow. "Why are you surprised? You never get to make a first impression twice, and I always dress to impress."

Sophie smiled. "Good point."

Donovan ripped a piece of Sophie's toast from her plate and tossed it to the pigeon that landed near his feet. "You hungry, flying rat? Here's some carbs."

A sign above them warned guests not to feed the birds. "Eh-hem." Sophie cleared her throat, pointing.

"So we're choosing which rules to follow now?" he said with a devious smile. "Because I'm pretty sure we're not supposed to be participating in certain cruising activities."

Sophie plunked a bite of eggs in her mouth. "I'm not saying nothing."

"Don't talk with your mouth full. And don't lie to me using double negatives. I'm not dumb."

Sophie rolled her eyes. "Then why do you pester me?"

His eyes smiled. "Because it's fun."

Sophie pushed her plate back and stood. "I have to grab my laptop so I can finish some work while we meet for training this morning. See you in a bit."

Donovan raised his mug. "*Adios, mi amore.*"

Sophie took the stairs. Maybe a little exercise would clear her thoughts. Though grateful for Ryan saving her last night, she could not allow herself to think about him . . . or the way he held on to her, making sure she was okay. The way his jacket smelled like his cologne. The way he handled the staff so she wouldn't get in trouble. But worse, the way he conjured old feelings, making it doubly impossible to sleep last night.

Sophie shut her stateroom door and leaned against it. The reality of what could have happened shook her again. She could have gotten him killed. Guilt coiled in her chest. She wouldn't have been able to live with herself had she caused him harm. He wasn't even supposed to be there—or on this ship at all. Yet had he not been, she could have died.

She swallowed the bile that rose up her esophagus. She would *not* purge. It wouldn't solve anything except making her feel like a fraud to her girls.

She forced her mind back to the scavenger hunt and considered what it would take to win. Ryan couldn't know about it, so she needed to stay away from him. Her mind drifted to how he kept her warm against the coolness of the night. Against the shock. But that was him being nice. She squeezed her eyes shut. She especially needed to stay away from that. Far, far away.

She would avoid him at all costs today. Scratch that, she would avoid him at all costs for the rest of her life. *And* she would locate today's scavenger hunt items. She retrieved the flier she'd received earlier that morning outlining her mission, grabbed her laptop, and made it to the conference room with thirty seconds to spare.

Ryan stood at the front of the room, leaning against the first table, all tall and sinewy and heroic. He made small talk with Tyler Scott, but his Caribbean eyes glanced her way. Somehow they seemed to say all the right things. Things she wished he had said ten years ago, instead of what he did say—or wrote, rather. Sophie bit her lip. Nope. *Far, far away.*

Ryan ambled toward her and sat at the edge of her table. "You feeling better today?"

She never knew it was possible to blush from the tips of her toes to the top of her head. Dear God, it was only eight in the morning and she'd already failed miserably at avoiding him. And the bigger problem was some rogue piece of her heart didn't want to.

Chapter 11

Ryan—freshly showered and feeling renewed after an intense run—exited the ship in hopes of exploring Ensenada. But when he saw Sophie flailing at a crewmember at the excursion podium near the ship's debarkation ramp, he stopped. She looked as if she was about to go postal on the employee. Curiosity got the better of him and he headed her way.

"I'm sorry," the bubblegum-snapping twenty-something blond said, looking anything but apologetic. "That tour is sold out for the day. You should have booked yesterday. You can try for another tour on the main strip, which is a short bus ride from here, but here I can only check people in. Now please excuse me," she said, motioning another couple forward.

Ryan hung back, watching Sophie sift through different brochure options. This morning he'd attempted small talk, but she'd only offered him a slight smile and then sat in the back and spent the entire hour typing on her keyboard. Clearly, she was fine, except for acting distracted. After the training ended, she left in a hurry.

Now here she was, her hair pulled back in a tight ponytail, looking unbelievable in a red tank top and white shorts. The last decade had been good to her. She had lost weight. Not that she'd needed to. But whereas her clavicle was once hidden beneath her neckline, it now framed her neck and shoulders. Her arms were slimmer and her waistline smaller, but the most obvious change wasn't in her appearance. Her confidence now dwarfed the shy girl he once knew back in college. The mental snapshot stored in the back of his mind was that of a young, timid girl.

Even still, as confident as she was, he detected a fracture in that façade. Just like he did a decade ago when she abruptly cut him off.

Stop. He wasn't here for that. For her. As soon as this cruise was over and the transition complete, he'd be back in San Antonio. And that was best for everyone.

Amy slid up behind Sophie wearing a pair of dark sunglasses. She had sunscreen in one hand and a beach towel in the other. "It's full?"

Sophie stepped back from the podium, her eyes still glued to the brochure. "It would appear so."

Amy placed a hand on Sophie's shoulder. "Pity. Sorry, Soph."

Sophie glanced at Amy and then did a double take. "Why are you dressed in a bathing suit? You can't wear that on our tour today." She eyed her friend up and down. Amy's red bikini with black polka dots beneath a swim cover was clearly not excursion-appropriate.

"I'm sorry to bail, but I don't think I can go into a foreign country where I don't know the language or the culture. It's poolside for me."

Sophie furrowed her brows. "What are you talking about? More people speak English here than they do Spanish. This is tour central. They probably know your culture better than you do."

Amy glared at her. "Okay, fine, you caught me. I drank too much last night and all I see are the black dots behind my eye lids. My head is killing me, and I'll be awful company. All I want to do is lie out and relax. But we'll catch up tonight before the cocktail party."

Sophie eyed the top of the ship. Loud squeals from kids echoed from the Lido Deck. "You'd rather endure that level of torture over a tour today? Was it at least top shelf stuff you drank? Never mind, it doesn't matter. Leave me in my hour of need."

"You'll survive. And you'll cover more ground without my hair getting in the way. But if you really want someone to go with you take Donovan."

"No, he'll just want to bar hop and shop."

"Um, how about Terri and Lori?"

"Did you seriously just suggest them?"

"Hire a tour guide."

Sophie glared at Amy. "That's how you end up on an episode of *20/20*."

Amy shrugged her tiny shoulders. "I'm just offering suggestions."

Gobs of people walked by the clearance area where a drug-sniffing dog checked everyone. This didn't seem like a place they wanted people to gather to decide what to do with their day. Ryan ambled toward Amy and Sophie. "I'll go," he said before he could think twice about what he was offering.

Amy's eyes met Ryan's first, a wicked grin splitting her face. "Yeah, take him with you." She wagged her eyebrows suggestively. "He doesn't seem as bad as you make him out to be."

Ryan wasn't sure what made him offer to go. It was clear after last night Sophie didn't want him around. But the idea of her alone in Mexico seemed wrong.

Sophie turned toward him.

If looks could kill, he'd be lying dead on the ground. Probably with a jagged dagger in his eye. Not a terrible way to go, Ryan mused. Maybe not the most pleasant, but since he'd returned, he had yet to do one thing to earn her approval. Apparently, saving someone from drowning didn't count for much these days.

"No thanks. It's okay." Sophie leaned over the excursion desk again, her cheekbones flushed with frustration. "Excuse me, what do you mean book a tour on the main strip?"

The staff member seemed slightly annoyed now. "That's where you book excursions. Like I said, I'm just checking people in and telling them where to go."

"I'm going to head back," Amy said. "Good luck. We'll catch up tonight. Love ya."

"You too." Sophie exchanged a fast cheek kiss with Amy.

"Hey, Sophie," a voice called from among a gathering of camera-laden tourists sporting sun hats. Asher Hughes stood below an ATV tour sign watching Sophie with a sordid look. The guy rubbed Ryan the wrong way. "I think I got the last spot."

"You have something sticking out of your pants. Oh, I'm sorry, it's a stick shoved up your—"

"—And why don't we find something else to do, Soph," Ryan offered. "It's not like there aren't a ton of other tours to check out, and I hear Señor Frog's serves incredible drinks." And the perfect excuse to steer her away from Asher. If Ryan knew anything about grade-A jerks in the journalism industry, it's that shady ones like Asher are only effective if they get in your head. Ryan had a personal vendetta against guys like that, and he wouldn't let this guy have that over Sophie.

Again, if looks could kill. "Then go," she chided. "I appreciate the offer, honestly. But it's okay. You don't have to do that. I'm fine now. Sorry about last night." She returned to the itinerary.

Ryan frowned. The way he saw it, she didn't want to ask for help, but she needed it.

Not this time, sister. Ryan stepped around the podium forcing her to focus on him. "Let's go."

Her brows narrowed. "What?"

"Come on." Ryan took her hand and guided her away from the podium and toward the main road where a city bus would take them to the main strip.

"What are you doing?"

"Don't let him get to you. Trust me."

She finally softened. "Look, Ryan, I get it. You're trying to help, but I can handle this. I have to get on that tour."

Ryan pointed to the group of tourists now pulling away in the bright red and blue bus. "That tour?"

"No!" She threw her hands up and then slammed them on her hips. "That's just great."

"Why would you want to go on a tour with him anyway? I get the feeling he's a jerk."

"You wouldn't understand. I just need to go off-roading where I can collect some . . . objects. For the girls back at the café." She shrugged. "I promised them some unusual souvenirs."

Ryan recognized a lie when he saw one. Sweat pooled at the back of his neck. Was this about the scavenger hunt? "I'm sure there are other options."

"Pssst." A hoarse voice caught their attention. A man standing off to the side nodded for them to come closer. He stood all of five-foot-seven wearing an oversized wife-beater. An old, dingy bungee cord held his shorts above his hips and the fact that he was slithering among the other tourists spelled trouble with a capital T. "You need to rent ATVs?"

"No," Ryan said at the same time Sophie said, "Yes."

Sophie flashed a hopeful look his way, but Ryan shook his head.

"What do you have?" Sophie asked.

He gestured for them to move away from the tourist-filled pathway. "I haves jus' the thing," he said in a rich Hispanic accent. "I am Luis. Follow me."

"Sophie," Ryan warned. She seemed hell-bent on this ATV thing but something about this shifty guy screamed dubious.

"Ryan," she answered, mirroring his tone. "I'm just going to look."

"You have cash?" Luis asked, leading them along trail leading to an alleyway.

"How much for an ATV?"

"No ATV."

"What?" Sophie retorted. "I thought you had some for rent."

Ryan scanned the immediate area. Following a stranger to a garage off the main walkway in a foreign country was not smart. The guy was about as stout as a green bean, so it wasn't a mugging that concerned him, but the sleaze ball way he so easily lured Sophie off the main road.

"Journalism one-oh-one, Soph," Ryan whispered. "Don't chase stories where you can be backed against a wall."

Sophie creased her brows, shushing him.

"No, what I have is better. *Se maneja muy rapido.*"

"Huh?" Sophie asked.

Luis, if that was his name, looked a little south of Sophie's eyes. Ryan slid in next to her. Towering over the ogler suddenly made his gaze turn true north. *There we go, big guy.*

"Um. Fast." He smiled and nodded. "It goes very fast."

He led them inside the garage and pulled a plastic tarp off six brand-spanking new Ducati motorcycles. Ryan's jaw dropped. These were fully equipped—160 horsepower, 9,500 revolutions per minute, with a sporty suspension setup and decision support system mapping.

Sophie's mouth was as wide as Ryan's eyes. "Wow!"

At this moment a feather could have knocked Ryan over. These bikes flew rocket fast, clocking in at 200 miles per hour. He used to own a Ducati. It made his commute to work feel like mere seconds. He actually rode this very model when he interviewed Jeff Gordon last spring.

"No way." Ryan nudged Sophie, reining her in. "There's no way these are legit."

"Shut it, Dad." She shot him the slitty eyes of death, which seemed to be her go-to when looking at him.

Dad? Ryan met her gaze and held it, daring her to walk away. *Please let her walk away.*

"How much?" she asked.

"Uh, two hundred dollars," Luis answered. "Per hour."

The air seemed to deflate from Sophie's sails. "I don't have that much."

"We can make . . . other arrangements," he drooled, dropping his eyes again.

Did I hear that right? Ryan started to step in front of Sophie, but she raised her hand against his chest, halting him.

"How about fifty bucks for two hours and I don't kick you in your junk for saying that."

Luis laughed nervously and his eyes cut to Ryan. "She for real?"

"I wouldn't test her."

"Okay." He smiled, flashing his gold and silver teeth. "You a lucky man."

Sophie handed Luis the cash and bounced over to the bikes.

Ryan sauntered behind. "You know these things are stolen, don't you?"

"I just want to do a little sightseeing."

"But what about an ATV? A much safer, four-wheeled ATV?"

Sophie's exaggerated sigh told him he'd better get with the program or go sip cocktails alone on the ship. Despite their past, something about Sophie drew him. Or maybe it was because of their past. Who knew? Either way he didn't feel like fighting the urge. What would it hurt to catch up?

"I'm trying to avoid sightseeing on public transportation and I want something that can move," she said.

"Can you handle one of these things? They go incredibly

fast. You'll lose your hair if you're not careful." She'd lose a lot more than that if she lost control.

"Yeah, I rode a little after college. I almost got my class C, but decided against it."

"This is not like riding your run-of-the-mill motorcycle."

"I know, right?" She approached the Ducati closest to her, running her hand over the slick, leather seat.

"No, no!" Luis hustled toward them with some form of paper work in his hand. "No *señorita* drive."

Apparently, Sophie hadn't convinced Luis of her crotch-rocket driving skills.

"Why not?" Sophie raised her voice. "I can drive."

"No," he said again, a crisp harshness in his voice. He looked at Ryan. "Is too much power for her. She's a girl."

"Excuse me? I know how to ride a motorcycle."

Luis tried to hand back Sophie's money. "No. My sister crashed into the wall and broke her leg." He jutted his chin toward another motorcycle in the corner. "It no run now. She thought she could handle it, too. And guess what? I'm out eight hundred bucks."

Ryan cocked his head. "You paid eight hundred American dollars for each one?"

Luis bared his gold teeth. "I know a guy." He turned to Sophie. "Here. You take your money. Go back to the bus."

"I guess that's that," Ryan said, barely able to contain a twitch at the corner of his lips.

"Wait! Can he drive?" Sophie reached for Luis's wrist. She bit her bottom lip, and purred, "Please."

Luis eyed Ryan, rubbing his chin with his finger and thumb. "Yeah, that is okay." He pocketed the cash and walked off.

Ryan hiked a brow and lowered his voice. "Are you flirting?"

"Journalism one-oh-one: Use whatever assets you have to get a story . . . or in this case a nice bike."

"It's not just any bike, *Sophia*. It's a Ducati. I think they come equipped with their very own souls."

"Oh, pulling the 'Sophia' card." She offered an enigmatic smile and mounted the back of the Ducati. "Note to self, don't call a Ducati a bike."

Ryan rolled his eyes, but slid onto the seat in front of her.

"Put your arms around me, okay? And hold on tightly."

Sophie scooted forward so her body was flush with his and wrapped her arms around him, locking her forearms together above his waist. "Like this?"

He could feel every curve of her body. Ryan swallowed hard. "Yes, but first you need to put this on." He was not happy with the poor quality helmet, but at least the chinstrap was better than nothing. "Don't grab the straps on the seat. They will do nothing to help you stay on."

"Okay."

"When we turn, I need you to lean into the turn, even if you feel like you're falling. If you fight against the turn, we can crash. Got it?"

"Yes, can we go already?"

"And if anything is wrong, I need you to pat my thigh. I may not hear you, so that's how I'll know to stop."

"Okay, okay, I get it."

"So where are we going?"

Sophie signaled Luis. "Where would you suggest two tourists go to see the best your city has to offer?"

"Ah." Luis smiled, his gold teeth glistening. "You go to La Bufadora. Is the most beautiful sight."

"La Bufadora?" Ryan asked. "You mean the blowhole?"

"*Si*. You will never see a more grandiose place."

Ryan could think of more than a dozen sights grander than a blowhole—Taj Mahal, any of the hundreds of Egyptian pyramids, or even the Grand Canyon—but he didn't respond.

Sophie tapped Ryan's thigh. "What do you think?"

Her touch startled him. Jolted him, actually. "Um." His voice cracked like a fifteen-year-old boy. She was just following his directions, sarcastically, but he'd take that as a rocky start. He cleared his throat. "Right. It's true. I'd say it's worth a trip."

"Sounds great. Let's go."

After they signed a few papers and Luis offered vague directions in broken English, Ryan checked Sophie's grip around his waist. He dropped the throttle, squeezed the clutch, and popped the Ducati into first gear.

It had been a very long time since anyone's close proximity quickened his pulse. Hell, it had been too long since any woman had been in this close of proximity. And he hated to admit, the fact Sophie pressed up against him might have something to do with that quickened pulse more than anything. Her breath against his neck only added to his already searing internal temperature. He slowly released the clutch as they glided out of the garage.

He was uncertain where they stood after all these years. But part of her must still trust him. Why else would she be on the back of this bike holding on to him?

He'd messed up years ago with that article. He'd own up to that. The article had been motivated by trying to make sense of his own desperate pain. If he had the opportunity now, with ten years of growing up under his belt, he never would have written it. But she had dumped him, and for no reason that he could figure out other than he had poured out his heart and she didn't like what she saw. Ryan clenched his jaw. *Let's not forget who charred whom.*

Regardless of their past, he was certain of one thing in this moment. He liked her arms wrapped tightly around his waist more than he cared to admit.

Chapter 12

Ryan drove the Ducati slower than a grandma pushing a baby buggy, which, she was pretty sure, went against its creator's religion. Normally, Sophie would be okay with just taking in the beautiful scenery, but not today.

Today she needed to kick butt finding the perfect scavenger hunt item.

During this morning's meeting, she'd logged on to her email, hopeful to hear back from any of the grant applications. But when she checked, there was nothing, not even a hello from Grandmoo.

The warm air blew dust into Sophie's eyes. She rested her head against his shoulder and clamped her eyes shut. The guilty pleasure would remain her little secret. Something she wrapped up tightly and stuck in her back pocket. Because no matter how right he felt, she reminded herself he was *very* wrong.

This morning's scavenger hunt instructions clearly indicated she had to collect a unique item while touring, and the item had to be native to the land but could not be purchased. *Unique, creative, and thought to be valuable by the panel, which included a pre-selected group of carefully picked cruise employees.* She suddenly felt the time crunch.

"Can we go a little faster?" Sophie yelled over the hum of the engine.

"No."

"Why not?"

Ryan turned his head so she could hear him over the wind. "Because there are a slew of people and the driving laws around here are a little less formal than the States." He paused momentarily. "Do you want to see anything else along the way? I don't think they have much for off-roading on the beaches here, but we can ask some locals for some trails along the coast if you want."

"No," Sophie said. No use wasting precious hunting time sightseeing. She wouldn't be able to focus anyway. Not with the pressure to beat Asher, and well, focusing with Ryan around was growing impossible. "Just head to La Bufadora."

The highway signs offered little for directions, and the wind was mercilessly stabbing her in the face.

Ryan must have felt the same about directions because he yelled over his shoulder, "Did the guy say to head south or west?"

"South. No, west. No . . ."

Ryan slowed the bike into a turnout. When he stopped she pushed off the seat and nearly collapsed; the engine's powerful vibration had numbed her legs. She shook them out and removed her helmet. Ryan effortlessly dismounted in one swift, steady motion. *Of course he did.*

Cars roared past, the thundering reverberation rattled pebbles on the ground. Sophie grabbed the bike, keeping her balance until her equilibrium cooperated. "What are you doing? We're going to get killed."

"Relax, *Mom*," he said, laying the city's map over the Ducati's seat.

A bus roared past, making Sophie stumble. "I'm reassured, thanks."

Ryan directed her to the opposite side of the motorcycle. "Stay clear of the roadway."

Sophie peered over Ryan's shoulder as he smoothed out the map. "It's in Spanish. Great, we're lost." She slumped.

"No, we're not," he said with an air of assurance.

"Since when do you read Spanish?"

"I understand more than I speak, but I can read a map. It's close enough to English. Just give me a few minutes."

A few minutes she didn't have. They had to be back on the boat by five tonight, which meant every second he spent playing map-reader, was one she didn't have to search for the winning item.

A tour bus darted past them, kicking up debris and wind, forcing them to duck. Sophie watched the bus speed past, but it didn't take more than a second for bus's advertisement to resonate. "There," she hollered over the thundering rumble of passing cars. "That bus is headed for the blowhole! Let's go."

They mounted the bike and Ryan peeled out, sending gravel flying.

From that point on, the ride was smooth. Or maybe Sophie had gotten used to it. As Ryan sped up to catch the bus, Sophie relaxed against his shoulder. White, sandy beaches peppered the background. The salty air cleared Sophie's clouded mind, and it was too easy to feel the power not only beneath her, but also in front of her. Ryan steered the bike like it was a part of him, smooth and confidently.

His muscles flexed when he squeezed the throttle and Sophie liked how they tightened against her. She sunk deeper into the seat as the vibrating hum of the ride soothed her into a relaxed state. The combination of Ryan's feel, his smell, and his insisting to come with her summoned the Ryan she once knew. The one who she had locked away in the furthest corner of her mind because the mere thought of him made her stomach turn.

But leaning against him now tapped into a sensation she'd let go of a long time ago. It reached into her core where hatching butterflies reassured her that she belonged. Like she had when they were together so many years ago.

Midway through her senior year of college, Sophie fell in love.

That Ryan Pike would pay her any attention, let alone ask her to winter formal, had fairy tale written all over it. Sure, girls spoke of butterflies and swooning lady parts and classic first-kiss-leg-lifts, but she was not one of those girls.

She was north of a size ten, and thus dropped into the "good personality" category. Not pretty . . . well, not the sort of pretty boys like Ryan typically went for. Not that it was all her fault. Grandmoo, who raised her from age twelve, was from the Deep South, and fed her accordingly.

But despite her physical flaws, having the right things in common could draw in a good-looking, kindhearted boy like Ryan just the same. At least that's what Grandmoo said.

Sophie wiped her mouth and stuffed the guilt of having just chowed down on Crawford State University's cafeteria's idea of grilled cheese on Texas toast, slathered in butter and extra cheese with a side of fries. It was nothing compared to Grandmoo's fried chicken—made with bacon grease—and canned greens smothered in butter and brown sugar, but it would do for school food. She stepped into the spring air, the sun shining on the buildings, when someone caught her arm and spun her around.

Ryan Pike looked handsome as ever—tall, wavy dark hair, ocean blue eyes, Caribbean blue, not Pacific blue— even with the uncharacteristic flush on his cheeks. He looked . . . nervous. What did the Nice Playboy have to be nervous about, and where was his latest flavor of the month?

Sophie clutched her books in front of her waistline, concealing what she wished wasn't there, and hoped her breath didn't smell like cheese. "Hey, what's up?"

He swallowed, then in a rush of words said, "Do you want to go to a party with me? It's something my fraternity puts on. A themed thing," he added.

Sophie blinked at him. He must want something. Boys like him didn't talk to girls like her, and they certainly didn't ask them out. Maybe he needed access to the dean's office, where she worked part time, to alter his grades?

This was probably just some fraternity prank. "I can't. I'm sorry." She moved to step past him but he met her step-for-step. God, he smelled so good.

"Why not? I know it's totally lame to go to these things, but I thought it would be fun." He smiled, his perfect lips parting in that teasing grin. And she was done for, practically swooning right there on the stairs. "It's an '80s theme party, which makes it even dumber. But, you know . . ."

His words trailed. He wanted an answer. And maybe, just maybe he was being sincere. After all she nicknamed him the Nice Playboy for a reason.

Freshman year, they shared a math class together. She had slipped out of class for a moment to use the restroom, and when she returned, her saltine crackers were smashed to bits in their plastic baggie where she had left them on her desk. The gorgeous Leggy Blonde Ryan was dating at the time snickered in front of her. A knot in her throat threatened forbidden tears, but she bit her lip hard and stared at her crushed crackers.

Not two minutes later, Ryan tapped her on the shoulder and handed her a pack of peanut butter crackers, the ones from the vending machine. That grin made her heart flutter. "These ones are better anyway," he said.

After class, Sophie saw him and Leggy Blonde arguing outside. They stopped dating, and Sophie tried not to care. Though the gesture was not lost on her. She gave him the "nice" nickname, but then it wasn't even a week later when she spotted him with his arm around another one of those girls. The ones she could never compete with in looks or dress size. Dagger. In. Heart.

So why would he be asking her out? Maybe he needed tutoring?

"I'm not that smart."

"Excuse me?" His eyes narrowed in confusion.

Those Caribbean eyes would be the death of her. "I wouldn't be a good tutor. These upperclassman courses are tough."

He laughed. Not in that condescending way, just in that's-not-what-I-meant sort of way. "No, I just want to take you out. Get to know you." He tentatively grabbed her hand and tugged it. "Honestly."

And before she could think better of it, before she could come up with an excuse, "Bon Jovi," squeaked from her lips.

His smile blinded her. "What?"

"I love the eighties, I mean. Bon Jovi practically raised me. I'd love to go as a punk rocker." Sophie internally clamped a hand over her mouth. Word vomit was not necessary.

"Great. I'll meet you in the quad tomorrow at seven. See ya, Sophie."

And before she could stop him, tell him she didn't mean it, he was halfway across campus. The view of his backside wasn't too shabby either.

By seven the following evening, Sophie was ready for anything. She added an iconic eighties' wig to accent her sequined dress that showed just enough leg—but not too much to suggest she was one of *those girls*, and then fixed the pair of oversized sunglasses she'd picked up a secondhand store earlier that day over her eyes. She had also shaved everywhere, and dabbed a little of her roommate's Brittany Spears in a bottle on all the important places. Being she was the only girl in the universe who hadn't been with a guy yet, she didn't want to assume anything.

By 7:05, Sophie began to break out in hives. He wasn't there yet. He stood her up. *Why did he ask me out in the first place? What sort of sick game is he playing? What if he asked me here to murder me for my trust fund? I don't even have a trust fund.* Sophie decided to hustle back to her dorm room.

"Ready?" his smooth-as-butter voice called from behind.

She shivered at the sound of his baritone and her knees threatened to buckle. When she took his arm, she wasn't sure if she should laugh or ask him where he had found a time machine because he was dressed as if he'd just stepped off an eighties' rock band stage. "Oh, my gosh, where did you find leather pants?"

His smile made her sequins quiver. Or was that her legs? "Same place I found this matching vest and wig."

"Your bandana is awesome," Sophie said on a laugh.

"Thanks." He moved into her personal bubble. And she surprised herself by letting him. "Your dress is amazing, by the way."

All insecurities subsided as he cupped her hand in his warm, secure grip and escorted her to his awaiting carriage. Well, 1998 Ford pickup, but it may as well have been a carriage. She was no princess . . . or rock star, but no one could convince her otherwise.

By the end of the dance, she knew everything about him. He was interested in sports journalism—something they had in common—well, the journalism anyway. When he spoke of a future, his face lit up like a Christmas tree and he came alive. He dropped names like Bear Bryant and Babe Ruth and spoke of chasing athletes like a greyhound chasing a rubber rabbit. It was all so fascinating. His goals in life were sure and steady and amazing. He wasn't only nice, he was self-assured and gentle and sweet.

So, when the lights went dim, and the live band started playing "Time of My Life," Ryan's fingers brushed Sophie's cheek, sending goose bumps down her legs. He wrapped his hand around the back of her neck and drew her closer. His other hand, warm and strong, set on the small of her back. His breath summoned her lips to his.

When she opened to his coaxing, she fell into his spell. His mouth explored hers, reaching down and touching the depths of her soul in a way she'd never felt before. Sophie didn't want the kiss to break, but suddenly the song had ended, and only then did she realize they'd kissed the entire four minutes and twenty-nine seconds. Why Patrick Swayze wasted all that time dancing with Jennifer Grey when he should have been kissing her was beyond Sophie's comprehension. Because it was far better.

He brushed his thumb over her bottom lip. "Want to go?"

Words stuck in Sophie's throat. So when she nodded, what she meant to say was that she would have robbed a bank with him if he'd asked her to.

His hand dropped into hers, holding it as gently as if he held her heart, which he did. Sophie didn't care everyone watched as they left the party. And she certainly didn't mind the scorn from Leggy Blonde as Ryan held the door and escorted her to her carriage.

Sophie blinked back to the present and subconsciously stomped on the memory, refusing to get swept up in the moment. Her *been there done that had the baggage from it* tee shirt was currently at the cleaners. She'd chalk today up as a one-time only situation since Luis wouldn't let her drive her own Ducati.

A group of horseback-riding tourists waved at Sophie and she almost waved back, except Ryan must have felt her loosen her grip because he fastened his hand over hers at lightning speed, squeezing it back in place. The feeling of his hand securely holding hers did something to her insides to which she wasn't exactly opposed.

"Got it, don't let go." After that, Sophie relaxed. She closed her eyes and allowed her other senses to come alive. Unfortunately, the moment she completely relaxed, the memories of their past spurred seeds of old fears and insecurities. He was too nice and that scared her. The last time he was this easy to be around he used her for a story. There had to be a catch. Why was he here? What did she have that he wanted? Everyone in the office seemed to like him. Even Amy.

Or maybe it was nothing. *Ficus*, she hated mind games. She'd promised herself no games. Today would test her theory. She'd give him the benefit of the doubt. If he planned to manipulate her again, she would know. For now, that plan was enough to settle the nausea twirling in the lowest part of her belly.

Chapter 13

Minutes later, they pulled off the main road onto the partially paved parking lot, following a few tour busses. Ryan whipped out a bill and paid the entrance fee. Sophie's stomach quaked at the gesture. It wasn't a date, no, but that didn't negate the chivalry any less.

"That wasn't such a rough ride now, was it?" Ryan pulled the Ducati to a complete stop, drawing Sophie from her quiet thoughts. "I mean, it's not an ATV, but it got the job done."

"You're right, it was a beautiful ride."

Ryan helped Sophie off the bike, then turned her around. "You see that?" he asked, leaning alarmingly close and pointed at the ocean. The cliffside looked as though an artist carved it from the side of a mountain.

Her heart jackhammered and she yearned to fold into his chest, because, well, she didn't have any common sense, as evidenced by driving around in a stolen rocket. "Mmm." Did she just moan? She pressed her lips together. *Get it together, Sophie.*

"It's home to the second largest marine geyser in the world."

"Thank you, Mr. Jeopardy know-it-all." Sophie stepped away from him creating a little space. "How do you know all this random stuff?"

He grinned and pointed to a nearby sign. "Because *Geyser Facts* says so."

"Oh, so it does."

Ryan mouth curved upward and Sophie thought she may need more than just a little space if his smile kept doing things to her. He secured the bike with a cable he found in the tire wheel, fastening the ends together like a glorified bike lock. "Let's go."

An old, standalone gateway sign made out of dark wood with painted white letters reading *Bienvenidos A La Bufadora* separated the parking area from the bazaar-style flea market. Tourists and local venders haggled for merchandise, families laughed, and in the distance, an echo from the geyser spraying the sky lent its soft lullaby to the jovial atmosphere.

Now to find the perfect, unique item. Sophie put on her game face and followed Ryan into the bazaar.

Ryan's hand brushed against hers, sending a lightning bolt through her core. She didn't mean to flinch but whipped her hand behind her.

"Sorry," he uttered.

"It's okay. The ground is uneven and sometimes I have two left feet and—" *Cough, cough. Shut up, Sophie.*

She eyed Ryan through lowered lashes and saw the corners of his mouth pull upward. She was happy to not be alone. Ryan may not have been her first choice in a companion, but without him, she very well could have been road kill. Then again, maybe he was just being *nice*.

Sophie reached for her phone, hoping to check her email, but at the same time she patted her empty back pocket, visualizing right where she'd left it in her cabin. *Ficus*. What if something was wrong with her girls? How would they reach her? Sophie filled her lungs. *They're fine.*

"Nice ride, friend," a vender with a booth flanking the parking lot called to Ryan. His T-shirt featured Gene Simmons's foot-long tongue and a black and white painted face. His booth was packed with sun hats, scarves, backpacks, knives, knock-off Rolex watches, and in case the moment lent itself, ukuleles. Sophie felt reassured this tent would suffice if she ever got lost in deep terrain with Bear Grylls.

"Thanks. It's on loan." Ryan glanced back at the Ducati and narrowed his eyes.

Sophie's eyes followed.

Ryan faced the man again. "*Cuanto cuesta?*" How much?

Sophie was lost. "How much for what?"

The vender rubbed his fist over his chin. "*Cincuenta dolares.*"

Ryan hiked a brow. "Fifty? How about twenty?"

"Twenty-five."

"Deal." Ryan handed the man a couple bills.

What just happened here? "Did you buy something?"

"Just a little peace of mind. You ready?"

Sophie raised an eyebrow at the man as he stuffed the bills in his pocket.

He nodded back at her with a twenty-five-dollar smile.

"Oh." She offered a *well-played* smirk. "He's going to babysit the Ducati."

"Yep."

"Did you pay him enough?"

"He's selling five-dollar trinkets and knock-off watches. We have an understanding. The bike will be fine."

Sophie shrugged. "Okay." Now to find her scavenger hunt item. But as they strolled through the bazaar, Sophie found basically the same junk souvenirs at every booth. Nothing unique here. A twinge of unease settled in her gut. Asher was probably uncovering some Mayan artifact while she wasted time in this tourist trap. Maybe she'd find something of value near the blowhole.

Finally, they reached the end of the flea market where a rail guarded against a steep fall straight down into the blowhole. On one side of the geyser stood a crescent-shaped rocky cliff, on the other side the wide ocean sparkled in the sunshine. *Breathtaking* was an understatement.

"You hungry?" Ryan asked.

"No," she said, taking in the panoramic view. Frustration ate at her. She'd wasted precious hours, where could they go to find something unique? She leaned her elbows on the worn red railing and hung her head. And there, just out of sight, an old sign for a guided tour al la kayaks. *Kayaks!*

She straightened back up and faced Ryan who was leaning his back against the railing. "What do you want to do?"

Sophie bit her lip. That tour sign led to something promising. Very likely ample, untouched *unique valuables* would be everywhere. Maybe she'd find a priceless artifact washed ashore on the beach. But how could she slip down to the shoreline unnoticed? She huffed as the kayak sign grew more promising than just a stroll on the beach. A plan formed in her mind, but first she needed to ditch Ryan. She didn't want him tagging along to try and talk her out of it.

She scanned the vendors, searching for a diversion.

A long line snaked from a standalone, refrigerated cart with an umbrella shading it. A six-foot-tall pineapple cardboard cutout stood next to it advertising some sort of pineapple smoothie goodness.

"Actually, I'm parched." She gestured toward the cart. "Those drinks look really refreshing. Mind getting me one?" She batted her lashes for good measure.

"Yeah, sure. Anything to eat? Looks like your only choice is fish tacos, wrapped in a fried tortilla.

"Gross."

"Suit yourself. I'm starving." He graced her with a heart-stopping grin then disappeared into the crowd.

A twinge of guilt swirled through her. He was being so nice, and she was ditching him. But for good reason. He had been very clear last night that the scavenger hunt was off limits, not that he was her boss. But if he knew what she was up to, it would put him in an uncomfortable position.

He'd have to pick loyalty to her or loyalty to his job. And she knew from past experience, Ryan was a career first kind of man.

But her girls came before anything. She shoved the guilt aside and ducked behind a tall man with an oversized straw hat, shadowing him until she reached the stone stairs that led down to the beach.

"Would you mind taking our picture, miss?" a nerdy tourist-to-the-T asked, shoving a gargantuan camera in her hands, breaching her bubble.

Sophie took a huge step back and apprehensively accepted the Nikon. She'd seen enough *Dateline* episodes where con artists use the non-threatening ploy of asking favors of an unsuspecting stranger before they put a pillowcase over the tourist's head and ship them to a foreign country.

However, between this guy's enthusiastic nodding that bordered Tourette's, and his overly white legs blinding her, he lacked way too much stealth to be an efficient kidnapper.

"Of course." Sophie grinned, using this as an excuse to make sure Ryan was in line. And he was. Sophie held the camera up and brought the family into focus. All four members looked disturbingly alike. Four redheaded, freckled-faced lookalikes with glasses and cherry lips stared back at her. They were like a little pack of nerdlings.

"Say cheese." As the family came into focus so did the details of what she would use to find her winning scavenger hunt item. Down the steps that led to the far end of La Bufadora's shoreline, her opportunity waded in the water. Four snapshots later, she handed the camera to the littlest redhead who had more freckles on his face than sand on the beach. *Cute little nerdling.*

A group of tourists in kayaks floated by with a tour guide directing them when to paddle and how to maneuver. She followed the tour sign to a booth made from driftwood and two-by-fours. Its wood was cracked and faded from the sun, which convinced Sophie the business had been around long enough to offer safe boats.

She approached the guy manning the kayaks, ignoring the momentous warning sign flashing in the forefront of her mind.

So what if she had never operated a kayak in her life, how hard could it be? Kayaks peppered the ocean, their occupants looked like they were having the time of their lives. If these tourists could do it, so could she. She'd just do what she always did . . . sink until she swam.

~ ~ ~

"You ever operate one of these?" a tour guide asked. He handed her the release and liability paperwork on a clipboard.

"Absolutely," Sophie lied. If she had a nickel for every fib she'd uttered on this trip, the café's debt would likely be paid in full.

"I'm Jaime." His fresh face and thick eyebrows pegged him about twenty years old. His lack of a Spanish accent told Sophie he'd worked in tourism his whole life. Probably the family business.

Jaime cupped his hands to his mouth and yelled to an older man with salt and pepper hair helping a couple into a two-seater kayak, probably his father. "Papa, which kayak?"

Yep, father and son duo. Sophie subconsciously patted herself on her back.

"Only have number nine right now," the dad hollered back. His accent was thick. "Unless she waits an hour."

Jaime narrowed his eyes. "Just how good of a kayaker are you?"

What an odd question. "How good do you want me to be?"

His crooked smile may as well have been a forewarning. "I'm asking because we only have one kayak available right now. It has a bit of split personality, if you get my drift."

Sophie shook her head. "Not exactly."

"Well, it occasionally pulls left when you direct it right, hence the 'split personality.' But if you're experienced, it won't be problem." He took the clipboard back from Sophie and scribbled some notes. "If you wait an hour, another group will be back and you can have a perfectly well-mannered kayak."

Part of Sophie's job included snap decisions. She'd never heard of kayaks with split personalities. She had learned tennis and bocce ball in one afternoon. In fact, she was bocce ball junior champion her senior year of college. She'd pick up kayaking just as fast.

"Of course," she lied again. "I kayak all the time. Like *all* the time. In rivers, oceans, streams, swimming pools." *Pools?* "Ah-hem, I mean, you know, all sorts of water. I'm a great kayaker," she finished lamely.

Jaime narrowed his gaze and handed her back the clipboard.

Her heart sank. *Rejected.*

"You didn't put down an emergency contact." He pointed to the empty space on the form.

"Oh." She feigned a smile. "Right. How could I forget that? Safety first, right?" Taking the clipboard she couldn't think of whom to put down. Amy's number was in her cell phone, which was probably mocking her from her room. With Grandmoo's health, she couldn't help even if she wanted to. Red was in the States and likely still unavailable. *Ficus.*

She gritted her teeth and scribbled Ryan's name and cell number before good sense had a chance to set in. His contact info was on the itinerary when they boarded the ship. Sure, her photographic memory kicked in now.

Jaime handed her an XXL-sized life jacket. She eyed the beast and wondered if he noticed the problem.

"Um, Jaime?" Sophie dangled the life jacket over the

kiosk desk. "Do you happen to have a smaller size?"

He slid his sunglasses down his nose. "Sure, sweets. If you wait an hour."

Sophie sighed. "Never mind, this is perfect. Thanks."

She pulled the straps as tight as they would go, but she still swam in the orange tent. Oh well, details and all.

The older man pushed kayak number nine into the water, and then smiled, gesturing for Sophie to get in. He held out his hands mimicking holding the paddle and swayed his arms from side to side.

Sophie mirrored him. "Like this?"

"*Si*." He placed one foot on the kayak and kicked it into the slow current. Figuring out how to paddle was the easy part. Learning the oversized plantain would only go in circles was a bit more of a challenge. When the kayak banked left, she stabbed the water, forcing it to the right. But it still drifted left. "Split personality my butt," she bit out. "This thing is full-blown bi-polar."

Sophie's face grew hot as she continually dipped the bright red paddle on the right side of the kayak. She bit out a curse when it formed a figure eight. "What is the matter with you?" she asked, as if she expected an explanation for its behavior.

Sophie's arms grew heavy and tired. This was worse than hard labor. She'd once shoveled wet cement when helping Grandmoo pour a driveway, and that required less effort than this. She dropped her chin, glaring at her problem. The life jacket. It refused to give her the maneuverability to fight the bi-polar banana. She squirmed out of the vest and tossed it in the empty space behind her. Finally she could move.

While a few perfectly seasoned kayakers pointed and laughed, she finally got the beast to straighten out. With a little cooperation, the oversized yellow banana glided smoothly toward the blowhole. It had mustered manners under her watch, thank you very much.

Now that she had control, Sophie searched the likely untouched shore for something unique. A yellow warning flag flapped in the light breeze. Under it was a sign cautioning: ALTO/STOP. Yellow signified proceed with caution. Red was a command. Sophie lifted a shoulder. No red flags here.

Ignoring the additional two lines of miniscule printed words about changing currents, she paddled toward the shore. Maybe she would find ancient pirate's treasure or a Victorian ruby or an eighteenth-century fishing lure. Did they have lures back then? Who cared? As long as she didn't stumble upon any human remains, she'd be happy with whatever.

Just yards from shore, the kayak veered toward the blowhole. She stuck the paddle in the water to turn. At first, it pivoted back toward her waiting booty, championing Team Sophie. Until the beast jerked hard.

Adrenaline pelted warning shots straight through Sophie's skin. "No you don't." She clenched the paddle, assessing the water's new route.

The current apparently also suffered from bi-polar disorder. It abruptly changed directions like a train jumping tracks. She stabbed the water with the paddle blade and fought. "No you don't, I said!"

Sophie squirmed in her seat, leaning against the side closest to land. The harder she pushed against the current, the easier the paddle leveraged her body, lifting her as if she weighed nothing. Her muscles screamed while the vessel pulled in the wrong direction.

With her back now facing the blowhole, it didn't take a nautical genius to explain how very dangerous this was. "Stop it!" she yelled at the kayak. Her palms burned against the hot, plastic shaft as she tried to adjust course one more time.

"No, señorita," a voice called in the distance. It was

Jaime. "You've gone too far."

Thank you, Captain Obvious. The boat swirled around, and the blowhole opened its mouth to spit in her face.

"You okay?" Jaime hollered, sounding more like a laugh than a concern. "Just sit straight and paddle backwards," he said, all calm and stupid and stuff.

"I can't," she called back. "How do you turn it?"

"Put your vest back on."

Good idea. It didn't matter the floatation device was big enough to fit the Loch Ness monster. Better she wear it than end up meeting Nessie in the depths below the blowhole.

Jaime's voice neared but Sophie didn't dare turn around to see how close. She reached for the oversized life vest, but her paddle slipped off her lap and into the water. "Dang it!"

She swung back around to grab it, but the current moved too quickly. The paddle was just an inch away. Sophie leaned further. Further. Just as her fingertips nicked it, the kayak tipped, dumping her into the water.

"Ficus!" Cold water snatched her breath away like a punch to the gut. The current pushed Sophie in the direction of the blowhole. Then something slimy and squirmy touched her foot. "Ew!" *A shark . . . or an eel . . . or a corpse!*

A million tiny needles stabbed every inch of her body. The current tugged her under and she nearly choked on a mouthful of salt water. What was it with her and water?

Sophie gritted her teeth against the cold and kicked her legs. "Gawd, that's cold!"

The kayak drifted in the opposite direction, mocking her on its way to the blowhole, taking the life preserver and any hope she had of finding an item with it. Had the water been as Caribbean blue as Ryan's eyes and the temperature a balmy eighty-six point five degrees, she might have tried to save it, but not now. Only the truly insane would swim toward the blowhole without a life vest or boat or tequila shots.

The blowhole would eventually suck in and then spit

out the kayak. That was the good news. The bad news . . . well, there went her deposit. Flushed down the deep, dark, proverbial toilet. With no unique item to show for it.

Resolved to not freeze to death like in her all-time favorite movie *Titanic,* she bit down on the cold and put her butt in gear, cutting through the frigid water toward shore.

The girls' faces flashed through her mind, one after the other. Hot frustration set in. How could she give up so easily? She couldn't let them down. She needed a stupid trinket. Something she certainly wouldn't get now.

Not unless . . . What if she got something mundane— like a rock or piece of coral—and a story? Sophie grinned as the idea took hold. She stopped swimming, took another deep breath, and like a stupid tourist, dove underwater.

An abrupt tug on her tank top thwarted her forward efforts.

"Let's go, Nemo," Jaime said. He'd come out of nowhere in a scanty, motorized raft.

Sophie jerked against his hold. "But I need— just give me a second."

Jaime's lobster grip wouldn't relent, but he laughed. "So, you're an expert kayaker who can't navigate a piece of plastic that turns on a dime?"

She did not appreciate his condescending tone. "That thing did *not* turn on a dime."

Jaime, an infuriating grin on his face, shook his head. "Hold on, I'll help you in," he said, angling the boat toward the wrong shore.

Sophie's teeth chattered as she looked over her shoulder at the abandoned beach that stole all her hopes and dreams.

Hot tears welled up against her icy skin. She had come so far. She'd sacrificed so much—near drowning in the ship's pool, Asher's smug confidence, Ryan searching for her with a melting pineapple smoothie, and all the lies. She groaned.

So many lies.

Something shinny floated near her leg. Was it unique? Creative? She had to have it.

Sophie lurched forward. Wrapping her fingers around a slick, hard object, just as a *rip* had her sucking in another lungful of salt water.

Jaime stared at her bobbing half naked in the ocean, then at her tank top still in his vise grip. A slow grin spread across his face. "Don't move."

She glared at him. How could she when she was too busy covering her chest?

He whipped out his cell phone and snapped a picture. The grin turned devilish as his thumbs raced across the phone's screen. He flipped the phone around so she could see his Instagram account. *Finding Nemo* captioned her picture. "Some things that happen in La Bufadora don't stay in La Bufadora."

Ficus.

Chapter 14

Webster's Dictionary could most definitely portray Sophie's face beneath the definition of "humiliated." Not only did she fail to find anything for the scavenger hunt, but thanks to Captain Jaime with his vise grip of death, it also robbed her of a trinket opportunity and left her shirtless. *This could not get any worse.*

"Sophie?" She locked eyes with Ryan. His perfectly square jaw tensed as he waited next to the kayak kiosk. *Seriously?*

A knot wound in Sophie's chest. *Now* things couldn't get any worse.

He held a pineapple drink in either hand. His brows pulled together as if to ask a million questions, none of which would be helpful at this moment. He landed on the safest question. "Are you okay?"

She wrapped her arms around her chest, the stinging vulnerability of her situation in plain view. "You bet."

His sunglasses were set on top of his head, the look of concern etched in his Caribbean eyes. His fitted shirt accentuated his broad chest and his denim jeans wrapped firmly around his thighs. He looked like a rugged, exotic model posing for an island getaway brochure.

Someone who looked like that should not be waiting for a wet, matted dog like her. She set her jaw. She was not that twenty-year-old anymore. She was a grown adult with self-respect. Well, as soon as she found a shirt, she'd find some self-respect and she would rock it.

Sophie stepped out of the motorized raft. Her soaked shoes squeaked with each step. A rush of cool air, or maybe a cold sweat, reminded her that her tank top was lost at sea, God rest its soul. A twinge of vulnerability stabbed her in the gut. Not the purge twinge, but the crawling under a rock twinge.

"Here," Jaime's dad, who had a caterpillar under his nose posing as a mustache, growled. A stress vein bulged from his red forehead. He tossed her a towel and a fuchsia-colored shirt, then helped Jaime drag the raft onto dry land.

"Thanks," she mumbled and stepped behind the kiosk. Wishing she could summon the patron saint of humiliation to douse her with brimstone and firewater, Sophie all but accepted the shirt's graphic as her penance: a gloriously illuminate yellow arrow pointing directly at her face. It read: 'I Kayaked With Stupid.' *Appalling . . . and yet, weirdly appropriate.*

She rolled her eyes and yanked the shirt over her head. It hung to her mid thighs. Two of her could have fit in it and still be roomy.

Sophie bunched the fabric together and tied the side of shirt into a knot so at least her shorts were visible.

Now to face Ryan. She took a deep breath and stepped onto the path. He stood there looking too handsome and too touchable. She forced her feet forward, aware of each step like she was on a walk of shame.

His firm mouth curled as his eyes dropped to her shirt. "It's a good color on you."

Sophie narrowed her eyes to thin slits. "I'm sure it is. How did you know where I was?"

He nodded toward the kiosk. "They called me a few minutes ago. Told me you fell in."

"I hardly fell in. And it was hardly worth mentioning. I'm surprised they did that."

"I'm surprised I'm your emergency contact."

"Oh, well . . ." She shifted her feet. "I, um, had to put something down." She dropped her eyes and tucked some of her wet hair behind her ear. "I left my phone on the ship. Your number happened to be the only one I remembered."

"Oh, really?"

She scowled at him. "Don't get too excited."

Ryan raised his hands in defense, still holding the drinks. "I wouldn't dream of it. Thirsty?" he asked on a half-smile. He stepped toward her.

"Don't even," she warned. "You laugh and you'll be wearing those pineapples. And I don't mean in a pineapple bra sort of way."

"Duly noted." He smiled anyway.

Jerk.

Sophie gratefully accepted the drink. The dry, salty ocean taste burned her mouth. But before she could indulge in the fresh pineapple juice Jaime's dad called out, "Hey. *Policía* here."

"The police?" Sophie whipped around so fast her wet ponytail slapped her in the eye. "Who called the police?" More importantly, why would they do that?

The caterpillar under the man's nose twitched. He pointed behind Sophie in the direction of the stairs. And sure as this never-ending day was long, a red-faced officer descended and made a beeline for Jaime's dad.

Sophie didn't speak a word of Spanish aside from the normal pleasantries learned as a child, and she knew for certain whatever he said did not include pleasantries. He pelted what she could only assume were foreign insults faster than bullets from a semi-automatic.

On two different occasions, the police officer gawked at Sophie, raising a judgy eyebrow, then nodded.

"Do you have any idea what he's saying?" Sophie whispered to Ryan.

Ryan shushed her and continued listening to the conversation.

"Do you understand?"

"A little," he whispered.

"What are they saying?" The hair on the back of her neck stood on edge. What if they sent her to jail? She couldn't go to jail. Not in a foreign country. She would be fresh bait in there. Did they even separate the men from woman? American prisons were probably like day spas in comparison.

Ryan smirked.

She elbowed him. "What? What's that smirk for?"

"I didn't smirk," he said, pushing Sophie a few feet away from the police officer. "Just relax, it's fine."

Sophie bristled, and something squeezed in her chest. Nothing was going as planned, and now the police were involved. *How is this* fine? Sophie stabbed Ryan's chest with her finger. "No, it's not *fine*. The police are here. So, don't use *fine* with me when things are obviously not."

"Don't worry about my dad," Jaime said from behind Sophie.

He shook Ryan's extended hand. "You here to collect what I fished from the ocean?"

"It would appear that way."

Sophie recoiled. "Excuse me? I'm standing right there."

Jaime winked at Sophie. "She put up a fight, but I reeled her in."

Ugh. Boys and their fishing innuendos.

"Hey," Jaime continued, "you're Ryan Pike, right?"

Ryan grinned. "I am."

Seriously. In Mexico? Where did Ryan's tentacles not reach?

"Great articles, man. I follow your blog and love the interview you posted with Jeter."

Pet a man's ego and he turns into a blimp. Sophie was so irritated with the unbelievable bromance, she nearly forgot there was talk about her future criminal record taking place ten feet away.

"Excuse me, boys," she interrupted, "can we please get back to what's happening over there?"

"Oh." Jaime shrugged. "He's not even talking about you."

"Wait. What?" Sophie didn't follow. "Then why is the police officer looking at me?"

"I don't know. You're kind of cute, I guess."

Sophie's jaw dropped. Then she closed it and studied the men talking. "Then who called him?"

"My dad did," Jaime said. "But that was more because he was angry about the lost kayak and then there's tourism protocol and all. But we dragged you back to shore. No worries. Now he's telling Officer Jorge that the chalupas his wife gave him made him sick."

"So are we done here?" Sophie asked.

"It appears so." Jaime's grin spread into a full-forced smile. "Feel free to keep the shirt as a little memento reminding you about your amazing adventure here, and drop a Yelp review if you wouldn't mind."

Sophie wrapped her arms around her front. *Doubtful*. The sooner she could tear this shirt off and burn it, the better. "No problem." She smiled tightly. "Sorry again about all of this."

Jaime waved his hand. "No worries. We never see this much excitement."

At the top of the landing, Sophie walked ahead of Ryan, but wasn't prepared for the gawkers. At least down by the kayaks she was without an audience to witness her walk of shame. Now, dozens of sets of eyes followed her, many with their smart phones at the helm.

"So what happened to you?" Ryan asked, his soothing voice a low hum. He tossed their now warm pineapple drinks into a garbage can.

Sophie dropped her head, watching her shoelaces bounce against her shoes as she placed one heavy, wet foot in front of the other. "Don't ask."

"Hey, Mommy, there's the lady that took our picture. You said we couldn't swim here." The littlest nerdling from the family she'd met earlier pointed and ogled, along with everyone else. "Is she going to jail?"

"Probably," the mother answered. "That's what happens when you don't follow the rules."

Sophie shot the woman a scowl so harsh, she was certain that whole nerdling family felt it.

Ryan must have caught the scowl because he wrapped his arm around Sophie, and she surprised herself by letting him. Actually, it felt nice. Having him with her felt *nice*.

Ryan's phone buzzed in his pocket. He kept his arm around her and answered. "Ryan Pike." After a brief pause his eyes dipped to Sophie. "It's for you. She sounds upset."

For her? Who was upset? A sinking feeling sunk in Sophie's gut like an anchor. She took the phone and slid away, feigning some privacy. "Hello?"

"Hey, Sophie, it's Tanya." Her edgy voice shook with each word. "I couldn't reach you on your cell, so I called Red and he gave me Ryan's number and said he'd be able to find you." Her words came in short, forced spurts as if she were out of breath.

Sophie's insides froze, except for her heart. She gripped her chest as a million worst-case scenarios raced through her mind. She wasn't sure what a heart attack felt like, but this had to be close. "What's wrong? Is anyone hurt?"

"I don't know, ask Deidra," Tanya said, with a bite.

"What's wrong with Deidra?" It'd occurred to Sophie that in the years she'd ran the café, she'd never been gone longer than a day or two. And only when Donovan or Amy could cover. She should have known the place would fall apart without her. Any number of things could go wrong. Her eyes cut to Ryan. His brows creased together as he mapped her face with concern.

Sophie held up a finger and then turned around, walking double time back through the flea market. Whatever was wrong in the café most definitely required her presence pronto. From her end of the call, even though she could still hear the geyser and the hustling of her surroundings, she sensed that the café was unusually quiet. Music or conversation almost always hummed, so quiet meant mischief or trouble. "Where is everyone?"

"Deidra has the pukes," Tanya hissed into the phone. "She's in the bathroom praying to the porcelain god."

A softball size knot formed in Sophie's throat on those trigger words. "Oh my God, Tanya. Are you for real?" Sophie didn't realize her voice carried so loud. Ryan, with unease etched in his expression, lightly gripped her elbow as if he were asking her to explain.

She jerked away, not meaning to be harsh, but wishing she could wring Tanya's puny little neck. "Why aren't you in there? What's going on?"

"Sophie, I don't think you understand the severity here."

Holy cow. Sophie felt the sweat pool at the back of her neck. She was ready to hijack a race boat at this point and channel the Pacific. "Tanya, stop telling me that something is wrong, and tell me what is going on."

"My shoes, Sophie. She upchucked all over my shoes, and I just bought these. They are three-hundred-dollar Khloe Kardashian flats with real cheetah print trim. And I want to know who is going to pay for them."

Sophie stopped dead in her tracks and Ryan nearly ran into her. Her head spun six different directions from sideways. Any bile or bulging knots buried deep in her chest turned into burning fury. "What?" She snapped.

"Yeah, this is bull crap. I'm here on my time, and the fat little twit got upset about something and then stuffed her face with so many marshmallows and God knows what else, she billowed up like a balloon and freaking spewed all over my shoes. Three hundred dollars, Sophie!"

If it was possible for someone to be so infuriated they actually saw red, Sophie would be seeing deep crimson scarlet dipped in blood. Tanya's blood at that. She squeezed the phone until her fingers tingled and then slowly moved it away from her ear and put it directly in front of her face. "If you ever scare me like that again, over something so stupid, I will personally take your shoes and shove them so deep down your throat that you'll be crapping shoelaces until your proctologist begs for mercy."

Sophie took a deep breath. Tears threatened to fill her eyes. She felt like she just aged a decade. How could someone mean so much to her that any hint of failing them instantly flung her off the ledge, head first? All the anguish that had built up inside her released, leaving her spinning like a top. The girls fully relied on her to help them, and here she was hundreds of miles away, trying to do something, anything to help, and she couldn't even come up with one meager scavenger item.

"Why are you so mad at me?" Tanya mewled.

Sophie summoned all the patience she could conjure. "Because you are responsible for the café *and* the girls while I'm gone. Did you call Deidra's aunt?"

"Charlie did."

"And where is Charlie?" Sophie asked, surprising herself by remaining calm.

"She's in the bathroom."

"Don't you think you should be in there, too?"

Tanya exhaled loudly. "I was. I was cleaning my shoe, and they kicked me out. What was I supposed to do?"

Sophie pictured what that must have looked like and smiled to herself. Charlie was a bit of a scrapper, so if she chased someone out of the bathroom, that person would know they were in trouble. "Why was Deidra eating like that? Where were you?"

"I don't know. I was watching *Downton Abby* while I waited for business in the lobby. You can't expect me to go running in there every time a girl starts crying over a boy."

A boy? Blinding fury rose in Sophie's eyes again. She heard Tanya chomping on something. A carrot maybe.

"Tanya!" Sophie barked into the phone.

"What?"

The words caught in Sophie's throat so tightly she was surprised she didn't choke getting them out. "You're supposed to call me when there's an issue! That's what you do. Not sit on your butt and watch British TV." Sophie grabbed the back of her neck, squeezing as if she could summon the right thing to do. She was too far away to be of any help, and Tanya was officially elected the mayor of Uselessville.

"I tried," Tanya said, raising her voice. "And before you yell at me, the person who's actually here when I should be home cooking dinner for my cat, maybe you should answer your phone."

Sophie's blood surged. She wanted to call Tanya out for being the most incompetent person to ever walk the face of the earth. But she was *right*. Her stupid phone was next to her computer where she'd spent the first part of the morning trying everything she could to raise money. This outreach was not a one-woman job. She needed a team. A reliable team. But what she had was sitting on their fat tail watching TV.

Ryan hadn't taken his eyes off her. And his concern strewn across his face was giving Sophie a migraine. She held the phone away from her ear and cupped the bottom of it. "It's fine. A little mishap at the café. I have it under control." No she didn't. But Ryan wasn't the person to confide in. Even Amy couldn't help right now. She just wished she could be at the cafe. Everything would be okay if she were the one consoling Deidra. Not the half-wit Tanya.

Ryan didn't say anything, but his knowing eyes said he understood.

Good. She picked up her pace, barely noticing that Ryan was left to follow her without any idea what was happening. She'd fill him in after she processed what was happening in her absence. Of course she knew nothing herself . . . other than she shouldn't have come. She should have told Red she had the walking flu. The symptoms were easy enough to fake. "Give the phone to Charlie."

"Okay, Sophie. Calm down. I'm upset too, you know."

"If you even utter the word 'shoe' . . . " Sophie held her breath until Charlie's calm voice answered.

"Mrs. Croft?" Charlie said when she came on the phone.

"No, it's Sophie."

"Oh, hey! How's the cruise?"

What? Who cares? "How's Deidra doing? Are you with her?"

"Yeah, were sitting here. Deidra's head's on my lap and she's seriously regretting the Chinese she ate for lunch."

"Chinese? That's not what I mean. What triggered her?"

"I don't know. Salmonella? I'm waiting for Deidra's aunt to come get her before her food poisoning gets any worse."

Wait? Salmonella. "Like, she's got food poisoning?"

"That's what I said. Are you even listening to me?"

Food poisoning! That's all? The ten thousand pounds of bricks that had been crushing Sophie's chest cavity suddenly lifted, igniting a bout of nauseated relief. "Food poisoning? Oh, oh, man, that's just great."

"Great? How's that great? I've cleaned up two splash attacks already. It's about as far from great as possible. She ate bananas, Sophie. Chow mein, marshmallows, and bananas. You know how I know that? It was all over the bathroom and my shoes."

"From food poisoning, though, right? Tanya is under some guise that she overate because of a boy."

"Well, yeah. There was a thing with a boy. But don't worry about it."

Sophie was eternally grateful Charlie wasn't a typical teenager. It wasn't fair to plant adult-sized problems on her tiny shoulders, but she handled them with twice the aptitude of an average adult. Ten times the aptitude of Tanya. "But she didn't"—Sophie lowered her voice so Ryan wouldn't hear her—"force herself to vomit."

"Not that I know of. Though maybe the combination of what she ate was all the force necessary to projectile like that. She did binge on the marshmallows after . . . You know what, we'll talk about it later. Her aunt needs to get here in case the food decides to head for the southern exit."

Sophie sighed. Guilt swirled in her belly. She should have been there, plain and simple. She slowed her pace and noticed Ryan was still by her side. He wasn't crowding, but he was there. Warmth reversing the chills from her dip in the sea sent gooseflesh up her arms. She wasn't used to someone by her side in moments of chaos. Especially when she barked at them. False alarms or not. This was . . . nice.

Sophie's muscles relaxed and though she was grateful for the misunderstanding, it clearly reminded her that the café must stay open. The girls needed her. So what if this time was just food poisoning. Next time it might not. She calmed and summoned her cool, composed voice. "Can I call anyone else for you, Charlie?"

"No. I have it under control. But thanks."

"Okay, I'll let you get back to her. And I'll check in tomorrow. Okay?"

"You better bring me home something good."

"Done." When Sophie disconnected she had to stop. It was all too much. The rush of emotion from the last few hours felt like cymbals clashing together in her brain. It hurt so much she bent over and cradled her head.

"Hey. Are you okay?" Ryan crouched down and placed a hand on her knee.

She looked up and caught his worried eyes. "It's fine. I'm sorry. I . . . Here." She handed him his phone and stood up. A light breeze reminded Sophie she was still damp and now cold.

"Not to pry, but is everything okay at home?"

Ryan looked as sincere as she felt dreadful. The last thing she wanted was to share details of what it was that made her heart beat—the girls. She didn't want him to see her like this, because she didn't want to see herself like this. She didn't like feeling so helpless, but that's exactly how she felt. And over an upset stomach, not even a real crisis.

"Everything is fine. One of the girls got sick." Sophie slowly stood and ambled back through the dirt lot.

"Like sick, hospital sick? Or sick, soup and crackers sick? Because I thought someone died just a moment ago. Or that you were going to kill someone. I'm not really sure." The corners of his lips quirked up and Sophie's heart thudded in a different direction. Not one she was emotionally up for feeling right then.

Sophie knew she'd overreacted. Though, at the moment it wasn't an overreaction to her. Not until you've lain on a bacteria-riddled tile floor, hugging a toilet because you're too weak to get up after nearly cracking a rib from convulsing. Sometimes overreaction was the only reaction. So, considering what she knew from firsthand experience and why the girls were in the group, it wasn't a far reach to assume puking meant purging. "Soup and crackers," she said. "Don't worry about it."

Ryan pressed his lips together and nodded. Sophie knew he was probably thinking she'd lost it. But he didn't say anything like that to her, so it wasn't fair of her to assume. And he wouldn't say anything because he was the *nice guy.* Though, not nice enough to sign the card his office sent her when she won an award this past spring for her piece on senior citizens and orphaned dogs.

Still, he was nice enough to walk with her, even though she was still wet and people stared. But now she needed some space. The more she dwelled on Deidra and the café, as well as a hundred other potential problems, the sicker she felt.

They walked the rest of the way to the Ducati in silence. But not the kind of quietness where you're wondering what the other person is thinking. It was where the other person is diagnosing everything about you. Coming here with Ryan was a mistake. The scavenger hunt was a mistake . . . and it irritated Sophie to no end that she thought she had a chance to win.

"Are you mad at me?" Ryan asked, unlocking the Ducati.

"No. I'm drenched." *And quite humiliated.*

"You want a cab?"

"I want to get back to the ship and take a nap." Actually, she wanted to check her email. Typical response time for locally sponsored grants ranged in the forty-eight-to-seventy-two-hour mark. It had been several days.

Ryan didn't respond. He walked up to one of the waiting cabs and said something in Spanish, then slipped the cabby ten bucks.

"What was that?"

Ryan grinned sweetly and for some reason that caused bile to seep up.

"I just arranged a comfortable ride back to the ship. You don't want to ride back on this. You'll chafe for days."

Okay. *Way too nice!* What was she missing? "I can pay for my own ride back." She reached in her pocket and found it empty. She stifled a groan. Her money was fish food at the moment. "Never mind. I lost my cash."

"Don't worry about it. It's not a big deal, Sapphire. I'm just trying to be nice."

There! He'd said it. *Oh, God I'm going to be sick.* "Thanks." Sophie ducked around him so he didn't feel like he had to hold the door for her or hug her goodbye.

Her attempt at not letting him touch her failed. His warm hand pressed into her shoulder anyway. And as much as she wanted to give in and give up, she couldn't. But she waved the white flag anyway. He was the handsome hero all over again.

"Sophie, are you all right?" His steady voice was calming, but at the same time stirred something in her stomach that she'd long thought she'd defeated.

One trick she'd picked up from years of the mean girls walking all over her was to keep her head high and never let them have the satisfaction. "Thank you for the cab ride. I'll pay you back at the event tonight, okay?"

Ryan opened his mouth to say something but Sophie didn't let him. She didn't want him to say anything else. It'd been a long day, and after spending all this time with her ex, who'd managed to strum her heart like a runaway roller coaster, this was more than she could handle right now. "I had a lovely afternoon. I mean kind of crazy that I fell in the water, but you know . . . accidents happen. So, if you'll excuse me, I don't want to keep this guy waiting. Have a good day."

She gently closed the car door, its audible click reverberating in her head, and left Ryan with his incredibly sad Caribbean eyes staring blankly back at her. This was the right thing to do. She didn't want him to have to go over and beyond his call of duty. He was here for training, not to mend any hurt that she was so over she didn't even consider it a "thing" anymore.

That thought squeezed her gut until she was certain the bile was going to surface. Her smile felt so tight it didn't come close to meeting her eyes, but that was okay. She smiled right through the pain and squeezed her eyes until a single tear traced her cheek and landed on her clenched fist.

As the cab pulled away, Sophie slowly opened her eyes. She'd conquer this . . . just like every other challenge in her life. She'd go back to the ship, check her email for good news and regroup. And though the scavenger hunt today proved unsuccessful, it wasn't over. She'd figure out the next logical step and charge forward. Just like always.

She could do this. But when Sophie saw Ryan's reflection in the rear-view mirror, his grave expression took her back to the night in the bed of his truck. That same look promised her the world. *Before page seventy-four*. Her mouth went instantly drier than the Sahara. Her heart pounded faster than ten galloping horses. She gripped her gnawing stomach as if it was about to claw out of her skin.

Sophie recognized this. If she were honest, she'd tell herself she was no more recovered from bulimia than any other functioning addict. She'd only managed to white-knuckle it long enough until the right trigger found its mark. The horrifying cocktail mixing all-things-Ryan with losing the café and letting so many people down sent her spiraling.

If Ryan with his nice eyes wasn't the smoking gun, he'd certainly pulled the trigger.

~ ~ ~

Four months after Sophie had given herself to Ryan, someone anonymously mailed her a copy of *Sports Now*, page seventy-four dog-eared.

Ryan's magazine. He had taken that coveted job at *Sports Now* in San Antonio, and she was finishing college, making up the work she missed when she took a leave of absence at the end of her senior year.

Did he send the magazine and leave a hidden message? Was he trying to apologize? Because, you know, that's what nice guys did. And she was ready to apologize for essentially shutting him out. She did owe him a huge explanation.

Hadn't they talked about a future together? The memory of those best-laid plans kept her wound quite tightly. In all the good ways, of course. Maybe he'd just needed a break— some time to get situated at his new job. And he had to know she didn't want to actually break up. She just had a lot going on, too.

Turning to the folded page, she didn't find an apology. In fact, what she read in that article was an apology's direct enemy. It was gossip. Worse, it was her gossip. It was her story.

Larger Assets, Lesser Access—How Women in Sports View Themselves.

He didn't even bother to change her name. He'd written about her, adding sensitive details relating to woman in sports. The article highlighted how the industry wasn't fair to woman. Especially women who ate too much. And there it was. In black and white. Her name. How he felt about her eating. And how she scampered away behind food.

Even now, the food in her stomach felt like a belly bomb ready to explode. It didn't surprise her that she wanted to rid her body of this bomb. No, what surprised her was how quickly she eased that discomfort by gaining control. It was numbing and comforting and exhilarating. The pain stopped hurting so much when she learned how to gain control. By sticking her finger down her throat.

So the nice guy wasn't so nice.

Had she always been *just* a story?

Chapter 15

Ryan watched the cab until it was out of sight. He shoved his hands in his pockets and mounted the Ducati. He couldn't put his finger on it, but something was definitely off with Sophie.

She seemed a little embarrassed to have fallen in the water, which couldn't have been more than fifty-five degrees, poor girl, and then the call from work had really upset her. Yet, she shook it off and said it was fine. But he'd missed *it*.

Again.

Had it really been nearly a decade since he'd last missed it. Not even sure what it was, but *it* had been the beginning of the end for them. For what he'd had hoped would have been so much more. That was, until he screwed up and threw it all away.

Ryan kicked the starter and revved the engine. He needed this forty-five-minute ride back to the boat. He only hoped Sophie was okay too.

A few months after Ryan had taken Sophie to his frat party, they'd curled up together on a nest of blankets in the bed of his Ford truck to watch for shooting stars. He pointed out a number of stars by name.

"You see that one?" He wrapped her up and pointed to the Big Dipper.

"Yeah."

She smelled so good. He was falling for her, and he was pretty sure she was already in love. Something he'd never really understood. Love wasn't an emotion he'd seen much growing up. But Sophie wasn't the kind of girl to hide hers. She pretty much wore her emotions on her sleeve. He liked that.

"Did you know it's not a constellation? It's a group of stars that will eventually face the opposite direction."

"Really?" Sophie said. He was shocked she was enamored with astrology. None of the girls he'd dated before cared.

"Yes. In about 50,000 years, give or take a few." He kissed her temple. He knew each constellation's unique history and every formation by heart. He could even recite the history of how they earned their names. This was useless information he'd retained since childhood. But tonight, he loved how this bit of knowledge served him well. She was eating it up, so he'd enjoy dishing it out.

"Hmm." Sophie's burrowed deeper into him. She fit perfectly next to him. "That's so fascinating. How do you know all this?"

"My dad. We spent summer nights stargazing." A dormant flame ignited in the pit of Ryan's stomach. "It was our thing before . . . well, before he changed."

"Changed?" Sophie's soft hands toyed with the buttons on his shirt, eliciting an expected response from his lower half. He didn't want to assume she was ready to sleep with him. He knew she was a virgin, but her touch felt nice. He stroked the back of her hand with his fingertips.

"Um, yeah. We don't talk anymore. My dad and I don't exactly see eye-to-eye on anything." That was the first time Ryan mentioned his dad to any girl. And though he sensed an easiness with her, he hoped she didn't probe. His mom was a much safer subject, but he generally avoided talking about his parents at all. He'd never forgive his dad anyway, so why rehash all the reasons his dad was a prick?

"I'm sorry to hear that," Sophie said, a hint of sadness in her voice.

Time to change the subject. He pointed to another constellation. "You see that one?"

"Which one?"

Ryan pulled her closer so their cheeks touched. He held up her hand and aligned her vision with his. She smelled sweet, his mouth watered and his body ached. "That one. Follow the Big Dipper's handle about forty-five degrees south and then look really hard. You can only see this one on a clear night during fall equinox." Sophie squeezed in so close he thought she was going to crawl on him, which he wouldn't have minded, but if she did his brain would probably go numb and do something they'd both regret. She wasn't like any of the other girls he'd been with. She was different. More fragile. He refused to push her into anything she wasn't ready for.

Sophie's breathing slowed and then stopped. "I see it," she said enthusiastically. "What is it?"

His fingers drew her face to his. "It's yours."

"Mine?" Her eyes danced. The two shades of green mixed with a speck of blue locked on his and he thought how easily he could get lost in them. "What do you mean?"

Her breath was sweet too. He breathed her in and it took everything he had to refrain from kissing her right then. "I have something for you."

She tensed as a hint of hesitation washed over her. Did he scare her? Something about her screamed that she was a kicked puppy, and every time they were together, he was careful not to spook her. "What's wrong?"

She shook her head. "Nothing. I-I thought we were looking at stars tonight, and it's not my birthday or anything."

"Does it have to be your birthday for me to give you something?"

The corner of Sophie's lip quirked up and he felt her relax. "No."

"Good. But you do have a birthday coming."

Her smile widened. "It seems to be an annual occurrence."

Ryan tucked a piece of her hair behind her ear. "I can wait if you want. Give it to you on your actual birthday."

Sophie bit her lip and a thrill shot down Ryan's back. He loved when she did that. It was usually followed by a kiss. But she rolled her eyes instead. *Oh well.* "Um, I don't want to be rude or anything. I mean you brought it, so . . ."

He tapped her nose with his finger. "That's what I thought." Taking the time to stroke her cheek, he placed gentle kisses around her face. "Here." He reached beneath the blankets under her head and retrieved a sheet of paper.

She took the paper and lifted herself onto one elbow, reading it beneath the glow of the crescent moon. It was a certified document with her name and the location of the constellation and a star, which he named after her: Sophie's Sapphire.

"It means wisdom. Your name, that is."

"You named a star after me," she whispered.

"Yeah. That one." He pointed to it again.

"You got me a star that can be seen by the naked eye."

"I didn't realize your eyes were naked," he said, brows raised.

She hit him. "Such a guy."

He smiled.

Sophie blushed still looking at the piece of paper. "I didn't mean to fall so hard, but you're kind of perfect. Which sort of scares me."

"Why?"

She squeezed her eyes. Throwing off the blanket, she revealed a creamy patch of skin. "Because of this."

"What?" He shrugged. "You have a belly button ring I'm not aware of?"

She giggled, pulling the blanket up to her chin. "No."

"A tattoo? Is it lame? Do you have your ex boyfriend's name stamped there and you're afraid to show me? It's okay, I have six girl names on my back."

Sophie's eyes went wide.

"Just kidding. Only three." Ryan laughed and then covered her hand with his. He knew she was referring to the fact she wasn't pencil thin. The ultimate girl hang up. "I don't care, Sophie. You're beautiful."

"I just have a little . . . extra. In comparison to Leggy Blonde."

"Who?"

She sunk in the blankets. "Never mind."

She was referring to the girls from his past. But that was just it, they were in his past. A past when he was still pissed at his dad for being a mean drunk and was trying to numb the pain with girls. It didn't work. He wanted something more than a fling. He wanted to be with a girl with substance, who he could have a conversation with and buy a star for because she was interested in him. All of him.

He softly stroked her back, drawing her into him. She surprised him when she kissed him. The kiss lingered, and he savored every moment. She made a small sound, and he backed off, only to feel her press deeper. He took that as permission.

Slowly, he reached up the back of her blouse and unhooked her bra.

"I've never—" she started.

"I know," he said softly, not breaking the kiss. "We don't have to."

"No, it's okay. I love you. Don't leave."

Where would he go? "I'm right here," he assured. And if she were willing, he'd give her everything that she felt she was missing. He'd show her how he wouldn't leave. Not now. Not ever.

They'd made love. And it was amazing. Well, a little awkward, as expected for the first time, but really good, too. He knew it'd only get better. She rested against his chest, he stroked her arm, goose bumps shivering beneath his touch. The only sound was the restlessness of the trees and each other's beating heart.

Sophie had been quiet a long time. He didn't want to interrupt her thoughts, but desperately needed to know about her. He wanted to know everything. For someone who talked a lot about her grandmother, he didn't know anything about her parents. It was a good place to start. "Hey, Sophie?"

"Hmm?" Her naked flesh rested perfectly against him. He kissed the top of her head. "Tell me about your parents."

Sophie's entire body flinched. It was like he'd hit an exposed nerve. He didn't like talking about his family, and with a reaction like that, he bet she never talked about hers either.

He gently squeezed her arm. "You okay?"

Her breath hitched, and Ryan knew immediately something was wrong. She wasn't facing him but when she opened her mouth, he could hear the tears in her eyes. "I . . . um, don't remember much."

That was a lie but maybe her lying about it was easier than reliving it. "You don't have to tell me, I'm sorry I asked."

Sophie wiped her face with the blanket. "No, it's okay. I can."

"Don't force it, I was just curious."

Sophie dragged in the deepest, most unsteady breath he'd ever heard her take. "Mom was beautiful. She read Jane Austen to me every night and took me to the ballet in the City every year on my birthday. We'd dress up in formal gowns we bought at the Goodwill and have our nails done. Dad worked a lot. I didn't see him much, but he loved us.

He'd send me flowers from wherever he traveled. He was in telecommunications."

"How'd they die?" Ryan asked using his most sincere voice.

"I, um, I can't . . . please."

Sophie shook. He felt terrible and realized he'd pushed her too far. "Shhh, it's okay. You don't have to say anything." He grabbed an extra blanket and wrapped her tightly, turning her toward him and pulling her into his chest.

She cried into his neck. "Um, car wreck. In Tahoe." A few tears seeped down his bare chest.

"I'm really sorry," he whispered. "I know that must have been hard."

"There was a fire and I think my dad tried to get out, but was overcome by the flames. Mom died from smoke inhalation. She couldn't even breathe." Sophie clinched his arms so tight, he knew she'd leave a mark, but he didn't care. After a moment, she let him go. "I want to go home." She sniffled.

"Yeah, sure. I'll take you." He slid out from under the covers and slipped on his pants.

"I'm sorry." Her voice cracked.

"Don't be." Ryan swallowed hard. Leaving one blanket with Sophie, he wadded up the others and tossed them to the side. He hopped out while Sophie got dressed and started the truck, blasting the heat and opening a bottle of water for her.

Honestly, he didn't know what to do. This was way out of his comfort zone. No girl had ever cried after they had been together. He'd also never been with an inexperienced girl. What was he thinking? God, he hoped he didn't hurt her.

When he'd asked her out tonight he hadn't planned on being intimate, at least not physically. Sure, he'd expected her reaction when he gave her the star certificate, but he didn't expect her to fall apart.

Ryan barreled down the road, speeding, watching for cops. She stared out the window and he didn't know if he was supposed to hold her hand or talk to her or just turn on the radio and let that do all the talking.

At some point he'd have to tell her about his offer to *Sports Now*. It was in San Antonio, but it was an offer he couldn't refuse. It could be really good for him. For them— if she wasn't breaking up with him, that is.

"So, you know, I thought I was okay," she whispered, breaking the silence. "Parents die all the time. But sometimes the pain hurts. My stomach would twist and I didn't know how to make that pain stop. They gave me medicine but that made me dizzy and tired. I learned if I ate something, my stomach wouldn't twist so much. So I just . . . ate. And for a while, the pain went numb."

Ryan set aside his news, aware this was not the time for that conversation, and set his hand over her arm. She didn't pull away, but somehow the energy between them had changed. He took his hand back and firmly placed it on the steering wheel. Ten and two, just like Driver's Ed suggested. "That's a tough break. No mother to guide you through those awkward years."

"Awkward years?" She cut her eyes to him. "What do you mean?"

He shook his head. "I didn't mean anything. Just, you know, I remember how mean some of the girls were to you. It's a small school. I noticed things. So what if you ate cupcakes and fries to numb the pain?"

Sophie covered her face with her hands. "Oh, God. That's really embarrassing."

Ryan's jaw dropped. What'd he say? "What?"

"You saw me eating?"

No big deal. He knew girls her size who ate upwards of twenty-five hundred calories a day when training. Girls handled food differently. That last girl he dated refused to eat in front of him. Sophie didn't seem to care. He liked that. "Don't be embarrassed," Ryan said. "You didn't have a mom show you how to dress for your bone structure and wear makeup and handle the girls in class."

Sophie yanked her hands down. "But you used to date those girls."

He looked at her and then back at the nothingness of the night. "Used to," he murmured, not sure why he had to defend his past.

"Why are you with me?" Sophie's question hung in the air like dead weight.

Ryan blinked. Even in the darkness of night, he could see her biting her lip, and he felt bad for her. She was questioning the wrong person. He should be asking her why she agreed to go out with him if she was that insecure with their relationship. "Because I really like you. I don't know . . . maybe even more than like you."

"Why?"

"I just do. You're not like those other girls." Oh, damn. Wrong answer.

"What? Like pretty and thin and dressed in the latest fashion?"

"Sophie," Ryan said, flipping his turn signal as he pulled on to her street. "I wasn't insinuating anything. I think you're beautiful and full of life. I'm sorry about your mom. Trust me, I understand and I'm glad you told me."

"I can't," she uttered.

Ryan pulled up to the side of her house and jammed the truck in park. He turned to face her. If this conversation was happening, it would be face-to-face. "You can't what?"

Tears slid down her cheeks, landing in his gut like a sucker punch. "I should go."

"No, don't." Ryan reached for her hand, but she threw open the truck door. "Sophie, wait."

"Please. Don't. I need to go."

He unbuckled his seatbelt and opened his door, not willing to let this conversation end like this. "Sophie, I'm sorry if I said something to upset you."

"I need to go. I just . . ."

Before he had the chance to get out of his truck she had disappeared up her front walk. He ran both hands through his hair. Where the hell did all that come from?

He turned around to close her door and saw the certificate on the bench seat. He snatched it and before he thought twice about keeping it, he walked it up to the front step and shoved it under her doormat.

Ryan was almost to the truck when he heard her scream. He almost ran back, wanting to knock down her front door and make her understand that he did love her. That she wasn't just another notch in his proverbial belt. That she meant more to him than any girl, er, woman, he'd ever had. And he wanted to tell her about his offer and how they could do this together. That he wanted her to come with him. But she had made it clear she didn't want him around. So much so she was screaming at him.

He hopped in his truck, unaware that would be their end. If he had known, he would have kicked down that door.

Ryan slowed the Ducati to a stop in Luis's garage. A large rock loomed in his path. He swerved, narrowly missing it. "Argh." He clenched his teeth together. Something that size would have launched him off the bike. He needed to get focused on the present, on his job. Sophie had already broken his heart. No use letting their past distract him from so much he crashed and broke his body too.

"Where's that sweet little thing you had with you earlier?" Luis all but drooled.

Ryan stared at him for a second, wishing he could land a fist against his mouth and add more color to the plated gold and silver. But instead he tossed him the keys and signed off on the return.

Chapter 16

Walking back to the ship, Ryan's mind replayed the whole day in its entirety.

Something was definitely wrong with Sophie, but he couldn't put his finger on it. Was it the café and the kid who had food poisoning? She did freak out about that. Or was it something more? The decade old guilt lurched deep in his gut told him she probably didn't trust him, but knowing he had to go back to San Antonio soon, he didn't want to leave things like this.

He broke it and needed to fix it. She could trust him. He needed to show her how.

Tomorrow they would visit Avalon, and there laid his opportunity. It was such a beautiful little island. At least it was when he spent his summers there as a teenager. He would invite Sophie along to meet the woman who took him in when his dad couldn't look him in the eyes any more.

Tia was his source of security when his world spiraled out of control. And she was long overdue a visit. He yanked his phone from his pocket to give her a call. As soon as he looked at his screen, he saw he'd missed a call from Phil. *Damn.* He'd left two more messages this morning and had told Lola to have Phil call him back. Ryan must have missed the call while he was on the Ducati. No voicemail though.

Something was up. Whether it was a merge—which wasn't necessarily bad—or a complete shutdown—which was—Phil owed him answers. It wasn't like Phil to throw him into a situation where he was unprepared.

Ryan rubbed the back of his neck. Unless Phil had been blinded too.

He unlocked the phone and called.

It didn't even ring before Phil answered. "Hey, Pike. Sorry we haven't connected yet. I'm swamped here. How's the training?"

"Fine. But that's not why I called. Level with me. What's the news on the merge?"

"Yes, about that. Things are picking up around here. I've had six meetings since yesterday about it."

"Holy hell. Over what?"

"*Jazz's* focus group is assembled, so the Chair is interested is moving forward way faster than predicted. They figure if they close *Up Front* by fiscal year end, it will bode well for our shareholders. This will look good for you once we vet who stays and who goes. Speaking of which, how goes it?"

Like shit, Ryan wanted to say. Vetting people for a company-wide termination was not part of his job. "What do you mean by who stays and who goes?"

Something about this conversation didn't sit right. He'd made tough calls in the past; it sort of came with the territory. But this was different. The prickling up his back festered as he tried to sort this new information in his head. At no point was he under the impression that a merge meant firing people within a week. And if that was the case, who was on the chopping block? Just people from *Up Front*? Or was *Jazz* and *Sports Now* going to see a ripple effect too?

"We have some changes coming down the shoot," Phil said amicably. "So use your training opportunity there to do some vetting. Again, this will look good for you. A merge will allow our strongest team players an opportunity to grow ratings."

Changes? Throwing any sort of curve ball at this point could be detrimental. "What changes?"

"Well, the committee is moving faster than expected. "We should know more in a few days. May even have some severance contracts drawn up by then."

Ryan cringed. "Just like that? Cut them loose?"

"That's business, son. You'll get the hang of it."

I hope not. "How fast?"

There was a pause while Ryan heard shuffling of papers from the other end. "*Jazz* has an estimated date for the focus group to beta read by the first. We need our ducks in a row for the board by then. A full re-launch is scheduled for next month."

"The first?" Ryan swallowed a lump. "That's two weeks, Phil."

"Be the first or be the best, and we intend on being both. With Harpoon Inc., launching their e-mag next quarter, we want to have ours trending first."

"Where can I find the minutes from the board meeting? You have to at least give me a chance to read the verbiage." Ryan hoped to find something that could pertain to keeping jobs. New Age journalism was too cutthroat. If they did follow through with a layoff, there'd be a good chance there wouldn't be other jobs to go to. Not with freelance journalism.

"I'll have my assistance shoot you the minutes."

"Thank you. I'll keep you posted, but this is a great team here. I'd rather not see any of them cut."

"Nature of business is a beast. But you'll see it's what's best for the company. And it goes without saying this is all confidential. We haven't even told Red."

Ryan almost felt numb when he replied, "Understood."

"Atta boy." Ryan could hear Phil smiling. "Listen, go view those minutes and start making me a list of who you think's a good fit here. I want to have something to present to the board and HR ASAP. And give me an update tomorrow. Maybe by then I'll have more information. Just know things are moving fast around here. These are exciting times for Over the Top. We'll be the first to have a number one e-mag on top of a specialized genre magazine if all goes as planned. We have the edge. And we have you, son. Don't let me down."

Ryan scrubbed his hand through is hair. "Okay, boss."

Phil must have heard Ryan's tone. "Hey."

"Yeah?" Ryan was down to one-syllable answers. This conversation sucked the life out of him. He cleared his throat.

"Go have a drink. It will settle your nerves."

Ryan didn't like the idea of using alcohol as a crutch—a way to numb cognitive thinking when that's exactly what he needed—to be clear and focused. Alcohol was his dad's crutch, not his. And it often reminded him of the night his dad found the private letter from Ryan's sister, Nicole telling him not to let Dad push him into astrophysics. She encouraged him to follow his dream of journalism and Dad would understand. But Dad felt slighted and Ryan broke his middle finger when his dad, drunk and angry, launched at him. That night he learned exactly how much of an affect alcohol had.

"My nerves are fine."

"Bull. Remember we've all been where you are and this gets easier. It's all part of the job. Trust me, the opportunity will leave you high on the hog." Ryan paused, how could he possibly know how to respond to that. "Have a drink," Phil repeated.

"Got it."

The call went dead, but it took a moment for Ryan to lower his cell from his ear. He rubbed his hand over his mouth, scratching his stubble. He needed to shave before tonight. Or not. He didn't really care.

He showed his key card to the cruise attendant and walked through the metal detector. "Any way I can check to see if my friend made it back yet?" He realized he hadn't heard from Sophie. Not that she was supposed to check in with him, but he was a little worried.

The attendant gave him a wry look.

"Guess not." He slipped his card back in his pocket and stepped on board. Of course Sophie was here. His mind was messing with him now. He briefly considered just going back to his suite, but the thought of what was in the board meeting minutes made him cringe. That could wait. He'd eventually get to it. And he'd do the right thing by this company. He always did the right thing. He just needed some time to build trust with this group so when the merge was completed, they could still be friends in adversary. He'd offer to write letters of recommendation to anyone who asked. That was all he could do.

For now, a drink was in order. Phil was right about his nerves. An extra drink wouldn't hurt. After all, he was not his dad.

Chapter 17

To gag or not to gag?

Sophie stared at the porcelain throne in her tiny cabin, her stomach swirling with anxiety that needed to be purged.

It had been a long time.

Too long.

She'd hit the trifecta—almost drowning, Ryan's disapproval, and of course failing the girls by botching the scavenger hunt today.

Her stomach rumbled again, her anxiety dialed way up.

She shouldn't do this.

But it would reset her control. She could release the anxiety and regroup.

Her stomach grumbled in sync to her rambling thoughts. The epic failure rehashed old wounds and threatened to upend what little food she had thought to eat for breakfast. It would reset her control in the matter. Control she needed since she'd just read that a dozen of her much-needed grants did not meet the requirements to move on to the next stage in the process. Yes, there were still several more to hear back from. But when? Disappointment swelled inside.

Staring at her reflection, Sophie could almost see her heart pounding through her chest. Its thumping pulsed like horse hooves on a cobblestone road.

The toilet's ceramic aroma exploded through her, dropping her to her knees. The urge detonated inside her. Her chest tightened. This was like riding a bike. *Isn't that what all addicts said?*

She lifted the toilet lid, and leaned in. A mixture of chlorine and sulfur filled her. Placing her index finger as far back as it would go, she bowed and gagged.

Again.

This time her muscles spasmed, and tears sprang to her eyes.

This used to be so easy. A simple thought could summon the ritual. That's when she knew she needed help back then. Walking to her car after lunch one day, she vomited without even a second thought. But now, she looked around for something she could use to help things along and spotted her toothbrush. She shoved it deep in her mouth, triggering a gag reflex.

It was as if the past several years hadn't closed this door.

The burn of the bile seeping its way up her esophagus was a terrifying thrill. She thought of Ryan. The sensation of her arms wrapped around him, the feel of him as he maneuvered the Ducati, the rush of nuzzling his back and breathing in that old, familiar scent.

His cologne. It took her back to when she would rest on his shoulder, breathing him in. He always smelled like cedar and heaven—at least what she imagined heaven would smell like. Ryan and The Ritual. The two went together.

In little more than a moment, it was finished. Exhaustion took over. Sophie staggered to her feet, flushed, and trudged to her bed. So tired, all it took was falling into her soft, crisp pillow before she drifted into a dreamless sleep.

~ ~ ~

Thud, thud, thud.

Sophie jerked awake then groaned, squeezing her temples. Why was someone jackhammering her head?

Thud, thud, thud. "Sophie? You in there?"

Oh, not a jackhammer. An Amy.

Sophie slowly sat up, scanning her surroundings. Her eyes stung, her throat was on fire, and her shoulders throbbed. She cringed, Aftermath pains. She forgot how terrible they were.

Thud, thud, thud. "Sophie! Let me in!"

Her lips came apart with a sticky *pop*. "Hold on!"

First order of business: find water.

Sophie sighed heavily. What had she done? Had this been one of her girls, she would have been sorely disappointed. And Charlie . . . oh God, she couldn't think about Charlie. She'd be so disappointed.

Fingers drummed against the door. "Hey, Sophie. Wakey, wakey. Time to get ready for the cocktail party."

"I'm up. I'm up. I'm coming."

Sophie's legs hit the floor like anchors. Standing sent her head spinning. She grabbed the bottle of water. It burned going down, but quenched the fire at the same time. Each step toward the door was a little easier than the one before.

Sophie cracked the door.

Amy barged in, smelling like coconut and hot Pacific Ocean. She still wore her ladybug-patterned bikini beneath a sheer swimsuit cover. For a petite girl, she had abs of steal. "Oh my gosh, you have to try these." Amy shoved a greasy paper bag filled with soggy peanuts in her face.

Sophie nearly fell into the tiny bathroom . . . or dove. Anything to get away from the reeking nuts. She batted the bag away. "Those are disgusting."

Amy looked Sophie up and down, her golden hair taller than usual, probably from all the sunrays. "Suit yourself. Boiled peanuts are amazing."

"They smell like death."

"Speaking of which"—Amy wrinkled her nose and plopped herself on the unmade bed—"what's that smell?"

Sophie closed the bathroom door, hoping Amy's sense of

smell wouldn't lead her to contemplate any past, ritualistic behaviors. "It's your nuts."

"No, it smells like hot mildew."

Sophie pulled her matted hair into a messy ponytail. "No clue. I don't smell anything."

"That's because you're bathing in it. I hope you plan on taking a shower before tonight. Where have you been anyway?"

Sophie's heart sped up. "Just here. I took a nap."

"Oh, really? How'd your day go?" Amy raised her eyebrow.

Sophie swallowed hard. "Fine."

"Don't use the F-word with me," Amy said. "I'm not a dude, I'm your best friend. Now spill it or I'm going to start chucking nuts at you." Amy grabbed the TV remote and flipped through channels, landing on a Nicholas Sparks flick.

Sophie pushed off the wall and dropped into the chair. She was not ready to discuss this right now. Not after just spewing all over the toilet bowl. "I don't know what you mean."

Amy narrowed her eyes. "Yes, you do. You were with Ryan all day. Why are you hiding in here, while he's out roaming the Lido Deck sparking up conversations with our peeps."

Sophie jerked her head toward Amy too quickly; things got fuzzy for a second. "Really? What did he say?" Did he tell her about the kayak? How she'd acted like a fool? How she completely lost it over Deidre?

The voices of people laughing hysterically came from the hallway outside her door.

Amy pealed a boiled nut and threw it in the air before catching it in her mouth. Sophie wanted to gag for her. "He didn't say anything to me. I was working. Well, actually I was pretending to work, but really I was watching him. And the gossip queens in case they got any swanky ideas about putting their hands near him."

Terri and Lori—gossip girls and office flirts. Sophie grabbed a bottle of Tylenol from the desk and swallowed a couple. Her throat still burned. "I'm sure he was. Probably work stuff."

"I don't know. I can't imagine he was working the way he was laughing and carrying on."

"Why, what did he say?" He wasn't telling everyone about her dip in the ocean, was he? He wouldn't. He'd seemed so concerned. So *nice*. But he'd spilled her secrets before. Page seventy-four. Sophie wanted to die.

"I don't know. I didn't talk to him." The start of a smile tipped at the corners of her mouth. "But Donovan listened in on his conversations with some of the others. You should ask him." Her smile grew a devious mustache, to which Sophie pictured Amy's fingers twisting at the ends. "He seems to think Ryan is promoting in the company. Possibly even transferring here."

Sophie made a disapproving face. "Wait, what? No. Impossible. What makes him think that?"

Amy peeled another peanut and Sophie wanted to gag. "Would that be so bad? Donovan's our first line of defense. He seemed to like the guy. And if he gets a pass from our very own fashion diva, he's good with me."

Donovan had warned Sophie that Asher was a scuzz from the bottom of the barrel. She wished she'd had listened to his warning then. She narrowed her eyes at Amy, realizing she was clinging a little too tightly to her words. What did it matter who he was talking to or about what? Unless, he was still laughing at *her*. "Never mind, it doesn't even matter."

"What doesn't matter?" Amy muted the movie as Ryan Gosling hung from a Ferris wheel in an attempt to get Rachel McAdams' attention. She swung her legs off the bed and sat up. "How are you doing with him here? Is he driving you a little . . . wild?"

"Oh, please."

"People only say 'oh, please' when they don't have a real argument."

Did it just jump ten degrees in here? "No, they don't. If Ryan's promoting to the Bay Area, I'm saying someone should consider Red and his feelings. You know Red's my couch potato."

"Your what?"

"My couch potato," Sophie said. "My comfort zone."

"Oh, yeah, everyone knows that."

Sophie chewed her thumbnail but only bit skin. She had chewed that one off earlier. She switched to her other thumbnail and gnawed on it for a moment. If Ryan promoted here, she'd have to leave. End of story. "Ryan can't come here. We would know. Secrets and media are like wine and chocolate. You can't have one without the other."

"I'm not so sure. The way Donovan was talking, it sounds like Ryan was asking a lot of questions."

The room was now sweltering. There was no way Ryan would relocate to *Up Front*. The stacked boxes in Red's office didn't mean anything. Sophie assumed Donovan had stopped by his office threatening another extreme office makeover: editor in chief edition. Red would absolutely tell her if he planned on leaving. Wouldn't he? Before she started spending six nights a week at Chicks 'n' Slicks her Friday nights were spent with Red at Muy Caliente where they'd share a plate of jerk chicken nachos and a pitcher of beer. They were close.

Of course he would tell her, Sophie resolved. They were a family. She would know if something were askew. Everyone at *Up Front* played a necessary role. Even Ash-hat's job as *antagonist jerk turned problem child* had its place. And Red was her couch potato, dang it!

Besides, Sophie thought, swallowing dryly, it took all of one afternoon with Ryan for her to succumb to her illness. A part of her life she was certain she'd nipped in the bud. If he joined the *Up Front* team, who knows what that would mean?

Sophie tucked her hair behind her ears. "He's here for field training. Nothing more. I'm certain. Red would have said something otherwise."

When Sophie's eyes cut to Amy's, her friend gave her a sidelong gaze. "I don't know. Maybe Red doesn't know. It's not like he's here, if you didn't notice. And he was the one who said this was mandatory."

"I did notice. But that doesn't mean anything."

"Okay, forget I said anything." Amy curled a few strands of hair around her finger and eyed Sophie. "So, what *did* you do all day?" A sly smile crept over her face. "With Ryan."

Sophie's stomach swooped. "I didn't do much. Not really."

"Liar."

Sophie scowled at her friend. "Hey! Whose team are you on?"

"Just tell me what you need. If you want me to be the icy friend who henceforth shuns him, I will. But if you want me to be a voice of reason and give you permission to kiss him . . . there's that too."

A bit of heat swelled on Sophie's face. "What? No. Why would I do that?"

"Because I haven't seen you this worked up over something since I found you four years ago with your finger down your throat and you couldn't even say over what."

Sophie shook the ugly memory. She stood, and stared at her reflection. She'd failed today. In more areas than she cared to rehash. But the girls still needed her. They needed the café. She wasn't giving up on the scavenger hunt that easily.

Amy bumped Sophie's hip, shoving her way into the cramped mirror space. She picked at her tower-high hair. "Oh my God, is that a gray hair?"

"Probably, want me to pluck it?"

Sophie could have been running a dog-fighting ring and wouldn't have received a meaner glare. "No, you may not," Amy exclaimed. "Don't you know if you pluck one, ten more grow in its place? Or has Donovan not had that conversation with you?"

"Apparently not. But I'm not the one with gray hair."

Amy scoffed. "We are not talking about this. We are talking about you and why you're being so defensive about Ryan."

Sophie sighed. "I don't know. Maybe he seems normal now. But you never read what he wrote about me. Then again, you don't become the top-rated journalist at one of the biggest magazines by being a jerk."

"Maybe that's *exactly* how you become the top-rated journalist at one of the biggest magazines."

Sophie flinched. *Same team. Amy is on the same team,* she reminded herself. Amy was the best sort of friend. She'd play devil's advocate and let Sophie work out her feelings.

Amy must have read Sophie's face. "I'm not necessarily saying he's a jerk," she said softly. "Did you ever ask him about it?"

Sophie's bare toes clawed at the carpet and she shook her head.

"All I'm saying is guys change. And you have a lot to offer. You're not the same girl you were ten years ago. And he can't be the same guy. But I can say at least this guy doesn't have you hiding in the back of Sergio's picking at pizza while you mark him for a hit."

No, he just has me purging. "True. We had an interesting day. Let's just say that."

"Did you at least enjoy yourself?"

She felt herself flush with a sudden fluttering in her chest. She smiled, recalling how his fingers felt against her skin when he held her hand. "Mostly, yeah."

"Then why are you alone in your room like a reclusive hermit? I figured you two might be back together or something. Guys like that grow into men. Seriously, Soph. Guys like Ryan last. I don't see a flaw in his chiseled, handsome face. And trust me, I'm looking."

Sophie stared at the picture above her bed of a sinking ship about to be swallowed up by a huge wave. Why did she feel like that ship? *Or they laugh at you when you're already humiliated.*

"Give him a chance, Soph." Amy used her best-friend-telepathy thing to tell her exactly what she needed to hear. "I promise you I'll throw him overboard if you need me to. I'm team Sophie all the way. But maybe he can help secure financing from Over the Top for the café. I'm sure he knows people."

"No thanks." Sophie swallowed hard, grateful the burn was nearly gone. "I don't need him to rescue Chicks 'n' Slicks."

"Okay," Amy said, not pushing the idea. "So then, back to winning the scavenger hunt. What'd you come up with today?"

"Ugh," Sophie mumbled. "This." She picked up the evil T-shirt from the desk and tossed it at Amy.

Amy held it up, eyeing Sophie. "So, is there a story here?"

"Not one I'm willing to share without a bottle of red."

"That bad?"

"Worse."

"Bummer."

"You're telling me."

"Well, cheer up!" Amy said, tossing the shirt on the floor by the bathroom. "It's cocktail party night and that means open bar and now that you're a single lady, it also means you can flirt with Ryan and blame it on the alcohol."

Sophie tossed her head back. "You're unbelievable, you know that? Besides, I can't. I've got to find some easy sucker points!"

"The scavenger hunt list?"

"Yep," Sophie said, popping the *P*. "I'm sure I can find most of what's on the list at our party. Tonight's loot includes a drink umbrella, cocktail napkin with bartender's signature, a book of matches, salt and pepper shakers, and the drink of the day menu."

"I will be stationed at the bar with a straw permanently situated in a bottomless glass of fruity libations, so I can get the umbrella and the menu for you."

"How generous of you."

Amy stepped into Sophie's bubble and cupped her face in her coconut-lavender-scented palms. "You can do this. I have every confidence in you. You're a scrapper."

"Thanks, bestie."

"What are you wearing tonight? I want to coordinate." Amy headed for the door.

Pep talk over. Well, good, at least The Hair settled. "Probably just a casual dress and cardigan. I need to be nimble and free to roam comfortably."

Amy paused at the door.

"Soph, try to relax and have a good time."

Sophie sighed heavily.

"Trust me," Amy said. "You want to know what I think?"

"Not really." Sophie smirked. "But I'm sure you're going to fill me in."

She raised her eyebrows. "I think you're letting something that happened ten years ago speak for you now."

Sophie picked at her fingernails. "Please don't diagnose me, Freudette."

"I think you're scared."

Sophie shook her head. "Not scared. Determined."

Amy stepped across the threshold, doorknob in hand. "At least slow down long enough to have a drink with me. You need to relax." She smiled. "Meanwhile, I need to go tame this hair."

"Yeah, you may want to look into that gray one."

Amy stuck out her tongue and closed the door.

Sophie locked the door behind her friend and stepped into the cramped bathroom. A combination of bleach and bile wafted in the air. She twisted her lips, her stomach heaving again. No. No more of that.

Ignoring the toilet, she turned on the shower and freed her hair from its messy ponytail. She pulled her shirt over her head and tossed it to the corner of the tiny bathroom. The souvenir shirt was wadded up outside the door, mocking her. That shirt would likely get a watery grave sometime tonight.

A knock on the room door startled Sophie. She wrapped a towel around her, assuming it was probably just Amy with more hair-brained advice.

"Hold on," she said, hugging the towel tighter. Stubbing her pinky toe on the edge of the bathroom doorframe, she stumbled the last foot or so and fell into the door. *Ficus*. She unlocked the door and opened it enough to poke her head though. "Oh, it's you." She narrowed her eyes.

"Nice to see you too," Asher said, fully decked out in a tuxedo with an oversized bowtie. He looked uncannily like a circus penguin. His chest puffed out as if he were a blowfish ready to blow. Or maybe he resembled a peacock spreading his elongated tail feathers. Although, that would be the *only* elongated thing about him. He held up a cruise napkin that not only had the ship's charismatic logo on it, but . . .

"Is that who I think it is?"

"The one and only. And let me tell you, the man stays in character the whole time."

"How did you get a signature from Johnny Depp?"

Asher leaned against the doorframe a little too comfortably. "Fun fact." He gloated, his teeth sporting a whitening strip. "The role of Jack Sparrow from the first Pirates movie originally belonged to Antonio Banderas. I know this because we spent the afternoon in a hole-in-the-wall joint that had margaritas the size of basketballs. He's filming something new around here."

Sophie sucked in what little oxygen she could find. Asher managed to take all of that away from her, too. "What do you want, Asher?"

"Just showing you what I'll be turning in for today's hunt."

Sophie thought of the pathetic treasure she achieved and what it took to get it. No points offered for effort.

"I mean, what were the odds that reading one tweet from Johnny would change my game?"

Of course Asher followed actors on social media. That was his editorial job.

"One call to a friend who works with a producer at Bruckheimer, and, *bam*, I had his location."

"That's called stalking." Sophie snuffed a flame of jealousy that burned in her chest. Why couldn't she think of something so brilliant? Why did *he* have to be so good at these games?

"No." He winked. "It's called winning."

"Good for you, She-Ra." Sophie pumped her arm in a hoorah gesture. It was a petty gesture, but he was a petty man, so there you go.

Asher tried to peek his head through the tiny door opening. "What did you find today?"

"Bye, Asher." She slammed the door in his face, but he caught it with his foot.

He grinned at her devilishly through the foot-wide crack. "Did you happen to see anything of interest trending on YouTube today?"

A sudden heat crept across Sophie's cheeks.

The blowhole! Did he know?

"Your shoe is in my way," Sophie said from behind gritted teeth. Would she be quarantined for killing a passenger?

"Did you seriously fall out of a kayak into the ocean? I mean, no offense, but it's seriously hard to fall out. It looks like you're okay and all. But wow, that takes talent. I'm impressed!"

"Move your foot."

"Ah, come on, Sophie." Asher smirked. "It's all in good fun."

"Well, have fun with this!" She pulled the door all the way open and slammed it against his foot.

He cussed, yanking his foot free.

Sophie stifled a laugh then gently shut the door, locking the latch with a resounding *click*.

Chapter 18

The cruise director had set the cocktail party in a cozy, jazz-inspired lounge. It served as the perfect location to stage a company dinner. Appetizers and drinks didn't actually constitute as dinner, but the drinks were courtesy of Over the Top, Inc., so Ryan was sure the employees could care less if there was a three-course meal or not. Fried food and bottomless liquor would suffice.

Dressed casually in a sports coat, button-down shirt, loosely done tie, and blue jeans, Ryan moved into the sports bar, which was adjacent to the lounge.

"Rum and Coke," he ordered from the bartender. He leaned against the back of the bar and scanned the room. Not that he was looking for Sophie, per se, but he was concerned.

The bar tender slid him his drink and Ryan signed the slip. "Thanks."

"Don't mention it."

Several people in the bar section were cheering at the game. Three of the TVs broadcasted the championship game he was supposed to be covering right now. Ryan homed in on one. Game four was in full swing. Bottom of the fifth. Giants up by three. He wondered if his replacement, Johnson was on the field or in the locker room. He hated to miss this game. He hated more that Johnson was bootlegging his pennant interviews with rookie closing pitcher Doug Murphy. He'd have to settle for catching the highlights later when he updated his blog.

Ryan downed his drink and ordered another. For the next forty-five minutes, he did his best to put on a smile and concentrate on the task at hand, which included vetting the current talent from *Up Front*. He scanned the room a few times making pleasantries along the way, but really, he was watching for *her*.

"Hey, Ryan, there you are." Lori from the gossip column approached. "Can I get you another drink?"

After returning to the ship, Ryan had spent the later part of the afternoon on the Lido Deck getting to know some of the team. Lori and her coworker Terri seemed to hang on his every word, and had followed him around like a puppy. He had to literally spell out he was using the restroom when he excused himself so they wouldn't follow him there too. It was no surprise that though they had a lot to talk about, very little of it had to do with the magazine. "No thanks," Ryan declined.

"So, Ryan." Terri popped up from behind Lori. "I meant to ask you, what's this we've heard about you transferring to our little neck of the woods?"

Ryan held his poker face. "Not sure what you've heard, but that's not the case."

"Are you sure?" Lori said, brushing a strand of red hair off her face. "Because, um, our sources say it's true. And since you've never come to a retreat before, it looks a little suspicious."

Ryan flinched at her forwardness. He could smell alcohol on her breath and detected a bit of accusation in her tone. "What sources?"

"Ah, so it is true?" she said with a flirty tone. "Sorry, I don't kiss and tell my sources."

Ryan stepped back before he got a contact high from her breath. "Sorry, ladies, don't mean to disappoint, but check your facts."

"Oh, come on, handsome." Lori circled around and brushed invisible lint from his coat. "You can be honest with us. Did they really fire Red?"

Fire Red? Ryan's eyes stared at her hand resting on his shoulder until she moved it. "I'm sorry for any misunderstandings, but I have no idea what you're talking about."

"Come on, Ryan." Terri batted her eyelashes. "We had a good time this afternoon getting to know each other. You can be honest. We just want you to know when you come on board with us, we'll help you get adjusted."

Her expression implied the innuendo.

Ryan cleared his throat and stepped back. "You're right. It was nice chatting with you today, and I'm sure you have a lot more to offer the magazine, but I was asked to head the training and that's it. Nothing more."

"Thelma, Louise." Donovan swooped in and hung his arms over the girls' shoulders. "Stop suffocating the poor guy."

"Oh, Donnie." Lori grinned and kissed his cheek. "You know we like to be in the know."

"Well, I happen to know those two gentlemen are over there are crashing our party and vying for your attention."

Terri and Lori both craned their necks simultaneously as if they were trained Siamese cats.

"Really?" Terri said.

"Most definitely," Donovan said, winking at Ryan. "I already checked them out. You should go say hi."

"We'll see you around, Ryan." Lori waved her fingers like a 1920's flapper. "Do tell us if anything new surfaces." She batted her lashes. "See ya."

"Well, Ryan, my friend." Donovan turned to watch the girls shimmy across the room. Their matching sequined cocktail dresses sparkled against the dim, florescent lighting. "I see you got the full dose of our resident, uh, welcoming committee."

Ryan blew out a sigh of relief. "I guess so." Usher blared from the speakers, but Ryan could still hear the sports announcer in the bar section behind him. He veered his attention in that direction. Top of the seventh. Tied score. His insides churned at the thought of what he was missing. Ryan threw his drink back, expecting to take a huge gulp only to realize his glass was empty.

Donovan slapped Ryan's back. "What are you drinking, my man?"

"Rum and Coke."

They moved into the bar. Donovan raised his free hand to beckon the bartender. "Rum and Coke for the gentleman please. I'll have a piña colada on the rocks."

Donovan's slick bowtie and oversized fuchsia eyeglasses fit the man's smooth appearance. His position with Over the Top, Inc., was more than secure. According to the file Phil sent over, he pulled in over twenty-five percent of the readership on his own. In fact, they may have to offer him a bonus to keep him if the merge was executed. Ryan would be lucky if Donovan chose to sign on with *Jazz*.

And Ryan flat out liked the guy. "Are you enjoying the cruise?" he asked as they both took a seat at the bar.

"I could ask you that very same question." Donovan sipped on his fruity cocktail-concoction, heavy on the coconut with a huge umbrella. "I was on the Lido Deck today observing while you spoke to some of our team."

So, Donovan was analyzing him while he was vetting the group? Yep, Ryan knew he liked the guy. "Why didn't you join us? You could have added input on the analysis."

"Well, you are the guest of honor and since you were rather elusive at the office last week, I figured I'd let the others talk to you while I hung back and waited for an opportunity to meet with you. So, to what do we owe your company visit? The rumor mill is hinting at a promotion, but I'd rather hear any such news from the source."

Promotion? "I hate to burst any bubbles, but I really am here for industry training." Ryan absently turned his new glass in circles. It was the truth. Not the whole truth, but semi-truthful anyway. "How are things in the fashion world?"

Donovan eyed him for a moment before answering with a genial smile. "Fabulous as always." Donovan flicked his hair off his shoulder and adjusted his glasses. "I scored a spot on the Red Carpet for the *Red Glam* awards and an interview with the six-foot-two Russian twins who have taken the modeling world by storm."

"The twins, huh?"

Donovan nodded. "Indeed." He jutted his chin toward one of the televisions on the wall not broadcasting the game. It showed football highlights from years past. "How are things in the wild, wild world of sports and athletes? Better yet, tell me what's up with all the uniform design changes with the NFL?" Donovan rolled his eyes as if the monochrome jerseys offended the fashion world.

Ryan smiled, swirling the liquid around his glass. "I don't know but they are different."

Donovan offered a canned laugh.

Ryan scanned the jazz room again. "So tell me about your job at *Up Front*—"

And there *she* was. Across the room, wearing a floral sundress under a light sweater, her hair pulled to one side. She walked across the room like a woman on a mission and sat at a corner booth just below a life-sized framed picture of Dizzy Gillespie. Alone.

Donovan's fingers snapped in front of his face.

Ryan flinched. "Did you just snap at me?"

"Did you hear a word I just said?"

Touché. "Sorry, I got sidetracked."

Donovan turned to see what—or who, rather—he was looking at. "Ah, I pegged that one on your first day."

Ryan cocked an eyebrow. "You did what?"

"You best just leave that little hummingbird alone while her heart heals."

"I wasn't looking at anything."

"Sure, and I just happened to have been born yesterday. Gay *and* Jewish, if you can believe that, so I'm intuitive and honest. I read faces and emotions like I read the front page of a newspaper."

Ryan cocked his other brow and took another pull of his drink. This time he drank a little longer just to watch her again.

"That little girl was done fifty shades of wrong, if you know what I mean."

"Not exactly." Ryan straightened. Who better to fill him in with whatever that story was than one of Sophie's best friends?

"Oh, brother, sit back and listen. You may need another drink for this one."

"No, I'm fine. Three's my limit when I'm working." Though tonight may call for more.

"Oh." Donovan let out a deep, flirty grin. "A man who knows his hard limits. I like that."

Ryan frowned. "You were saying?"

"It was a pretty nasty thing for Asher to do. Almost the entire office saw it at our soirée. Which I coordinated." He, straightened his bowtie. "Sophie wasn't planning on attending, as she was tied up at the café. But then she did show up. Just in time to see Asher openly kissed our own little Trixie-Done-Her-Wrong-Bell." Donovan clucked his tongue mid-sentence. "I don't know what angered me more. That Asher did that right then, or after all the work I put into making that party top notch. We had a nothing budget, but I worked my magic and it was flawless, right down to the tiny Golden Gate Bridges as the centerpiece for each table. All the effort I had in the place settings—"

"You're getting off track." Ryan's gaze darted to Sophie, who seemed to be staring at nothing, but concentrating hard.

"Anyway, she was seriously caught off guard and walked right up to Trixie. You could hear a mouse peeing on a cotton ball, it was so quiet in there."

"And?"

"And she snapped. Oh, the poor butterfly."

"Snapped?"

"Tell me you're the one percent who hasn't seen the YouTube video?"

"No."

"Oh, well, let me fill you in. Sophie walked right up to Trixie, grabbed her by the hair, and the two of them dropped to the floor, flopping around like delicate angelfish out of water. Sophie, that is. Trixie was more like a piranha or a cougar fish."

"That sounds . . ." Ryan searched for the word. "Dauntless. Bold, maybe."

Donovan pressed his straw to his mouth and gave Ryan a wry look. "Well, Ryan, we can hardly blame her after what happened in college. Perhaps she had a bout of PTSD."

Ryan cringed. Of course Donovan would know about their college days. At least her side of it. "Where's Trixie Bell now? I was under the impression this was a mandatory event."

"From what I hear she's on assignment shooting rare pictures of some endangered wolf in the foothills or something." Donovan paused and sipped his umbrella straw. "Mmm, that's the best rum I've ever had! Anyway, Sophie didn't even shed a tear. She just moved on, and did what she does. She's a fighter, that one. So"—Donovan's head tilted—"when I say leave that little butterfly to heal, I mean it. I don't want to question your intentions, but she's fighting a bigger battle than you and I. Especially with that café. And I won't have you causing any undue pain."

Ryan sipped his drink, his focus fixed on Sophie.

"All I'm saying is she doesn't need any more boys complicating her life. Not with what's going down with her café and all."

That piqued Ryan's attention. Aside from the rent hike and wanting to sock Asher in the gut right now, he was curious. "I'm a little foggy on the details. It's just the company outreach, right?"

"Don't you say that to Sophie. Not if you want to live another day. She lives and breathes for that place. I mean, don't get me wrong, I love those girls like my very own nieces, but Sophie would jump in front of a bullet for them." Donovan looked at Ryan skeptically. "You've never heard the story how the café was born?"

"Can't say I have."

"The idea for the café fell into Sophie's lap, really. Or rather, Amy fell into her lap four years ago at the office when she caught Sophie with her ass in the air, deliberately puking her tuna on rye."

"Really? She was vomiting on purpose?"

"She was. Amy called her on it."

A knot in Ryan's chest made him uneasy. He knew she had body image issues, and that ten years later she'd dropped a few dress sizes, but Sophie was bulimic? Was she still bulimic? He replayed the day in his head and couldn't help but think how sullen she was when he put her in the cab. Was she still vulnerable?

"Amy took Sophie to a recovery group for bulimia."

Donovan stirred his drink and continued. "Imagine a group of nine ladies, all in their late forties, exploring why they felt the need to regurgitate all their stomach contents."

"I'd rather not. But I'm not following," Ryan muttered, his level of discomfort peaking at DEFCON three.

"They weren't teen friendly. I mean, discussing Mother

Nature's natural, southward progression on their once youthful bodies is not teen appropriate."

"Teen girls needed a place to go," Ryan affirmed what Donovan was alluding to.

Donavan nodded. "And that's when Sophie came up with the idea to run the company's community project for bulimic girls. She started a crafting club and it morphed into a café that focused on healthy choices. But really it's about the camaraderie."

Ryan narrowed his eyes. No wonder Sophie's fixation on the café trumped everything, even her job.

Donovan placed his drink on the napkin in front of him. "I like you. I think you're good people. And you could be good for her. But for now, you may want to steer clear. However, if being with her is what you truly want"—Donovan gestured toward the TV where the announcer was screaming over a double play—"then you better treat her right. And if you will, you have my blessing."

Donovan stood, dropping his gaze at a guy at the end of the bar who was eyeing him. "I, on the other hand, have nothing to lose, and us talking right now is giving off the wrong impression to my future evening plans. I will catch you later."

Ryan nodded. Then he looked over at Sophie. The call today was from someone at the café. No wonder she'd lost it over some food poisoning. Had that been an emergency, she would have had every right to want to leave. Ryan felt for her. The pressure to keep it all together while running a pretty significant outreach, which was likely on the chopping block, would keep anyone on edge.

Ryan frowned. He really should heed Donovan's advice. But he couldn't. He was drawn to her. He closed his eyes. What would it matter in a few days? When he was back in San Antonio, and she was, well, what were her plans? Only one way to find out.

He retrieved his phone and checked his app's live-streaming of the game. Bottom of the ninth. Tied game. Bases loaded. He could count on one hand how many times he'd seen a walk-off home run in a championship game.

This would not be one of those times. He'd have to chime in at some point, but not now. He also needed to touch base with Phil again and prepare his notes for tomorrow. That could wait as well. He clicked his phone off and shoved it into his pocket. Johnson could cover this one.

As Ryan approached Sophie, she scanned the room before slipping a set of salt and pepper shakers in her purse.

Odd. He ran a hand through his hair and straightened his sports coat. As if on cue, Louis Armstrong's "What a Wonderful World" hummed through the speakers.

Ryan gently tapped her shoulder. "Care to dance?"

Chapter 19

The touch on her shoulder startled Sophie. When she glanced up, Ryan's gorgeous eyes stared back at her. That crooked smile was growing on her.

Even still, her mind remained clouded. "I don't think that's such a good idea." First of all, she didn't trust her emotions around him. Second, she still needed to gather a few items on her scavenger hunt list before it was time to turn in today's loot. Third, why was Ryan asking her to dance anyway?

Her eyes cut away from his and she stared at his extended hand.

"Why not? It's just a dance between colleagues."

Colleagues? Is that how he wanted to describe it?

The way pressing against him on that motorcycle made her feel, she didn't think being in his arms was such a great idea.

He added a raised eyebrow to the smile. "One dance, Sophie. Please."

Oh, his compelling, Caribbean eyes. Sophie bit her bottom lip. "I don't know. I wouldn't want you to be caught dancing with stupid and all," she said, referencing the gawd-awful shirt from earlier.

"Let's just say I'm a pretty good judge of character, and stupid you are not. Or"—he grinned mischievously—"we could discuss your need to season your purse with salt and pepper."

Sophie's jaw dropped. Literally.

Ryan took her hand, leading her to the dance floor. He leaned in and whispered, "Just one dance. For the kids."

"The kids?"

He nodded toward Donovan who sat at the bar with another gentleman. Donovan glanced over and feigned wiping a tear from his cheek as if they were part of a reality show. He caressed a half-empty daiquiri, complete with a drink umbrella for her loot.

"So, you doing okay?" he asked softly, releasing her long enough to gently tuck a loose tendril behind her ear.

His hand in hers made her quake, but she wanted to laugh. *Okay? Sure. If you call humiliation followed by a shameful ritual that caused more pain than it relieved, then sure, yeah.* "I'm okay," she said.

Sophie closed her eyes. *What are you doing?* His familiar smell, touch, hold. It took her back to their days of watching meteorite showers and finding constellations, and the star he named after her. And then the jagged knife to the heart when he left her.

Careful not to delve too deeply into that moment, a moment where the thought alone made her stomach churn, she hurtled herself back to Earth. To the present where there were no painful memories of stargazing and intimacy. This was just a dance and he was still Ryan Pike, the *nice* guy who chose a career over her.

They stepped onto the dance floor, and he pulled her into his arms.

"You're not talking."

She pursed her lips.

"Hey." His fingers curled under her chin. "Talk to me. Are you okay?"

His touch sent a wave of chills down her spine, like a warning signal. Dancing was one thing. It was safe. People did it all the time. But the way he wrapped his fingers around her chin felt too intimate, too sensual. What was he trying to do? And did she want him to do it?

No. Maybe. She wrapped a hand around his, pulling it from her face, not sure she could trust herself. "I'm good. I think I'm just tired."

Ryan took the hint, but instead of releasing her, he pulled her tighter. "I have an idea," he offered, changing the subject. "Later tonight there's a luau on the Lido Deck I was going to check out. I hear a world-renowned chef prepares the food. Maybe some fresh air will help—"

"All right, you guys." The DJ's game show voice cracked through the microphone and his white tux with a white bowtie more than qualified him as the cheesy announcer for a cheesy game. "This just in. For those of you participating in the cruise's fifth annual scavenger hunt, we have an extra bonus tonight only!" His voice carried the words like he was singing. "Our captain just announced a very special walkie-talkie is hidden somewhere on this ship and he will be on the other end to tell one lucky participant the location to a valuable triple-bonus find!"

Sophie's heart flipped, and her grip on Ryan's shirt tightened. If five grand weren't the pot, she'd have laughed at the other passengers who hung on his every word.

"The clues to the location are as follows: Follow the trail that leads to fun, where liquid flows and stars bask in the sun."

Sophie's attention whipped back to Ryan, whose eyes locked on hers. His lips tugged at one side, hinting at his striking smile. "Well, looks like the crowd just thinned out a bit."

Sophie watched as no less than a dozen bodies scrambled for the exit. One head ducked out so fast, Sophie almost missed it. But his sandy-colored head and obnoxious tuxedo gave Asher away.

Being riddles were his unspoken language, she knew if she had a chance at beating him, she'd have to let him lead her to the find.

"I have to go," Sophie said, releasing her grip on Ryan's shirt.

Ryan squeezed her hand. "You want to follow that crowd while they run over each other?"

"I'm supposed to meet Amy but she never showed. I'm going to look for her."

Ryan dropped his hand, and a twinge of something swelled up in her. Dancing with him felt better than she cared to admit. But she had to try to find this stupid walkie-talkie. For the girls. "I'm sorry. Thank you for the dance." She turned on her heel and hugged her purse tightly to her side. Heading toward the exit, she stopped in front of the freshly lacquered bar where Donovan sat perched on a stool. "Thank you," she said.

"For what?" he asked, his voice three octaves higher than usual, even for him.

"For this." She plucked the umbrella from his fruity cocktail. Turning toward Ryan, she watched his brows lift in confusion. Then she stuffed the umbrella in her purse and rushed out of the room to find Asher.

~ ~ ~

Asher was long gone, and everyone else scurried off in different directions. Sophie repeated the clues in her head. Without Asher, she'd have to fend for herself. But where to start? The clues said something about stars basking in the sun and flowing liquid, right?

But what did that mean? Stars clearly meant the sky. And flowing liquid could easily refer to the Milky Way. Sophie's heart drummed in her chest and she headed for the observatory on the Panorama deck, which was the tenth floor. That's where she needed to start.

The lingering scent of Ryan's cologne clung to her skin like fingers hanging on a railing overlooking a canyon. Her thoughts shifted to him. She could still feel his arms locked around her. *Focus, Sophie—the café.*

Ryan said he'd be at the Lido Deck later tonight. Clearly the clues didn't lead there. Everyone and their mother would likely be at a pig roasting. Or, at least some semblance of a roast, she didn't expect the ship would allow open flames on a lacquered wooden deck, so there was no reason to meet him there.

Except that he was there.

Sophie's heart inched toward her throat. Why did she want to see him again? He'd tortured her enough in the silence after Grandmoo's accident. Were the endless hours spent crying in her pillow and starving herself until she nearly passed out, only to drive through a fast-food restaurant and order the left side of the menu—followed by vomiting so that she'd feel something—not enough to remind her how this ends? She'd shed enough tears over him, she didn't plan to shed anymore. Yes, he was her first love. But the other six billion people on this planet had a first love, too. Almost none of who actually married that person. And that's okay.

She was okay.

So what if her head spun while they danced? Perhaps somewhere in the very back of her mind, deep in the temporal lobe where Ryan lived and breathed and gave her heart a cardio workout, she wanted to believe he had changed. That he had realized it took a decade of never filling that hole to remind him what could have been.

Then again, that was *her* hole. Not his. And the consequence of another rejection was not worth exploring. Especially since spending one afternoon with him sent her over the edge.

Sophie's stomach constricted. That sort of pain—the gooey, messy, first love kind—left pain so intense, she'd rather have a root canal, performed by a Captain Hook, with his eyes closed, and the crocodile still attached to his wrist than allow Ryan to hurt her again.

Besides, the way he made her feel now was just remnants from when she was twenty. This wasn't real.

He was that nice guy who got along with everyone. So what if he spent the day with her? He also hung out with the others when he got back on the ship. Because he was nice, and dammit, that's what *nice* people do.

Stop! Sophie's mind raced so fast she forgot which direction she was headed. This obsessing was going to cost her the game. Time to focus. Girls, café, walkie-talkie. No more Ryan. Period.

The observatory wasn't hard to find, but something seemed eerie. She stopped in front of a closed door with a gold-plated sign that read in black letters 'Observatory: Open to guests from dusk till dawn,' and it occurred to her that nobody was around. Could it be that someone already found it? No, of course not. She was the only one that headed this way. Maybe she was the only one who put the clues together. Or, God forbid, she completely missed the mark.

She tried to open the door, and found it was locked. A sign posted near the door read that the room was closed due to renovations. Believing the walkie-talkie had to be in there, she assumed it was locked by accident. She jiggled the doorknob harder, twisting it and trying to make it open. This had to be a mistake. Why wouldn't the door open?

Unless she was wrong. But she couldn't be. The clues clearly stated it was where the stars were basking and flowing. You can't see more stars than through the lens of a telescope! "Open up, you stupid door!" She banged the window and threw her shoulder into the door as if she could channel the Incredible Hulk and get in.

"Can I help you?" asked a high-pitched voice.

Sophie turned. The high-pitched voice belonged to a scrawny, and very likely inexperienced crewmember. The kid had a volcanic blemish on his chin which quite possibly had its own zip code. He couldn't be a day older than eighteen-years-old.

She pushed herself from the door and stood tall, dwarfing him by a good three inches. Maybe she could trick him into letting her in. She glanced at his nametag and said, "Good evening, Todd. Maybe you can help me. This door is locked and I would like to get inside."

Todd craned his neck toward the sign. "It's closed."

Sophie tried the door handle again. "Yes, but as you can see it's supposed to be open because I'm betting the captain placed a hidden walkie-talkie in there and I'd like to check. Just a peek, Todd."

"Yeah, sorry, ma'am. That's not going to happen."

"Well, why not? I'm just asking for a minute." Determination was like a broomstick holding her up. He had to let her in.

"Because the sign says so." The pimple on his chin clearly mocked her.

Sophie tried to level with the guy. "Come on, Todd. I'm just asking for one minute in there. I won't touch anything. Please."

"Sorry. I follow the rules but I can get a supervisor for you."

A loud cheer erupted from the Lido Deck just below them. Both Todd and Sophie shot to the railing, stretching their necks to see what was happening below.

A spotlight haloed around Asher, who was standing next to the pool Ryan had dragged her out of last night, holding the walkie-talkie high above his head. Next to him were cardboard cutouts of Leonardo DiCaprio, Marilyn Monroe, and Justin Beiber. *Stars. Stars basking in the sun where the liquid flows. Oh, how did I miss that?* He found the walkie-talkie because he was a freak of nature when it came to games. And Sophie spent her time trying to break into a fortified fortress.

A faint thread of hysteria caught in her voice. "No. It can't be."

"Well, that guy seems happy." Todd and his zit, which grew a goatee and aged about ten years, seemed suddenly buoyant. "The observatory will be open tomorrow. Have a good night."

Todd scampered away, and Sophie leaned against the desolate room, desolate like her hope for saving the cafe. She refused the tears that welled up. "It was a stupid game and a long shot anyway."

"Sophie?" Ryan said.

She shivered at the sound of his voice.

He stood in the shadows of the ship's immense fin, and for a moment she longed for his comfort. His arms strong around her, his skin soft against hers, his lips making her forget. She clenched her jaw. But fulfilling that desire was about as probable as winning the money for the café. She sunk down next to the door. "How did you know where I was?"

"I didn't. I'm headed to my room." He pointed toward the sliding glass doors that led to the balcony suites.

"Oh. Okay." He needed to go. Immediately. She needed a good cry—not a purge, thankfully—and she couldn't do that with him here. As the nice guy, if he saw even on glistening tear, he'd stay. But then what? He would leave, because his job was in San Antonio, and he would ultimately end up with another woman anyway. Her heart couldn't handle one more ripple.

Sophie watched the ground and held her breath. Ryan's shiny black dress shoes did not walk toward his room as expected, but rather approached her. Her feelings for him intensified with every step. She looked up and offered him a tentative smile. "Have a good night then."

Ryan slid down and sat next to her. He didn't say anything, but wrapped an arm around her and pulled her in to him.

And something deep inside her broke. She sobbed. Didn't even try to contain it, but let her hurt explode all over his overpriced shirt. She was grateful the observatory was closed, because sitting in the darkness away from the crowd allowed her a moment to regroup. She didn't let the girls down on purpose. And there was still hope. But it was one failed attempt after another. And with each letdown, she felt the café slip further away.

Ryan reached into his coat, pulled a handkerchief from his shirt pocket, and handed it to her.

"Really?" She sniffle-laughed. "You carry a handkerchief in your pocket?"

"Well," he said into her hair, "you never know when you'll find a pretty young lady who has something in her eye."

Sophie relaxed her head into his chest. "Thank you."

"You're welcome." After a moment of silence, Ryan tucked his fist under her chin and lifted. "I don't know what's wrong, but if you want to talk about it, I'm here."

"I'm okay. I just needed a minute."

Ryan was silent for a moment before asking, "What are you thinking about?"

Sophie smiled. So much for giving her a minute. "I'm not," she said. "I'm listening."

Ryan looked around. The air was calm. The festivities below on the Lido Deck had simmered. The night was coming to a close. "To what?" he finally asked.

"To the rational voices in my head reminding me how the last time we were together, things . . . didn't fare so well."

"You're the one who stopped dancing."

"I'm not talking about dancing, Pike."

"Now, now. No need to use my name in vain. But I think things can fare a little better given whatever was in your eye seems to have come out. It was an exciting day for you. But maybe no more kayaks for now."

Oh, those dimples when his whole face smiles. She'd forgotten how they made her breath catch. "Right," Sophie said. He was too close to seeing her vulnerability. "About that. The day just got to me. I'm pretty sure I can never show my face in that city again."

"Well, I wouldn't say that. They'd be lucky to see your face again."

Sophie blushed. Her legs quivered. "You don't have to be so nice to me. What happened between us was a long time ago. But I appreciate the gesture."

Ryan blinked. He looked at the door and then stood up, pulling Sophie with him. He looked through in the window and placed his hand on the handle.

"It's locked. I tried to get in."

Ryan's eyes smiled. "Then you didn't try very hard." He took his wallet from his back pocket and removed what looked like a miniature toolkit.

As he tucked his wallet away, Sophie followed his hand movements to his waistline. When he saw her watching, she blushed again.

"Eh-hem, my eyes are up here," he said, pointing two fingers to his deep blues. The darkness changed them grayish. His fingers caressed her cheek. "You have a little something right here." He lightly brushed off a tear.

Sophie's stomach danced and she bit hard on her lower lip, hoping to gain control of her traitor body. But she couldn't resist a smile.

Ryan carefully put a thin, long piece of metal in the doorknob's keyhole, carefully maneuvering his thumb and forefinger in a circular motion. He then added a second tool.

"What are those?" Sophie asked.

"A tension wrench and a pick."

"Is it even legal to have those tools in your wallet?"

"Have what?"

"You know what I'm referring to, Pike."

"Again, with you and using my name in vain." After a moment a click sounded and he leaned back on his heels, smiling. "I like to be prepared." He pushed the door open and Sophie stepped inside.

Once in the room, Sophie's eyes ballooned at the sight. The observation deck contained what Sophie assumed were about fifteen top-of-the-line telescopes evenly spread out around the room, all pointing toward the night sky. They were black, and beautiful, and their sturdy tri-pods stood erected side-by-side, holding each telescope carefully as they dutifully guarded the night sky.

Ryan's fingers curved under her chin again. That touch sent a merciless quiver through her.

Chapter 20

"Ryan, this is beautiful."

"Have you ever looked through one?" He placed his hand on the curve of her back and guided her in, closing the door behind them.

"No, never," she said. "You used to tell me about them when we stargazed, but that was as close to the night sky as I ever came."

Ryan grimaced. He had never taken her to see his telescope because it was at Tia's, still was. Back then, he wasn't ready to reclaim something that triggered such a difficult memory. But now it was time. He wanted to show her the star that bore her name, Sophie's Sapphire. "Would you like to now? See the stars?" *See your star.*

Sophie studied him for a moment, then answered with a tantalizing smile. Ryan took that to mean 'yes' and gently laced his fingers through hers and led her to the center telescope.

This telescope, though a newer model, was the same enormous reflector telescope his father bought him as a kid.

He positioned Sophie directly behind it and rested his hands on her arms. Hundreds of goose bumps edged against his palms, and Ryan couldn't help but smile. Was it his touch, or, "Cold?"

"Not really."

"Hmm." That gave him immense satisfaction. "You want to see what's behind door number one?"

Her eyes widened slightly. "Only if you want to show me."

The tease in her voice quickened his already racing heart and he forced a dry swallow. *Okay then. Here goes nothing.* Dropping his hands, he slowly reached around her and carefully led her hand onto the massive apparatus. Being a reflective telescope, it had an eight-inch aperture, allowing enough light to see clusters of stars that a plain refractor telescope could only dream of seeing. Using this piece of equipment demanded respect for the universe and its unconceivable power.

Sophie gasped in awe. "Do you know how to work it?"

A smile tugged at his mouth. "I do. I had one very similar to this," he said, placing her hands in the correct position.

"You *had* one? What happened to it?"

"I still technically own it. But it's at a friend's house."

"Why?" she asked.

Her question couldn't be answered without delving into the full story. But he shoved it so deep into the no man's land part of his mind that it seemed like a bad dream.

So, he decided on the abridged, safe version. "For safe keeping. It was my twelfth birthday present and after I went to college I stored a lot of my belongings with a family friend."

"You got a this for your twelfth birthday?"

Ryan lifted a shoulder. "Well, yeah."

Sophie shook her head. "All I got was a set of R.L. Stein books and a Lite Brite set."

Ryan laughed. "Lite Brite, huh?" He ran his fingers along the optical tube, familiarizing himself with it, until he reached the aperture. Though he didn't appreciate his gift as a child, he did now. "Well," Ryan said, gripping the telescope by its stand, "what you don't know is my present came with a consolation gift."

He reached over Sophie. Her flowery perfume all but consumed him as he carefully directed the scope toward the dark sky. Billions of stars stared back at them—beautiful now as the first time he saw them.

He withdrew a cloth from a bag hanging on the tripod and cleaned the lenses, adding the correct filters in place. He assumed when the observatory was open, crewmembers assisted with this part. Once finished, he went to work on finding a reference point. He knew the night sky very well. That was one assurance he could count on; the sky would barely change throughout his lifetime. He pointed the scope toward the moon and then directed it to his left.

Sophie stood in front of him, cradled between his arms. He could hear her steady breathing and he changed his breaths to match hers. Her creamy skin was just a touch away and he had to hold himself back from moving his hand to caress her neck.

"What do you mean by consolation gift?" Sophie whispered.

Ryan looked in the finder scope and answered. "It also came with a crap load of guilt, wrapped up with a pretty little bow." He didn't mean to sound so harsh.

Sophie's brows creased, and he sighed.

"Let's just say Dad had a plan for me. He gave me my telescope and together we designed and polished the mirror to give it more edge. I loved it for the first few months, but then my interests waned. And Dad's plans for me didn't exactly include what I wanted. Of course who knows what they want at twelve years old?"

"It's okay," Sophie said, reaching for Ryan's forearm. "You don't have to talk about it, but if you want to, I'm a good listener."

Ryan stopped messing with the telescope. He allowed himself a long look at Sophie, and knew he'd once asked her about her family but never shared his. He'd felt if he kept his life private, the parts that hurt the most wouldn't. But maybe that's what chased her away. He had asked her to be open and honest with him, but had he ever returned the favor? Ryan sunk to the floor, this time Sophie met him there.

"Winter solstice," Ryan said.

Sophie's kind eyes were soft "I'm not sure I follow," she whispered.

"Every winter solstice, Dad and I dressed in our warmest pajamas, sipped on hot cocoa with nine marshmallows each, one for each planet . . . we still included Pluto, and watched as the shortest day of the year came to an end. It used to be fun in a believing-in-Santa Claus sort of way. We watched the sky change from fall to winter while my junk froze like a snowball. Eventually it was as amazing as watching paint dry."

"Sounds like, um, fun. I guess."

Ryan smiled. "It was for a while. At six years old, I was a proud, card carrying, bona fide junior astronomer. I think I still have my membership card somewhere." His chest gripped again and he licked his incredibly dry lips.

He subtly glanced at Sophie, who looked straight ahead, carefully listening. He stared ahead, too, catching the refraction from the moonlight that danced against the furthest wall. Then he told her something he'd never told anyone since that night. He told her his story.

"I told you before that my sister Nicole was an art prodigy. Dad couldn't be more proud. He had two kids on either end of the talent spectrum. Nicole was his artist. She could paint a canvas that would make the Mona Lisa cry. And then he had me. I happened to test at a genius level since third grade and was enrolled in the GATE program for the nerds.

"But school was a means to an end for me. I knew that about myself as soon I was old enough to walk to the liquor store on the corner and find my escape in *Sports Now*. I mean," he said on a laugh, "the annual swimsuit edition was where I lost my innocence, but I ate up the articles."

"Swimsuit edition, huh?" Sophie scrutinized Ryan with a playful tone.

"Don't judge. I was like eleven or twelve."

Sophie laughed. "Boys."

Ryan couldn't help how much she captivated him. She deserved to know everything. For now, though, she'd have to settle with knowing about the night his dad disowned him. Ryan squeezed Sophie's hand and continued. "When I was fourteen, Nicole was eighteen and studying abroad. She and I resurrected the lost art of writing each other letters, and I made the monumental mistake of keeping them." Ryan paused, the tightness in his chest welled up to a knot just below his throat. "I was an ass to my dad. I was mad that he kept pressing the astronomy program, and I just wanted to do my own thing."

Sophie looked at Ryan with an understanding gentleness he didn't feel he deserved. "You were a kid, Ryan. No matter what you thought, he can't be mad that you disagreed with him."

Ryan's hand began to sweat and he shook from her grip. He stared at the telescope. "No, that's not it. We exchanged inside jokes about how astronomy was a dreamer's paradise and a waste of time. So much so, even NASA was being defunded. My real dream was following sports. All the sports. I loved everything about athletes, and I wanted to tell their stories and follow their careers the way my dad wanted me to follow his."

Ryan peered out the observation window. The stars where so peaceful, he felt more relaxed than he had in years. He recalled his mother's soft demeanor, knowing Ryan was not cut from the same cloth as Dad. "Mom knew me better. She always placed the sports section of the daily newspaper under the *Time* magazine at the breakfast table with my bowl of Wheaties. It always had to be Wheaties because that's what the athletes on the cover of the box ate. Mom never uttered a word against Dad's wishes for me, but it was our unspoken language."

Ryan dragged in a long, ragged breath. He recalled that night as if it happened just yesterday. Ryan swallowed a lump remembering his mother's cries. But his dad pushed him too far that night.

Sophie set her hand on his thigh. "It's okay. You don't have to talk about it."

Ryan nodded but he needed to tell Sophie. "Eventually, the lying caught up. Nicole and I continued to exchange letters. We wrote about the Eiffel Tower, the Dodger's crap season, and how Americans have it all wrong when they say New York is the greatest city in the world. And how I had been making a fool of Dad, having every intention of attending a small, private college for journalism, our school." He smirked. "So it was no surprise when that very lie not only caught up with me, but exploded."

Ryan explained the scene as it unfolded in his memory. How Dad stormed into the family room after returning home from the lab. He held the letters in his hand and asked if they were some sort of joke.

"My mom pleaded for Dad to stop. His rage was like nothing I had ever seen. I felt something inside me snap." Ryan's voice hitched and Sophie squeezed his leg again. "Dad found the letters in the garage. I don't even remember how it came to blows but I do recall my mother's shrieking and begging Dad to stop. Only I didn't know my own strength. I was angry, frustrated, and stupid. I threw the first and only punch. Having thrown back a twelve pack of Bud, he collapsed, crushing a wooden bar stool on his way down."

Ryan swallowed dryly. "Mom screamed but I was so angry I almost kicked him when he was down. Who does that?" Ryan shook his head. "I stood over Dad, willing him to get back up so I could knock him down again."

Sophie pressed her hand against his shoulder. "Ryan, it's not your fault. He was drunk. You were scared. You were just a boy."

"He told me in no uncertain terms that he was done with me."

Sophie cupped Ryan's face, her nose only inches from his. He could smell her sweet perfume, the heat in his chest morphing from anger to want, need.

"So," he sighed, drawing her into his arms, "Mom went to Dad's side. I stood there seething. I couldn't understand how she would stay with a man who chose an addiction over his family. That was the only time I ever thought of her as weak. I told her as much too. When I turned to leave she called my name. You know what she said to me after all that?"

Sophie intertwined her fingers in his.

Ryan squeezed. "She told me to be the best sports journalist ever. She told me to make a name for myself and my father would be prouder of me than she was at this moment."

"She loved you dearly, Ryan. You have to know that."

Ryan caressed Sophie's cheek so she had to look at him. He wanted her to see that he was wrong. That it was his fault and he was to blame.

Her eyes drifted from one to another and he gave her a rueful grin.

"Some things are hard to accept. Like how a father can allow his career to turn him into a raging alcoholic. Or how cancer can suddenly come upon your mother and take her life within six months."

"Oh, Ryan. I'm so sorry."

"It's okay. I'm actually okay, but I wanted to tell you."

"I . . ." Sophie whispered. "I'm glad you did."

Ryan gave her an almost smile. "Tomorrow we arrive in Avalon. I have a very good friend there I want you to meet. Say you'll come with me."

Sophie's face paled. "I-I don't know. I need to check on my girls, and I have my next article to research." She inched back, and Ryan was afraid he asked too much of her. Maybe she was still apprehensive after everything that had happened today.

"It's okay. You don't have to." Ryan couldn't help it, he cupped her chin and stroked her cheek with his thumb. She was so beautiful. "You want to see something amazing?"

Her eyes dropped to his lips and she opened her mouth to say something, but just a squeak came out. He'd take that as a yes. He helped her off the ground and directed her back in front of him. Taking her wrists in his hands, he said, "Be a puppet."

She swung around, eyes narrowed.

He laughed. "Trust me."

Something like pain flashed through her eyes before she turned back to the telescope. What was that about? But her arms went limp in his hands. He shook them a few times to make sure she'd let him play puppet master. "Good, now place one here." He gently set her right hand on the eyepiece, softly running his fingers up her arm.

Gooseflesh rose beneath his fingertips. His inner man smiled. "The other one goes here." He placed her left hand on the optical tube for balance. "Now close your left eye and look into this hole here. Use this little doo-hickey to adjust the focus."

"Doo-hickey?" He could hear the smile in her tone.

"Would you prefer focuser? Because if I start talking terminology, there might be a quiz at the end."

Sophie looked at him and cocked a brow. "Oh? What happens if I fail?"

"You'll be sentenced to a date with me."

She smiled. "What happens if I pass?"

"You'll be rewarded kindly."

"Maybe I'll just skip class and you won't have to follow through on either."

Ryan grinned. "Easy now. There's an extra penalty for cutting class."

A shooting star shot across the diamond-filled sky, and Ryan watched as Sophie's wide eyes sparkled in the slight glow. "Don't make threats you don't intend to enforce," she said, still watching the sky through the massive window.

"I never do. Now stop stalling and look through the eyepiece."

Sophie dropped her head so her eye lined up perfectly. She adjusted the focuser slightly, which told Ryan her vision wasn't as perfect as his.

He waited a moment and then felt her go stiff. She gasped. "Ryan, is that what I think it is?"

He couldn't help the want that shot through him. "Sophie's Sapphire. In the same place I left it ten years ago."

"It's perfect. I don't want to stop looking at it."

Ryan resisted the urge to stroke her back. He rested his hands on her shoulders instead. "Well, maybe I'll have to get you one of these fancy devices so you can look at it whenever you want."

Sophie lifted her head and turned toward him. A smile played in her lips. He fought the urge to kiss it off her lips. He didn't want to scare her away. "I still have the certificate you left for me."

The one he left on her porch. He homed in on the diamond-shaped dimples under her lips. He needed to kiss each one right now, just to remind her exactly how beautiful she was. Her skin glowed in the moonlight, providing just enough light to see her heartbeat pulsing through her neck. He wanted to kiss that, too. Resisting, he said, "We should go."

"Yeah," she agreed. And Ryan wished she would've asked to stay. But being she didn't, he missed his chance to try and talk to her. Talk about her café, and possible changes, and what the future could hold if she'd give him another chance.

Details about exactly how things ended ten years ago were foggy. They could start fresh. He could take care of her. And her grandmoo. She just needed to trust him.

"Thank you for showing me my star." Sophie's cheeks pinked sending shockwaves through him.

"You're quite welcome."

Watching her walk away, he struggled with the idea of letting her go. Away from the possible merge, and away from his life . . . again. He needed a drink. A big one.

Chapter 21

Six hours later—or was it only two—Ryan woke half dazed on a chaise lounge with a killer headache. He pushed himself into a sitting position and wiped the drool from his cheek. He'd been lying face down in a puddle of it like a teething toddler.

A soft wind floated up from the sea, bringing with it the echo of squawking seagulls, tickling the hair on the nape of his neck. Waves sloshed a rhythmic melody against the boat.

His tongue felt like sandpaper and begged for water. He patted around his unbelievably stiff body and felt a plastic water bottle. He'd caught the end of the luau and only meant to have one drink after Sophie left him reeling last night. But then he got to chatting with some people from the San Fran office, and that drink turned into a few more.

An air horn blew, rattling Ryan's brain. The ship must be docking in Catalina. Ryan had spent six summers on this tiny island. The silver lining in missing the first couple pennant games was visiting the woman who was like a sister to his mother and, in all the ways that counted, a second mother to him.

Rubbing the sleep from his eyes, Ryan reached for his phone to read his schedule for the day.

It was dead.

Great.

He knew he had training at eight and he owed Phil an update. Ryan worked his fingers into the rock-hard knot in his neck, which prevented him from looking left. Or right, come to think of it.

"Rough night?" asked a middle-aged, pot-bellied man. He was wearing a too-tight Speedo with a towel tossed over his shoulder. He looked as greasy as the fattened pig roasting at the luau last night. His disheveled hair told Ryan that the man might have had a "what happens on International waters stays on International waters" sort of night.

Ryan's thoughts flashed to Sophie. How she felt cradled in his arms and how she'd left him lonely again. "Something like that," Ryan said, kneading his fingers deeper into his neck.

"Those hula dancers, right?" the man said. "It was my lucky night. They were here for a bachelorette party. You get enough fireballs in them, and wow, they can plow you harder than a harnessed ass on a Kansas field. Know what I mean?"

Ryan felt his face tighten, trying desperately to stop the images burning in his mind. "That's enough, man." Ryan held up his hands with a desperate plea to protect his ears. "I'm good on the details."

Except he wasn't good. He couldn't remember much after Sophie left.

How had he'd ended up sleeping on the Lido Deck, on a hard, plastic lounge chair? He loosened his tie and remembered Sophie had walked to her room. After he *almost* kissed her.

"Wicked awesome night." The pot-bellied man guffawed before setting off.

Ryan stepped over the chaise lounge next to his and knocked over two empty bottles of scotch. He tensed, he hadn't ordered those, right? He couldn't have. He'd vowed long ago not to be a drunk like his father. He'd have to check his bill later.

The eardrum-bursting horn went off again and Ryan ducked as if someone just hollered "Fore" on a golf course.

He cringed. *What happened last night?*

"Welcome to Catalina Island," a crewmember in a crisp, white uniform said as he passed Ryan, reading something on a clipboard.

"Hey," Ryan called after him. "What time is it?"

Without stopping, or looking up, the guy answered, "Quarter to six."

"Thanks." Ryan stood and shook off the rest of his aches. He would go back to his suite, change, and pop some Ibuprofen for his headache. Then, he thought with an unsettled pull in his chest, he'd call Phil.

~ ~ ~

Watching the massive, two hundred ton ship dock from the quiet, padded, obnoxious running track—*I mean really, who exercises on vacation?*—gave Sophie perspective. She clutched the banister, twisting and massaging her dry palms against the smooth wood like a reflexology treatment, and looked out at the peaceful city in the glowing horizon. The repetitive twisting somehow settled the softball-sized knots building in her chest.

She'd decided to quit the scavenger hunt. Continuing the game seemed futile, not to mention deceptive, and it was stirring too much anxiety. She couldn't afford to lose control again. She'd figure out another way to pay rent. But lying wasn't it.

Spending time with Ryan last night made her come alive. The comfort of his touch and the feel of his breath against her lips . . . it made the scavenger hunt seem juvenile and senseless.

Sophie smiled to herself as she replayed last night's stargazing in her head like a movie trailer. She touched her lips wondering how sweet his kiss would have tasted. As much as she wanted him to kiss her, she wasn't sure that was a good idea. They had too much history, a subject neither of them broached. Which was probably for the best.

Especially when the thought of their past compromised her sobriety, sending her stomach swirling into the great abyss. History had a weird way of repeating itself.

Plus, he would be back in San Antonio soon. Even if she were willing to give them another chance, she couldn't, knowing that he was leaving. It didn't make sense to fall for him again, no matter what her heart felt. Her feelings didn't matter. Grandmoo always said 'feelings don't have brains,' and the logical side of her knew that.

"Catching the morning sunrise?" Asher's voice drew her from her memory and sent a prickle down her spine.

She turned to see Asher in running shorts with a towel over his shoulder. *Ficus.* What does it take to lose this guy?

"You'd be surprised how fast I can still run, even with an injured toe, thank you for that again, by the way."

"Oh yeah? Can your injured toe swim, too? Because that water looks mighty inviting."

Asher laughed and leaned over the railing, folding his hands.

Sophie slid a step in the opposite direction. "What do you want, Asher?"

"I've just been thinking."

"Does it hurt?"

Asher stifled a laugh and turned so his back was leaning against the rail. "I get it. You're pissed. I deserve that much."

Sophie narrowed her eyes. What was he doing? Of course she was pissed. He'd spent the past week torturing her. Why was he acting all chivalrous now? "I'm going back to my room." Sophie pushed off the rail and headed for the steps.

"I owe you an apology. I messed up when I kissed Trixie."

Sophie froze. Was he kidding? An apology? The

YouTube video with its hundreds of thousands of views said as much. His hands on Trixie. His mouth covering hers. The prickle grew barbs as it tore flesh at the memory. She turned around. "No." She shook her head. "I don't accept."

"I don't blame you. But I've been thinking about it. And I'm really sorry. I'm a guy. It happens."

Sophie scrunched her forehead. "Excuse me? What happens?"

"Trixie came on to me. You were too busy to even attend the party, and that put me in a vulnerable position. Trixie walked over to me, handing me a drink. I didn't want to be rude so I accepted. We started talking, and one thing led to another . . . You were at that café, and I was alone."

That café? If he was trying to apologize, calling her lifeline 'that café' was not a good place to start. "I was working."

"Like you always are. But it wasn't my fault. She kissed me. I didn't see it coming. And I didn't expect you to be there."

This had to be a joke. Sophie half-expected a cameraman to pop out and some stupid prankster yell 'Surprise!' "But you kept kissing her. And then you pretty much dumped me."

"I didn't dump you. I just said we weren't exclusive. That's all."

Sophie rolled her eyes. "No, when you kiss another woman and stick your wandering hands where they don't belong, that's a non-verbal gesture expressing the end of a relationship."

Sophie didn't know who to feel worse for. Herself for being dumb enough to get involved with Asher, or him for being the stupidest Neanderthal to walk to Earth. He'd been busted for cheating on her and now he was trying to explain his behavior away. But why? "What do you want?"

Asher shrugged. "Nothing from you. But I do want to

warn you."

Warn her about what? Sophie sighed, not sure why she was giving him any of her time. "I'll give you thirty seconds."

Asher inched closer to Sophie's bubble. "No doubt you heard by now I took the triple points in the scavenger hunt last night."

Sophie writhed. "Are you here to rub my nose in it? That doesn't follow an apology very well. Besides, no doubt you heard, I don't care. I quit, and you should too since we're not supposed to participate."

"No, I'm not trying to rub your nose in anything." Asher stepped in front of her and folded his arms. "Just thought you should know your boy was getting mighty comfortable with our office teases after the luau."

Sophie scoffed. "So, you're spreading rumors now? Nice. You're about as reliable as a gold-digging source looking for a quick buck." Asher was probably baiting her, and she wasn't about to take the hook. Not this time. "Ryan is free to do as he pleases."

"I call it like I see it, Soph."

But her heart still sped with the visual of Ryan with Thelma and Louise. A bolt of anger shot through her. "And you have a knack for seeing it wrong."

"So then it wouldn't bother you that he was at the bar last night drinking it up with them?"

"Go away, Asher."

"Hmm." Asher shrugged. "All right. Just sharing what I saw. Don't shoot the messenger."

Sophie headed for the stairs. "I'm not involved with Ryan. And since last Friday your word is no longer good with me. I see your mouth moving and immediately wonder what you're lying about. So, goodbye."

Feeling all *I am woman hear me roar*, Sophie made an abrupt turn and took to the steps with a little too much gusto. Just before she hit the bottom, she lost her footing and slipped, missing the last two stairs. She landed right on her tailbone. Hard.

"Hey, are you okay?" Asher called down.

Sophie jumped up, rubbing her butt. Anger flooded through her like a roaring fire thirsting for gasoline. "Fine."

"Seriously, that looked painful," Asher said, slithering down the steps.

"I'll live." She rubbed it for a good moment and decided it was just her ego that was bruised. She could have lost an arm in a shark attack and wouldn't have asked Asher for so much as a Band-Aid. She did, however, smile at his slight limp from where his foot met her door. *I hope your foot gets gangrene and you have to amputate it.*

"Listen, take it for what its worth, but I thought you'd like to know what was in an email I received from a news channel up north I applied for."

Asher was seeking new employment? This was good news. "You're leaving?"

Asher lifted a shoulder. "It doesn't take rocket science to see where *Up Front* is headed. Not with subscription rates plummeting."

"What did you hear?"

"That Over the Top, Inc., is going another direction. That includes closing the café, which is why your funding was cut. I thought you should hear it from someone who cares."

Sophie's eyes narrowed until they were mere slits. "Stop talking about things you know nothing about. No one can close the café because *Up Front* carries the business license and pays the bills—not Over the Top. So, I'd appreciate it if you left me alone."

Asher threw his hands up. "Okay. I know the timing sucks, but you should know I do care. I know you're mad at me, and I'm sorry for that, but you should at least know.

Ryan's not as perfect as he seems."

That's it. Sophie had heard enough. She inched up to Asher and stuck her finger in his face, the fire building within boiling over. "Don't. Talk. To. Me. And stay out of my café's business."

And she walked away. But even as she did, she couldn't unhear what Asher had said. What if he was even partially right about Ryan and the café? And what if corporate did close *Up Front*? What would that mean for the café and for her job?

For everyone's job?

Chapter 22

"Here." Amy placed a steaming cup of coffee in front of Sophie's nose. "Double shot, vanilla soy frothy goodness. It's good for the soul."

"You're a godsend." Sophie took the microscopic porcelain cup and let the steam open her nostrils. "And a terrible friend, I might add. Where were you last night?"

Amy sat next to her. Sophie had arrived at the training a few minutes early so she could secure a seat in the back. The room was efficiently set up like a classroom with a wall-to-wall white board in the front. It had eight tables in all, two rows with four tables each. It was cramped, which was probably typical for cruise ships. Who wanted to waste space on a meeting room when they could add a climbing wall or a useless running track for the guests?

"I'm sorry. I flaked, I know."

"You missed the party and then when I looked for you, you were nowhere to be found. What happened to our plan?"

Sophie took a long sip of her coffee and let the warmth fill her soul. After listening to Asher's lies this morning and still not hearing any good news regarding her grants, her nerves were on edge. Coffee may not be the best idea for settling her jitters, but an elephant-sized tranquilizer wasn't available.

"I was, um, caught up face-timing with Mark. I had to go to the back of the ship to get any reception. And it was so beautiful and quiet, I just lost track of time. Before I knew it, it was midnight. You forgive me?"

The room slowly filled as her coworkers trickled in. Even Asher slithered in, sitting in the furthest seat from her. *Good.*

She sipped her coffee. "I don't know. What's in it for me?"

"I'll name my firstborn after you."

"Done. Tell Mark to get busy. I need my namesake before I get too old to be the cool auntie."

"I'm planning on having enough kids to form a softball team."

"You have fun with that. I'll stick with the two point five kids I'll statistically have."

"Good morning, everyone," Ryan said, moving to the front of the meeting room. "I hope everyone had a good time at the cocktail party last night."

The gossip girls, who sat at the first table closest to Ryan, giggled.

Sophie made a face behind her cup and slid deeper in her chair.

Amy leaned over. "Why are they giggling? What'd I miss?"

Sophie sneered. Her chest tightened. She was not good at the jealously thing. "I don't know," she whispered. "Asher said they were being friendly with Ryan last night."

"Tramps."

"I know, right?"

"Don't let it get to you," Amy reassured Sophie with a nudge. "And don't listen to Asher. I bet he'd pit his parents against each other if it'd get him what he wants."

Bless that head of hair. Sophie could be in prison for knocking over a 7-11 and Amy would make it seem as though it was the 7-11's fault.

"He's got eyes for you. Trust me."

"He almost kissed me last night," Sophie said, hiding

behind her cup. She sipped her coffee and let that little nugget soak in.

Amy's head snapped her way so fast, you'd think she would have injured her brain. "Shut up! What happened?"

"Shhh," Tyler from the entertainment department warned.

"Is there something you two would like to share with the group?" Ryan asked. He'd displayed an image of a bar graph on the white board from his laptop and was pointing to *Up Front's* numbers versus competing magazines. Ugh, graphs and numbers hurt Sophie's head.

"Sorry," Amy answered for both of them. "We were discussing how to enhance readership with the younger generation."

Amy nudged her phone and motioned for Sophie to continue the conversation via text.

Tell me everything.

Nothing happened.

Bull. U better spill it.

Seriously, he didn't seal the deal and it's a good thing. I can't get involved right now. There's 2 much history and I can't go there. Not with the café hanging on by a thread and besides, he makes me crazy.

Amy scowled. *That means he's perfect. A man who doesn't evoke emotion is wasted time. If Ryan has U crazy, U need 2 explore that.*

Sophie stared at the words on her phone's screen. She couldn't. Even if she wanted to, the timing was off. Something with Ryan still felt off. And until a grant or miracle came through she needed to think about how to pay rent this month.

Sophie changed the subject. *What are we doing today? I am not leaving without you. Yesterday was a mess.*

We'll come back 2 this conversation, but I know. I wasn't

going 2 say anything. But wow, YouTube sensation 2x in a week. New record.

Sophie dropped her phone. "You saw it?" she whispered.

"Last night. Mark tagged me."

Sophie rubbed her eyes. "Ugh, what is wrong with lookie-loos? Can't people just do stupid things in the privacy of their own bubble and leave it at that?"

Amy offered a sincere smile. "Not for you, I guess."

"Whatever. So, want to go horseback riding? I hear that's the thing to do here."

Amy dropped her eyes and played with her phone. "Don't hate me."

Sophie darted her a look of distain. "Then don't try to tell me you're not coming."

"Eh-hem." Tyler shot them a death stare. Ryan stopped talking again and looked from Amy to Sophie.

"Sorry," Sophie said this time, using her best *don't be mad you wanted to kiss these lips last night* smile.

Ryan's return grin sent a swirl of delight through her core. His dimples were nearly impossible not to gawk at. She'd imagined herself feeling the natural indents in his cheeks just before she'd kiss him. *God, what is he doing to me?*

Amy slid a piece of notebook paper toward Sophie. It read:

Have to work. Got an email from Red insisting I add the Golden Gate Color Run and some crab feed to my column by deadline. He wants the whole piece rewritten. Sorry, bestie.

Sophie figured Red was probably stressed. He wasn't usually so anal, but this just proved that something was up.

I'll just hang back and help then, Sophie wrote back.

"No you won't. You need to get out of here and do something fun." When John—*Meal Time on Your Dime* column—looked over at them, Amy held up a warning finger and he looked away, grumbling.

Sophie twisted her lips. "What I *need* to do is check in with the girls." And as if she conjured the call herself, her phone buzzed. The caller ID read Charlie. "I need to take this." Sophie quietly slid her chair back and slipped out of the room just as Ryan was lecturing about being present in the moment and limiting distractions. *Sorry,* she shot him a thought-apology and closed the door behind her.

"Hey, Charlie, what's up?"

"Don't freak out," Charlie squealed.

Sophie's stomach instantly sank. She hesitated a moment, as if replying too fast could detonate a bomb. After the false alarm yesterday, she tried to relax a bit and not jump to worse-case scenarios. But the sound in Charlie's voice was anything but relaxed. "What's wrong? Are you okay? Who's dead?"

"No one's dead," she croaked. "Yet."

Oh, dear God. In the background Sophie heard someone chanting. Charlie stayed silent.

Sophie gripped her cell phone so hard her fingers tingled. "If you don't say something, I'm going to freak out."

"We have a small situation. Emphasis on the small."

"Okaaaaaay, just how small?"

"Like really small. You know . . . beady-eyed teeny-tiny."

What was Charlie talking about? Maybe someone else could explain. "Is Tanya with you?"

"Tanya's a little freaked out right now. She's on a chair in the corner of your office with a broom and a crucifix reciting the 'Hail Mary.'"

And that would explain the chanting. "Why is Tanya on a chair with a broom and cross?"

The milliseconds elongated to an interstellar time lapse. "Charlie?"

"Because the small problem might be of a rodent nature."

"Oh, jeez. Oh, God."

"Yeah, that's what Tanya's saying"

"Charlie. Rip off the Band-Aid. What's going on?"

The few key words Sophie did catch served as a vise clamping onto her swollen chest. Words like "unintentional" and "health department" and "rats."

Chapter 23

Ryan closed the door to his cabin and pulled out the collective notes he made on each employee for how they would fit with *Jazz*. Not that the merge was finalized—though it was just a matter of time, but Phil would want answers.

He tossed the files on the bed. Squeezing his eyes shut, he cracked his neck and sucked in a deep, rigid breath, releasing it slowly. Sophie seemed like she'd seen a ghost when she walked back into the meeting after taking a call. He looked for her, but she and Amy slipped out right after the meeting was over.

He checked the time and grabbed his cell phone, quickly dialing Phil in San Antonio.

"Phil speaking." The bad connection on the other end of the line shrieked. Ryan jerked the phone from his ear and put it on speaker.

"Just checking in, boss," Ryan said, slipping on some khaki shorts and grabbing a shirt out of his luggage. He never bothered using the empty drawers when traveling.

"You got anything for me?"

Other than a slight headache from a hangover I don't remember earning and a touch of unease over my old girlfriend? "Just getting ready to head to shore for a bit. I'm going to visit an old friend."

"Well, I have news. Great news, actually."

Ryan stopped moving. "What's that?"

"The merge is approved. We'll likely be ready to transition by the end of the month. Next month's periodical will be *Up Front's* last."

Ryan jerked his head toward the phone. "Say that again."

"I know. I haven't seen a merge approved that fast in, well, ever. It was a unanimous decision."

"But what about the team here. The training we've done and their individual lives. I mean we're talking about health insurance and little league and college tuitions. These people need time to figure out how they're going to make ends meet."

Phil's gravelly voice broke through the sketchy speaker. "It's not personal, Ryan. We have a bottom line and are required by law to do what's best for our stockholders. Finish up the training like nothing has changed, we still want to keep our best writers."

Ryan raked both hands down his face. His stubble scratched his palms. "It's just so soon."

"I know. And you're doing a good job, son. I'm sending you a file with merge info on it. Read it over and get back to me with your thoughts. I'll be there next week to address the office. We expect to extend a handful of positions over at *Jazz*. But as you know, most of the work is freelance."

"But the rest? What about them?"

"That's why we need you to vet our best. You're the eyes and ears for Over the Top and I'm relying on you to get the job done. Make good notes. Over the next week, you can review their employee files and make time to meet with our best prospects."

Next week? Ryan lurched his whole body around and about pulled a calf muscle. There was no way he could make that sort of decision with a few days' notice. He snatched up the cell phone and clicked off the speaker. "I need more time, Phil. I need to do background checks, look over stats, check records. This isn't my area of expertise."

"You'll be fine."

"And then what happens?"

"As a board member, I'll do Red Goldberg's exit interview Friday morning since he's retiring anyway. That way this will ensure a smooth transition when I introduce the newest e-mag team members to *Sports Now's* next editor in chief. The rest will be handed over to HR. They will handle the severance packages and complete the layoffs. You can start Monday morning as the interim while *Up Front* finishes their last run."

"What about the Series? What about my app?"

"You will have people who can handle that."

People? Ryan didn't want people to do his job. He shoved a hand through his hair. *Damn.* He wasn't even sure he wanted the editor position. Not at the cost of all these jobs. The jobs of people he'd gotten to know. It was all happening too fast. "Just like that. The magazine closes?" He trudged into the bathroom and grabbed a few more ibuprofen, dropped his head back and tossed them in. This quick phone call just turned his slight headache into a pending migraine.

"You sound surprised. It's okay, son. I was nervous the first time I had to let an entire team go, too. Things are moving fast due to a breach of info. Didn't you get my email?"

Between the cocktail party and seeing Sophie, he hadn't thought to check his email again. "Not yet."

"It's all outlined there," Phil continued. "Read it over."

"Shouldn't we privy *Sports Now* to my promotion first?" If he accepted it.

"Ideally, but you're already there and we can't cut a main artery without immediately clotting the bleed."

Ryan pressed his thumb and finger in his eyes. "English, please."

"The board doesn't want to announce closing *Up Front* without simultaneously announcing the revamp of *Jazz.* It would turn into a cluster."

Ryan racked his brain. The last thing he wanted was to jump the gun and make a wrong decision. "I need more time to weigh pros and cons. I need to fly back to my office before you come to the Bay Area office. Give me a week."

"We don't have a week. The breach came from inside *Sports Now.* I bet it was Johnson, that prick. You have two days."

"Come on, Phil. You want to lose all moral here? These people are a tightknit group. Give me five days."

"Three. Hang on, got another call."

"Fine." Ryan clenched his teeth. He crouched down, stretching his aching calves. *Son of a . . .* This was all too soon. He wasn't sure he wanted this. Well, hell, who doesn't want to run an entire magazine? It was a huge opportunity.

But not like this. This sort of burn in the industry follows a man. He'd carry a stigma. And he'd worked so hard to ensure he was a respected member of the journalism community.

He had drawn up notes on *Up Front's* team in the event of an "unlikely" merge. But now that it was happening, Ryan didn't know what to think. These notes were entirely for him so he could keep their strengths and weaknesses in mind as he worked through the training. Because that was why he was here.

All the notes lined his bedspread. He picked up Sophie's, which had her name and nothing more than a large question mark. He turned the page over and thought they didn't deserve her. He continued his notes and wrote three simple words. *Too much passion.*

"You there, Pike?"

"I'm here," Ryan said flatly.

"It's a good thing. This merge. Remember that."

"Sure, boss. I'll be ready," he lied. Ryan disconnected the call without saying goodbye. He chucked the phone across the room, watching it skid along the synthetic fiber carpet and slam against the wall.

Adrenaline pulsed through every fiber in his body. He needed to burn off some steam before he imploded. Shoving the chair out of his way, he grabbed his running shoes and slipped on a different pair of shorts. He checked the time. He had about an hour before he wanted to leave the ship. He needed to clear his mind to make room for some hard and fast decisions. His breathing evened as he formulated a plan. It was obvious what he had to do. What better place to do that than here and now?

He would regain Sophie's trust. Today. He had to explain himself before the merge leaked. Because if he didn't, he'd kill any chance he had with her. Hurting her was not an option. If he let this play out without giving her a heads up, he'd for damn sure hurt her.

He grabbed his phone and scrolled through the employee roster. He typed Donovan's number.

Donovan answered on the first ring.

"Donovan, it's Ryan. I need a favor. Call it a professional courtesy."

Chapter 24

An hour after the training, Sophie and Amy hovered over Sophie's cell phone in the ship's main atrium Googling the crap out of rats. The service in her cabin was terrible so they brought the conversation here.

Sophie wanted off this ship. Rats in the café was the ten-thousand-pound straw that broke the camel's back. As soon as she got the rats under control, she would find a way to leave. Meanwhile Google was all she had.

To make it worse, Donovan was acting like a spaz. He kept wringing his hands like a father about to marry off his only daughter to the crown prince.

His panic put Sophie on edge. "Donovan," she spat. "Man up. It's just rats. And from how Charlie described them, they sound domesticated." She knew Donovan could handle anything except spiders and rats. So his response shouldn't have surprised her, yet he stuck around torturing himself. Torturing her.

"Bleck. So gross."

"Either leave or stop pacing," Sophie said over her shoulder. "I have this under control." *God bless Google.*

Donovan pishawed. "Don't be silly. I mean rats. It's rats." He wrung his hands again. "We have to save the girls."

Sophie rolled her eyes. Men. Even gay men. It was a wonder they ever learned to make fire without a woman at the helm. Of course, Donovan could easily make a love seat and ottoman out of a rock and fig leaves so when the women figured out fire, he'd have a place to roast marshmallows. "Okay, Charlie, you still there?"

"I'm here and I have the peanut butter."

"Okay, good. Place a heaping spoonful inside the trap."

"Done."

Donovan squirmed. "Don't get too close, Charlie. They carry rabies."

"Donovan," Sophie chided. "Simmer. She's fine."

"I'm just cautioning her. They're intelligent creatures that scamper. Charlie, do you have a blow torch?"

"Okay, enough with you." Sophie pushed his head away from the phone.

Amy scrolled through the instructions on her phone and showed Sophie the next step.

Sophie continued to read. "Now turn off the lights and leave the room. Our homemade trap should work. How many did you see?"

"I can't be sure. Maybe two or three. They scurried when I flipped on the lights earlier."

"See, they scamper," Donovan interjected.

Sophie slid him the side-eye.

Amy took Donovan by the arm and led him to a couch across from them. "Chill. In fact, why don't you take off? Go find a bar."

"I can't," Donovan said.

"Why not?" Amy said.

"Because I'm supposed to wait here."

Sophie looked up from her phone. "Wait for what? Are you meeting someone? Did you meet a guy?"

"No," Donovan said, crossing one leg over the other. "You didn't hear it from me, but I'm supposed to babysit you until your prince arrives."

Sophie stiffened. *Wait? What?* "Charlie." She returned her attention to the phone. "You okay now?"

"Yes, I have four plastic tubs with peanut butter under each one. They will collapse when the rats go for the bait."

"I still say call an exterminator," Donovan said.

"Exterminators lead to paperwork and health departments, which lead to expenses we don't have. Plus, we've never had rats. Never had more than the occasional ant. If this doesn't work, we'll call someone, okay?"

Donovan rolled his eyes.

"Good." Sophie subconsciously pat herself on the back. "Charlie, after you catch them, don't touch them. I have an old friend coming to dispose of them. His name is Bob Jamison."

"Aw," Charlie squeaked. "Don't kill them. They don't seem mean."

"Well, they don't get to stay. I'll be sure to tell Bob to take them to a rat sanctuary where they will get proper care and housing."

"Really?"

"No. Now turn off the lights and wait outside until he gets there."

"Whatever. I gotta run. Deidra's eating all the peanut butter."

Sophie dropped her phone in her lap and glared at Donovan. "What's this *prince* business?"

Donovan looked at her and feigned zipping his lips closed.

"Talk."

"My lips are sealed."

"Your lips are about to bleed if you don't talk," Amy threatened.

"Don't get your panties in a bunch, Hair. I had a great conversation with my man Ryan this morning, and you will wait for him because I still believe in the magic of true love."

Sophie threw her head back. One crisis at a time. She didn't have it in her to deal with rats and Ryan. The parallel of the two shocked her. Both were cute, intelligent species. But both had terrible timing—and showed up in the wrong place at the wrong time. She could dispose of the rats with peanut butter, but Ryan was another story. As much as she longed for him to make her heart flutter, she couldn't do this to herself. It logically didn't make sense.

"Ooh, Ryan." Amy's eyes lit. "Okay, I'm switching to team Donovan. Sorry, Soph. We'll strong arm you to keep you here."

Sophie narrowed her eyes at Amy before shooting darts at Donovan. "What do you mean I will wait for him?"

"You're not getting anything else from me. You didn't listen to me about Asher, so you owe me this. Just wait here."

Sophie's insides stood at attention. How very chauvinistic of him. Ryan had sent Donovan to wait with her? Why? So she didn't escape? How far could she get? She was on a ship!

As if rats and Ryan didn't produce enough turmoil for the morning, Terri and Lori walked up. Terri was dressed in something Sophie was certain would qualify as a nighty, and Lori was dressed in half that.

"Good morning, my fabulous coworkers. How is everyone?" Lori chirped.

Amy shot Sophie a careful look. Sophie rolled her eyes, but since the girls addressed her specifically, she wouldn't give them the satisfaction of a cold shoulder. "We're good. And you?"

Terri fluttered her lashes. "Ah-mazing."

Sophie turned her back to them. "That's nice. Have a nice day."

"Don't you want to know about our night?"

"Not really," Amy said. "We're busy working. You should try it," she said on a smirk.

Donovan, forever the gentleman, chimed in. "What can we do for you ladies?"

Lori was the first to throw fuel on the fire. "I just wanted to ask if Sophie and Ryan were a thing."

Sophie tsked and then looked up. She wanted to give Lori the stink-eye, but settled on a snarl. "No. That's in the past, not that it's any of your business."

"No, it's not," Terri added, "but we wanted to check because we are all on the same feminist team, even you, Donovan."

"Um, thanks?" he said with a raised brow.

"We don't want to go after a man spoken for. We're not Trixie," she said, kicking some salt on an old wound. "But if you're saying there's nothing between you . . . well then . . ." Terri slid Lori a vexatious glare.

Heat swelled in Sophie's chest. She wanted to set a few rabid rats loose in someone's cabin right about now. Instead, she forced a smile. After what Asher had said about last night, what if his lying mouth had a hint of truth attached? It wouldn't be the first time Ryan couldn't wait for her during a crises and decided to look elsewhere. "Whatever. We're not together. He's leaving in a few days anyway, so why bother."

"That's exactly why we bother," Lori exclaimed.

Donovan stood. "Hush, child," he said to Sophie. "As for you two. Trust me when I say Ryan is not a good match for you. He's looking for a different sort of relationship."

Terri giggled. "Not after last night."

Sophie shot the girls a *death by eye gouging* glare while a sinking feeling pooled in the pit of her stomach. Why did it bother her so much? It didn't matter what Ryan did. She'd pushed him away last night. He had every right to do as he pleased. But still, a part of her wanted him to do as he pleased with her. Not a couple floozies from Parties R Us.

The masochist in Sophie wanted—or rather needed—to know. "What exactly does that mean?"

The girls shared an annoying laugh.

"We don't kiss and tell," Lori said.

This time Amy's face turned the color of rage. "So you made out with Ryan last night?"

"Well," Terri said, "not exactly."

"But you kissed him?"

Lori bristled. "I already said we don't kiss and tell. I'm just saying things may have happened."

Donovan shrugged. "What things?"

"None of your business. We have to go."

They strutted off and Donovan turned to Sophie. "I stand corrected. Rats don't scamper, *they* scamper. Don't listen to them, Sophie. Nothing happened between them and Ryan except for what they conjured up in their heads."

It didn't matter, Sophie decided. She had to leave. She couldn't focus here any longer. Everything with the café and the magazine had her mind constantly occupied. Add in Ryan, and her entire body was one confused, wrecked nerve.

She could scream all day that she didn't care what the gossip girls were up to, but even the fact Ryan gave them the time of day was suggestive.

And therein lay the problem. She did care. The idea of Ryan with someone else, especially someone like Tweedledee and Tweedledimwit, took her to a dark place. And what she needed was a two-thousand-watt bulb lighting her path out of her dark cave.

She doubted he kissed either one of them, but why would he hang out with them? Ryan had been on his way to his room when he ran into her, so why did he go back to the bar?

These were all questions she didn't have the time or the heart to invest in. She needed to get home. That was her goal. But if she were honest with herself, rats gnawing on the girls' ankles were no longer a threat, the café would still be standing in two days when they returned, and on the off chance one of the girls had a setback, the number to the emergency therapist was in her office. So, technically, all disasters averted.

Ryan was an impending disaster she couldn't avert. Not here, at least. He was too much of a trigger and a loose cannon. He'd been incredibly sweet last night, and maybe that's where she needed to leave it. It was closure of sorts. He'd told her about things from his childhood. It made sense. He was a broken kid, and broken kids do stupid things. As for now, she couldn't risk falling for him again, just to have it blow up in her face. Whatever he and Donovan were planning, she would squash right now. Before her stomach contents threatened to make an encore appearance. Which is why she needed to go home. Immediately.

Sophie hugged Donovan. "You're the best, but I need to go."

Donovan cocked his head. "Like go back to your room? Or go home, go?"

She smiled sadly. "Home."

Donovan sighed. "Those girls are dumb. You know this, Sophie."

Her chest tightened. Yes, she knew this. But she didn't care. There was a twelve-thirty flight home. She wanted to be on it.

Amy shook her head. "I think leaving now would be a huge mistake. It's only two more days. And I promise if any other catastrophes arise short of California breaking off the continent, we can handle it from here." Amy's voice of reason was beginning to rub her raw.

"I already have someone looking into getting me off this ship. I should get back to the café. The whole place is falling apart and now that I've bowed out of the scavenger hunt I need to get back and figure out what I'm going to do about the rent hike. I can't think here."

"Because two more days on this ship will make or break it?" Amy questioned. "We've done everything we can. We filled out every grant known to man, we contacted all our sources, we even put some items up for sale. We just have to wait and see what happens. You can wait here where you at least can be distracted with work and a little eye-candy, or you can go back and pace the floor while driving the girls nuts."

Sophie bit her lip. She still hadn't told Amy or Donovan about her little regression into the deep, dark place that she needed to stay far, far away from. "Because two more days on this ship may break my heart if I have to look at Ryan and not do anything about it."

"Oh, Sophie," Amy sighed.

Donovan pressed his hands to his hips. "Sophie, I love ya, girl, but you are making a momentous mistake." He wrapped Sophie in a bear hug. "A guy like that comes around only once in a lifetime. Trust me. I know."

Sophie stepped back. Guilt played desperately at her heartstrings. Ryan had been nothing but nice to her. But that was his Achilles tendon. He was *nice* to everyone. And she couldn't have that. Not with the girls, and the café, and the gigantuous fact that they lived in two very different worlds. They didn't fit together anymore. Better to leave now.

"What do I tell Ryan?" Donovan asked, holding his phone out.

Blood rushed to Sophie's head. She snatched Donovan's cell and powered it off. "You don't say anything. Either of you." Sophie directed her attention to Amy. "Tell him you lost me. Do this for me, okay?"

Both Amy and Donovan nodded, though Donovan looked as if he'd been personally rejected, which ate at Sophie's conscience. "Look. I can't do this again. I've been down this very same road. Don't potentially put me through that again. Because if this doesn't end well, I'll never recover."

"I tried to tell him to leave you alone," Donovan whispered. "But true love doesn't listen to reason. Okay, you have my word."

Amy's phone buzzed. "Sorry," she mouthed. "It's Mark. I have to take this."

"Okay, bye," Sophie mouthed back. And gladly. One less distraction.

"Call me if you leave," Amy said.

"Will do." She smiled as Amy took off toward the elevators. Then she turned her full attention on Donovan. "I'll call you too, okay?"

"Be careful, sweetie," he said, leaning in to kiss her cheek. "Just be careful. I'm here if you need."

Sophie offered him a reassuring smile, feeling anything but reassured. Her insides twisted with gut-wrenching doubt. Should she leave? *Yes*. Her girls needed her. Right? Charlie was at the helm running everything as if Sophie was no longer needed. She shook her head. Of course, they needed her. Or, Sophie swallowed dryly, was it she who needed them?

Chapter 25

Sophie tapped her fingers impatiently along the ocean-blue marble countertop of the concierge desk. The gum-snapping, ponytail-wearing dingbat Natalia typed away on her *state of the art but absolutely no help* computer. "How are there no available flights? I thought you said there was a twelve-thirty."

Moments after Amy took Mark's call and Donovan headed to his room, Sophie wished they were here to help strangle this woman.

"Nope, sorry, hun, nothing's open."

Hun was used in one of two scenarios: A. When someone was talking to a child, or B. When a child-like twenty-two-year-old was trying to sound like a grownup.

"Let me keep checking," she said, clicking away.

Blood vessels in Sophie's head threatened an aneurism. She tapped her fingers on the counter to Strauss's "Blue Danube," then Beethoven's "Für Elise"—at least the first sixteen counts that she remembered—and then, before she lost her good-girl Catholic upbringing, the Jeopardy theme song. "It's Catalina. We're a stone's throw from California. If not the twelve-thirty, surely one seat is open to one of the five surrounding Bay Area airports in the next few hours."

Natalie popped her gum. "Ah, here's the problem. Nothing's open. The airport grounded all flights because of a cargo fire."

"A what?" Sophie threw her hands in the air. "Are you kidding me?"

Natalia jumped. "Nope, lookie here." Natalia pointed to the flat screen monitor as if Sophie had summoned x-ray vision.

"No flights in or out of Catalina until the situation is contained. Expected to reopen by 3 p.m."

"What about a boat?" Sophie said from behind clenched teeth. "It's an emergency." Not exactly an emergency, but the particulars were of little significance. The tightness in her chest squeezed. Even though the emergencies had been diverted, and she may not be as needed at the café as she thought, the idea of staying another day on this ship was not an option. She just wanted to get home. Her heart and sanity begged this of her.

"Mmm, sorry, hun."

Say "hun" one more time . . .

"We don't book boat rides back to the mainland. But I'm sure you can find a private party on the Island that will take you. It's about an hour to Long Beach and then you can find a flight there to take you back to Frisco. But before you debark, we have to sign you out and contact customs."

"Customs?" Sophie pinched the bridge of her nose hoping to relieve a budding headache.

"We *were* just in another country, you know. Protocol and all."

"Forget it. I'll figure something out."

Natalia busied herself with some stacks of paper. Apparently, Sophie had been dismissed. "Will there be anything else, hun?"

Before Sophie could finally lose her religion and slap the "hun" out of Nattie's vocabulary, the girl's half-assed attention suddenly came alive. Her eyes grew as big as the ship's fancy dinner plates and she fell onto the countertop, swooning. A grape flavored puff blew out of her mouth. *Gross.*

Sophie followed Natalia's gape to Ryan as he entered the atrium. Sweat made him sparkle like a vampire. His shirt hung over his left shoulder, revealing his broad chest. *Good God, Father Time was way too good to him.*

"Oh, my!" Natalia said and snapped her gum. "His muscles should require a permit."

Donovan is going to die a slow, painful death. The traitor. Even still, Sophie looked a little longer than she liked. "Well, I've seen better," she said to Natalia for no reason other than to squelch the bit of jealousy of another girl looking at Ryan. *No you haven't,* her logical half argued.

Sophie sighed. *Time to go.* She backed away from the counter, searching for cover.

"Sophie," Ryan called, just as she ducked behind a shelf of excursion brochures.

"You know him?" Natalia said a little too loudly. "What's his name? Can you get me his number?" The grape-tinted drool foaming at Natalia's mouth appeared a little rabid.

Sophie gawked at Ryan's broad chest, which was as carefully chiseled as Michelangelo's sculpture of *David*. She gulped and forced her eyes north. She then pictured him with Terri and Lori. Her gulp caught in her throat.

Ryan slipped his shirt back on—pity—and approached her. The shirt clung to his body like a glove and his hair dripped with beads of sweat that sent a tingle in the pit of her stomach. How was it possible for someone to perspire so much, yet smell so fabulous?

She needed to escape. She couldn't talk to him. What would she say? *Sorry you almost kissed me last night because I'm sure whatever you did with the gossip twins was much better. Also, you're so gorgeous I can't think clearly around you. Oh, and by the way, remember the café I live and breathe for? Yeah, it has rats.*

Shut up! Sophie told her less-than-logical half.

"Rats?" Natalie said.

"What rats?" Sophie spluttered.

Ryan crossed his arms exposing his too perfect biceps. "You said rats."

Oh. My. Ficus. "No, I didn't."

"Whatever." Natalia turned her full bubblegum attention on Ryan and extended her hand "I'm Natalia, but you can call me Nattie."

A piece of paper was exchanged from her hand into his. Sophie frowned. "Did you just slip him your number?"

"What do you care?" Natalia shrugged. "You said you've seen better."

"Better, huh?" Ryan slipped the paper into his pocket and his lips curved with an unfair advantage.

His morning stubble upped his "yummy" appeal about four hundred percent. She didn't notice that this morning. And really, she didn't want to notice that now. Not with her mind reminding her how he played spin the bottle last night. She didn't kiss him, so he went looking elsewhere.

"Did you need something?" Sophie asked, fighting her blush. *Why did he have to be so charming? So nice?*

"Oh, right." Ryan cleared his throat. He directed Sophie away from Natalia. "You okay? You seemed awfully distracted this morning during our meeting. Then you disappeared."

Sophie raised her eyebrows. Her stomach clenched tightly, and she almost couldn't summon the words. "Something came up. But I'm taking care of it." She needed to get out of there. Let Natalia have him. She'd played with fire and had been burned. It was best just to leave now. She'd find her own way off the island.

"Thanks for the stargazing last night." Sophie's mouth twisted into a carefully censored smile—she could play nice too—and she stepped past Ryan to catch the elevator. "Bye."

"Wait."

Slowly, she turned. "What?"

Ryan frowned. "I thought we could go see my friend on the island."

Right, he'd asked her to go with him. "I'm sorry, I can't."

"Why not?"

There was no way he could be that dumb. And though every bit of common sense urged her to leave, she had to play this out. "What? You almost kiss me in the observatory, don't close the deal, so you turn to the gossip girls instead, and think we can just pick up where we left off?"

"The who?"

Ugh! The shock on his face gave her pause. But she plowed on, forgetting to filter her thoughts before her mouth got the "dumb". "You broke my heart once, Ryan, I can't let you do it again." She clamped her mouth shut. *Shut up, Sophie!* God, she was a liar, because even though she tried to guard her heart, it was pretty much exposed for all eight hundred and fifty-five passengers to see.

Ryan's eyes pleaded, filled with unsaid words. Maybe she was off base? Had interpreted it wrong. "I broke *your* heart?"

"It doesn't matter."

"Yes it does."

"But it doesn't. I'm truly sorry for my part in all of this. I think once upon a time, you found a scared little girl who ate too much and needed a little attention. But then when things got hard, you left."

There. She said it. Word vomit was just as vile as the real thing. Nothing felt good right now. If he were wise, he'd turn around and leave. Like he did before, because as soon as things had gotten hard the first time, Ryan left her for a job and then used it to hurt her.

Yet he stood unmoved, and though his brows furrowed and his eyes searched hers, she knew her words were the truth.

Ryan stared at her, his mouth agape. He was all sexy and chiseled and nice. So damn nice, and she didn't know why. But she couldn't let herself fall for that. Not again.

Sophie planted her hands on her hips. His move. If the first words out of his mouth weren't "I'm sorry" then she'd know for certain he was still as self-centered and playboy as he was when he wrote *that article* for all the world to see.

"Sophie," he said, stepping closer. "I'm so sorry."

Well damn. "What for? For ten years ago, or for showing me my star last night and making me fall for you again?"

A smile played on his lips. Why couldn't she ever stop while she's ahead?

"Falling for me?"

"Not after I learned about you and Terri and Lori."

"Who?"

"You know who. The girls who fawned all over you and you couldn't resist?"

"You mean the ones who invited me to their after party, to which I vehemently declined. And then I found myself sleeping on the Lido Deck so they wouldn't get the wrong idea and follow me to my room."

This time Sophie stood with her mouth dropped. "Oh."

Ryan's eyes widened, but he didn't release her hands. "Yeah. *Oh* is right. What did you think I did? Throw myself at you, and then when you turned me down, you think I ran to them?"

Well, when you put it that way. His words unfairly hooked her in.

"Sophie, you have to trust me."

She wanted to shrink into oblivion. "But you were so nice. They thought it meant something different."

"That's too bad, but I never gave them any sort of inclination I was interested. And of course I was nice. I'm always nice. Try growing up with someone who is angry all the time. It's not fun. So, I'm nice. Is that so wrong?"

A cinderblock dumped onto Sophie's chest, and she wanted to wither away. She didn't turn him down last night. She just didn't know if that's what she wanted. And what about when they were dating. He wasn't so nice then.

Sophie gave him a careful look. His knowing eyes seemed to take her in as if letting her absorb his words. Absorb him. His steady breathing comforted her. Suddenly going home didn't seem so urgent.

"Ohh," Natalia swooned, elbows on the countertop, head leaning into her hands. "You can't leave the island after a man says something like that!"

Ryan frowned. "You're leaving?"

"No. I . . . I was . . . Yes, I have to go," Sophie said, almost in a squeak. "I have a small rodent problem at the café and then what if one of the girls need me?"

"Charlie's there, right?"

"Yes."

"And Tanya?"

"Yes, but she's pretty useless."

"But she's there?" Ryan took Sophie's hand. He squeezed. "Right?"

"I guess."

"Then let them handle it. I'm sure they are fine. But if not, they know how to get help."

"I—"

"Why don't you come with me today? Get your mind off things. I really want you to meet a friend of mine." He caressed the soft skin between her thumb and forefinger.

"I don't know if that's a good idea."

"Trust me, Sapphire. Stop worrying. I promise to bring you back by curfew and if there are any further concerns with the girls, we will come straight back and I will personally find a way off this ship. Even if I have to highjack a lifeboat and row all the way." He cupped her chin in his fingers. "Okay?"

"That's so sweet!" Natalia chirped.

Ryan returned a polite smile, but gripped Sophie's elbow and moved several feet away.

"Call me," Natalia said, grinning like the Cheshire cat.

"Isn't there some rule against the staff hitting on the guests?"

Ryan smirked. "You're not jealous, are you?"

"You're not keeping her number, are you?"

Ryan laughed and dug the paper from his pocket. He glanced at Natalia, who was busy with another guest, and dumped it in the potted ficus next to them.

Sophie couldn't keep the sides of her lips from curving upward or the heat in her core from swelling. She only wished she could take back her earlier words. How could she have been so far off base? He cared about the girls. About their concerns. And that very likely meant he'd care just as much about keeping the café for them. The sincerity in his voice suddenly jump-started her vision of her future. *Yes, you can father my children.*

"Do you trust me?"

Sophie swallowed. He traced his fingers up her arms in a zigzag pattern until they found her hair. He threaded his fingers through, interlacing them together behind her neck. He gently brought her face to his, and she could taste his breath with each word he enunciated. She shuttered. Of course, she *wanted* to trust him. But could she?

"Come with me." He kissed her forehead then her nose and then the side of her lips. "I promise you'll have fun." He slowly drew his fingers from her neck and cupped her cheeks in his hands, luring her in so close she could see her reflection through his deep-set cerulean eyes.

"Ryan," she started, but hesitated. And when she put her hands on his chest she surprised herself when she gripped the fabric rather than pushed. His warm breath released a hint of mint and sweetness and his eyes locked on hers.

"Shhh." He claimed her lips with his.

She heard herself moan. It wasn't a leg-lifting sort of kiss, but rather more of the leg-buckling, fall into a coma kind.

He adjusted his grip to hold a lock of her hair, and she felt his other hand skim down her back until it settled just above her hip. He firmed his grasp, drawing her against him, his body as strong as an iron anchor. He pushed deeper into the kiss and her mouth opened under his, giving as much as she took. He tasted sweet and savory. A fully satisfying rush.

The kiss was as persuasive as it was convicting. Her lips tingled as they separated and Sophie could feel the heat from his breath as it quickened her own. Her heart thumped erratically, and a delightful shiver of want ran through her. When he broke the kiss, he pressed his soft lips against the side of her mouth once. And then again.

Her breath quivered and she couldn't tell where her bubble ended and his started. They were in a searing bubble together. His kiss wrapped her whole body in a warm hug she desperately needed. He kissed her until she thought she could see her star through his eyes. Until she trusted him again.

She broke for air, remembering how all this started. "So, nothing happened with those girls last night?" she said with a tantalizing tone.

He softly pulled her away just enough so their noses brushed together. Sophie's insides tingled beneath the feel of his warm breath. "No," he said.

He pressed his lips into hers, but she kept her hands against his chest, staving him off. She believed him. And yet, she wanted him to tell her again. "You're sure?"

"I'm not that guy, Sophie. It's been a long time since that guy was around."

"I know." The pit of her stomach whirled. But in the best sort of way.

His eyes remained locked on to hers, the desire for another kiss swirling between them.

"Let's go to the island."

Sophie nodded. "And no other girls, right?"

Ryan grinned. "Trust me. I don't frolic with girls when there is a woman to be serious with."

Chapter 26

Thirty-eight minutes after Ryan's kiss deprived Sophie of enough oxygen to set her back a few nonessential brain cells, she waited impatiently for him at the debarking bridge. He needed a quick shower after his run, though Sophie tried to convince him it was not necessary. For some reason, he didn't share her opinion of how incredibly delicious his perspiring body smelled.

Her phone buzzed. It was Charlie.

"Finally." She pressed the phone to her ear. "Charlie."

"Hey."

"What's the status on the vermin?"

"They're gone. Your friend is awesome."

Sophie sighed in relief. "Good."

"But, Sophie, they were so cute. And really tame. Your guy thought they might be someone's pets. There was a little brown and cream colored one. Can I keep—"

"No!"

"But he was so cute."

"If it stays then you go."

Charlie sighed. "Fine."

"Good. You sure you're okay?"

"Yes. Stop worrying about us. Go have fun. Let loose a little. Get drunk or be irresponsible for once."

Charlie laughed and that sound sent a calmness through her. It untangled the knot in her stomach. "Okay. Sorry Tanya was such a tool. I'll kill her when I get back."

"No killing necessary. You don't do prison orange well, or so Donovan would say."

Sophie sighed and smiled. The smile was for Charlie; the sigh was because deep down, Sophie wasn't sure how she felt about Charlie handling the crisis without her there. It bugged her. And she didn't know why. "Okay, sweetie, you sound like you have it all under control. I'm still going to try and get home."

"Don't."

Sophie pulled her brows together. "Why not? I should be there. What if next time it's not rats in the café, but vipers, or massive, prowling tigers?"

Charlie's laugh burst through the phone. "Don't worry. If I see any snakes, I'll burn the place down."

"You wouldn't dare."

"Goodbye, Sophie. Go play in the sand and we'll keep the fire extinguishers on hand." Charlie paused. "Unless there's a viper. Then it's poof."

Charlie disconnected before Sophie could argue. She held the phone in front of her face and scowled. "Rude."

"What's rude?" Ryan's smooth voice came up behind her.

"Charlie." Sophie turned. Ryan was dressed in a button-down shirt and cargo shorts, looking every bit as yummy as a mouth-watering dessert. He had a dozen red roses in one hand and a brown paper bag with a bottle of scotch in the other. She recognized the red label on the bottle's neck as scotch. Sophie raised her eyebrows, her insides buzzing with excitement.

He stepped aside to give her a path toward the tender that would lead them to Catalina Island. "Are you ready?" Luckily there was no line so they could board right away.

Ryan's fresh shower smell coupled with his cologne kicked her heart into turbo speed. "I am."

He wrapped an arm around her waist and guided her toward tender.

Sophie eyed his other hand and raised a brow.

He must have read her expression because he said, "Actually, these aren't for you."

"Oh," she said, almost disappointed. But then again, scotch wasn't her thing and roses hinted at assumptions she wasn't ready to have assumed.

"Don't worry. I peg you for more of a wine girl." He gave her his crooked smile, making her lightheaded. At this rate, she'd need a pacemaker to get through the remainder of the cruise. "I'll explain later," he said.

Sophie nodded.

"Be back by six-thirty p.m.," the crewmember reminded guests as they loaded the shuttle.

Ryan took Sophie's hand. His palm was warm and strong. She didn't need his help down the steps, but it felt nice to hold him. Ryan led her toward an open bench seat. "Did you get everything squared away with the—uh— uninvited guests?"

Sophie sat and Ryan slid in next to her, placing his flowers and scotch on his opposite side. He reached his arm around the back of the seat and Sophie allowed herself to fold into him. Her insides praised her with a friendly burst of excitement. "I did, thank you."

"That's good. What did you do?"

"What any other thirty-one-year-old girl would do. I Googled the crap out of the situation."

Ryan nodded. "Clever."

"Turns out little beady-eyed critters can't resist peanut butter."

"And what'd you do with the bodies?"

"Had them removed. Far, far away."

"That's too bad." Ryan mused.

Sophie scowled. "Filthy, disease-filled rodents spell horror for the food industry."

He smiled wryly. "I can promise you one thing." Ryan fixed a pair of sunglasses over his eyes. "Rats are awesome. You just don't have any boys to show you."

"Nope, nope, disgusting, and just nope."

"They're actually pretty smart."

"Maybe. Charlie said they seemed tame and actually wanted to keep one. That was vetoed real quick."

"You think they were placed?"

Sophie shook her head. "I think me being here and not there is a big mistake."

Ryan's brows creased. He teased the back of Sophie's hair and gently pulled her closer to him. "I hope it's not all that bad."

Sophie bit her lower lip and allowed herself to lean in. Her belly swirled as he threaded his fingers through her hair and found the nape of her neck. He gently caressed her skin with the pad of his thumb, making her body heat. Like a tropical waterfall, the thrill of his touch sent chills cascading down her back.

It took a second, but Sophie finally found her voice. "No, not so bad."

She turned her head into the wind. The salty air swept her hair into her face, whipping and stinging her cheeks like little pinpricks. She watched the waves approach the boat, then dive under it as they neared the dock where they would climb a narrow ramp to the island. Now that the rats were gone and the girls were okay, she could breathe. A cloud of financial doom loomed over the future of the café. But for the moment, while she was on this beautiful island with a man who made her heart beat out of her chest, she would relax.

Chapter 27

Ryan paid the driver, whose car was actually a golf cart, and waved goodbye.

"Where are we?" Sophie asked.

"This is a very special place to me."

"Okay." Sophie had a note of hesitation in her voice.

Ryan had purposely been slight on the details of their destination. He'd also been slight on mentioning his promotion. He knew that was something he needed to tell her. He owed her the truth, but that could wait until later today.

The cruise ship had its formal dinner tonight and Ryan hoped to tell her then.

Today was about visiting Tia and surprising Sophie with the farm. He wanted to let her experience the same awe he felt when he first visited. It had been years since he'd seen Tia, and though dropping in unannounced wasn't initially part of his plan, plans had change.

He tried to gauge Sophie's expression to get a feel for her thoughts. This part of the island was very different from the horseshoe shaped alcove, peppered with sailboats where they made port. The entire island was like a funnel with million-dollar homes stacked on top of each other on the outer edge and a forest of trees in the center.

Most of the roads were so narrow they only allowed one car at a time, but the route near the golf course and Wrigley's Memorial didn't make claustrophobic people nervous. Tia's small farm was just off the golf course's beaten path.

Not clear whether Sophie's silence was due to apprehension of her whereabouts or him, he took her hand and led her forward.

"How do you know the people here?" Sophie murmured, staring at the sturdy, 1930s Portuguese-style bungalow, sitting in the middle of farmland. "It's mesmerizing."

It had that effect on him, too, when he'd first seen it. "I lived here for a time. Played ball across the island at Joe Machado Field when it was first built."

Sadie's apprehension made sense. The farm was big enough to appear intimidating but small enough to seem out of place. The house was about thirteen shades of red and brown, with a wraparound porch straight from the *Gone with the Wind* era. Three ceiling fans hung beneath the overhang with wires poking out from every possible crevice. The tattered, wooden corral that he'd helped build had been replaced with a new white plastic one. The barn's original red paint had faded to rust orange. Dry-rot had settled in the barn's eaves, but other than that, it was the same.

"Are we expected?" She clung to Ryan's arm. He like that. He also liked how her sweet perfume lingered.

"No," he finally answered as a horse neighed in the distance. "But Tia's always home."

"Isn't it rude to drop in unannounced?"

"Don't worry," he said, brushing his arm against hers.

"How do you know this lady? Is she an old, um, acquaintance? I think most girls pass on scotch. You probably should have brought a sweet red if you wanted to impress."

Are we jealous now? "Oh, Tia's no lady," he assured.

"So, you're bringing flowers to a guy?"

Ryan snorted. "Not unless it's for his wake. But no, Tia is most definitely a woman, hence the name Tia."

"But you don't have any aunts."

He guffawed under his breath. "True. But you asked if she was a lady. Don't get caught calling her that." Ryan took

Sophie by the hand again. "No, Tia is like a mom to me. And she always treated me like her own."

Sophie stiffened at that comparison, and Ryan hoped he didn't dredge up any raw emotions. That was their one common deep-rooted pain. He squeezed her hand again, suddenly missing his mom. He stared at the barn he helped restore. "I used to spend the summers here with my family. And then after my mother passed away, my dad sent me here for the summers before I went away to college. Ryan grimaced. *More like my dad dumped me here after I officially became his greatest disappointment.*

Sophie bit her lip. "I'm sorry."

Ryan waved his hand. "I'm not. It's in the past, as they say, right?"

Sophie somberly stared at the barn. "Your past is part of who you are."

Ryan squeezed her fingers. "Don't get all philosophical on me."

Sophie stopped dead, tugging her hand out of his.

Ryan almost stumbled over her. "What's wrong?"

"I think you should have your reconnection moment without me. I'm just going to wait back here, okay?"

Her hesitance was not lost on him. He never considered she might be uncomfortable. He nodded. "Okay, I'll be just a minute." He kissed her knuckles and grinned. "You'll love Tia, I promise. She's a different sort of flavor. I'll be right back."

Ryan headed for the front porch. His thoughts lost in the memories he built while working the farm. Hauling hay, scooping manure, mastering tools, the nights spent reading sports almanacs and stargazing on the beach.

He was almost to the porch when he heard the faint sound of fast-approaching hooves clomping against the dusty earth. He whipped around to see Sophie gazing in another direction. "Sophie, look out!"

And no one, especially Ryan, could have predicted the sequence of events that followed. A loud bleating cry, the blur of a wire-haired creature, the blue, flannel pattern jumpsuit it wore. The goat, no bigger than a cocker spaniel, headed directly for Sophie.

Ryan dropped the roses and scotch. "Sophie!"

~ ~ ~

At the sound of her name, Sophie lurched back. Too late. She registered the pounding of hooves as way too close. She tried to run, but her sheer fright and forward motion had her tripping over her own feet, landing face first in the dirt before she had a chance to see what had jumped on her.

It nuzzled her neck, then nibbled on the collar of her shirt. "Ficus! Get it off, get it off!"

The thing leapt off her back and licked her face. Its coarse tongue exfoliated her forehead, then nibbled her scalp.

Sophie pushed up to her knees but the goat didn't see that as a deterrent.

Not. One. Bit.

It slid its slimy, and somewhat hairy, tongue across her forehead, ensuring it conquered its quest to lick every bit of dead skin off her face.

"Fligggh," she managed. It dipped its head from side to side, sliding that long tongue through the strands of hair that fell in front her face.

"Oh! For the love of all things . . ." Sophie finally found her bearings and flew to her feet where she had a hard time distinguishing the thing's godawful bleat from Ryan's laugh. "Are you seriously laughing at me?"

"Hey, hey. Shoo. Get away." Ryan's laugh echoed across the entire farm, and had Sophie not been dusting herself off and fixing her hair, she might have socked him.

Ryan bent down and held out his hand, still laughing.

Actually, it was more of a giggle. Very manly. "Come here, little goat."

Of course, the goat obliged by licking his palm. He pet it, then wrapped an arm around the belly of the creature, picked it up and held it against his broad chest.

"I'm going to beat you, Ryan," she warned between swipes.

Sophie lifted the front of her shirt to dab at the saliva on her cheeks. The combined texture of woodchips and dirt and possibly coffee grinds hung in her nose.

He didn't respond.

She stared up at him.

He gazed at her bare stomach.

"Are you for real? I have a brush with death, and you're gawking at me?"

Ryan met her *should I kill you now or later* stare. "No, not at all."

Sophie blew a strand of hair out of her face. The goat had settled into Ryan's arms. Its tiny flannel outfit was complemented with quarter-sized bows fastened to the top of its floppy ears. She hated how her legs quivered at their cuteness.

She relented and pet its diamond nose, earning a less forceful lick. "Other than almost scaring me to death, the thing is kind of cute. Points for being well dressed too."

"Dolly!" A sizable Samoan man, wearing only tweed pants, cargo boots, and billboard-worthy tattoos from the neck down hollered as he leapt over the fence in a single stride. He stopped within an inch of Ryan, tugging the goat from his arms. "What are you doing to my pygmy?"

Ryan relinquished the goat.

The goat offered the man a long-tongued kiss.

Sophie scrunched her nose. *Ugh, ick, blech.*

He set the goat down and she trotted away. He turned his

full pro-wrestler bulk on Ryan and stared him down. "Why you messing with a man's goat?"

Ryan raised his arms in defense. "Your goat jumped on my friend. I grabbed her off. That's it."

The man looked Sophie up and down. "She likes blondes." He turned back to Ryan. "Who the hell are you?"

Ryan narrowed his eyes.

Sophie didn't want Ryan getting pummeled. "You know what?" Sophie put her hand on Ryan's chest, feeling it flex. *Oh, she should feel his chest more often.* "I'm fine. Your goat is fine. We should just go."

The behemoth frowned. "You owe my goat an apology, dude."

Ryan recoiled. "An apology? For what? Your goat just assaulted my friend."

"Your friend is on her property."

Ryan's jaw tensed. "It's a goat. She doesn't have property."

"She is a pygmy goat. Her name is Dolly, and you scared her. I don't come to your house and torment your animals."

"Your house?" Ryan's face turn crimson. "I don't think so."

Are we at the wrong house? Sophie knew this could go bad real fast.

The snap like thunder made Sophie jump and instinctually duck behind Ryan's shoulder. Her gaze darted toward the sound.

"What's going on out here?"

On the front porch a corpulent woman towered, holding a bullwhip like Indiana Jones. Her stout frame commanded attention, and she strode down the porch stairs like a lion tamer about to break up a very menacing, testosterone-laden catfight.

"We have trespassers, Tia."

"Trespassers?" Ryan shot back. "Hardly. I practically lived here!"

"Ryan?" Tia glanced Sophie's way, then ran over and wrapped him in a bear hug. "*Mijo*, how are you? What are you doing here?"

"Hi, Tia," he said, kissing her cheek.

"You know this wanker?" the behemoth said.

"What did you call me?"

"Boys," Tia warned, pushing them in opposite directions. Her bullwhip curled neatly in the hand pressed against Ryan's chest. "Act like men. Ryan, this is my stable hand, Jamba. Jamba, this is my best friend's son, Ryan."

Ryan shifted his eyes to the empty corral, regret flitting through his eyes. "Your stable hand? Since when do you need help, Tia?"

"Since I got the sugars and can't run this place on my own."

Sophie knew *sugars* was slang for diabetes.

Ryan stared at her, and Sophie rested a hand on his shoulder. It was hard to hear when someone you loved was ill.

"Now tell me why you're here. I'm sure you didn't leave your big shot office in San Antonio to come all the way down to my neck of the woods to play with Jamba's goat."

Ryan shook his head, squinting at Jamba. "Yeah, what's up with that?"

"You have your sports and traveling, and Jamba has his . . . uh, Dolly." Tia's face softened. "Jamba's auntie and I play bridge every Sunday. He's not very good with conversations, or even with new people, as you can see, but boy can he tell you about goats and pretty much anything you would need to know about farming. He works here during the week."

"Damn right I do," Jamba said with child-like enthusiasm.

"Jamba, why don't you go check on Dolly and water the horses."

"Sure, Tia. Ryan." He dipped his head.

"Jamba." Ryan nodded back, his gaze softening.

Ryan reached for Sophie's hand. "Sorry about that. I didn't foresee a circus act today. You okay?" He swiped a stray hair from in front of her face.

Sophie parted her lips to say she was fine. But that little touch tied her tongue. To say that the goat gave her more excitement than she had had in pretty much forever would not have been an exaggeration. But she just smiled and nodded, while her knees quivered.

"All right, Sapphire. I want you to meet my dear friend." He kissed her forehead.

"So, is this the one?" Tia winked.

The one? Sophie kind of liked the sound of that.

"I'm Dolores Cardoza. But call me Tia. Nice to meet you, dear." Her smile widened across plump, copper cheeks. She had a thin gap between her front teeth and freckles dotted either side of her nose.

"Very nice to meet you. I'm Sophie Dougherty."

"A pleasure. Now let's get inside and you can tell me all about this beautiful lady."

~ ~ ~

"I come bearing gifts," Ryan said, pulling Sophie along.

"Firewater?"

"Gold Watch."

"Perfect, *mijo*. That's why you'll always be my favorite."

Tia took the scotch and stuffed it under her arm. "Thank you, *mijo*."

Sophie leaned into Ryan and whispered. "I like her."

He pressed his lips to her hair sending a shiver down her back. "Everyone does." Sophie could hear the smile in his words.

Tia opened the bungalow's door to a time warp. Circa 1969 to be exact. The far wall paid exceptional homage to the original Woodstock. Sophie would recognize these famous prints anywhere. Except they didn't appear to be mass-produced. There was no way she had original copies. *Was there?* Among other framed and autographed legends, epic stills of Janis Joplin, Santana, The Who, Keef Hartley Band, and—wipe the drool from her chin—Hendrix, quite possibly God's only forgotten son, dressed the wall.

In one print, Jimi Hendrix's arm was draped around a much younger, and quite smaller Tia. They were both laughing and posing with Hendrix's guitar in front of them. His signature across the sound board of the guitar was clear enough to read, even from the poor-quality picture.

"You met Jimi Hendrix?"

"Met him?" Tia scoffed, tossing the bullwhip onto a chair that appeared to be held up with past *Sports Now* magazines. "Ever hear of groupies?" she asked as she dawdled in the kitchen.

"Um, yeah," Sophie coyly answered, suddenly warm.

"Well, I wasn't one, in case that's what you're thinking." Tia cackled. "Got ya, didn't I?"

Sophie grinned. She most definitely liked this lady.

"Want some iced tea? Just put a fresh brewed pitcher over ice. No sugar, though. The doctor's added torture to my dietary plan. They told me to use sweetener. I told them where they could stick that sweetener." Tia banged around in the kitchen before returning to the living room where she set a wooden tray stacked with four tall, mismatched glasses and a pitcher of iced tea on an Elvis-topped coffee table—the 1960s version of the King.

"No, I was part of the cleanup crew at Woodstock. If you ever want to see a bigger group of slobs," she said, pointing to the wall, "well, I tell ya. That was slob headquarters."

Tia poured a glass of tea and handed it to Sophie. "Hendrix and I . . . well, we had an understanding."

Sophie grinned behind her glass and glanced at Ryan who pursed his lips in a *don't ask me* way.

Tia sat. Her worn leather chair donned strips of duct tape holding the seams together and piles of old magazines from *Red Book* to *National Geographic* stacked neatly in rows next to it. "The fascinating part was after he played his last set, he approached me! Oh, talk about a girl and her dream come true. He handed me one of his autographed guitars—that one there," she said, pointing to the picture—"in exchange for going out on a date with one of his roadies, Edwin, my future husband."

"Oh. Wow. That's not something you hear every day."

"Yeah." Tia handed Ryan his tea and poured herself a glass. "That boy tried talking to me for two days and I wouldn't give him the time of day. Come to find out, he worked as a traveling stagehand for the legend. And *handle* me well, Edwin did. That was back when love and romance meant something. It was a fantastic Age of the Aquarius movement. Now people type in something on their fancy iHookup device and *bam*, iRomance. No offense to the tech world, *mijo*."

"None taken."

"It's also where I met Ryan's mom." Tia winked at Ryan and smiled. "I sure do miss Mary."

Ryan's smile faltered, and Sophie had the urge to wrap her arms around him. "Me, too."

"But, I don't suppose you came all this way to reminiscence about my hippy days when I was a twig . . . and smoking them. What brings you to my island? Unannounced, I might add. Not that I'm not happy to see you. But you dying or getting married or something?"

Ryan choked on his tea.

"Or not." Tia handed him a napkin.

Just then, the front door swung open and Jamba clomped in, Dolly wrapped around his neck like a scarf. She wore a shimmery pink ballerina costume with layered tulle at the bottom.

"You changed her clothes?" Ryan asked.

"And?"

Sophie and Ryan shared a *well okay then* look. She was never one to play dress up even with Barbie or paper dolls. So the idea of playing dress up with a goat never crossed her mind. Ever.

"Um, never mind," Ryan said.

"Tia." Jamba unwrapped Dolly and started rocking her in his arms. "Looks like rain. I'm going to throw tarps over the hay and shovel a moat around the barn so the rain don't flood Joplin's stall. Can you watch Dolly so she doesn't go swimming in the lake again? I just bathed her."

"Sure, honey. Thank you."

Jamba put Dolly down and clipped a pink, diamond-studded leash to her outfit before giving her to Tia.

"Are those real?" Sophie gawked at the goat's bling.

Jamba jerked his head in Sophie's direction. "Don't be ludicrous. Who would get their pet diamonds?"

Sophie smothered a smile.

He turned back to Tia. "After I'm done, I'm going to head to town."

Jamba clunked out the door.

"He seems great," Sophie said.

Tia scratched Dolly between her nubs, and the sparkling goat turned in a few circles before lying down at Tia's feet. "He's pretty handy to have around. I just love him to pieces and he takes great care of my horses. The world isn't easy on him. So I'm glad he has a place here."

"That's wonderful, Tia." Sophie smiled warmly.

"So, Ryan," Tia redirected, "to what do I owe this visit?"

"Actually, this is a legit case of we just happened to be in town."

"But you're not dying?"

"No."

"Not eloping?"

This time Sophie choked on her tea. "No, most certainly not."

Ryan's Caribbean eyes challenged her claim. "Would it be that bad?"

Sophie suddenly visualized herself signing her name Sophia Pike. *Whoa.* "Absolutely," she said on a hard laugh.

"How do you know Ryan?" Tia asked, squeezing lemon into her tea.

Sophie snapped her eyes back to Tia. "We, ah, we work under the same organization," Sophie said. "He's with *Sports Now*, as you know, and I'm a columnist for a smaller magazine called *Up Front*."

"We also dated ten years ago and she's starting to fall for my rugged good looks again."

"Ryan!" Sophie elbowed his ribs.

"What?" He did his sultry half-smile thing.

"You two are going to make beautiful babies."

"Tia!" Sophie scoffed, but couldn't help the tinge of hope brewing deep in her stomach. Maybe one day. The rogue thought caught her off guard. "I also coordinate a non-profit café for girls with eating disorders. Mainly bulimia."

"Oh, that's insightful. Is that something you have a personal connection to?"

"Um, w-well," Sophie stuttered, then laughed nervously.

Ryan took her hand and intertwined his fingers with hers, calming her nerves but threatening to explode her heart.

"I just do what I can."

"And how is that going?"

Sophie squeezed Ryan's hand, not sure how to answer. "Well, it's had a bit of a financial . . ." Sophie paused, thinking the right word was "death" but went with the safer word, "setback. But we'll be okay."

"I'm sure you will." Her eyes skipped to Ryan. "How's your dad?"

This time, Ryan's fingers squeezed hers before they released altogether. He crossed his arms over his chest and squirmed. "Honestly, he's been trying to call me, but I haven't had the time to call back."

"You haven't had the time, or you haven't made the time?"

Tia did not beat around the bush, Sophie realized.

Ryan's face didn't crack. He held Tia's gaze, and only the slighted twinge in eyes told Sophie that he didn't appreciate the accusation. "It's not that simple, Tia,"

"Honey, I never said it was. But he's your dad."

"Right. And still in Paris with Nicole. Hasn't picked up a phone in years and now he's calling? I don't really care."

"The phone works both ways, sweets."

"Got it," Ryan said through gritted teeth. He cleared his throat and stared at Elvis.

"He'll come around. He just needs time to adjust."

Sophie tried to make herself disappear into the couch, not wanting to intrude on their conversation.

"He's been there for twelve years. I doubt it's an adjustment and more like an avoidance."

"Well, we all wear our grief differently." Tia filled his cup with more tea.

Ryan cleared his throat again and moved to the edge of the couch to grab his tea. Sophie heard a familiar pain in his voice. "He wears his as far away from me as he can."

"Now, now. Give him time."

"He can have it." Ryan looked at Sophie, his hard eyes softening. "You still want to go horseback riding?"

"I thought it was going to rain."

"Rain won't come for a few hours yet," Tia chimed in. "Take Joplin and Santana. They're my tame mares. Steer clear of Hendrix. He's sniffing the wind, if you know what I mean."

"You don't mind, Tia? I don't want to bail right after we got here, but I'd love to show Sophie the area."

"Go on. You're interrupting my *Days of our Lives*. I have an old pair of chaps in the barn that should fit you, Sophie. You'll want those. And by old . . . I mean I outgrew them before you were even born."

Sophie laughed. "Okay. Thanks."

They headed for the front door.

"Hey, Tia." Sophie stopped in front of the door. "What happened to the guitar Hendrix gave you?"

Tia swung her finger in a large horizontal circle. "You think we could have afforded all this on a technician's salary?"

"Well, it's a beautiful farm," Sophie said, looking at the shrine again. "I can tell it's well loved."

"Oh, sure. Just don't go digging up the ground. You may find a buried body or two." Her hoarse cackle startled Dolly. She sat up then shook her tail, which was caught in the tulle, and jumped in Tia's lap.

A vision of a baby, instead of a goat, slung across Tia's lap surged through Sophie's mind. Warmth swirled inside her. She blushed. Not that it would be *her* baby. Ryan hadn't even hinted at the *where this was going* conversation.

But the possibility of a baby with Ryan? And an extended family like Tia, who would tell stories about Ryan as a child. It all seemed within reach. Only it was within Ryan's reach, not hers. Sophie shook the thought. That's what fantasies were for: hopeful wishing stuffed deep within the boundaries of her mind.

"I told you she was great," Ryan whispered in her ear, sending a buzz down her back. He pushed the screen door open and they stepped out. "Thank you for coming with me." His big, fat, irresistible grin stretched across his face, and Sophie sighed. He was going back to San Antonio in a couple of days. Letting her heart roam wild and free with the possibility of *them* was asking for heartbreak. But for the moment, she let the fantasy win.

"Nowhere else I'd rather be." She tucked her hand in his and for the first time in God knew how long, felt at ease.

Her mind cleared, allowing her a thought she hadn't considered in four years: perhaps her café was not a lifeline for the girls, but a crutch holding them back. Holding her back—she squeezed Ryan's hand—from what she *really* wanted.

Chapter 28

Ryan held the barn door open for Sophie. It took a second for his eyes to adjust to the dim lighting, but everything inside was just how he remembered. Dust particles hovered in the air and the smell of manure and straw burned his nose.

There were eight stalls in all. Four on each side. The first one to the right housed the tack and the feed. The left side held his past. He turned purposefully to the right and peeked into the stall. Sure enough, as if time hadn't touched a thing, the halter and lead line for all the horses hung neatly against the wall next to the bridles. Four saddles sat atop saddle racks along back wall and years of blue, red, yellow, and white award ribbons adorned the far wall.

Sophie tucked her hands behind her back as if she were afraid to break something and slowly strolled down the center of the barn taking it all in. She barely made it to the first set of stalls before she stopped, homing in on that stall dedicated to his past.

Ryan stood at the threshold, not ready to cross that line. He watched her carefully circle around his delicate scope covered by a bulky canvas drape. Just how he'd left it.

She inched closer and carefully placed her hand on top. Dust specks erupted into the air and the sunrays made them sparkle like tiny diamonds.

"What's this?" she asked in an almost whisper.

"Regret."

"So, this is it. This is your telescope?"

He came up behind her and laid his hands over her arms. At his touch, her shiver pricked against his hands, and Ryan couldn't help but smile. "You want to see what's behind door number one?"

Her eyes widened if only slightly. "Only if you want to show me."

The tease in her voice quickened his already racing heart and he forced a dry swallow. *Okay then. Here goes nothing.* He slowly reached around her and removed the cloth from the full-sized, black, pristine, reflector telescope. Untouched by human hands for over a decade, it still maintained its wonder and mystery.

Sophie gasped in awe. "Ryan, it's beautiful."

"Thank you."

She spread her arms wide, gesturing around the room. "All this is yours? From your home?"

"Just a few items I didn't want Dad to sell before he moved to Paris. Tia's home is . . . well . . ." He found he couldn't say the words. Couldn't speak them. *Tia's home is my home.* So he shrugged again. "I rather my things stay here for now." And since I travel so much, I didn't dare leave these stashed in my spare bedroom. I only keep a few personal effects, as well as a few things my mom loved, here."

"In a barn rather than your home?"

Yeah, Ryan understood the paradox. "Tia's home is safer and well loved."

She quietly took in the rest of the items in the stall. A stack of *Astrology Times* magazines, a signed football jersey displayed in a glass case, a box of vintage toys. A dusty Pound Puppy hung over the box. Sophie picked him up and held him to her chest. "Yours?"

Ryan took the stuffed toy and shook it. Its droopy ears waggled. "I forgot about him. I begged my parents for a real one. I must've played with this guy until his stuffing nearly disintegrated. I did eventually get that real dog."

"I didn't know you had a dog."

A cold sweat percolated on his neck. "Yeah, his name was Jasper. My dad dumped him with a neighbor before he moved."

"Oh." Sophie's voice carried a sympathetic tone. One Ryan didn't want. She pet the Pound Puppy as if it were his real dog. "I'm sorry to hear that."

"Yeah. It sucked. Anyway . . ." Ryan carefully set the toy back in the box.

Sophie's eyes settled on something, making the corners of her lips tug upward. "Is this your mom?"

A framed picture of his mother and him from his eighth-grade graduation rested against an antique gold-plated mirror. He could see her reflection. Soft, pink cheeks, almond-shaped green eyes, gazing intently at the camera, and a look of longing that he couldn't quite place. "Yeah," he said.

Sophie smiled. "You were close to her."

Ryan pursed his lips and nodded. His throat tightened.

Sophie took a hand from his face and caressed it. "It's okay." She brought him the few short strides where several bales of hay stacked neatly against the side of the stall. She sat down and pulled him next to her. "What was she like?"

"Ha." Ryan's chest burned with memories. "Mom was something else. Whereas Dad worked for the astronomy institute, and had always hoped I would pursue, Mom loved my passion for sports."

"She sounded incredibly supportive."

Ryan half-heartedly smiled. "I think she was hyper competitive, so she understood what drew me. We had to stop playing Monopoly when I was twelve because she'd own all the good property while I inevitably sit in jail. Not once did she let me roll my way out. I always had to pay the fine."

Sophie laughed, dropping her head, and Ryan curled his fist under her chin. "Would you like to go riding with me?"

She nodded. Her lips were inches from his, and he could taste her sweet breath as if she were breathing life back into him. Then she pulled away, eyes darting as she took in the whole stable. "This place really is a diamond in the rough."

"You like it?"

"I do." The horse in the stall next to them whinnied, and Sophie jerked her head in the mare's direction. "Can I meet her?"

Ryan caressed her cheek. *Can I kiss you?* "Yes," he said instead. Stupid mare and her impeccably awful timing.

Sophie bit her bottom lip and stood, taking Ryan's hands and pulling him up with her. Outside of the stall, she grabbed a handful of grain from a mesh feed bag and clucked at the mare. The horse nickered before plotting over and stretched her neck through the iron bars, investigating. The plaque on the stall door read SANTANA. Sophie opened her palm under Santana's muzzle and she eagerly lapped up the grain. *Lucky horse.* Ryan stepped away to the tack stall. He grabbed a halter and lead line off the hook, and the chaps, which sat on top a western saddle.

Sophie turned around. "You know how to get the horses ready?"

His lips twisted. Partially because he wanted that kiss he'd started in his head and partially because he loved that she seemed impressed that he could saddle a horse. "Did this for years." Ryan leaned against the stall door and gazed at Sophie. She seemed so relaxed and happy. He wanted to offer her a lifetime of feeling this way.

"You're so lucky."

Ryan chuckled. "I didn't feel so lucky when I was a fourteen-year-old kid shoveling manure. That's purgatory for the male teen."

"Oh, yeah, I guess so."

"Have you ever ridden before?"

"No, never."

"Well, you're in for a treat. Nothing quite compares to riding a horse. In fact," Ryan said, handing her the brown, leather chaps, "yesterday you rode your first Ducati and today your first horse. I'd say this trip has been educational in many ways."

Sophie blushed, and that gave him smug satisfaction. She stared at the chaps, and he realized she had no idea how to put them on. "May I?"

"Um, yeah, thank you." She handed them back.

Ryan set down the halter and unsnapped the long line of buttons. Newer chaps had zippers, but these old, leather ones resembled chaps from a John Wayne movie. And Ryan wouldn't miss the opportunity to assist.

He took her leg and propped it up on his thigh. Her leg was smooth and her calf muscle flexed in his palm. He wrapped the chap around her leg, snapping the first button at her ankle and worked his way up to the top of her thigh. Then he repeated the same motion with the other leg.

There are two things a young man won't forget: The first time their father hands their ass to them from wrecking the family car while drag racing, which he'd won, and the first time they touch the woman they want to marry. Ryan's thoughts shifted to the night he made love to Sophie. Though years had separated them from that night, he still recalled exactly how her skin felt against his palm, and how it was no less perfect now than it was in the bed of his old Ford.

When he fastened the last snap, he stood, allowing his hands to trail the back of her body.

She pressed into him, and her breathing quivered.

"That's a good look for you."

"Yeah?" Her breath caught. She lightly pursed her lips together and set her hands over his biceps. "Thank you."

"My pleasure." Ryan skimmed his fingers all the way up her back until they reached her shoulders. He gently pulled her hair, tilting her face upward to meet his. Her velvety skin smelled like fresh air and juicy pears. He saw his future in her eyes.

She bit her lower lip.

Easy, Ryan. She's nervous.

Her nails dug into the back of his arms, and he inched her in closer until his lips brushed against hers. "You smell incredible."

Her lips parted just enough for his mouth to cover hers, and he pressed into its softness. She moved her hands to the back of his shirt and gripped.

He lifted her to her tiptoe and pushed her flat against the stall door, searching every part of her mouth. It was silky and giving, allowing him to navigate and rediscover a place he once knew so very well.

Her breath hitched, and she threaded her fingers into his hair, arching into him.

His passion rose to meet hers. If he didn't stop now, he'd be tempted to take her on the barn floor. Conjuring every ounce of self-control he had, he broke the kiss, drawing back and searching her eyes.

Ryan brushed his thumb against her flushed cheek. "I like this look on you." When her eyes beckoned him to come closer, he obeyed.

"Hey, guys," Jamba called.

Damn! Thought he was gone.

Ryan grunted and pushed himself off the stall door.

Jamba's head peered out from a stall at the end of the row. He wore a Patriots shirt and a Mets baseball cap. His timing may be way off, but at least he had good sports sense.

"What's up?" Ryan answered.

"Bad news. Joplin's out. She has hives."

"Huh?" Sophie's eyes were still dilated. Ryan felt a thrill of pleasure knowing he'd made her feel that way. "Is she going to be okay?"

"Horses get hives all the time. She just can't go out today if you were hoping to ride her. I'll give her a dose of meds and she'll be good in the morning."

Sophie slumped against the stall door and Santana stuck out her head, nuzzling her hair. Sophie patted the side of her jaw. "Good girl," she cooed, coaxing Santana's neck further out of the stall. "I guess we don't get to ride. That's a bummer."

"You can ride." Jamba walked past them. "Double up on Santana. She's a gentle quarter horse so you won't need a saddle." He ducked into the tack stall and brought out a bridle and a Clemson orange bareback pad. Handing it to Ryan he offered a couple quick tips and left the barn.

"You won't need these then," he said, pointing to the chaps. "You can take those off."

"I liked it better when you did it," Sophie teased.

Ryan grinned. He tried to maintain a cool front though his insides scorched. *Me too.* Sophie removed the chaps and handed them to Ryan. He dumped them on the ground. "Shall we?" He unlocked the metal latch to Santana's stall, and Sophie stepped inside.

She cocked her head at the horse. "So, what do we do?"

"Just trust me. I'll take care of everything." As he uttered the sentence, Ryan hoped she would remember those words long after they finished riding.

Chapter 29

Sophie, having never ridden before, and still completely dazed from that earth-shattering kiss, felt incredibly incompetent on top of this beast with nothing but a bareback pad keeping her from the hard ground. It was one thing to see a quarter horse up close; a completely different thing to be that high off the ground. Luckily, her competent cowboy sat behind her. And with his arms firmly wrapped around her hips and the reins secured in his grip, she could ride like this for days. Darn Henry Ford and his invention anyway.

"It's incredible out here," Sophie said as they walked along a canyon trail. Dried barren trees appeared to have popped up from scattered seeds with no worry about where they grew. She longed for that sort of simplicity. As far as she could see, the landscape looked like a scene from an old western movie, varying shades of browns and reds cascading throughout. Aside from Ryan, the horse, and the distant sound of a city too far away to gauge actual distance, she felt she was in her own island within an island.

"I'm glad you're having a good time," Ryan said, his lips pressed to her ear. "Happy you stayed?"

Sophie sighed and leaned against Ryan's solid chest. She ached to touch him, to explore him, to try again. "Mostly." No matter how hard she tried to disconnect, the café's financial woes seeped into her thoughts. "But I'm worried about the future of the café. The company doesn't seem to value it. But I care. If I can't make them see the vision, I'm going to lose funding."

"Have you had a meeting with the board?" Ryan's hand caressed Sophie's as she stroked Santana's mane.

"They stopped taking my calls a long time ago. But I'm waiting to hear back from grants. And when I get home, I think I'm going to organize an outreach fundraiser."

"You really care about them."

"Yeah, we're a family."

"What would happen if it closed down?"

Sophie thought about it for a moment. Asher's warning about the café closing replayed in her mind. "Nothing good, that's for sure. To understand the girls, you have to really understand the disease. There's not a lot of awareness out there to help troubled teens who throw up on a whim."

"And you understand it?"

Sophie shrugged. She wasn't ready to tell Ryan about her experience. There was no way he could understand.

"You know I've followed your career," he said out of left field.

Sophie twisted so she could clearly see him. "Really?"

"Absolutely." The blue in his eyes turned crystal clear. His sincerity was unmistakable. "When I read your work I feel like I personally become a part of your story. You have a way of writing that evokes emotion. That's hard to do in a space of fifteen hundred words."

Sophie couldn't imagine Ryan reading her work. "How come you never told me? Usually when another journalist reads and likes a column, they comment on it in the internal loop."

"I don't know. Maybe because I didn't want you to know I was reading it."

She wasn't sure if she believed that. "Okay, what's your favorite story of mine?" She scanned his expression, looking to see if his face would betray his words. When it didn't, she waited for him to answer. When she saw his lips curl up and the smile spread across his face, she knew exactly which one. All of them.

Ryan adjusted his seat on the pad. "I have read every one of your articles for the past ten years."

Sophie heard herself swallow. If that didn't make a girl want to kiss a guy, what would?

"But my absolute favorite was your four-part series on how reading memory-jogging articles and classic books to the elderly increased their appetites and boosted their morale. The part about reading old Sunday morning comics like Li'l Abner and Peanuts really struck a chord."

Wow. She owed that article to Grandmoo. Grandmoo spurred her heart for seniors. She found reading old articles like the opening of Macy's in New York and personal accounts of meeting JFK brought smiles to lonely faces who had no idea what was going on in the present.

So, she wrote the series to honor Grandmoo, as well as Donovan's mother whose dementia had worsened.

"Ryan, I had no idea. Thank you."

"So, will you tell me something else?"

Sophie relaxed back into his chest. "Okay."

"Tell me about the girls in your café. I want to know about them."

The calm wind gently danced around the leaves. A few shoots broke loose and glided to the ground. "When you have your face in the toilet, and you slowly wreck your intestines one heave at a time because you feel it gives you a measure of control, it slowly kills you. But really it takes control of you. That's what I'm fighting with these girls. Control over the disease. Not the disease itself."

"Wow. And they all struggle?"

"In some form or fashion. Charlie was the first to join our group and stick around. Not willingly at first. The judge gave her the option to join or complete a thousand hours of community service for a minor vandalizing offense. Then came Joy, Erika, Jasmine, Quita, Dominique, Deidra with her unpredictable mood swings, and Jenny who is quiet. Though girls have come and gone like a revolving door, the core group stuck around. All of them have something special and unique about them." Sophie relaxed against Ryan and breathed him in. He smelled good enough to eat . . . or kiss.

"You don't need a license to run a group like that?"

"No. I'm not diagnosing anything or dispensing medicine, and the magazine more than obliged funding the standard three-thousand-per-year stipend after an office petition went around adopting the idea. I wrote a few articles highlighting the outreach as more than just a community project. It was a local safe haven; it didn't take long before word got out."

"That really puts our outreach to shame," Ryan chuckled, threading his fingers through hers. "We just do office tours and backpack drives. Are all your girls success stories?"

Sophie inhaled sharply. "No. Suzie didn't make it."

"Suzie?"

"She was our youngest at only eleven years old. She came to us a twig, and I was so far out of my element, the idea of even considering mentoring her was out of the question. But Charlie wouldn't hear of that. She absolutely loved Suzie. And Suzie loved the 1950s café theme and even championed the fundraising for our vintage custard machine."

"Sounds driven."

"She was. She earned the unofficial title of café's sweetheart. But unfortunately, only a month after the custard machine joined the family, she lost her battle with bulimia."

"I'm so sorry."

"I fear if the café closes, they won't have anywhere to go." Sophie hated feeling so helpless. She would do everything in her power to not let that happen.

Ryan grew quiet. Sophie felt his breathing and the soft tempo of his heart serenaded her through his chest.

"Soph?"

"Yeah?"

"Do you see yourself in those girls? Was that you? I mean is that how you lost so much . . ." He gulped. "I mean, your commonality with them. Does it have anything to do with this disease?"

Sophie stiffened at his question. She played with Santana's mane, yesterday's guilt budding in her gut. She nodded.

He kissed her hair. "It's okay. We don't have to talk about it. Just know I think what you're doing is amazing and I want to help. I *will* help."

She quietly kneaded her fingers around the coarse strands of Santana's mane.

Ryan rested his cheek on top of her head. "Sophie?"

"Hmm?"

"Would you be willing to tell me something else, though?"

The budding guilt twisted into a knot that swelled in her stomach. It wasn't what he asked, but the tone in which he asked. Shame from her stupid purge the day before made her want to crawl into a hole and disappear.

Something that she once used to gain control suddenly had its control over her. "Like what?" she asked hesitantly.

"It's okay if you don't want to talk about it, but I was wondering if you would be willing to tell me what happened?"

An unsettling angst flickered within. "What do you mean?"

"I mean ten years ago. I dropped you off at your grandma's house and that was it. I barely heard from you again. What happened?"

Sophie bit her lip, not sure if the words would come. "I—I tried but then I saw you with—." She paused. "You're right I don't want to talk about it."

"Okay." His understanding voice wasn't fair. The truth was after her grandmother was in the hospital, Sophie couldn't pull herself together to even so much as brush her teeth. She ate her pain away and turned into a sloth. Refusing Ryan's calls was self-preservation. He couldn't leave her if he couldn't talk to her.

A week later, when her grandmother was released, she still couldn't pull herself together enough to see Ryan. A few weeks after that, she forced herself to go to him because how do you call someone after weeks of nothing. And he had been so nice, leaving her incredible sweet voicemails. He'd understand. But then she found him at school, his arm was wrapped around Leggie Blonde.

Santana's gait bounced her from side to side, making her suddenly nauseous. Confusion and anger and desire swirled within, making her dizzy, and her stomach heaved. Unable to stay upright a second more, she rested her head on the horse's neck.

"Whoa," Ryan commanded, pulling the reigns tight. "Do you need to stop? What's the matter?"

"I'm dizzy."

Ryan slid off Santana's back and pulled Sophie into his arms. Though she felt secure, she also felt carsick. And sick with emotion.

Santana headed to a nearby patch of grass and began grazing. Ryan settled Sophie in his lap next to a eucalyptus with a wide trunk and sufficient shade. "Talk to me, Sapphire."

Oh, that name when it resonated from his lips. It lulled her into a relaxed state. What could she say? The last night they were together had transformed from the best night of her life to an unimaginable nightmare. Then he left her. And now here she was sitting in his lap. What was she thinking? She needed space. She was about to move, but then his soothing voice coaxed her into staying.

"Sophie?" He brushed her hair away from her ear and whispered. "You can trust me."

A hot tear rolled down her cheek, and Ryan wiped it with his thumb. *Trust him?* A stab of fear pierced her through. How could she trust the person who catapulted her into a disease she was still clearly fighting? Why did she let him kiss her like that? She didn't want to talk about their breakup, couldn't stomach hearing that he finally realized she was just a story, so she veered to safer ground. Grandmoo's accident.

"That night I found my grandmother on the ground unconscious and bleeding. She'd had a stroke."

Sophie blinked rapidly, trying to hold back the burning tears that escaped. She couldn't look at Ryan. So much about who she was today stemmed from that night. Some of it was good, sure, the girls and the café and meeting Amy. All of those were good, and they happened because of him. But the pain and the shame and the controlling manipulation all originated from him, too.

"Do you want to talk about it?"

Sophie watched Santana chomp on grass. The horse seemed methodical in her approach. She'd sniff the grass, rip a huge chunk of it from the ground, and chew. Then rinse and repeat. She didn't have a care in the world. Sophie envied her.

"I slipped the key into the lock like always. Grandmoo always waited up for me, but when I checked the reading room, her sappy Silhouette title sat on the chair, and the room was dark.

"I went to the kitchen for a glass of milk. I needed to calm down. I felt bad about how we left things. I was going to call you as soon as I went to my room and apologize." Sophie paused to catch her breath. Her heart picked up speed and the knot deep within her twisted, cautioning her brain to not go there.

Ryan squeezed her hand gently as if saying he would wait patiently for her to continue.

"The kitchen was still dark when I walked in, but something was off. It smelled like iron. When I stepped in warm thick liquid, I knew." Sophie gulped hard.

"It's okay, sweetheart" Ryan stroked her hair. "Take your time."

Sophie appreciated his patience, but she needed to get this out. "Grandmoo hit her head on the counter top. There was blood. A lot of sticky blood all over. I screamed. I didn't know what to do." Hot tears slipped out, and her throat tightened making it hard to continue. "She was like my mom, you know? More than a mom."

Ryan wrapped his arms around her like a warm, winter coat. He rocked her back and forth until her involuntary trembling slowed.

"I don't remember calling 9-1-1, except I was suddenly on the phone, hysterical. It was an eternity of minutes before help arrived."

The tears mercilessly streamed down her face. Sophie couldn't understand why retelling this story hurt so much after all these years. She'd lived it, processed it. So why was she crying? She lay motionless, listening to the crackling of autumn leaves swirling just above the ground. Everything was quiet, save the cawing from seagulls in the distance. Ryan stroked her hair, and she felt a measure of calmness run through her body as Ryan stroked her hair. Her hot face cooled as the breeze brushed against the dried tears on her cheeks.

"Grandmoo gave up everything to raise me. She worked at the state department in Sacramento. But rather than make me move to her, she relocated so I didn't have to leave everything after I lost my parents. Then after her accident, she had to stop working for the county. I can't help but harbor some of the guilt for making her change everything for me."

"Soph, you cannot hold yourself responsible for a stroke. It was a terrible accident, but that's exactly what it was. An accident."

Sophie wiped her nose. "It was one of the hardest times in my life."

"Why did you shut me out then?" Ryan whispered. "When you needed me. I could have held your hand through it."

Sophie hung her head. *Why did you use me for a story?* Her skin prickled at the memory, so she pushed herself off his lap and walked to Santana. "I thought my grandmother was dying."

Ryan stared at her for a moment before standing. He slowly stepped toward her but Sophie laid her head on Santana's soft coat. "I could have helped you," he said in a soothing tone.

"You would have left me if you saw me." Actually, he did leave her. "I was a mess. It was pretty awful. School didn't even matter. I ate my way through everything in the hospital cafeteria the week my Grandma was in ICU. And then I binged on Chinese takeout for the next several weeks at home." Home had become an empty shell, void of warmth and comfort. Food filled that void.

"You didn't give me a chance, Soph."

Tears threatened, as her memory took her back to the shell of the girl she had been. "But I didn't want you to see me like that."

Ryan stepped around the horse and she could see that his expression remained a surly shade of confused. "Why not? Why not let me in?"

"Because I *couldn't* let you see me like that. I couldn't stand the sight of myself. And then when I finally built up the courage I saw you . . . you were with *her*." Sophie didn't mean for her voice to crack but the pain brewing inside fractured at the memory.

Ryan's eyes pelted her with a quizzical look that almost made her think he didn't know what she was talking about. "Sophie, I thought I'd hurt you that night we'd made love— like physically hurt you. I knew I was your first, and I just thought I'd done something unforgivable. Why else wouldn't you return my calls?"

Sophie stared in disbelief. "I didn't take them at first because I didn't know what I wanted. I couldn't stop crying or stop stuffing my face." She threw her hands up and covered her eyes. "Oh, God, I can't believe I'm telling you this."

"Sophie," his voice pleaded, "I would have been there, blotchy face and all."

"I was so in love with you." Her voice cracked and the tears flowed freely. "Every fiber in my core longed for you but you didn't want me."

"Sophie, I had no—"

"Don't you dare say no idea. You knew. I know you knew. I just needed space for a few weeks. Yes, I screwed up, but I didn't cheat on you." Sophie dropped her hands, her gut wrenched. "I saw you with her, Ryan."

"With who?"

"Amber Whitman! Leggie Blonde. Remember her? The *acceptable* girl you probably wasted no time jumping into bed with. The girl who was so mean to me. The one you had your arms around when I came to you to tell you about my grandmother."

Ryan's mouth clamped shut. His expression was pained. He closed his eyes and breathed heavily then skirted around the horse so he was next to her. Sophie refused to look at him.

"I meant to say I had no intention of leaving you. Not for Amber or anyone else." His voice was calm and Sophie hated how much control he had. "I don't know where you got your information from, Soph. But I did call you. A lot. You refused all of them. I went to your dorm room. I also checked your grandma's home. But no one answered the door. I didn't know what happened to you! I even emailed your school account."

He seemed so genuine but that didn't explain why he had his arm around Leggie Blonde or why he used her for a story. "Ryan." She finally faced him and broke down. The forgotten tears, the ones she'd refused to shed back then welled up with more force than that blowhole. "I messed up. I did. But then I saw your arm around her and I got the message loud and clear.

Ryan's eyes narrowed. He lunged into her space and though she backed up, he met her step for step. All that calm control dissipated. "That is not fair. You don't get to play victim, Sophie. I'm sorry about what happened to your grandmother, but you're wrong. That day you saw me with Amber had been when she twisted her ankle. I was helping her to the dorm. Which was where I was headed anyway to see you."

Sophie was out of breath. Her throat felt like she'd swallowed needles and her head threatened to explode. If she had any food in her stomach she'd throw up. She had accepted the truth long ago. She had convinced herself he'd given up on her. Because she was just a story.

Sophie's eyes stayed trained on his, trying to process his words.

"I went to see you a handful of times, but your roommate brushed me off and fed me lines like you were out with some guys and you were over us. She's the one that told me to email you and she'd give you my messages."

Sophie's arms went limp. "Molly said that?" How many times did Molly tell her that Ryan was above her grade? She'd been so supportive with Grandmoo's stroke. *The wench!* She had to know Sophie didn't use the school email. "She told you I was out with other guys?"

Ryan ran both hands through his hair. "Yeah. She said you made it very clear you didn't want to see me."

Sophie's eyes burned with fury. It all made sense now. Molly liked Ryan. Couldn't understand that Ryan actually liked her.

The searing pain in her chest was doused by the truth. How could this have gone so wrong? And what about all those wasted years. Sophie's voice was barely audible when she spoke. "I-I had no idea. I should have called you, but when I saw you with Amber . . . I just lost it. I refused to answer your calls after that." *I purged.*

"But that's just it, Sapphire." Ryan's voice hummed. "I figured after we made love you were upset, or at the very least repulsed by me for whatever reason. I wanted to tell you about my job offer in San Antonio. I had three weeks to report, covering the inside of the Cubs' locker room. But when I couldn't get to you, I had to make the decision. The opportunity was a once in a lifetime chance. I thought we could go together. Or at least talk about it. But I was a kid with a million-dollar opportunity I couldn't pass up. So, I left you a final message and then I left right after graduation."

Sophie shook and hugged herself. The tears wouldn't stop. She wouldn't have known. She stopped checking his voice mails.

He wrapped his arms around her. He was her cocoon and she was his butterfly.

She sobbed. She couldn't help it. All those years of sticking her finger down her throat all because maybe, just maybe, she didn't allow herself to be loved. Her parents had loved her, but they died. Her grandma loved her, but she almost died. Ryan said he loved her, but she'd seen him with another girl. Love was supposed to be effortless, but maybe she turned it into something unattainable.

Maybe she didn't know how to let someone love her.

Sophie slowly arched back. Her hair stuck to her face,

but she didn't care.

Ryan wiped the strands from her cheeks and kissed her forehead.

"Do you want to head back?" His question was more of a suggestion. The clouds were rolling in and Sophie was exhausted.

"Yes."

Ryan helped her on the horse, then led Santana to a boulder, which he used to mount her.

The start back to Tia's was quiet, and for that, Sophie was grateful. Because there was still one more thing left unsaid. But she didn't have the words. Did he even know she knew?

Her blinking slowed. It was the part she couldn't manage to relive verbally. A month later, after everything was grandiose and antiplatelet medication coupled with the occasional aspirin kept Grandmoo on the mend, Sophie saw it.

The article.

That's when she'd learned how to take control . . . by whatever means necessary.

Chapter 30

Ryan gently held Sophie's hand. She'd leaned against him and he took that as the first step in rebuilding trust. She'd just unloaded a decade's worth of pain. And he couldn't help but regret that he'd played a destructive role in her life.

His chest felt heavy at the thought of leaving in a couple days, but that wasn't his call. He was on assignment. A lot of people counted on him, and his promotion was days away. He needed to tell Sophie.

But Ryan was torn. He was here for work and needed to do what was in the best interest of the company that served him well for a decade, but another part of him—the much larger part—was in love with Sophie.

Ryan started at that realization. Yes, he had deep feelings for her. But this longing for her rattled in his core.

Santana's gait rocked them from side to side and Ryan squeezed Sophie tighter between his arms to help steady her sway. "You okay?"

She nodded. "What are you thinking?"

About my promotion, he wanted to say, but couldn't. Maybe he could ease the topic with some hard facts. "Did you know I spend about two hundred days a year traveling?"

Her upper body twisted and their eyes met. "Seriously?"

"Yeah. Crazy huh?"

She turned forward again. "That is crazy. And lonely."

She had no idea. He was definitely ready to settle down. Up until now it had been all about chasing the game. He wouldn't miss an inning or quarter. The chase was endless but his blog and articles were better because of it. "Yeah, many lonely nights."

"I think they have a one-nine-hundred number for that." Ryan could hear the smirk in her voice.

"I'll pass, thanks."

"How did you do it?"

Good question. Ryan thought a moment. "I guess pure adrenaline. When baseball and football season overlapped, I lived on Red Bull and vending machine cuisines. Never took any of the synthetic alternatives I was offered. I like to keep my head clear." Plus, he'd be damned to follow in his father's substance abuse shoes.

"That must be really hard. Ever think about not traveling."

And there was the ten-thousand-dollar question. One that was in the works of being answered for him by way of a merge, layoff, and promotion. None of which he could to tell her. But he wanted to. He needed to be vague for now, so he answered, "It's crossed my mind."

She stared off in the distance where a trail of tourists in golf carts drove past the Holiday Inn. "I guess you'll know when the time is right."

Part of him felt deceptive. A huge part of him. He needed to tell Sophie the truth. Tonight. The merge was happening. He couldn't let her find out through someone else. She'd never trust him again. Stupid Johnson and his loose, vindictive lips.

The conversation tapered off, and Ryan reflected on Phil's caution that this transition would be hard, yet Red Goldman's heartfelt *been there done that* warning burned in his mind. *Don't put your career over your heart.*

Sophie leaned against him again, and he settled one of his hands over her thigh, breathing her in. He had to let her know about the merge before the rumor mill got to her first.

She fell apart in his arms because everything built up and crashed down on her. How long had she been holding that in? She was such a strong woman, yet she had limits. He didn't have the heart to tell her that whether she raised five thousand dollars or a hundred thousand dollars, the café would shut down.

She'd be devastated more about the café closing than what the merge meant for her career. And before he returned to San Antonio, he was determined to help her figure out a way to keep its door open.

She shifted on the saddle pad.

"You comfortable?" Ryan adjusted his seat so she could move. Riding horses made butts numb.

"I'm fine. Just a little embarrassed still. I think everything caught up with me. I'm sorry."

Ryan squeezed his eyes. His own regret dwarfed anything she could ever tell him. In fact, he wanted nothing more than to fix what he'd done to her. "I'm glad you told me. I just wish I would have known."

Sophie shook her head. "No more secrets, okay?"

Shit. "I agree." Only, he still had one. And he needed to tell her about the merge and his promotion tonight. This time, they would figure out their impossible situation together.

When they got back to the barn, Jamba clomped out of Tia's house with Dolly slung around his neck.

"Have fun?" Jamba plucked Dolly from his shoulders and gripped her like a football. "Want some help?"

Ryan hopped off and Sophie slid down behind him, wobbling unsteadily at first. "Numb legs, right?"

"Uh, yeah," she said, rubbing her thighs.

Ryan handed the reins to Jamba. "Thanks." The goat bleated as Jamba tossed Dolly on Santana's back.

"I'll put her away and then I'm taking off. Sorry about the pummeling threat earlier. You seem all right."

Ryan smiled. "No worries." The goat eyed him and bleated again.

The back of Ryan's pants vibrated, and he pressed his cell to his ear. Phil. *Damn.* "I'll be just a minute."

Tia stepped out on to the porch. "*Mija*, come in here, you have to see this!"

Ryan's chin jutted, letting Sophie know he'd be right behind her. Then he turned around. "Pike," he answered.

"Change of plans. I need you to open the email I just sent."

"I'm not on the boat, Phil. I can't get to a computer just yet. I'll check my phone and read it."

"No, that won't do. It's a huge file and I want to talk you through it. It's a huge cluster so get to one ASAP and call me back. I need to go over a few changes."

"Phil, I'm a little indisposed. Can I call you tonight?"

"This is important, Pike. Just get to a computer and call me. Okay?"

"Sure, Phil." A chill shot down Ryan's back. "I'll call you back as soon as I can."

Ryan tucked his phone in his back pocket just as Jamba opened the door to his Chevy pick-up. Dolly trotted to the front porch. "Any chance you can give us a ride back to the ship right now?"

"Sure. Jump in."

"Great. I'll go get Sophie." Phil's urgency made Ryan uneasy. He'd never had him drop his plans to answer an email. And after the conversation they had this morning, Ryan's hackles stood on end.

Ryan swung the front door open and a blur of Dodger blue burst through his legs. Dolly jumped on the couch and circled a few times before she collapsed. Sophie and Tia sat on the floor laughing over a photo album. "What's so funny?"

Sophie glanced at him, her face red from hysterics. This, he thought, was a much better look on her. No more crying and sadness.

"You're so cute in your superhero cape . . . and nothing else." She snorted and fell back, laughing hard. Dolly raised her head in curiosity.

Ryan rolled his eyes. "Really, Tia? You have to show her baby pictures?"

"Naked pictures," Sophie said, nearly hyperventilating.

Ryan pointed at Sophie. "Not funny." Then he stabbed an even sterner finger at Tia. "And inappropriate."

The girls burst out laughing.

"Ha, ha," he said. "Get your kicks now. Just know that little stud there turned into this stud here." He flexed his biceps, and the laughing only intensified. "You guys are terrible. Wait until you need a spider stepped on. You can forget about asking me."

Sophie pressed her lips in a hard line, but the hysterics made her convulse into another bout of laughter.

"Whatever. Come on, Sophie, we have to go. My boss needs me to read an email pronto and apparently the attachment is too big to read on my phone."

Sophie pouted. "Really? We have an hour before we have to be back, and the ship is only fifteen minutes away."

"I know, but I have to go. Jamba's waiting."

Sophie slouched, pursing her lips. "We were just getting to know each other."

Something in Ryan swelled with hope. If she wanted to get to know Tia better, could it mean she wanted to be a part of his life? No way he wanted to end this bonding moment between them. Even if it did involve embarrassing photos. But his job. He scrubbed a hand through his hair.

"I'll take her," Tia offered.

"Really?" Sophie's gaze cut to Ryan.

"Okay, yeah." He crossed the Woodstock shrine and gave Tia a hug. "It was wonderful to see you, and I promise not to wait so long until next time."

She waved him off. "Yeah, yeah, I've heard that one before. You journalists are all the same."

"Hey," Sophie objected. "Not all journalists."

"*Touché*." Ryan kissed the top of Sophie's head. "Would you join me for dinner tonight for the formal dinner? Maybe we can pick up where we left off in the barn." He winked, and Sophie blushed.

Jamba pounded on the doorframe. "You ready?"

"I prefer guys with tattoos, I decided." She winked back.

"How about goats?"

Sophie punched him in the thigh. "How about charley horses?"

Ryan rubbed his leg, grinning. "See you at seven then?"

Sophie nodded. "Wouldn't miss it."

Ryan blew them both a kiss goodbye and jogged after Jamba toward his truck. He was going to take care of whatever Phil was throwing at him, but then he needed to talk everything out with Sophie. She deserved the truth. And he needed to find a way to break the news to her without compromising her café, his future with *Sports Now*, and hopefully, his future with her.

Chapter 31

To suggest Sophie was a *little* worried at this moment would have been the understatement of the century.

She checked her watch for the millionth time. 7:33:09 p.m. On the dot. He had to be on board. Right? They don't leave people stranded on desolate islands . . . not that Avalon was exactly desolate, but they had a date.

A date! Ficus, what could be holding him up? Ryan's face flashed in her mind. Where was he? Maybe his earlier call at Tia's farm had something to do with his family. Didn't he say his dad was in Paris? What if something terrible happened. What if he was already packed and off the ship?

Paranoia, much?

She sat at a two-person table on the Lido Deck, looking hot if she did say so herself. She was dressed in a long black gown, wearing Amy's dangly diamond earrings she had insisted Sophie use, with her hair twisted in one of those buns YouTube's *Pin it in a Minute* said would be easy. It wasn't easy at all. YouTube was quickly becoming her enemy, but her hair looked *really good*.

She stirred a mug of hot tea and checked the time again. 7:33:26. *Ugh.*

A coldness bit into her bones. Aggressive waves splashed against the side of the boat swaying everything from the teacup in her hand to the butterflies in her stomach. The rain hadn't started yet, but occasional drops of mist seeped into her pores.

Fidgeting her fingers, she played with the key card to Ryan's cabin. He'd dropped it outside the barn, and Sophie grabbed it on her way to Tia's small electric car. So she assumed he wasn't in his room, unless he got another key. But she had checked. Twice. It doesn't count as stalking until at least the third visit in thirty minutes.

A two-note whistle signaling someone else thought she looked hot came from behind. She turned around, fully expecting to see Ryan.

Who approached couldn't have been further from what she expected.

"Where's our fearless leader?" Asher said. His smugness was a bane to her existence. Why must he bug her incessantly?

"Shoo, tiny excuse of a man. I don't have any more time for you today and I don't feel like fighting."

"I'm not here to fight. I just wanted to say good game. And, damn, girl, you look good tonight. How come you never looked like that when we were together?"

"You were never worth the effort," Sophie chided. "And are you really bringing up the scavenger hunt again? Do you want a trophy or something? I quit, remember? So bye."

"Aw, that's too bad." He sat in the empty chair, Ryan's chair, not catching the hint.

She glared at him. "I didn't say you could sit."

"Why? It doesn't look like I'm interrupting anything."

His cynicism grated on her. "I said shoo."

"Humor me." He had a piece of paper in one hand and his stupid, beloved schnapps in the other.

Sophie checked the time again. Where was Ryan?

"This," he held up the paper, "is five thousand bucks with the name of my charity of choice to be added. My winnings from the scavenger hunt." He lifted his schnapps. "Here, here," he chorused.

Sophie narrowed her eyes and her muscles tensed. Visualizing throwing him overboard brought a ray of sunshine to this dismal night. "You're lucky you didn't get caught playing, though I'm sure you're disappointed you don't get to keep the money. Pity."

Asher rolled his eyes. "I don't care if they catch me. Whoever *they* are. They won't do anything anyway. It's a stupid rule. I was, however, awarded a complimentary three-day cruise in addition to the five grand. Sweet deal if you ask me."

"I didn't."

"Don't be sore." Asher smiled, or simpered rather, and tossed his winnings on the table. "It's just a game, princess. My Johnny Depp autograph gave me more points than everyone else combined."

"Bravo. You done here? Because I am."

"They actually asked if they could keep the autograph to frame it. I said no, of course." Asher mouthed the bottle of Schnapps and tossed his head back.

"Whatever, Asher. Like I said, congrats and all that. I'm tired. Go away."

"Here," Asher said, pushing his winning certificate across the table.

Sophie glanced at the certificate, her eyes snagging on the name of the charity. She stared for one moment, then two, not quite comprehending what she was seeing. "Is this for real?" Her eyes cut to his.

"It's just the chase, Sophie. Come on. You know me. I don't really care about the money. But your café needs it. The girls need it."

Sophie hesitated, baffled. "But why? You have been a number one, class-A prick for over a week now."

He shrugged, and a familiar smile draped across his face. The one he used to give her before he traded her in for an overly endowed Trixie Bell. "Ah, I was just messing with you, babe."

"Don't call me that. And no. You tormented me."

Asher leaned across the table. "Well, I'm sorry. Call it a lover's quarrel. We good?"

Disconcerted, she crossed her arms. "Cheating is far more than a lover's quarrel. Nobody hands over five thousand dollars. What's the catch?"

"Let me buy you a drink." He waved a server over.

Sophie lifted the certificate and rubbed the fibers against her fingers. She should probably decline the drink, but maybe this was genuine? Perhaps Asher's heart grew three sizes today. He basically just saved her café . . . at least for the short term. She could tolerate him through one drink. "Yeah. I think I can handle a drink." She could give him that.

"So, what happened?" Asher asked.

"What do you mean?"

"I mean you're here alone, looking smokin' hot, and obviously waiting for someone. Call it intuition, but something happened. Tell Uncle Asher all about it."

"Ew. Don't ever call yourself that again." She shook her head. "It's a long story."

"I've got time."

Even she didn't fully understand today. The last thing on Earth, nay, the universe, she would do is use Asher as a sounding board. Like ever. "I'm sorry, Asher. I'm just tired."

He took her hand from the tabletop and caressed it with his thumb. "You want to come back to my cabin for a bit?" He cocked his head to the side and raised his eyebrow like a bona fide sleaze.

"Absolutely not." She snatched her hand back.

"Come on. It'll be fun. We can just hang out or . . . explore. Nothing serious. No big deal."

Bile seeped up her throat. "Asher, has anyone ever told you you're like a tick that imbeds its head into your last nerve and then sucks the very life right out of you? Did you already forget? You broke up with me. You cheated on me. You pushed me in a pool, and before you deny it, I am sure

I can get security footage to prove it. So, no. I don't want to go back to your cabin and 'explore' anything."

He leaned back in his chair and killed his schnapps in one gulp just as the server brought them each a Mojito. "Don't think so hard, Sophie. You don't always need to read into things. It's just a drink. It's just a night of release. You and I both know something's askew with Captain Perfect leading the training. Let's just exercise some journalistic privileges."

"Journalistic privileges? That's not a thing. And trust me, you and I will never exercise anything together." She couldn't believe it, he was propositioning her like a whore. It was low, even for Asher. She glanced at the certificate. "Is that what this is?" Lifting it, she suddenly felt its immense weight. "Are you trying to coerce me?" she growled, "into bed with you?"

"Okay, fine. I can see you want to release your tension another way. Go to your bathroom and use your finger already."

As soon as Asher said it, his face went pale, and Sophie could see he knew he'd gone too far.

"I didn't meant that," he said. "I'm sorry."

"You said it. You meant it. You are a coward and an ass. And I can't believe I ever had a momentary lapse in judgment to go out with you." Sophie didn't feel the need to yell or scream or fight him. She felt calm, serene even. She'd never let him goad her again. He wasn't worth it. And she could tell that scared Asher more than if she went crazy on him.

"I'm really sorry, Sophie. That was uncalled for."

"You're right. You are sorry." She leapt to her feet and grasped the glass so tightly, her knuckles turned white. "So much so, you're not worthy of a response. Except to say you're completely out of line. Trust me, Asher, you did me the favor by ending us when you did. You must live in some fantasy world if you think you can buy me off with some two-dollar drink and dirty money. But consider this my direct warning to you. If you ever even utter a syllable to me about anything outside of journalism or work, I will slap a sexual harassment suit on you so fast, your head will spin on an axis even the earth can't compete with. You get me?"

Sophie shoved her chair back and took a long pull of her drink as the mist turned into a downpour.

As people began to run for cover, she threw the remaining contents in his face then crumpled up the certificate and threw it at his feet. "Ashface."

Chapter 32

Moments later, feeling like she'd just walked through fire and came out unscathed, Sophie approached the concierge's same blue counter top, with the same ever-lovely Natalia tapping away on her keyboard with a lollipop hanging from her mouth.

Natalia looked up. "Hey, hun, aren't you looking fancy-Nancy. How'd your day go?"

"Just peachy, princess, thanks."

Natalia yanked the sucker from her mouth. "Well, you're still here so your emergency must have worked out."

"It did, thanks. And my name is Sophie, not hun." She politely smiled.

"Oh, yeah, for sure. Like *Sofia the First*." She giggled. "What can I do for you?"

Sophie rolled her eyes. "I need help locating a friend. I'm not sure if he made it back to the ship and I'm worried. I have his key card so I don't know how he got back on."

"Oh, no problem, Fia. Can I call you Fia? I like Fia. It dazzles."

"No. My name is Sophie. Now, my friend?"

Natalia clicked the mouse at lightning speed. "I can tell you right now everyone's checked in and accounted for. They would have done a roster check if not. And any time a passenger loses a key, they just need their ID to get back on board." She plopped her arms over the counter. "Do you have any idea how much paperwork is involved when someone's left behind?"

"I can only imagine. But I can't find my friend, who I expected for dinner tonight."

Natalia stuck the lollipop back in her mouth. "Oh, that friend. It's a pity really . . . I mean, that sort of face should not endure such a catastrophe."

Wait? Catsatsa-wha? Sophie's stomach sunk. "What do you mean? What catastrophe?"

"Oh, you didn't know? I'm sorry, hun."

Didn't know what! Her limbs filled with tar but summoning all her might, she slammed her hands on the counter. "What. Happened."

Natalia jumped back, her eyes anchored at attention. "I don't know. I walked out of the break room, which is right next to the infirmary, as the doctor rushed him into Exam Room One. He was all blotchy and puffy. Not the chiseled fine specimen of a man I saw earlier today."

Sophie's gut wretched. Blotchy? "Are you sure?"

"You don't forget eye-candy like that."

Sophie's mind raced a million miles a minute. What could have happened? And if it was so bad, why didn't they call a medi-flight? Too many questions. She had to find him now. "Thanks, Natalia."

"You bet, Sophie. I'm sure he'll be fine. But here." Natalia handed her a key card. "It'll give you access through the employees-only deck. Do you know where that is?"

Sophie shook her head.

Natalie quickly scribbled a map on a piece of paper and gave her directions. "Good luck."

Sophie pivoted on her heel but before she dashed off, she turned back to Natalia. Opportunities to mess with Donovan only presented themselves once in a blue moon. And after the bromance scheme they concocted for her this morning, she couldn't resist. "Give me your pen."

Natalia obliged and handed Sophie the Colossal Cruise

ink pen. Sophie took Natalia by the wrist and scribbled a ten-digit phone number on the back of her hand.

"What's this?"

"My friend Donovan's number. Call him. He will take you out and show you the time of your life. He knows every hot bar in San Francisco."

"Oh?" Natalia's lollipop smile stretched from ear to ear.

"If he tries to make an excuse or tell you you're not his type, trust me, you are exactly what he deserves." She waved her hand in the air in a zigzag motion from Natalia's head to torso. "All of you. And if he fights it, tell him this is Sophie's thanks for attempting to hold her captive earlier."

Sophie winked at Natalia and rushed toward the elevator.

~ ~ ~

"You feeling better, Mr. Pike?"

Ryan sat on the hospital bed and pulled his shirt closed, needing to use more effort than normal to fasten the buttons. "Good enough, Doc," he said, rubbing his jaw. "I think the numbness is about gone." His jaw tingled, which was good. He'd read about the effects from epinephrine, but to experience it first hand was something else.

"You look a hundred percent better than you did when they dragged you in here. From now on, you need to carry an epi-pen."

"Got it, Doc." Ryan pressed his tongue against his teeth, it was still thicker than normal. He wondered if his speech sounded as off to the doctor as it did to him. Like how he sounded after having a cavity filled.

"Did you know you were allergic to bees?"

"I do now."

"It's not uncommon to learn about these things later in life, but you'll be fine. No alcohol tonight, and take it easy. As the medicine wears off, you may experience a few of these symptoms." The doctor handed Ryan a paper pamphlet and stepped out of the room, or really, the other side of the plastic curtain.

He briefly glanced over the pamphlet, which covered every possible seasick ailment from Norovirus to gastrointestinal illness. About halfway down the second section in a font too minuscule to register, Ryan read that side effects from epinephrine included difficulty breathing; irregular heartbeat; nausea; vomiting . . .

The sound of the curtain being forced open jolted Ryan. If angry had a face, she was staring right back at him, and, man, did she look good.

"So now you're dying on me?" Sophie invited herself in and pulled the curtain closed behind her.

"Hope you didn't start writing my obituary. You look absolutely stunning."

"Thanks, are you okay?" She prodded his body like a treasure seeker looking for the trap door.

Ryan took her hands in his. "I'm going to be okay if I don't chew off my tongue while I talk. Everything is still pretty numb."

"What happened?" She relaxed and leaned against the bed. "I half expected you to look like The Thing from *Fantastic Four*." Her touch sent a warm rush that countered the numbness of the anaphylaxis. The things her touch did to him.

"Sorry to disappoint."

"So," Sophie said, hopping up onto the bed. "What's the verdict?"

"Apparently, I'm allergic to bees."

"You didn't already know that?"

"I guess not. Or maybe I just wanted you to see me laid up like this so you could nurse me back to health."

"Keep dreaming." A slow smiled stretched across her mouth.

"Sorry I bailed on our dinner. You really do look nice. By the time I realized what was happening my fingers and tongue were too swollen to tell you."

"I figured something had to have happened. Did you get your call made? Do you want to go eat now?"

Ryan shook his head. Phil. He'd almost forgotten. "I'd love to but I still have to go to the conference room and call my boss. They have hi-speed Internet there and I need to look at some files he sent."

Sophie pouted.

"How about after?"

"Definitely."

Ryan stood to finish buttoning his shirt, but Sophie brushed his hand away. "Let me."

Who was he to argue? While she concentrated on his buttons, he concentrated on her face. He could get used to her hands on him. "Sorry if I worried you. Trust me, bee stings are no joke."

"I'm just glad you're not a corpse on your way to Davey Jones's locker."

Ryan gave her a thoughtful look. "About earlier today . . ." he started, but his voice trailed.

Sophie's cool hand grabbed his. "It's okay. I'm glad I finally told you." She patted his chest. "All done."

He smiled. With her in arms reach, he set his hands on her hips. She felt so perfect. She looked up at him and returned the smile. He wanted to fix her. Fix the girl who cried in his arms today. Everything that was about to unfold about the merge and the café closing needed to be gently unpacked. She had every right to be so invested in her outreach, but she was also vulnerable. She shouldn't find out by some office suit who didn't know her name from her employee number. The news needed to come from him. And he would do his best to make it right. "I want to talk about what happens after the cruise."

Sophie seemed to deflate. "As in you go back to Texas and I work on finding a cheaper location?"

Ryan cleared his throat. *I mean I want you to come back to San Antonio with me.* But he couldn't ask that. He had to make her come to terms with the café's closing. Or try to help her.

Don't put your career over your heart, Red's voice warned again. Medicine rushed to Ryan's head and he flinched. "I'll see you in an hour or so. Meet me at the jazz room? I'll get my call made and then change and see you there."

"Sounds good. I'm going to see if I still have a good enough signal to try Charlie again. That girl is going to get an earful from me about answering her phone. She's not teenagering right if she's not glued to that thing. That I pay for, I might add."

Ryan squeezed Sophie's arm. "I'm sure she's fine. It's good for them to have an opportunity to take care of things on their own."

"Still, I better call. You never know." Her lips were ripe for the taking, but he didn't trust his numb lips to follow through on an insatiable kiss, and he didn't want to give her anything less. "Okay, sweetheart. I'll see you later."

Her cheeks pinked, sending an uneasy ripple through Ryan.

As she turned to leave, he knew he had to tell her everything. And he would. Tonight.

Chapter 33

Sophie felt a little less heavy, almost jovial.

A bee sting. Wow.

Things were going well. If she had only taken his calls years ago, rather than assuming the worst, things might have been much different. A warm, swirly, euphoric sensation swaddled her like a newborn baby. Ten years was a long time. And even though he lived so far away, what's to say they wouldn't figure out a way to make this work?

She walked on cloud nine toward her room to call Charlie. Sophie was almost there when she realized she still had Ryan's key card. She meant to give it to him but then she got all caught up in his yummy hotness and, well, she plum forgot.

She checked her phone.

No cell reception and she never did buy a service plan for on board.

Perfect.

She glanced at Ryan's key card. He wouldn't care if she saved a few bucks and used his room line to call Charlie. He knew how much the girls meant to her. She'd sneak into his room, call Charlie from his line—surely no one would balk at him making calls to shore—and get out.

It would only take a few minutes. No one would know. And Ryan wouldn't care. Right?

Even as the plan formed in her head, Sophie knew it was risky.

Amy needed to validate this idea! Where was she anyway? She'd been MIA a lot on this trip. Regardless, she clearly wasn't here to champion Sophie's brilliance, so she'd have to wait for the *Reader's Digest* version later.

The Do Not Disturb sign hung on the door, but she knew he wasn't here, so it was safe. Sophie slipped in the key card, and slowly opened the door, sighing in relief that he hadn't replaced it yet.

She padded into his dimly lit room and closed the door behind her. Her heart pounded so hard she could feel it in her ears. Breaking and entering was a new thing for her.

The heady woody and Irish Spring scent loitered around her. Her face flushed imagining Ryan smelling that delicious. She set the key card on the desk and sauntered across the room to the French doors he'd left ajar. The floor just inside the balcony was damp, and the wadded-up shirt he'd worn that morning lay next to the door. *Men.* She pushed the door all the way closed and headed to the bathroom for a towel to place over the carpet so the room wouldn't smell mildewy.

When Sophie flipped on the light, she saw Ryan's shaving kit strewn about the sink and a towel carelessly tossed on the toilet seat, still damp from this morning. She blushed. He was a messy one.

She checked her hair, combing her fingers through a few strands the rain and displaced earlier and tucked the tendrils behind her ears.

She pinched her cheeks and checked her teeth. *Perfect.*

Back in the room, Sophie dropped a dry towel over the wet spot and turned on the desk lamp. She reached for the phone and saw a mound of paperwork scattered across his neatly made bed. Did he ever stop working?

She recognized the magazine's name, *Jazz,* and its trademark colors: purple and gold. Why would Ryan have *Jazz's* paperwork on his bed? Sure, they were part of the same corporation, but it was a completely different magazine. Was he transferring to *Jazz?*

She tried to pry her eyes from the bed, not wanting to snoop, but if he was leaving *Sports Now*, and moving to *Jazz*, she wanted to know.

She placed the handset back on the receiver and scooped up a few of the pages.

All of them were the same off-white, heavy-duty grade with Over the Top, Inc., letterhead. She wasn't looking at an internal job transfer. Not even close. The wording indicated a merge. More specifically, paperwork completely dissolving *Up Front* as an entity and folding it into *Jazz*. The printed words turned blurry, cutting into her like a dull knife, one that rips at the insides until the body bleeds out. Because this was as blunt and painful as an internal shredding.

Sophie blinked rapidly, unable to scroll down the entire page. She knew what a merge meant. *Jazz* was their online periodical. It meant ninety percent of their journalists were freelance writers.

And employees from *Up Front* would suddenly find themselves unemployed. No retirement. No health insurance.

Oh, God. She slumped onto the bed. Tears sprung to her eyes, blinding her from reading any further. Sophie cupped her mouth. Donovan's mom has Alzheimer's. Crap, he just took her to see *The Lion King*. He should have saved that money. He's her only source of support. What if he couldn't find a job for a few months?

Her heart pounded through her chest and, she couldn't find the strength to swallow the softball-sized lump. When she looked at the bottom of the paper, she noticed they were printed today, time stamped this morning. *After* the morning training to be exact. And before he kissed her.

Her grip loosened and the papers fell from her hands, floating back onto the bed. Ryan had used the conference room earlier and printed these pages. But why?

Another pile of papers with his sloppy handwritten notes

caught her eye. A list . . .

The dull blade twisted deeper. Each page started with a name. And then notes followed. Sophie couldn't stop herself.

Donovan—yes—everything Jazz *needs and wants.* She flipped to the next page.

Terri—no—she flirts too much and appears to copy Lori's work. Next page.

Lori—maybe—good articles. Next.

Tyler—no—terrible reviews.

Asher—no—just no.

Amy—yes—good fit for Jazz's "Fit and Flashy" column.

John—no—good guy, not going to cut it. Write a letter of recommendation.

Sophie kept flipping and reading name after name. When she turned to the final page, where her name was listed, she felt ill. But no words followed. Rather, a question mark. Probably a representation of what he thought of her.

I'm a question mark?

All that heaviness that she'd finally shed today came back with a vengeance.

Sophie wrenched her face to the side, wanting to unsee—*unknow*—what was right in front of her. She tried to come up with any possible scenario that suggested she was misreading this. But the thoughts scrambling in her head offered only one conclusion.

He lied to me.

Again.

A gut-wrenching pang tore through her. The familiar betrayal was like a knife shredding the soft layers of her vital organs. She dry-heaved and immediately covered her mouth with the back of her hand, refusing the impulse to purge. She gave him the benefit of the doubt, and he not only betrayed her, but he took her trust and squandered it.

"Oh, God," Ryan, clearly startled, said from behind her. She dropped the stack of papers and swung around, narrowing her eyes.

"Sophie, it's not what it looks like."

"Oh really, Ryan?" Sophie stamped her hands on her hips. "I'm a big girl. Why don't you tell me what it is, then?"

Ryan stood unmoving.

Heat rose in her face, and she could barely stand the sight of him. "How could you?" Her hoarse voice, barely above a whisper.

Ryan shook his head. "I . . . It all happened so fast. I had no idea about the merge until recently."

"Really, Ryan? No idea?"

"Nothing was solidified until today. It's been a rough few days."

"You're kidding right? Are you serious? Or are you just so delusional that you actually think *you've* had a rough few days."

"Sophie, this isn't personal."

"How can it be any less personal?" She waved her hands across the bed, encompassing everything there. "This is our livelihood." Her voice waned. "This is our family."

Ryan let out a sigh as if he were stalling to find the right words. Or cover up. Because isn't that what two-faced journalists did? Use five-dollar words in their cover stories to keep the opposition close? "I know, Sapphire."

She stabbed a finger at him. "Don't you dare."

"We've had to make some hard calls and do what's best for everyone."

Sophie scoffed at that. "Really, because every time you open your mouth I hear you back peddling and twisting this bull in your favor." Sophie's throat went dry. "And the worst part is you lied." Her legs threatened to give out. "But I defended you." *Oh, God. What would Donovan and Amy say? And of all people to be right about smelling a rat— Asher had pegged Ryan as being duplicitous.*

"Sophie, I know. And I'm really sorry. It's all very

hush-hush at the corporate office, but it's a corporate merge. I really did come to help with training, but things sort of moved fast. I'll be assisting with the transition."

"The transition?"

Ryan's brows creased. "The layoff."

Sophie's legs couldn't hold her. She slumped on the bed, the paper crinkling beneath her. "But you *lied*."

His face was sullen, his voice low. "I know. I didn't want to."

"When did you know?"

When he didn't answer right away, Sophie turned just enough to see Ryan shaking his head. "It's so very complicated."

"When, Ryan? Was it when you kissed me today? Was that your way of softening me up?" She held up the paper that bore her name. "What is this? Am I just a question mark to you? Tell me, is this a question of moral obligation or whether you should screw me all over again." She crumpled it and threw it at his feet.

He took a step toward her, supplication written all over his face. "No. Nothing like that. I want more for you. More than a low-rated magazine that if not merged, will close altogether. At least we can save a few jobs, and I'll write letters of recommendations and help find work for those who want to stay in the industry."

Sophie's stomach churned. She threaded her fingers together, pushing on her stomach to try and ease the pain. "I'm happy where I am. I love my job." Tears swelled and it only took one blink for her lashes to release a stream. "I love my outreach. The girls need me! And to think . . . I let you in. I told you about everything . . ." Sophie gasped. Realization hit her. With no magazine there was no budget for the outreach, which meant closing the café. There was no way she could afford rent on her own. Not with San

Francisco real estate. "How could you do that to the girls?"

"Sophie, you have to believe me," he pleaded. "That wasn't me. It's bad timing. Since I found out, I've been trying to figure out how to help the café."

A low guttural growl surfaced from somewhere inside. She enunciated each word carefully. "You stay away from me and my girls."

Ryan stepped toward Sophie, but she sidestepped. "I want to help. I believe in you and your cause. Trust me, Sophie, please." His beseeching eyes flickered in the dim light. "This isn't personal and it doesn't change one ounce about how I feel about you. Sophia, I lo—"

"No!" She stabbed her finger at him again. "You don't get to say that." She gestured at the strewn about papers on his bed. "And don't talk to me about trust, Pike. You lied about why you're here. You *lied to my face.* And then you had the nerve to kiss me."

Ryan shifted. He covered his head with both hands and then rubbed them through his hair. "This is not how I wanted to you find out. I was going to tell you tonight."

"Well isn't that convenient timing? I suppose you paid off that bee so you could avoid having this conversation. I bet you planned to get through the next twenty-four hours and say *au revoir*."

"Sophie, please. I didn't mean to hurt you, I promise. It's my job."

"Oh yeah? How much did you sell your soul for this time?"

At that, Ryan's face turned to stone. He looked at Sophie with his knowing eyes that in that moment turned tortured.

"That's right," Sophie said so calmly, she almost scared herself. "You threw me a sympathy bone to get your story last time. You turned a very private time of my life into an article and published it." She took a step closer, but Ryan remained anchored in place. "How could you?"

He rubbed the inside corners of his eyes and sighed heavily. "I wrote from my pain, Sophie. I had to process things. Why would a beautiful girl like you, with all the confidence in the world, stop talking to me all of a sudden? I thought you loved me."

Sophie listened but didn't buy his words.

"I had no idea they would publish it."

"Yes, you did. You know as well as I do that once the written word is out there, it's for the world to see." Sophie cringed from the heartache of those printed words. They were still imbedded in her mind like the Pledge of Allegiance or her social security number. "The article basically called me fat. It said I had a pretty face but valued my worth by my size. It said I scampered like a hermit crab. You said that."

"The editor took a little too much liberty."

"Don't you proofread those things before you submit? I know I do."

"No, not when you sign over the rights for a mere $250."

"You sold me out for $250?" Sophie could hear the strain in her voice, but hoped Ryan didn't catch it.

"No. I sold myself out."

Sophie threw her hands up. "Well, congratulations. You just did it again."

Sophie stormed past Ryan, but he reached out and snagged her arm, forcing her to turn around. "Don't leave like this."

Sophie snatched her arm back and leaned in, nose to nose. She had one question for the man who swooped in like he'd saved the world, but really only wanted to save face. "What would your mother say?"

Ryan recoiled. His creased brows drew together, and she knew she'd hit a nerve. A haunted look spread across his face.

"Enough!" Ryan's bark could have cleared a room.

Sophie flinched, not losing her lock on his eyes.

"I may not be perfect. I have my flaws, especially in the past, but I have tried to fix this. And for you to bring up my mother, it just shows you're weak."

Fire roared in her chest. Hot tears of frustration and disappointment and betrayal threatened to explode out of her. "I'm weak?"

"You need people to need you. And you can't let anyone else make a mistake or screw up without calling them on it. I messed up. And I was trying to fix it. I don't want this for you. But I don't make these decisions. Yet, you don't see that. You see that you have no control here and you're not willing to accept that."

"I do not need to have control."

"Oh really? Did you call Charlie yet? Is that why you're in my room?"

Sophie's jaw fell open. How did he know? "I was going to but then I saw all this—"

"Exactly. Control. You have no control over those girls, you don't have control over the magazine, you don't even have control over your emotions. And you won't let anyone help. You fight to hold that control. But it's all smoke and mirrors. Sometimes you have to accept what is and move forward."

Sophie's legs were cemented to the floor. She wanted to yell at him and scream that he was wrong, except a small part of her knew he had a point. She was out of control. The way she treated Asher? And why else would she have purged yesterday and wanted to do it again?

For control.

Sophie didn't have the words to argue. She dropped her eyes and looked away. "Maybe you're right."

Ryan's voice dropped to a whisper. "I want to be wrong. This is all wrong."

Sophie nodded. "I'm gonna go." Sophie turned on her

heel and made no effort to hold back the tears blinding her.

"Sophie, wait."

She turned, one hand holding the doorknob.

He swallowed dryly then quietly said, "Don't say anything to the others just yet. They need to hear it from me. I owe them that."

Right. Job first. "Don't worry. The last thing I want to do is talk about you to anyone. Goodbye, Pike. I hope the apple tasted just as good this time around."

~ ~ ~

Sophie held her breath. If she didn't breathe, she couldn't cry. But that didn't mean tears wouldn't stop streaming down her hot cheeks.

Ryan's room was closer to the stairs than it was the elevator. And though her eyes stung, she had to get as far away from Ryan as possible. She took the steps all the way to the fourth floor mezzanine, then bolted to her room. She barely slammed the door before sliding to the floor. With her knees drawn to her chest, she cried. Tears of anguish and defeat and frustration. Not just for her, but for her girls. The ones who needed her.

Or did they?

Ryan's words had struck a chord. He was right about her needing control. But still. If she didn't take care of those girls, who would?

She got up to wash her face, but when she stepped into the bathroom the clean smell of chlorine swirled in her gut. She fought the urge almost as much as she wanted to give in to it.

Her toothbrush lay next to the sink and she knew The Ritual would only take a moment. Her stomach grumbled, mad at her for missing dinner—something she'd plan to do with Ryan. A purge would turn that pang off too.

Not giving it a second thought, because second thoughts

led to regret, she grabbed her toothbrush and dropped to her knees. She slammed open the toilet seat and vise-gripped her toothbrush with all her might. When the familiar smell of porcelain and bleach danced up her nose, her mouth filled with the needed saliva to make this effortless. Her body convulsed, giving her permission to lean in and stick that brush in her wide-open mouth.

But her muscles seized.

What was she doing? How many times had she let the hurt define this moment for her? One? Two? Three? She shook her head. Four? Five? Six thousand times?

She sat back on her ankles and ran her thumb over her toothbrush's bristles. Its soft, synthetic blue and white fibers massaged her tender skin. She held it in front of her eyes, not willing for it to touch the back of her throat. Ever. Again.

Her thumbnail slowly flicked the quills, one by one, forcing each of the hundreds of tiny individual spines to pop up—each one a part of a whole.

A simple toothbrush, a tool meant for good, well, good hygiene at least, that she'd used for self-sabotage. She thought of her girls—individuals, who by themselves were amazing, but when working as a whole, changed each other's worlds for the better.

But if they were such a good unit, did they need her as much as she believed they did? Charlie was perfectly capable of taking care of Deidra the other day. Sure, it was food poisoning, but even if it wasn't, Charlie's calmness in the situation put what Sophie was doing right now to shame. So why did they need her so much? Or—Sophie gulped—grateful the urge to purge had passed, was it the other way around?

I need them.

"I do," Sophie said to her toothbrush, which happened to give her its undivided attention. "Love them and let them go?"

She shook the thought of releasing them to a pack of

gnarling wolves from her mind, but considered what Ryan had said. What if she'd simply just transferred her control from purging to being the mother hen for the girls? It was still her trying to control. But she couldn't always have it. Like Ryan said, control was a façade.

What if the girls really didn't need her as much as she needed them? What if she was holding them back from their growth and development? What if freeing them into the world would make a difference to the world and to them? They needed freedom. As long as she kept them in the café, they would continually look to her for guidance and strength. And in return she would feel loved and needed.

Oh my God. Was she keeping them in a rundown café, slaving over mediocre food, for her own benefit? She felt nauseous, but for a different reason entirely than purging.

After a moment, she crawled to her feet and stared in the mirror, taking inventory. It was clear that her spiral was not because of Ryan, or work, or even the café's financial problems. It was deeper. The girls were her safe place. A part of her believed that as long as she invested in them, they wouldn't leave her. They wouldn't betray her.

Was this how she allowed herself to be someone's question mark? She had guarded her heart and only shared it with those she could trust, people like her. She'd worked so hard to heal her heart, it had taken so long. But had she really healed? Or had she hid behind the thrill of being needed? Without another thought, she marched out of the bathroom and chucked the toothbrush against the fake window. She refused for it to have any hold on her. The toothbrush dropped without a sound. It was just a tool, useless without the power she gave it. And now it lay on the floor. Powerless.

She fired up her laptop and scrolled her curser over the 'To' line. She typed 'J. Tomilson.' She made a face. Stupid scuzzy landlord. His email address popped up. Then she scrolled down to the subject line. Her mouth pulled to one side, and as she typed, her one regret was not having done this a long time ago: Notice of Non-Renewal.

Chapter 34

When the passengers finally debarked the ship in the heart of the Bay, a full thirty hours after Sophie stormed out of his room, Ryan carried his lone, black travel bag off the cruise ship and to an awaiting cab.

The mid-morning fog was burning off and Ryan hoped to get back to the local office before anyone had a chance to catch him. Yesterday's final training went off without a hitch. Or Sophie's attendance.

It shouldn't surprise him by now just how easily he compartmentalized all parts of his life. His dad, his job, his friends, and of course Sophie. No one area could affect another. He once viewed that as strength, now it felt like a fault. *Damn.*

The cab pulled alongside the office building. Ryan paid the driver and had almost exited when Red pushed him back in.

"Not here," Red said.

"Not here what?"

Red scooted across the seat, right up to Ryan's leg, and shut the door. "Take us to 15th and Irving Street," Red ordered the driver.

"What's going on, Red?"

"Guess who just called?"

Ryan knew Red's exit interview was scheduled for this morning, but he didn't dare answer that question. Phil had already dropped a few A-bombs over the past four days. So Ryan went with the safe and easy. "Couldn't tell ya. Who?"

"Well, it's the reason our meeting won't be taking place in my office." Red's plump face stared out the window as they hummed through the City. "My former office, I should say."

Ryan froze. "Come again?"

Red turned to Ryan. "Really?"

Ryan looked straight ahead. Someone must've called him. Maybe Sophie. "Okay."

Red nodded. The driver dodged three near misses with other vehicles, weaving in and out of lanes, and played Rochambeau with bicyclists.

When the cab stopped, and Ryan saw where they were, he rolled his eyes. "What are you doing, Red? We have a meeting, and then I'm going to SFO."

"What time's your flight?"

"Not until five, but—"

"Then you have plenty of time to humor an old man."

"I don't understand."

"Just pay the man," Red instructed. "You make the big bucks."

Ryan sighed but didn't argue. "Is this necessary? I've had a long, hard week and . . ."

Red shot daggers at Ryan, and he clamped his mouth shut.

Oh, right. You were basically just fired.

Red exerted extra effort to hoist himself out of the cab, and Ryan followed. He handed the cabby a twenty and closed the door.

"Let's have a drink," Red insisted. "You and I need to talk."

Ryan sighed heavily. He hadn't slept more than two hours since Sophie found those papers. Torment gnawed at his conscience. He slung his bag over his shoulder and shoved his hands in his pockets, following Red into the Sports Bar.

Red beelined to the bar and gestured two fingers at the neon sign above their head indicating that specific IPA, then turned to Ryan and said, "You screwed up."

Red didn't beat around the bush. Ryan glared straight ahead at all the varying labels of rum, vodka, scotch. The red-labeled scotch took him back to the tender where he threaded his fingers in Sophie's hair and enjoyed her body's response.

Ryan cleared his throat and gripped the opened bottle the bartender slid to him. He pressed it to his lips and took a prolonged pull. The fizz felt better than it should.

"You going to just let that little girl go?"

"Sophie?" Ryan swallowed a lump. "Red, I really don't think that is any of your concern."

"That bad, huh?"

Ryan took another swing and put the bottle down, peeling the label. "Got anything harder than beer? It was a blood bath."

"That's what I heard."

Ryan glared at Red. "She rat me out to you?"

"She's like a daughter to me." His voice was gravelly. "So that makes this worse. But no. It wasn't her."

Ryan nodded and continued to remove the sticker from the bottle. "Donovan?"

Red nodded. "Remember we're a family. We have our share of black sheep, but we're still close knit. He did the right thing. He was straight with me. He's worried about Sophie. And he told me you two spent an awful lot of time together."

"Not to be rude, Red, but I'd like to keep my personal business private. We do, however, have some stats and ratings we can run through, if you'd like."

Red waved his hand through the air. "Seriously, Ryan, you *are* green. What's the point? The magazine is closing."

Ryan shook his head and shrugged. "I can't confirm or—"

"Deny that statement at this time?" Red finished his sentence. "Is that what you're trying to tell me? You're feeding *me* a line? Son, I invented that line." Red flagged the bartender to bring two more beers.

"Just one," Ryan said to the man. "I have to fly soon. I don't want to be impaired."

"Fine." Red wiped the corners of him mouth with his thumb and forefinger. "Let me give you a tip for free. Can I be candid?"

"Sure." It's the least he could do.

"You don't know shit."

"Excuse me?" Ryan frowned.

"Just what I said. You assume in all the years I've been here, news about my canning, or excuse me"—he curled his fingers together creating quotation marks—"early retirement wouldn't reach me? We both knew even before you stepped on that plane to come here, I was on the cutting block."

"So, when I saw you drunk in your office, you were already aware?"

"Hell yes, I knew. What? You think I get skunked in my office for fun?"

Ryan held Red's gaze. The man deserved the highest level of respect. Clearly Ryan had misread a few things this week.

"The answer is no," Red asserted, taking a drink of his IPA, and almost choking as he laughed. "No, actually, I had just got off the phone with my contact. And, well, let's just say, I took a trip down memory lane. Sorry you had to bear witness. Besides, why do you think I bailed on the cruise? I had to get some affairs in order."

"Oh." Ryan stared at his beer. It now seemed rude to look the man in the eye. Ryan spent so much time chasing his dream, he managed to pick up a hearty dose of egotistical misconception. "I just assumed you weren't invited."

Red blew a raspberry against the lip of his beer bottle. "See. You don't know shit."

"Stop saying that."

"Then stop acting like a spoiled child in this very adult game of journalism. Here's another freebie: this industry is dying. People don't want paper magazines to deliver them the news. They want their news via tablet additions and their politics via parodies."

Ryan knew that, which was part of the reason for the merge and why his sports app would eventually expand and cross over into all subsidiaries owned by Over the Top, Inc.

"Anyway, like I said, I spent the past few days getting my affairs in order before I sign on the dotted line. I'm going to enjoy this pension I earned."

Ryan nodded, not sure what to say.

"I called my lawyer, sold some stocks, made plans to travel to Israel. Always wanted to go there." Red pulled his wallet from his back pocket. "But here's my point." Red placed a tattered black and white picture in front of Ryan. The woman in the photo was young. Her hair was short, styled just below her ears. She wore a classic 1960s-era, one-piece swimsuit, donned an open-mouth smiled.

"She's beautiful. Let me guess, she's the one that got away?"

"No, she's my sister, Sandy. Dead nine years now."

Oh. "I'm so sorry."

Red returned the photo to his wallet. "No, the one that got away . . . we were married for eleven years. But she couldn't handle me never being home. I guess we grew apart. Funny though. Here I am, twenty-some-odd years later, scrounging around trying to find myself, and she's happily remarried. Living in Martha's Vineyard, with our kids close by. Don't blame them for staying in the Vineyard either."

Ryan finished peeling the label from his empty bottle and wadded it into a ball. "That's tough, but I don't see my life going in that direction."

"My sister, though," Red continued, "she was very sweet and ever the patient one. When she got sick, I justified my long hours so I could put money toward the best treatment facilities."

"Cancer?"

"Not quite. Lou Gehrig's Disease."

"Ah, jeez. That's awful. I'm sorry to hear that." Ryan was familiar with that one. Named after a legend. Every year *Sports Now* ran an article highlighting the degenerating disease and what their partnership with the Lou Gehrig's Disease Foundation did for medical research.

"Yep, me too. I was all she had left after our parents passed away. And rather than spend the precious time we had left together holding her hand, washing her hair, reading to her or doing whatever I could do to help, I stayed safe and sound in my office, telling myself I was providing."

"I see."

"I don't think you do, Pike." Red threw two twenties on the bar. "But that's all I got. I wish you well and I hope you take my words to heart—or to hell—doesn't really matter to me. But I'm worried about Sophie, and though I didn't support her cause near enough, I get why she fought for that café. I wish I would have fought harder for better medicine for Sandy when I had the chance."

Red slid off his stool and shook Ryan's hand. "Good luck, Pike. I'm on my way to Martha's Vineyard. I want to see my kids. My daughter is a mother now. Hmm, imagine that," he mused. "I'm a granddad yet I've only seen those bouncy brunette curls on the screen of my phone."

Red pushed through the bar's exit, midday light blinded Ryan for a moment, before the door closed behind him.

"Can I get you anything else, boss?" the bartender asked as he collected Red's forty bucks.

"Not unless you have a conscience tucked away back there. But I do have a flight to catch. Can you call me a cab?"

Chapter 35

Sophie knocked on Grandmoo's front door before unlocking it and walking inside. She brought with her the usual: roses, Bengay, and chocolates, which her diet didn't allow, but the woman was seventy-six years old. Who cared?

"Grandmoo?" Sophie called.

"In here, dear." Her grandmother's voice still sung like a canary's.

When Sophie walked through the kitchen, and into the dining room, a new nurse was preparing Grandmoo's dinner. Salisbury steak—probably no salt—*what's the point?*—red potatoes, and a spinach salad.

Sophie hid the box of chocolates behind her back. "Hi. We haven't met, I'm Sophie."

Sophie pegged the nurse in her mid-forties. Stout, heavy on the eyeliner, and short, gray hair, with purple highlights streaking her bangs. "Evening, I'm Darleen. Feel free to drop those chocolates on the table, I'm sure they're easier to eat when not tucked behind her your back."

Sophie stared. "Wait, is this a trick?"

The nursed smiled and went back to preparing Grandmoo's tray of food. "Women never joke about chocolate."

Grandmoo was a lefty, and Sophie liked how the nurse made sure the fork sat near her left hand. Since her stroke affected her left side, details like that mattered.

"I like you." Sophie tossed the chocolates on the kitchen table, where they landed with a thud. She grabbed a tiny, porcelain coffee cup, which was part of a post-World War

II china set, from the cupboard—and poured herself a mug. One thing about Grandmoo, the coffee was always brewed. "Not that I'm not already swooning over Darleen, but where's your other nurse, Grandmoo?"

"April? She went on maternity leave three weeks ago. I told her when she was ready to come back to work to bring that baby. At least *somebody* is making babies for me."

Sophie rolled her eyes. "I didn't realize April was that far along. And," Sophie said, pulling a dining chair out from the table to sit, "wouldn't you rather I be married and settled before I start breeding?"

Grandmoo shoveled a piece of meat in her mouth and chewed slowly. "Yes, but would it kill you to put a rush on that?"

Just a week ago, Sophie thought maybe something like that could be in her near future. But any relationship that had a prayer of lasting was built on trust. "I'll say an extra prayer for that tonight, *mmmkay*?" She dumped three sugar cubes into her coffee and sipped.

Grandmoo slipped a crystal saltshaker from her slacks and flavored her meat.

"I didn't see that either," Darleen said. "But keep it to a simple amount. I don't want any evidence left behind."

"Pretty sure I really like you," Sophie said behind a smile.

"Well, the feeling's mutual. I'll be in the living room if you need me, Barb," Darlene said to Grandmoo.

Grandmoo pushed her plate toward Sophie. "You want any? It's low cholesterol, no sodium, pretty sure it's gluten- and taste-free too."

Sophie eyed the food on her plate. She'd rather eat the plate. "I'm good."

"Me too. Let's break open that chocolate."

"Great, because we have celebrating to do."

Grandmoo's eyes glossed over with confusion. "I thought you told me on the telephone that *Up Front* was folding, you were closing the café, and moving out this weekend."

"I did, Grandmoo. But you know how it is. One idea has to die, be buried, get infested by maggots, and become long forgotten before a bigger idea can be born."

"So, we've murdered the café and now what?" Grandmoo's smile was only half of what it used to be. But both eyes still glistened when the right side of her face lit up.

Sophie set a packet of papers on the table in front of her grandmother. They included copies of already-filed forms—as of a week ago, thank you very much—with a name, articles of incorporation, request for an EIN, and a list of the newly appointed, and most fabulous, board of directors known to man. "I wouldn't say murder. I'd say more like putting an ax to our little club, that was really hindered by the fact it was sponsored by a for-profit company."

Grandmoo, who'd spent her entire career working for the state attorney general's office, opened the package. She still had ties there and knew everyone who'd worked there since the seventies—including the current attorney general, who was sworn into office just last year. "I know it's a stretch, but I think it'll work. I just need a little help."

Grandmoo stroked her tongue across the top of her teeth, most of which were still hers, reached across the table, and flipped the top of the chocolate box open. She grabbed a nuts-and-chews delight. Her eyes scanned the papers. "I see."

Sophie knew that "I see." She'd heard it when Sophie decided to go to the private college rather than an out of state school, because it was closer to Grandmoo. She'd also heard it when she decided to move out of the house after Grandmoo had mostly recovered from the stroke, and then most recently, when she put together the outreach for the café. It was Grandmoo's prelude to "Yes, let's do it."

"What's your game plan, sweetie, and how can I help?"

A thrill of relief washed over Sophie. "Just like that. No questions about why I want to do this?"

"Baby, you are just like your father. I raised him to make a difference, and even if his life was cut short, I had no doubt in my mind you would carry on his passion for what matters. And this matters." She set her hands on top of the papers and looked directly into her eyes. "I ask again. How can I help?"

Sophie wanted to fold into her grandmother. Sure, Grandmoo knew about her illness, and Sophie shared that she relapsed, but Grandmoo had never labeled her a bulimic. "I need the direct number to the attorney general."

Chapter 36

Ryan stared at the office microwave as his dinner spun slowly around and around. He spent the last week eating frozen TV dinners. He didn't even bother picking out a selection, he just randomly grabbed ten lemon chicken and broccoli combinations. It didn't matter. Food all tasted the same right now. Added bonus, they fit perfectly in *Up Front's* break room freezer. His empty hotel suite was the last place he wanted to be.

He'd been in San Francisco for a week, tying up loose ends for the merge and overseeing *Up Front's* final issue. The applications for freelance journalists were flying in and the team at *Up Front* worked solemnly on their final pieces.

The cubicles were now void of personal touches and any sort of life in the office ceased to exist. Ryan reminded himself a hundred times a day that this was not personal. It was just work.

His plan was simple: finish merging *Up Front to Jazz*, and then go home. He'd ask Lola to go shopping for some furnishing. Since his time on the road was coming to a close, he decided he might as well put some color in his two-bedroom apartment, even if he didn't have anyone to share it with. Since he did such a stellar job ruining relationships, he certainly didn't have a need for that second room, no family in his future. He made a mental note to check with his apartment management for a single bedroom.

The microwave dinged, and Ryan retrieved his dinner. Dry bird on a bed of fiber. It sounded as appetizing as it would taste. He grabbed a plastic fork from the community drawer, and charged back to his office. He had to blog about the pennant. Another Giant's World Series was on the mound. "Hmm," he mumbled to himself. "That's a good title."

"What's a good title?" a raspy voice coming from Red's former office said.

Ryan flipped on the light. He kept his emotions on tight lockdown, refusing to let surprise show on his face. His dad didn't deserve that. His dad sat in the chair. His clothes wrinkled, his hair thinning. A tattered travel bag rested against the desk. Ryan frowned at the bag. "Let me guess, you happen to be in the area?"

Ryan didn't mean for his voice to come across so cold, but then again, what did his dad want?

"No, son. I've been trying to reach you."

"I know. I get your messages. I just haven't had the time to call you back."

"Haven't had the time, or haven't made the time?" His dad swiveled in the chair.

Ryan tossed his dinner onto his desk. "Accusation or assentation, Dad, because I'm not sure you know the difference." He backed to the corner of the office and sat down on the leather couch Red had left.

"I'm not here to argue," his father said calmly. "I'm only here to pay you a visit. I didn't even get a hotel room. If you don't want me to stay, I won't. I'll head to Santa Clara tonight."

Santa Clara? That was over two hours away. Ryan cleared his throat. So his dad was putting the ball in his court. Forcing him to either take the high road and pretend the man hadn't walked out of his life over a decade ago, or sent him packing. Ryan smoothed his palm over his mouth. "How's Nicole?" Ryan asked, dodging his dad's peace offering. A classic "Steven Pike" move.

"Great." His dad looked him up and down before adding, "I'm surprised you haven't been in closer contact with your sister. You two sure didn't have a problem with that before."

"Get out." Ryan stood and pointed at the door. "You don't get to do that. I'm not twenty anymore. I didn't ask you here, and I certainly don't need to stand here while you throw shade in my face."

"I didn't mean that, I'm sorry." His dad held up his hands. "Just give me a minute to explain." The sudden crack in his old man's voice made him appear ten years older.

"What do you want, Dad?" Ryan leaned against the arm of the couch, crossing his arms.

"I, uh, I tried, you know?" His dad's gaze drifted, as if he were searching for the right words. Ryan hoped they didn't include "I'm sorry" because he didn't know if he could handle that right now. There was no way this man was sorry after years of little more than a few short phone calls. Mostly for his birthday, which he actually had incorrect. "I tried calling you. I left you messages. I wanted to write you, but there are some things you can't put into words. And this wasn't something I could just leave on a machine."

Ryan couldn't help the pull in his chest. He straightened, trying to shake the unease that prickled under his skin. After so long, his dad was coming to him with grave news. It wasn't that Ryan assumed something was wrong, he knew it. He heard the same tone when his parents came to him and Nicole with the news that his mother had only a few months left. "This what?" he asked in a small voice.

His dad turned away. It was as if looking in his son's eyes would kill him. Maybe his dad realized he'd lost permission to look directly in his eyes. It was a matter of respect. And Ryan had very little for the man who sat across the room. But somehow Ryan knew the next words from his dad's mouth would change everything.

"Cirrhosis of the liver."

"Jesus, Dad." Ryan rubbed both hands down his face. "What the hell? You serious?" He stood and ambled across the office to where his dad's face paled. "Look at me."

He complied.

"How long?"

"Long enough."

"How long do you have?" He nearly choked on that question. Years of alcohol abuse finally caught up with him. And now Ryan had to face the fact that both his parents would be gone. No matter the cause, when a man comes to you with impending death, suddenly little more matters than the time left.

His dad shrugged. "Ten minutes. Ten years. I don't really know. I've been local a few months now seeking treatment at the Liver and Disease Clinic. Your blog post this week placed you here. And then when I called your office to see if you were still here, your assistant told me where to find you. The door was unlocked, so I let myself in."

Ryan sighed. "Yeah, she's been on me to call you."

"And you didn't want to?"

Ryan feigned a smile. "Can you blame me?"

His dad's face grew somber. "I screwed up, Ryan." His dad pushed away from the desk and walked around to Ryan. He half sat against the desk, folding his hands in his lap. "My diagnosis isn't sudden. I've been dealing with it for a while. Your sister knows, but I asked her not to mention it to you."

"But, Dad—"

His dad held up a hand. "Just listen a minute. I've had great care in Paris going the natural route, but I need serious intervention now. I'm terminal, and if I want to prolong a few years, I need advanced treatment."

Terminal? God that word was like a hot iron down a man's throat. "Geez, Dad. Why didn't you say something?"

His dad pulled in a deep breath, and Ryan watched his eyes fill. Suddenly he knew exactly why his dad didn't tell him sooner. "Because you made it. Everything I ever told you was wrong. I couldn't let my health stop you from moving toward your dream."

That gut shot hurt. Apparently, he'd set himself up to become a soulless ass. He'd buried himself in work, just to prove his dad wrong. And now? Now his dad was pointing out the very thing Red had. The very thing Sophie had. What did work matter when you wake up thirty years later and find yourself alone? It reared its ugly head with Sophie and had ground in with his dad. What could he say? "And now?"

"And now I'm making my amends. I can't fix what I did or said to you before, but I am telling you now that I screwed up. I'm sorry. And though they are just words, I plan on spending the last bit of time I have here between treatment and my new job."

Ryan felt his brows furrow. "Job?"

"I'm volunteering at the Institute of Astronomy Academy as a mentor to young astronomers."

Ryan about lost his balance. "Wait, you're going back into astronomy? I thought you gave that up for good."

A shadow of a smile draped across his face. "You never give up a passion, son. I merely lost my vision on what was important and stopped trying. But there's a whole new generation of kids who get all their science from social media, and I intend on promoting this program to fix that FUBAR."

Ryan laughed. "Nice, Dad."

"Well, it's not like I have another ten years to screw up again." He paused and sighed. "I cannot express to you how wrong I was. Your job matters. What you do matters. The difference you make in journalism matters. Even if it is just about funny-shaped balls and bad referee calls."

Ryan forced a grin. He didn't need to tell his dad his own

FUBAR to know he had some work to do. He didn't need his rocket-scientist father to guide him. Forgiveness was a process, not a drive-through, have-it-your-way request. He needed to sit down and have a serious conversation with his dad. And Nicole, apparently. But that was for later. His dad was here. Trying. And if a man with a terminal disease with nothing to gain by tucking his tail between his legs could admit he was wrong, then Ryan could take a page from dear old Dad's book.

"Dad, I have to go."

His dad's eyes met his. He got it. "Then go."

Ryan tossed his dad a room key. "I'm staying at the Grand Bella Suites. It's a two-bedroom suite." He looked his dad over. "Why don't you call concierge and have that suit cleaned? And I'd say help yourself to the mini-bar, but don't. I'd like a chance to maybe check out a constellation or two with you."

His dad's smile warmed him. If decades-old pain didn't kill a man, then maybe it wasn't too late with Sophie. He grabbed his cell and scrolled numbers until he found one he hadn't dialed in over ten years. Barbara Dougherty's home number.

Chapter 37

Sophie stood in front of Chicks 'n' Slicks' bar top, staring at the café's hand-made sign. She would miss the charm of this place. And the memories. But nothing more.

Chicks 'n' Slicks closing was not Ryan's fault. She knew that. No matter how many times she crunched the numbers, the rent was impossibly high, even for San Francisco, and without Over the Top's stipend, it was in financial stasis.

Her chest gripped as she remembered the surprise in Ryan face when she'd seen everything in his cabin. He was shocked. But not because she learned about the merge, but because he'd hurt her—that much she could see from his expression. She knew he didn't mean to hurt her. And then he made her face some truths about herself. So much so, that back at the office, Sophie had quit without a second thought.

Amy reported that Ryan's downcast eyes matched his solemn mood. Sure, she and Donovan stayed on with *Jazz* as their day job, and were cordial to Ryan, but ultimately, she knew this was her calling—even if it did mean she was moving back in with Grandmoo for the interim.

Sophie shook the thought. It had no place in her mind tonight. No, tonight was their last night as a family. Scratch that. It was the last night they would be at the café as a family. After this meeting, she would lock the door one last time, and Slumlord Sam could have his precious, run-down building to do with as he pleased. They may have to meet in a parking garage or something for a while, but that was okay.

Today, it became official. Grandmoo, who was a long-time colleague and close friend of Jonathan Bosson, the newly appointed attorney general, not only walked into his office without an appointment—as anyone who knew Grandmoo kept an open-door policy—but spent an hour with him.

"Okay, ladies," Sophie said, feeling as giddy as she did nervous. "You all know I have been working on a secret project, and this is the moment we have been waiting for. I just got the call."

The room fell completely silent. The girls, who had helped pack up and spent the afternoon reminiscing about their many shared memories, had all eyes on Sophie.

Her smile could hardly contain her excitement. "As of 3:54 p.m. the attorney general has formally signed the required document cementing our status as a not-for-profit organization.

"I don't have a new location secured, I don't have the start-up funds raised, and I don't have a clue how this is going to go, but our board members are in place." Sophie winked at Amy and Donovan, and then nodded at Jenny's mom who helped recruit the rest of the bodies. "We have the passion and know-how to run this, and we have each other." Sophie's eyes filled and threatened to spill over. "I want you, my family, to be the first to see it. Drum roll . . . without further ado, I introduce to you *Fierce Magazine!*"

Sophie ripped the sheet from the tripod stand holding the cardboard cutout of the new magazine's look, this one complete with a recent picture of Charlie on the cover and lots of clip-art from her word processer. The room exploded into varying degrees of joyful tears, hoots, laughter, and a smidgen of disbelief.

"Calm down. Let me finish."

The girls obeyed, though a few snapped pictures on their phones and began tapping away.

"This is not just a magazine, but the Bay Area's only magazine that focuses solely on combating negative body image for teens while offering an entire online forum to express triggers and how to overcome them. Every month, the top ten stories from the forum, as well as editorial guidance from professionals in their field, will be featured in print."

Over the span of five years, Sophie hoped to expand the magazine, both geographically and editorially, allowing teenagers to have a voice and support each other without having to live in shame or fear. That way, thousands of teenagers who struggled with eating disorders, bullying, body image, and an array of other hurts and hang-ups would have a place to find help. She also planned on setting up an anonymous eight hundred number for struggling teens who needed help right away. "Girls, this is innovative. It will be a teen-inspired, teen-driven initiative."

"Can I go first?" Deidra's hand popped up.

"We will all have a part in this," Sophie answered.

"Yeah, but can I go first?"

"Of course you can." Sophie filled her lungs and looked around. No matter how beat up this building was, she and the girls had made it a home. So much so Deidra finally fessed up as the one who brought in the pet rats because she read they were a good-luck omen for businesses. Luckily, thanks to her friend Bob Jamison, they made their way to a pet store. But now it was time to let go and let her girls spread their wings. They would always have each other, and now they could be a part of something bigger.

The girls peppered her with more questions.

"How will we do this?"

Sophie answered, "One day at a time."

"When will it release?"

"I expect in the next couple of months."

"What will I wear to my photo shoot?" Diedre asked.

"Clothes, I hope," Sophie said on a laugh.

"Can I have a corner office?" Charlie rubbed her hands together.

"Sure. Would you like that overlooking the bay or are you okay with city view?"

Charlie sneered. "You don't have to be snarky."

"Well," Sophie said, "come back down to reality and I won't have to be."

Amy and Donovan passed out packets explaining how a magazine ran and for the next thirty minutes, the girls asked more questions. They even bounced around a few good ideas for fundraising.

And then it was over. Everyone had left in a chattering bustle of excitement, promising to see Sophie in a few days. The café stood silent, empty. The end of an era. Sophie let a few rogue tears fall. A healing, struggle-filled, hard, amazing, era. Charlie was the only person left, since Sophie was giving her a ride home.

"Are you all set?" Amy waited by the bar.

Sophie wiped her wet cheeks. "Yes. I release you back into the wild."

"Good. I'm off to see Mark. He wants to watch a movie or something domestic tonight."

"Ugh, that sounds fun," Sophie said.

"I'd invite you, but you tend to turn green when we start playing tonsil hockey."

"Gross. Get out. And don't forget your promise to name your firstborn after me. Get busy on that."

"Right away. Oh, and by the way, I set you up a GoFundMe account for the new project."

"You what?" Sophie said, not sure she agreed with asking for money at this stage.

"Well, I am the treasurer. And it's more of a Kickstarter for non-profits, and supporters get an ad in our magazine as long as they meet the approved guidelines."

"Wow," Sophie said, taken aback. "How's it doing?"

"I'd say pretty well after Ash-face donated five thousand dollars."

He actually donated the money? No sexual favors required?

Interesting. "Oh, so his ice-cold heart warmed a few degrees." Sophie's spiteful words held no remorse.

"Could be. But good riddance now that he's up north with that news affiliate."

"Good riddance, indeed. And I'm going to go ahead and veto any ad request he has. But we'll keep the non-refundable donation. It'll be good to clean the tar from his black soul."

Amy laughed, and Charlie raised her plastic champagne glass they had used to toast the evening. Well, sparkling cider impersonating champagne, but details.

"Also," Amy said, a hint of enticement in her voice, "there's also a hefty donation from a donor named Mr. Sapphire."

Sophie's jaw dropped.

"But we'll talk about donations in the morning."

"Amy Aaliyah Reedy. Don't you drop a bomb like that and walk out of here as if nothing happened."

"Tomorrow. I promise." She blew Sophie a kiss and turned to Charlie. "Later, smaller version of Sophie."

"See ya, Hair."

After the door closed behind Amy, Sophie stood with her hand resting on the doorknob. *Mr. Sapphire?* No, it couldn't be. She'd purposely held back the magazine details from Ryan because she couldn't handle it. No matter how many times she stitched her heart back together, anything concerning him threatened to rip it back open. She couldn't risk it again. Not with the new magazine.

The front door pushed open and startled Sophie mid thought. In the half second it took to recognize the face in front of her, she'd expected it to be Amy, but hoped it would be Ryan, she froze. If she could backtrack five seconds, she would have locked the door. Because the face in front of her was flaming red. His nostrils flared, and his breath reeked of alcohol.

"James Tomilson? I didn't expect to see you until tomorrow. What can I do for you?"

"You can pay me the seven thousand dollars you owe me."

Sophie turned her head enough where she still had an eye on her landlord, but wanted Charlie out of there. "Charlie, please wait for me in the kitchen."

"No," Charlie said. "I'm not leaving you."

"Charlie," Sophie said, calm but firm as not to scare Charlie. "Please do as I say."

Charlie slowly rose and pushed her chair under the table. She hesitantly backed into the kitchen. Once she was safely out of sight, Sophie stepped deeper into the dining area, if only to put some distance between herself and the foul smell that came from her drunken landlord. *Former landlord, that is.*

"Mr. Tomilson," Sophie started, "I emailed you almost two weeks ago that we were not renewing our lease."

He staggered closer, forcing Sophie to step back. "I know, sweetheart, but that doesn't mean you don't still owe me for back rent and for all the damage this place has sustained."

Sophie took offense. "Ohhh no you don't! This place was a rat's nest when we moved in. In fact, we used our own money to fix the floors, the walls, and update the fixtures. All of which you are legally bound to do."

"I never received a request."

Sophie eyed Mr. Tomilson closely. He was plastered. Any chance of a decent or even partially civil conversation would not be happening tonight. "I'm going to have to ask you to leave."

He slid further inside. "No, I don't think so. I want to know how you intend to pay me back. I have debts I have to pay, and you have to pay yours. Okay, honey?"

Sophie pointed at the exit. "You are technically on my rented property until tomorrow morning, as indicated by our rental agreement. So, I'm asking you to leave or else I will call the police and have you escorted off the property."

"Listen, honey. I own this hole-in-the-wall and will take payment in full right now. Collateral payment is fine too."

"Collateral?" Sophie asked, almost to herself.

"Yes, I have my eye on that vintage custard machine, and I will take that for now. You can work out the rest of the payment with my property management tomorrow."

The custard machine meant more to Sophie than any earthly item she owned. And it would follow them wherever their outreach took them. Because the custard machine represented Suzie, who'd died fighting something so much bigger than her seventy-three pounds. "Not a chance in hades that you'll ever get your hands on our custard machine."

"I'll have you arrested for fraud, little lady. I know that custard machine is worth a pretty penny. I'll give you two thousand in credit for it."

"Over my dead body," Sophie said firmly. "Now, if you don't get out I'm going to call the police."

Tomilson's bloodshot eyes narrowed. He picked up a chair and slammed in on the ground. "Go ahead, princess."

"Get out," Charlie's voice echoed over the linoleum. She had the baseball bat Sophie kept in her office for moments just like this. Except they'd never had a moment like this, and no matter how prepared you think you are, when someone's threatening you, you're not always bat-ready.

"Charlie, no!" Sophie yelled.

"You know what you're doing with that thing, girl?"

Charlie raised the bat over her head. "Get out before I show you."

Tomilson looked directly into Sophie's eyes, his intent was clear. "You heard her. That was a direct threat, and I'm gonna defend myself."

"No." Sophie shoved Mr. Tomilson just as he lunged past her, grabbing her arms and thrusting her into a table. Sophie slid off the table and rolled onto the ground.

She sat up, about to charge forward, but what she saw stopped her breath.

Mr. Tomilson had somehow snatched the bat from Charlie and had it cocked back, ready to strike. Charlie lay on the floor, hands raised in defense.

"Stop!" Sophie screamed.

A blur of a long, gray coat flew past Sophie and tackled Mr. Tomilson. *Ryan?*

Ryan's one arm wrapped around Tomilson's neck, and his other did some sort of twist move.

The slumlord dropped the bat. It echoed as it hit the ground. "You want to pick on a kid?" Ryan shouted in his ear.

Mr. Tomilson unleashed every curse word known to mankind in the few seconds it took for Ryan to escort him to the door like he was nothing more than a doll. The last sentence Sophie heard before the front door closed behind them was something about a lawsuit.

Sophie muttered, "Go ahead and try," and then rushed over to Charlie.

A few moments later, Ryan came back in. Sophie's heart kicked into high gear and she knew she owed him everything, yet didn't know what to say.

Ryan's eyes searched every inch of Sophie's body. "You okay?"

Physically, yes she was. She nodded.

"Your, uh, visitor won't be bothering you again this evening. But just in case, I'll hang here if you need anything." And like a true gentleman, Ryan pulled out a chair from one of the only tables left and planted his too sexy, heroic butt in it.

"Thank you, Ryan," she managed.

~ ~ ~

An hour later Ryan quietly knocked on the office door. "Can we talk?"

Sophie raised her head from her laptop and took him in. All of him. Ryan leaned against the doorframe with his arms loosely crossed. He seemed larger than life at that moment, like he filled up the whole room. Not that there was much space left to be had with all the boxes that lined the back wall. Only her desk and a few necessary office supplies were left unpacked.

She closed the laptop having just replied to a second grant that had been awarded to Chicks 'n' Slicks.

"Yeah. And thanks." She looked at Charlie peacefully sleeping on the couch. Ryan had carried her into the office after she had fallen asleep in Sophie's lap. "You know, for everything." Sophie's heart still thundered from what had happened. Or maybe it was because Ryan was still here.

He stared at her, but she refused to fall into his gaze. Not this time. Not ever again. His Biblical-worthy exodus out of town after the cruise spoke volumes. Sure, he'd came back to interim at *Up Front* as it closed, but he didn't try to see her, and that was for the best.

Though, she was grateful he was here when Tomilson went crazy, that brought up another question. "Why are you here?"

He stepped around the desk and took her hands, guiding her up. "I'm not asking you to trust me again. I don't deserve that. But I do want you to know how sorry I am. Enough that I will turn around right now and never bother you again. But if any part of you believes me, then all I'm asking for is a chance to prove it to you."

She swallowed a hard lump. His eyes captured hers and his gaze slowly traced her face, settling on her lips. And like always, it elicited a deeply rooted tingling. It also pained her. The last time he'd made her feel that was right before she'd entered his cabin on the ship. She'd longed to feel like that again. But he was an editor in chief now in a land far, far away.

Sophie shrugged. "How did you know where to find me?"

"Grandmoo."

"She sold me out?" Sophie frowned. "She's supposed to be Team Sophie."

"I can be pretty persuasive." Ryan winked.

"She's not as shrewd now as she was in her hay day, I suppose." Though Sophie knew it wasn't true. Grandmoo had just helped pull a modern-day miracle pushing through her non-profit magazine. Typical time frame was a minimum three months and she got it done in less than three days.

Ryan reached inside his coat pocket and withdrew some papers. "Here."

Sophie narrowed her eyes. "What's this?"

"Just look at them."

Sophie unfolded the carbon copies of what looked to be a contract. "Is this the same thing your HR department sent us? Because if so I have the copies in my drawer."

Ryan's brows furrowed. "What are you talking about?"

Sophie set Ryan's papers down and reached into the top drawer, taking out a manila envelope. "Your stamped signature closing us down is right here. It was a nice touch having it delivered certified mail. Your formal apology in the official letter was heartwarming. Did your assistant come up with that, or do you write your own Dear John letters?"

Ryan shook his head at the paperwork. A muscle tensed along his jaw. "This isn't my signature."

"Well, they have a fine copy of it."

"That's why I'm here, Sophie." Ryan leaned on the desk. "I resigned."

What? "You quit?"

"Yup."

"But why?" Her voice cracked but she couldn't hide her enthusiasm. "That was your dream job. It's what you killed yourself for. It's what cost you . . ." Sophie couldn't make herself finish that sentence. It's what cost him *them*.

"It's because of bull like this." He stabbed the packet with his finger. "This is not what I signed up for. It's all bureaucracy and politics."

"Oh." Sophie stared at the packet. Ryan's finger turned white from the pressure. She picked up his hand, not sure what their physical boundaries were.

He laced their fingers together. She didn't realize how cold she was until she felt how warm he was. "Listen, Sophie. I am going to say this as plain and clear as I can. No more holding back."

Sophie gulped. Why'd he have to use his deep, sexy voice?

"I love you. My day begins and ends with you in mind. I want every day to start and stop with you beside me. I thought I was doing what was right by my company, and in a roundabout way, by my father. I wanted him to be proud of me. But pride doesn't keep me warm at night. I want you. Need you. I'd give up my dream job a million times if it means having you forever. Can you find it in your heart to forgive me?"

Sophie's heart about exploded with want. Her insides melted at his feet. Every inch of her core longed for those words to ring true. She wanted more than anything to believe he was as sincere as he expressed. If only she could trust him. But that was the problem. She couldn't trust him. Even if he meant well, she couldn't give up any more for him. She was embarking on something great, and she didn't have it in her to mend another broken heart.

She was scared to try again. "Ryan, I . . . I don't know."

Ryan grabbed the papers from the desk and placed them in her hand. "Read this, please. You'll understand when you do. Then you can give me your answer. Or ask me to leave. And I'll respect it whatever it is."

Sophie snapped the folded piece of paper open and began reading. Line by line, word for word, as she read on, her brows raised. And then it clicked. She looked up in disbelief. "It's a rental agreement for *Up Front's* building. Good for another six months." She set the paper down and wiped her face.

"It's for your magazine."

"Ryan . . ." she started, her voice cracking and trailing. "I don't know what to say."

"You don't need to say anything." He took a step closer, his gaze trained on her lips.

Her breath hitched, allowing the fullness of him to overpower her fading willpower.

"There's more you need to know. I've leased an apartment here. I can live anywhere with my blog. I have the support, and I still own my sports app. But I will be here. With you."

Hot tears blurred her vision. He was staying here? For her? He quit his job? For her? Rented out *Up Front's* office space for her magazine? And donated a ton of money? She couldn't stop shaking. She slumped onto the desk not convinced her legs would keep her upright.

"I love you, Sapphire. I always have. And I'm sorry for not proving that to you before."

He was giving her his everything. And she loved him, desperately. Could she really let him go?

"What if . . . ?" Sophie's words stuck in her throat. "What if you came on board with us? I can't pay you or anything, and you'd be more eye candy and stuff, but it could be fun. And we rep a great cause."

Ryan's lips spread wide and he stepped into her personal bubble. When she didn't object, he threaded his fingers through her hair and leaned into her. He groaned like a man deprived of oxygen and devoured her lips with his. He was demanding and full of promise and Sophie answered back. *Yes. Always.*

When he finally broke the kiss—*pity*—he touched his forehead to hers. "How's that for an answer?"

"Ew." Charlie shifted on the couch. "Get a room."

Sophie smiled and fastened her gaze back on Ryan. "Sounds like the best idea I've heard in a long time."

Epilogue

Six Weeks Later

The high-resolution sign, FIERCE, INC., hung where *Up Front's* once did on the city building. The rich, red with a golden accent dwarfed the original sign. Ryan and Sophie couldn't have envisioned it better when they sent the specs to the sign maker.

Across the street, preparations for *Fierce's* debut were almost done. The stage looked massive, decorated with *Fierce's* bold insignia. Samples of the magazine's covers flanked the sides, and the bleacher seats blocked all of West Highland Street, but who cared? Today was as close to perfect as they came.

Thanks to The Department of Building and Housing, Mr. Tomilson's building failed inspection and was officially condemned. Renovation for *Fierce's* new office space drew publicity from all around the Bay due to its unique floor plan that included an aerodynamic sphere design, with a layout donated by a local contractor.

"She looks beautiful," Sophie said, standing with Ryan across the street, watching workers drill the new sign into place.

"Not as beautiful as you." He wrapped an arm tightly around her waist and kissed her nose, each cheek, and finally her lips.

She blushed every time he did that, which was a lot.

"Hey! You two. We don't have time for that. Get a-movin', we have two hours before the big reveal." Donovan grabbed a few more boxes from his white Prius and headed for the building. Ryan walked over to help.

Several of the former journalists and columnists from *Up Front* decided to join *Fierce*, giving Sophie the warm fuzzies. They could freelance with whomever. Some even decided to Uber people around the city, but they still wanted to remain active with this outreach, and that was more than Sophie could have ever hoped for.

Amy hooked her arm around Sophie's and dragged her to the other side of the street. "So, we have our sponsors in place, and both the online and periodical issues are set to launch in two months."

"Yep, and the daily blog from our professional contributor will help the magazine focus on relevant topics."

"Excellent." Amy clapped her hands.

"Sophie!" Charlie screamed, sprinting full speed down the street as if a twenty-five-foot spider was chasing her.

Sophie cringed, nearly trampling over Amy as they both ran toward Charlie.

Sophie patted the outside of Charlie's jacket, checking her for missing limbs. "What's wrong?"

Ryan and Donovan jogged over.

"Got a . . . had a . . . need to catch my breath." Charlie's cheeks were streaked with tears, and the attention of every person on the street rested on them, which was no easy feat in this city. The people around here were usually so glued to their technology, they'd only know that a bus hit them if they suddenly found themselves on the pavement squished and dead.

Charlie panted for a few moments before Amy handed her a bottle of water.

"What is it, Charlie?" Sophie's anxiety was dialed to full on panic.

"You're not going to believe this. I don't even believe it."

Sophie shook Charlie's arm. "What is it, girlie? Spill it."

"I'm going!" she cried. "I'm really going."

"Going where? Did you meet a boy? The answer is no. Right now I am your unofficial guardian and I say no."

Charlie rolled her eyes. "No, dingbat, I'm going to school!"

"What? When did this happen?"

"Like, thirteen seconds ago!" Charlie beamed, holding up a semi-crumpled piece of typed computer paper, Bethany's letterhead adorned across the top.

Sophie began reading, "'Dear Ms. Charlotte Williams . . . We are pleased to inform you . . .'" Sophie read further down coming to the important part . . . "Full scholarship!" She started screaming and scooped Charlie in her arms, dancing and jumping and screaming in circles around everyone.

"When do you leave?"

The bystanders moved along, probably assuming no blood, no fun.

"I'll start fresh in the spring."

"Okay, great." Sophie's internal mothering instinct sighed in relief. "But I was serious about the boys."

Charlie gave her a dirty look.

Sophie grinned, "I am more proud of you than words can say, which as a journalist, kind of says a lot."

Charlie beamed. "I know."

An hour and a half later, goose bumps rose on Sophie's arms and her nerves turned her stomach.

"You're gorgeous, toots." Donovan dabbed another coat of matte foundation on her face. "Listen, I'll be in the front row. Picture me in my underwear and you'll be just fine."

A fresh wave of shivers that had nothing to do with nerves made her nauseous. "No, I'm pretty sure I'll puke if I picture that."

"Well, I tried," he said. "Okay, you look fab. I'm out. See you after the ceremony."

"Bye." When he left, Sophie grabbed a handful of tissue and blotted the makeup. She checked her reflection for the umpteenth time, and when Ryan walked back in from checking on the crowd, she wrapped her arms around him.

He nuzzled her neck. "It's a full house out there."

She stuck her hand deep in his back pocket, where she'd put her notes since she didn't have a pocket in her dress, and with a little squeeze, snatched them out.

Ryan laughed. "You look fabulous and your notes are on point."

Sophie read them again anyway. "I'm so nervous. I want to mention it was your inspiration that started this magazine."

"Darling, you were the inspiration," Ryan said, kissing the top of her head.

He didn't need to know how intricate his role was, and it was probably best. She tucked her hair behind her ears and Ryan gently grabbed her wrists.

"You have nothing to be nervous about. Everything is as it should be." He put his arms around her and squeezed. "We're up in fifteen minutes. City Councilman Peterson just wrapped up how struggling teens with eating disorders will now have access to others just like them so they won't feel so alone."

A silken cocoon of euphoria warmed Sophie. "You pulled all this off."

"We pulled it off." He cupped her cheek and kissed her lips.

Not thirty feet from where Sophie stood, several members of city hall, a reporter with the local paper, an affiliate with *The Times*, Channel 2 Nightly News, *E!*, two contributing pediatricians, one contributing dietitian, hundreds of young pioneer readers, and a few ad sponsors showed up for the ceremonial ribbon cutting outside the newly renovated office. Sophie overheard someone from *The Times* mention that this was some sort of record for a magazine launch, especially a local one with an online app already up and running ahead of schedule.

"I'm so proud of you," Red said, walking in.

Sophie let go of Ryan and leapt to Red. "When did you get here?"

Red embraced her. Sophie had never seen him in a Hawaiian print shirt and khakis before. He had always been the epitome of black slacks and ugly ties. "This morning," he said. "And I'm heading back to the Vineyard tomorrow, but I wouldn't miss the launch of your new magazine for the world."

Sophie blushed. "I'm so nervous."

"That's a good sign. And this is what putting your heart into your career looks like. I couldn't be prouder."

"Oh, Red, thank you for everything."

He put his hand on her cheek. "You're my couch potato too." He glanced over at Ryan and stuck out his hand. "Congrats, man."

Some kind of unspoken understanding passed between them that was totally lost on Sophie. "Thanks, Red."

"Okay, I'll see you two out there in a little bit. I'm going to go bug Donovan about that haircut. Someone needs to." With a shake of his head, he turned and left.

Sophie smiled. "That was great."

Ryan whispered in Sophie's ear. "Just wait. It gets better." He took Sophie's hand. "Come here." Ryan discretely led her out of the dressing room and into their newly renovated office space swirling with nodes of freshly cut cedar and crisp, new paint.

"What is it? You didn't see a rat or anything, right?" Sophie laughed, placing a well-earned kiss on his nose.

When she stepped back, Ryan held a small ring brandishing a not-so-small princess-cut diamond. She clamped her hands over her mouth, stifling a squeak.

"About ten years ago, I made one of the biggest mistakes of my life by letting you go. Yet you forgave me. I let building my portfolio and making a name for myself come before the only thing I really wanted. But in all that time, I never stopped thinking about you. Never stopped loving you. I'm here now and I will never let you go."

Sophie realized if she didn't start breathing, she'd never get engaged.

"Sophie—" Ryan dropped to one knee. "Will you make me the happiest man ever?"

Ryan hardly got the question out before she screamed. "Yes! Yes, yes, yes, yes! Of course I'll marry you."

He stood, smiling with satisfaction. "Let's make it official."

"What do you mean?"

"Grandmoo, you can come out now."

"What? Grandmoo's here?"

Dressed in a fancy-sequined top with black slacks, Grandmoo shuffled out of hiding with the help of her walker. Ryan walked over and kissed her cheek. "After I asked Grandmoo for your hand in marriage, she told me about the funding account. I could only type in my donation so fast. I learned then about her visit with the attorney general, and your plans. And I very much wanted her to be a part of this moment."

"Wait." She pointed at Grandmoo. "You knew about this? For six weeks? And didn't say anything?"

"Babydoll, I wouldn't have told you if you threatened to put me in an old folk's home. Some surprises are worth the wait." Grandmoo pressed her lips together in a playful smile. "Though I did ask the boy to hurry up so I could get me some of those great grandbabies!"

"Aw." Sophie joined them and placed a sloppy kiss on her cheek. As always, Grandmoo smelled like floral-scented

Bengay. It was her personal fragrance. "I'm so glad you're here, Grandmoo."

"Wouldn't have missed this for anything."

"I know. I love you."

Sophie glared at Ryan. "So, even before you came into the café that night, you'd already talked to Grandmoo?"

Ryan smiled into Sophie's neck, leaving a kiss that nearly compromised Sophie's balance. "Like she said, 'some surprises are worth the wait.'"

The three of them ambled out to the staging area. Grandmoo had reserved seating up front and Ryan helped her to her chair before meeting Sophie on stage.

The press busily snapped pictures of magazine contributors and councilmen, and the speakers as they spoke.

At her turn, she stepped up to the mic where she nervously held her notes and cleared her throat.

The light breeze ruffled her hair and a bird cawed in the distance. Sophie tapped the microphone until it squealed to life. "Good afternoon," she said, her voice bouncing off the surrounding buildings. She looked at her notes again, but they were all twisted and looked like the letter 'Q'. So she dropped them and peeked at her new fiancé. A smile draped across her face and she began. "Twice in the recent past I managed to make a less than graceful appearance on YouTube. I strongly believe in the power of three, as it's historically a lucky number. So, ladies and gentleman, please get your cameras ready."

Sophie reached for Ryan's hand and brought him with her to the front of the stage. She then placed her palms on either side of Ryan's bewildered face, and rubbed her fingers across his stubble. "Are you ready?" she whispered.

"For what?" he asked in the same quiet voice, his Caribbean eyes searching hers.

"To go viral, of course." And then she crushed her lips over his with newsworthy fierceness.

The hooting and hollering cheers from her girls as well as the clicking sounds from the camera's apertures drowned out the thumping hums of Sophie's racing heart. Sophie kept Ryan's face in her shaking hands and only broke the kiss when she needed air. "Take that, YouTube," Sophie said, smiling against Ryan's mouth.

Deb Lee found her voice writing what others wish they could say. She channels it in the form of contemporary romance, with plenty of emotional baggage to give her readers all the feels. Deb has the perfect husband and four spritely children, who test her sanity daily. She's also an avid swimmer, which ironically enough, happens to be the one place her children can't find her.

Deb lives in Northern California with her family and enough animals to make people really start to question her sanity. Find her on her ever-changing-until-she-eventually-gets-it-right website at www.debbilee.com. Also find her on Facebook and Instagram at Writer Deb Lee. And please share stories about your crazy kids. She yearns to normalize her daily dose of children-induced insanity.

CPSIA information can be obtained
at www.ICGtesting.com
Printed in the USA
LVHW081056220419
615066LV00005B/261/P